Penelope Kanaar's working life has been mainly concerned with nursing, including both acute and elderly care. As a qualified nurse she went into nurse education, where she contributed articles to professional publications. Apart from her nursing career, Penelope has also been a pub land-lady, a village hall caretaker and a kitchen assistant! Other activities in her life have involved volunteering for a "talking newspaper"; Meals on Wheels; Riding for the Disabled and has formerly been a Server in the church she attends. She is an active member of two amateur dramatic groups, and a member of two writing groups, one of which is her local U3A Creative Writing Group.

She writes under her maiden name, having gained the approval of her siblings, one of whom thought their parents would also approve. She has one son, from her first marriage, and two grandchildren. She lives near Brighton, West Sussex.

To Libby and Brian, with many thanks for your support and the wonderful holidays.

Penelope Kanaar

AND SO IT IS

AUSTIN MACAULEY PUBLISHERS™

LONDON * CAMBRIDGE * NEW YORK * SHARJAH

A CIP catalogue record for this title is available from the British Library.

ISBN 9781398437838 (Paperback)
ISBN 9781398437845 (ePub e-book)

www.austinmacauley.com

First Published 2022
Austin Macauley Publishers Ltd®
1 Canada Square
Canary Wharf
London
E14 5AA

My thanks go to my sister, Elizabeth and her husband, Brian for reading several versions of this book and their input and corrections about life in France—all included inaccuracies remain mine. To Maxine Vlieland who read and critiqued an early version, offering constructive suggestions. And to Pat Squire, Gordon Reece-Davies and Michael Duck, all members of the Creative Writing Group, for all their input and encouragement. To the many people at Austin Macauley Publishers who work to produce a book and especially to the editors, for having enough faith in the book to agree to publish it.

Chapter One

She stood still clutching a train ticket in her hand, a small suitcase at her feet. Hanging rather incongruously round her neck was a string bag. Faded now, but some of the bright red colour remained, through which a brown paper parcel could be seen. Her dress was of good quality but appeared too small for her, as if it had been bought at the start of the summer and she had now outgrown it. She was certainly well nourished, her skin tanned and her blonde hair, groomed into a neat ponytail, had a sleek shine to it. A picture of youthful health clouded by her sad demeanour.

There weren't many passengers in the ticket office of this small railway station, no one acknowledged her as they passed, totally oblivious of the fear expressed in the large blue eyes which followed the progress of a man, wearing a well-worn agricultural jacket, walking towards her carrying a packet of sweets which she took, crumpling her ticket as she did so. She said something to him, he sighed, shaking his head. She spoke again but when he repeated the gesture, she clung to him and started to cry. He gently brushed her hair and drew her close to him, easing her towards the machine where train tickets had to be validated before starting a journey.

After two attempts to insert the creased ticket into the machine, the man became flustered. The girl tried to direct him away from the contraption, indicating they should leave. He shook his head fiercely and spoke with some irritation tempered with helpless frustration. She seemed to understand his internal commotion and nodded, stood on her toes and kissed his clean-shaven cheek. He was now trying to stem tears from large dark eyes.

They seemed to be in a quandary as to what to do next, so I went to them, excused myself and offered to assist. Gratefully, the man relinquished the ticket from his gnarled hand, I managed to flatten the paper sufficiently to get it into the slot; after the quiet click registering its validation, I handed the ticket back.

He nodded his thanks and I watched the once tall, now slightly stooping man and a young fragile girl walk hand in hand across the rail tracks to the platform on the other side where the train would come and soon separate them.

For how long and why?

I put my ticket into the machine and waited for the familiar soft clunk confirming I could travel legally and followed in their footsteps. Sitting in the shelter on the platform to wait for the train, I closed my eyes and enjoyed the warmth of the sun which was precious at this time of day in late summer. I was thinking over the events of the last few months when I was roused from my reverie by a gentle voice asking me a question.

'Excuse me, *Madame*. Please excuse me for disturbing you, but are you travelling to Narbonne?'

It took me a moment to realise I was no longer with the other visitors at the large house but back in the real world having to resume an ordinary life.

'Yes. I change at Narbonne then go on to Carcassonne.' I replied.

His face lit up.

Despite being fluent in French, I found following the conversation rather confusing due to his agitation, but it emerged he wanted me to care for his granddaughter, Suzanne, during the journey and put her off the train at Lézignan after we had changed trains at Narbonne. I protested that Lézignan was a stop before Carcassonne; I couldn't just leave a child at a station, goodness knows what might happen to her.

But I suppose anything could happen to her on the journey anyway travelling on her own so perhaps I was better than nothing.

When I agreed, the man pulled a piece of paper and stub of pencil from his pocket and painstakingly wrote something and gave the paper to me.

'My son, her father, will be at the arrival platform at Lézignan when the train gets there.'

I looked at the words written in beautiful script.

'And this is your son's name?'

He confirmed this as the train arrived and the couple made their painful, heartbroken farewells.

The girl clung to her grandfather. I picked up the suitcases and put them onto the train as he almost thrust his granddaughter at me. Even so, both were reluctant to part and stayed holding hands till the train doors started to close. Her grandfather raised his hand in a salute of thanks to me and blew kisses to his granddaughter. As the train pulled out of Elne, I saw him suddenly take a few steps forward and start to wave a piece of paper frantically, shouting something. Suzanne waved back until she could see him no more.

I selected a double seat facing the way we were to travel and directed the girl to sit by the window. She was very subdued and meekly sat where I'd indicated and let tears silently fall. She looked more distraught now than when I'd first seen her as her face was truly tear marked and her crying had caused a deep flush beneath the suntan. I felt for her loss and thought I should say something but, not knowing what to say, I said nothing for a while, then decided some conversation was needed.

So, I asked,

'*Quel age a tu?*'

She smiled, replying with the pride of the young as they get nearer to being a teenager,

'*J'ai neuf ans et deux mois.*'

Nine and two months, still young to be put on a train by herself—or thrown into the company of a stranger. Why had no one come to collect her or her grandfather not escorted her?

Suzanne turned to the window and watched the passing scene which, in this area, was predominantly agricultural with vineyards and small mixed farms. At one point she stood up, pointed out of the window and waved shouting, '*La ferme, la ferme. Papi, Mamie*', and then dissolved into tears once again. I put my arm round her shoulder, held her close and let her sob. Obviously, leaving her grandparents and the farm was an extremely traumatic experience for her. After a while, she relaxed and I realised she'd slipped into an exhausted sleep.

I watched the countryside pass. Beautiful flamingos, their pink colour to be enhanced later by the setting sun, salt flats sheltering from the sea and deep mussel beds, while above large flocks of birds were gathering in preparation for their nocturnal roost. After four months in a beautiful, but remote house, these sights were a pure delight and I mentally thanked Patience for sending me away with her blessing.

No, my future doesn't lie in a sanctuary shut off from the hustle and bustle of life. I must now review my future. Oh, I don't know what I want. My world emptied when Mark died.

I must have dozed off too as, nearing Narbonne, I was woken by the ticket inspector demanding our tickets. I offered her mine and asked a sleepy Suzanne for hers. Horror struck us both at the same time. '*Papi!*' and '*Grand-Père!*' we exclaimed together realising he wasn't just waving goodbye but waving her ticket as we left Elne. I explained the situation but the inspector was not at all sympathetic and just pointed out the regulations, adding rather sarcastically that if everyone had a forgetful grandfather, the train company would go bankrupt.

There was no option but to pay for another ticket plus the instant fine for travelling without a valid one. After the ticket inspector had gone, Suzanne smiled and clung to me. I could certainly afford the extra expense but, on principle, I thought I should be repaid, so I wrote my name and address on a page of my diary, tore it out and put it, with the ticket documentation, in her dress pocket to give to her father.

'*Pour ton père,*' I said.

§

We whiled away the time between trains at Narbonne by walking round a little square having put our cases into a locker. On one corner we found a small café where we hoped to have a drink. As the staff were preparing for the evening clientele, the waiter was reluctant to let us have a table but agreed, after Suzanne had charmed him by pleading travellers' weariness and promising to leave shortly for our train.

'*Papa, papa!*' Suzanne fairly flew off the train at Lézignan and was swept up into the arms of a tall man dressed in a black, formal, almost funereal suit, who smothered her in kisses. I realised I was looking at a young version of the man we'd left at Elne. While the older man's still thick hair was white, this man's was jet black. Further contrasts were the still straight back and the hands, unmarred by age or recent hard manual labour, with neatly manicured nails.

He looked at the papers Suzanne had passed to him and turned to me.

'*Madame* Birch, thank you for escorting my daughter. Now come, let us all get back to the house, it is getting late and my little Marianne will have dinner on the table.'

'I was glad to assist, *Monsieur*, Suzanne's grandfather was rather agitated. I must go; the train's about to leave. Oh wait, Suzanne's bag is still on the train.' I returned to our seats and found both suitcases had vanished and were on the platform. I moved to collect mine but was intercepted by a man in a chauffeur's uniform. I protested I had to get to Carcassonne, I was booked on the last flight out tonight.

'Did you not know?' asked Suzanne's father, 'the airport is closed, there are no flights tonight. A baggage handlers' strike, so come home with me for tonight and I will sort out another flight tomorrow.'

'There was no indication at Narbonne,' I protested, 'I'll go on to Carcassonne and either find a hotel or stay at the airport.' As I was saying this, the train departed.

'Oh! I'll have to find a hotel here.' I said, rather deflated.

'You will do no such thing—you have cared for my daughter so the least I can do is to care for you for one night. Anyway, my little Marianne will want to thank you for bringing Suzanne home safely.'

'No, I'll be fine in a hotel, thank you.'

'Oh, I see! An unaccompanied female stranded in the middle of France is being abducted by a tall dark stranger and being whisked to—heaven knows what! Am I right?' His seriousness made me blush but I managed to smile and nod.

He returned my smile, trying not to laugh and extended his hand, introducing himself as Ricard Ramon Letour.

His warm handshake was firm and I felt the pressure of his ring on my hand.

Why was I worried? Marianne, his wife, will be there.

'Do not worry yourself, my little Marianne lives in the house. If you wish, she will put her mattress outside your bedroom door.'

So, Marianne is not his wife after all. And the ring?—wrong hand!

His young smartly dressed chauffeur was waiting at the car, I got in beside Suzanne who was already in the middle of the backseat, *Monsieur* Letour got in the other side of Suzanne. The driver pulled out of the station and skilfully negotiated the car into the traffic lane he needed. We drove through a well-lit, modern looking town till we reached an area where the roads became narrow, the tarmac surface changed to cobbles and the lighting was supplied by only a few old-fashioned streetlamps.

At one point, we moved into what looked like a dead-end track barely wide enough for the car, at the end of which an oak gate opened and we entered a walled courtyard. *Monsieur* Letour waited for the chauffeur to open the rear door and Suzanne climbed over his knees, rushed out of the car and up a curved stone staircase disappearing into the house calling for Marianne, stopping only briefly to accept a kiss on her head from a slim girl wearing a white apron over her black dress.

She approached the car, made a bob curtsey to *Monsieur* Letour and took my case from the chauffeur. The gates closed automatically, obviously on a remote-controlled system, with a slight sound of wood against wood.

Well, I'm now isolated from the world—again.

'Lucille will show you to your room. Please ask for anything you do not have and need. When you are refreshed, please come down,' he glanced around the courtyard, 'I expect we will eat outside this evening to enjoy as much of the last of the summer as we can. Will half an hour give you sufficient time? And please, there is no need to change your clothing, we are informal, but I will discard my court uniform.' He indicated his clothes, then turned to the chauffeur.

'Well, Sven?'

'Sir?'

'How do you think it went this afternoon?'

I caught the first part of their conversation but not the chauffeur's response to the question.

The house through which I followed Lucille was obviously old and extravagantly restored and furnished with care to enhance the building and reflected comfort. This was a living house, comfortable but I felt something was missing. It felt, I searched for the word to describe it and came up with *bereft* but thought that may be too harsh. The large room to which Lucille finally led me was square and had a complete set of matching bedroom furniture. The material covering the massive double bed and couch complemented the heavy drapes. Lucille left me for a moment then returned carrying some towels which she placed in the adjoining bathroom. She hadn't spoken nor responded to my efforts at conversation, though she smiled slightly, then repeating the bob curtsey, left me.

14

I checked my watch. 'Half an hour,' I said aloud. My wash bag was easily retrieved from my case as it was the last thing I'd thrown in before leaving the house. When I was ready, I put the open case on the trunk by the side of the door. As an afterthought, I put my nightdress on the coverlet at the foot of the bed.

§

'So, Yvonne, what brings you to this part of France?' Ricard looked straight into my eyes as he posed the question. We'd disposed of the *Monsieur* and *Madame* and were sitting at the large table in the courtyard having a drink before the meal. I wrapped my arms round myself while I gathered my thoughts.

'Are you cold?'

'No,' I smiled faintly, 'I'm surprised how warm it is here now the sun has almost gone, it must be something to do with the thick walls of the buildings and the trees.'

'Yes, one needs to get warmth where one can,' he said with an edge to his voice, 'well?' He waited for me to respond to his question but before I could do so, Suzanne, Sven and Lucille arrived carrying everything needed for the evening meal, accompanied by a short, dark-haired woman.

'Thank you, Lucille. Off you go home now.' The woman spoke slowly and kindly to the girl who repeated her curtsey and left us.

'Yvonne, allow me to introduce Marianne, my housekeeper.'

We acknowledged each other, then to my surprise, both the housekeeper and chauffeur, who had changed out of his uniform, settled themselves at the table.

The servants eating with their employer! How strange!

Sven filled our glasses then a quiet came over the group. Ricard said,

'Suzanne, would you say grace please.'

She did so. Then, she raised her glass of fruit juice and said,

'And a toast to our visitor.'

They all repeated the toast and clinked glasses, looking at me. I blushed and thanked them.

'I was asking Yvonne how it is she comes to this part of France.' He turned to me, obviously expecting me to continue our discussion. I could hardly refuse so I started.

'One day at work Andrea, my boss' personal assistant, said he wanted to see me in his office. A second meeting with Patrick in one day was unexpected, but

15

I wasn't perturbed by this, as h$$e often wanted impromptu updates on projects and expected concise and precise responses. In business matters, he is one of the toughest men I know, but on this occasion, he showed an empathetic side to his character, saying he was worried about me and wanted me to take some compassionate leave, as he'd watched me throw myself into work straight after Mark's funeral. He said he thought I'd not given myself time to grieve.'

'Mark being?' The question from Marianne hung in the air.

'Mark was my husband,' I responded, 'I was lost without him and work helped me stop thinking; anything to ease the pain and loneliness I'd been feeling for the last two years and more intensely over the last five months.' I stopped speaking, sipped some wine and steadied my voice. 'So here I am,' I concluded, clamping my jaw to stop myself crying.

'He sounds like a nice man, this boss of yours.'

'Yes, he is. But enough about me, tell me about your days here.'

They realised I needed to change the subject and turned the conversation, giving me a little insight into their lives, everyone joining in and adding different aspects. At the end of the meal, Marianne and Sven cleared the table and excused themselves taking Suzanne with them.

'But why this part of France?' Ricard returned to the earlier topic.

'It's strange how you never really know a person. Even though I've worked with Patrick for several years and he's a close friend of father's, almost part of our family, I didn't know he's a bereavement counsellor and had picked up on my behaviour. He suggested a little time with his sister who owns a large house, a chateau really, just outside Elne, might do me good. She offers peace, quiet and retreats from the busy world. She very nearly took holy orders but changed her mind at the last moment. In fact, most of Patrick's family are connected with the church in some way—missionaries, army chaplains, parish priests—he's the odd one out but finds he can do as much good outside the church as within its formal constraints. I found the silent time Patience likes respected in the house, refreshing.'

'Is this a convent?' Interjected Ricard.

'No, but because of her background she holds the services of Compline at nine in the evening and Vespers at eight in the morning. These are held at the end and start of days in convents and monasteries with silence between.'

'For most of which you'd be asleep.'

16

'Not to start with. I'd not slept properly for months. Mark had not been well, for over a year, the last few months of which he was in pain and on a cocktail of drugs which gave him no relief, so there was not much rest or sleep for either of us, but yes, gradually I relaxed and found I was sleeping well. I fell into a routine of helping around the house, in the kitchen early in the morning, and assisting the elderly nuns, yes there were some nuns there, to get to the chapel. I found the peace beneficial. Then the time came I felt I should leave. I shall always be grateful to Patience and my fellow visitors for the support they gave me. But the life of a recluse is really not for me.'

'So, what now?'

'I go back and pick up the reins again, I suppose.'

'You don't sound very convinced.'

'You're right! I really have no strong desire to return, but doesn't everyone after a holiday?'

'This seems to have been more therapy than a holiday.'

I smiled in agreement.

I wonder if it has done me much good.

I'd been lost in my own thoughts when I realised the long silence, although familiar to me, was not the norm in company and I was being rude. I roused myself and smiled.

'What about you, Ricard? I'm here and knowing little of you except you let your daughter travel on her own, you have a housekeeper cum nanny, a maid, a chauffeur, probably a gardener and a wonderful house.'

Marianne joined us bringing another bottle of wine which she placed near Ricard.

'Suzanne is off to sleep and as it has been a long day, we are going to bed too. There always seems so much more to do when Suzanne is coming home. She certainly has grown during the summer; I will have to take her shopping for some clothes before she goes back to school on Monday,' Marianne paused for a moment before continuing, 'Grandparents Letour send their love and blessings to you, Ricard,' Marianne's tone of voice had changed as she said this and looked at Ricard, 'do not forget to look in on Suzanne as you go to bed. Welcome and goodnight, Yvonne.'

As she left, Marianne blew a kiss to Ricard which he acknowledged with a small finger movement to his lips.

17

There was an awkward reserve for a while during which Ricard refilled his glass. I felt exhausted and wanted to go inside and to bed, but felt he wanted to say something, so I sipped my wine and studied his face, not knowing either for what I was looking or expecting to see. His brow was slightly ridged in a frown, his smooth skin had few laughter lines round his mouth or eyes which were staring straight at me. I waited for him to break the silence.

'Marianne is Suzanne's aunt. When Charlotte, my wife, died, I asked her to come to look after Suzanne and help with the house. She had been married to a lovely man some twenty years older than her, he died several years ago. During their time here, she and Sven fell in love with each other.'

'Interesting!'

'Despite the age difference, they are devoted to each other and live together in their own self-contained apartment which is attached to the house but also has an entrance from the courtyard. So, if you are seriously in need of a mattress to be slept on as a guard to your bedroom door, I will call her, but I will not be responsible for their moods in the morning.'

'I can just imagine Marianne and Sven's morning wrath if they had to sleep on the floor.' I laughed which eased the atmosphere.

Ricard lifted the bottle towards my glass and started to pour, catching wine on my fingers as I put my hand over it saying, 'No more, thanks.'

Ricard took my hand and licked the wine from my fingers.

'Is that a family tradition when wine is poured on fingers?' I joked, hoping to break the tension I felt rising.

He smiled. 'Not one I know of, but it could become one!'

Still holding my hand, he stood, pulling me to my feet then holding me tightly, I was kissed gently but firmly by this stranger before being released.

'You know your way to your room, Yvonne?'

'Yes, thank you, Ricard. Goodnight.'

I felt his eyes on my back as I walked towards the stone steps. I turned at the top. He was still standing, watching me.

§

'Good morning.' I entered the kitchen where Marianne was making coffee. I felt a little awkward but her calm face and beautiful smile relaxed me as she ushered me to a chair at the large well-scrubbed kitchen table.

18

'Good morning, Yvonne, come and sit down. Did you sleep well?'

'Yes thanks, gloriously well.' I felt myself blushing.

'First time since Mark?' She asked placing a bowl of coffee and a plate of fresh bread before me. The forthrightness of her question was startling.

'Yes,' I agreed quietly, drawing the soft bathrobe around me, I breathed in deeply, 'this perfume is wonderful. Whoever used this robe last had excellent taste.'

'It was Charlotte's and yes, she had a knack of choosing absolutely the right thing. But be assured, no one else has worn it and even though it has been laundered, her perfume seems to linger. *C'est ça!*'

'Oh sorry, I didn't mean to offend, but it was on the chair by the bed.'

'It was left for you to use, so do not feel guilty. Eat some breakfast then get yourself ready, plenty of hot water for a bath or shower. I took the liberty of retrieving a blouse and skirt from your suitcase this morning and pressed them. Like most people returning home, you just threw everything into your case!'

Marianne's candour emboldened me to ask, 'Does Ricard …?'

'No, you are his first since Charlotte. So please be careful. You are still vulnerable and so is he. I did not think Ricard would survive after Charlotte's death.'

'We do survive, at the start it's all we can do. You survived after your husband died and now you have a full life again with Sven.'

'Yes, I am lucky, but people must get together for the right reasons. When Ricard first asked me to come and live here, I am sure he had no other thoughts than as a housekeeper and carer for his child. But in time he started to get close but I put a stop to it as I realised, not only was he still grieving and looking for solace, which is no basis for any long-term relationship, but it could not have been possible anyway. So, before you ask—no, we did not take things further, as I said, you are the first in nearly ten years, so please be careful and perhaps you should not read too much into it. Sorry to be blunt, but that is how I see it. *C'est ça!*'

'Ricard is very fond of you, he called you his "little Marianne" with such affection at the station.'

'Pretty obvious why! I am short, dark-haired with a tendency to roundness.'

'And Charlotte?'

'She was tall, slim and blonde. Enough talk now, have your breakfast or you will be late for the restaurant if you do not get a move on.'

'But I should be getting to the airport. Ricard said he'd enquire about another flight for me today. Where is he?'

'He went into the office early to reschedule his appointments for today so you can both go to Carcassonne for lunch. He wants to show you around the old city then take you on to the airport. He has fixed everything including a car to meet you when you land and take you to your home.'

I stared at Marianne with incredulity.

'Does he know how far West Hampstead is from Gatwick airport? It will cost a mint.'

'Yes, he knows, or should I say he has no idea, but he has arranged it regardless. And again, I say, please be careful. He is very charming and persuasive.'

Let alone foolish with his money. I hope I don't end up paying for the car.

I made my way to my room and into the shower. Returning, wrapping the bath sheet around me, I was surprised to see Suzanne sitting on the briefly used guest bed, clutching the red string bag.

'Did you sleep with my *Papa* last night?'

She looked me straight in the face. Again, I was stunned by the directness of this question.

Are they all so blunt?

But it seemed strange from this young girl.

'Yes.' I waited for her reaction.

'Why?'

I thought of creating some child-like reason to feed her but the look on her face was older than her years.

'Because I wanted to and he wanted me to.'

'That is alright then. He left you asleep when he went to the office early today. He looked different somehow.'

Guiltily, I asked,

'Suzanne, have other women stayed with your *Papa* overnight?'

'Oh no. If people come for dinner, he always sends them home. Especially if it is a lady on her own, Sven drives her to her home. But sometimes I go to see him if I cannot sleep and last night was the first time anyone else was there. You both looked so peaceful I went back to bed and my bad dream went away.'

'You had a bad dream last night? What was it about?' I adjusted the bath sheet and sat next to her.

'Some people were shouting and arguing. One of them looked like my *Papa*, but it was not really him, he does not shout or argue—except when he pretends in court. I love him and I bet he is the best *Papa* in the whole world. I have had the dream before and it does not seem to change.'

Suzanne slipped off the bed, saying I'd better get dressed, leaving behind her the string bag with the parcel still in it. I'd been led to believe children are very matter of fact, but this abrupt change of direction surprised me.

'Suzanne, your parcel.'

'Oh, *Papi* sent it for *Papa*, but he just looked at it and said he did not want it. I tried to give it to him two times yesterday, once at the station and again before dinner. But his face got cross—or sad—and he said again he did not want it.'

'You'd better keep it in case he changes his mind.'

'I wonder what it is; if someone sent me a present, I would open it straight away.'

'Well, as it's addressed to him, just put it somewhere safe till he does want it.'

'I will put it in my treasure box, I keep it under my bed.'

Sven was waiting with the back door to the car open when I emerged, I sat next to Suzanne who was already seated in the back and excitedly told me, after we had collected her father from the office, we were going to Carcassonne where Marianne, now sitting next to Sven, was taking her shopping for some new clothes. In the new town, she emphasised, not the historical old one which was boring.

I looked at the child who had been so distressed yesterday and thought about the resilience of the young and how life moves on for them almost without a second thought. New ideas, new clothes—a feeling of safety and security in a loving home.

But what about the recurring dream?

'Will you write to me, Yvonne?'

'Of course, but you will have to write to me first.'

'I want you to come and meet *Papi* and *Mamie* properly.'

Marianne stiffened slightly and said, 'It will be up to your grandparents to extend such an invitation, not you.'

'Oh, *Papi* would love to meet her again, I will give him the paper with your address on it.'

I caught Marianne's eye in the interior mirror and saw a warning sign. We stopped at an office from where Ricard emerged and joined Suzanne and me in the back seat. Suzanne leant into him and he put his arm round her shoulder, bringing her in to him, touching my neck in the movement.

We stopped in the shopping centre of the new town to let Suzanne and Marianne out. I kissed Suzanne on the cheek and said goodbye to Marianne before Sven drove to the old town where he left Ricard and me. We stood briefly in the street before holding hands and walking along the old cobbled roads.

'Last night—' he started.

'No, say nothing, please, it was wonderful. And I came to you, remember? Marianne and I have talked. The first for both of us for a long time so we must be careful, for our own sakes as well as each other's.'

We walked a little further and stopped outside a jeweller's shop.

'That's pretty.' I said, pointing to a pendant with an amber stone set on a heavy gold chain.

'Mm, but that one,' he pointed to another one set with a dark green stone I didn't recognise, 'would bring out the green flecks in your hazel eyes.'

'I haven't got green flecks.'

Ricard turned me to face him and looked straight into my eyes, took me in his arms and kissed my cheek.

'Yes, you have; beautiful almond-shaped eyes fringed with long lashes which do not need any mascara. Now, Yvonne, I can show you all the wonders of Old Carcassonne—including the tourist dragon den and knights in armour— but I do have an alternative itinerary—if you would agree.'

I agreed. After all, Carcassonne would still be there another year.

§

I must have slept as I woke with a start, knocking the glass Ricard was offering, spilling the wine down my bare chest.

'Oh, sorry!'

'No, my fault, I should have woken you more gently. I thought you might like a glass and something to eat before you fly.'

We sat comfortably, sipping wine which was cool and sharp and eating gorgeous warm pastries.

'You have time for a shower if you like,' Ricard said, leaning in to kiss me again, 'we will have to go soon if you are to get the flight.'

'It doesn't take me long to shower.' I reached for him; he didn't resist.

Later and reluctantly, we left the bed and went to shower. Shortly afterwards, we emerged from the hotel a few minutes before Sven drew up in the car. We sat close together as Sven drove smoothly to the airport.

'You could stay.'

'I could but I won't.'

'Will you come back?'

'Will you ask me?'

'If I did—would you?'

'Yes.'

We waved briefly as I went through the departure gate. He turned his back and was gone. His last kiss remaining warm on my lips as I boarded the plane.

Vulnerable. Yes. C'est ça! as Marianne would say.

Chapter Two

The plane had to circle for an hour before landing so it was gone mid-night before I got home. I was tired. On entering the flat, I felt it had the unwelcoming orphaned feeling of being empty for too long. The desolation without Mark hit me and I wondered what had come over me to behave as I had with Ricard. I suddenly felt miserable and guilty. Did I really feel something for him? Was it just the act of sex I was missing or the feeling of being in a man's arms? But despite the cold of an uninhabited flat I still felt the warmth of his lips from his last kiss.

I dropped my case in the hallway and put the heating on to the highest setting then wandered aimlessly along the hall through the living room, dining room, kitchen then to our bedroom turning on all the lights as I went. I was at a loss as to what to do feeling as bad now as I had before I went away.

I slumped in an armchair still wearing my jacket feeling utterly miserable. The benefit of the time with Patience seemed to have dissipated and I started crying. Great howls of grief.

What had been the point of it all? I'm back where I started.

After half an hour or so of self-pity and indulging in my wretchedness, I got up, took my case and put it on the spare room bed. Remembering the key to the case was still in my handbag I retraced my steps to where to I'd left it by the armchair and rummaged through the contents. To my surprise, I found a box in which was the green pendant on a chain Ricard had seen in Carcassonne.

I'd thought no more about it at the time; especially as we'd different ideas about the colour of my eyes, I'd thought it was just a passing comment, but obviously Ricard had bought it when he'd purchased the wine and food and placed it in my handbag at some point. If I'd had enough left, I'd have burst into tears again; as it was, I numbly put the box on the mantelpiece in the living room and took the key to unpack. I shoved all the dirty clothes into the washing machine and turned it on.

I looked in the wine cooler for a bottle of white wine, opened it and poured a small measure and placed the glass on the kitchen counter. I was beginning to warm up now and removed my jacket and hung it in the hall where I picked up the post I'd stepped through and was now scattered around the floor. Not a great deal of interest as far as I could see, four months of circulars which went straight into the recycling bin in the kitchen from where I picked up my glass and returned to the armchair with the remaining post.

Bills, tomorrow is soon enough for them—well, later today.

I put them aside and turned to the envelope with a handwritten address. I recognised the writing but couldn't instantly identify the writer.

Of course, it's Julie's. Why is she writing a letter? It's most unusual; of my three siblings, she is the most avid email user.

I ripped open the envelope, tearing it badly and heard Mark's reprimand for not using the letter opener. That recollection stunned me for a moment but I smiled weakly and said, 'Yes dear!' My voice sounded tired and lonesome in the empty apartment. I closed my eyes to conjure up his face and dropped off to sleep waking with a start, feeling chilled despite the central heating and still clutching the envelope.

Julie's news, under different circumstances, would have been wonderful. She was in her second year studying for her doctorate in bio-ecology management. She had flown through her first degree and been offered a postgraduate place to enhance her qualifications. She was a highflyer and we were all pleased for her. I looked for the date on her letter but resorted to the envelope, which of course I'd torn in my haste. She'd posted it during my fifth week away. She must have known she was pregnant when I left for France. Why did she wait to write and not say anything to me earlier? She said she was dropping out of the degree as she couldn't take all the stress with her disabling morning sickness.

I calculated she must be at least four months pregnant, if not more, and hoped she was having proper antenatal care. I was tempted to pick up the phone and talk to her but realising the time held off. I wondered as I took my glass to the kitchen and rinsed it, if the father, whoever he was, knew and if so, was he going to be involved or, as so many times with Julie, she'd fallen for a married man who would have no intention of leaving his wife. Oh, to give up such a promising career, what was she thinking about? Surely, she could do both. I wondered if she'd considered an abortion if the man was not on the scene, added to which if she wanted the baby there were employment laws to assist. Feeling even more dejected than before reading the letter, I turned the heating down, the lights off and fell into bed fully clothed.

I hadn't expected banners and flags but I'd not expected this on my home coming. Oh Julie, have you gone too far this time?

§§§

Sleep came, under the circumstances, remarkably easily and I was woken, rather crumpled at half past nine by the phone ringing. When we'd bought the apartment, long ago now, Mark and I had decided we wouldn't have a telephone in the bedroom so I wandered to the hall and picked up the receiver.

'Yvonne, oh good, you are back—how are you, my dear—have you heard from Julie? She's—taken herself off to America without saying why or goodbye—she sent a postcard last week—I've been waiting for you to get back to ask if you know anything—do you?'

I hedged for time, I needed to re reread the letter in case I'd missed something when I was so tired.

'Hello Mother. Yes, I'm fine, thank you, but I only got back early this morning and only just woken up. I've not had an email from Julie but I've not checked for messages on the phone answering service yet, I was too tired to do so last night.' At least these were not lies, but maybe I wasn't giving her the full picture and knowing how emotionally unstable she could be, I had no intention of telling her about the letter until I'd had more time to think. 'Mother,' I continued, 'I'm still not fully awake; let me get myself sorted out and I'll come over and see you. Are you home today or do you have a rehearsal or show on?'

'I'm home today—supposed to be studying the script—as if I can while I'm in this state—this is a "rest day" for the whole company—that's a euphemism for the fact the producer is still having problems finding sufficient funding to put the show on—please come over as soon as you can—I need you.'

'Alright, Dear. Let me sort myself out and I'll come over.'

Julie, what have you done and where are you? I can do without this hassle right now. So much for a peaceful return. C'est ça!

26

I took my time over coffee and having a shower before going over to the delicatessen where I was warmly welcomed.

'You look a bit brighter than you did a few weeks ago, a bit tired if I may say so but the tan suits you. Did the time help?' Phillippe, the owner, had known Mark long before I did and we'd became close friends with his extended family.

'Yes, I think the time has helped in some ways, but I had a late night—or early morning—so, yes, a bit tired. And mother was on the blower first thing!'

Phillippe grinned knowingly.

'Well, it's nice to be welcomed home by parents, isn't it?'

I returned his grin but only asked,

'Phil, have you seen anything of Julie recently?'

'Oh, not for about two months, I should think. She came over one day saying she was looking for you. She was a bit distraught and seemed to have forgotten you were away. Is she OK?'

'Exactly what I'm trying to find out. Can you give me some of your special pastries—I'm off to see mother.'

'I'll get some of the extra special ones. Her play is imminent in the West End, isn't it? Any chance of first night tickets?'

'I'll try, but from what she said this morning, it may never hit the boards.'

He handed me a box which I took. 'Pay you tomorrow, Phil.'

'You get the tickets and the pastries are on the house.'

Before I went to see mother, I returned home, had another coffee while I read Julie's letter again. Apart from sounding somehow frantic, she didn't give any indication she was leaving the country. I needed to find out exactly what information mother had, which was going to be difficult in her state, before I could do anything.

Since our parents' four children had left the large house set in a couple of acres of the Sussex countryside, they had sensibly downsized to a four-bedroom flat in London. It was a wrench for father as it had been his family home for three generations, but sense prevailed as none of us was likely to need it or indeed afford to keep it up; it was beginning to look tired and in need of a lot of maintenance. Father now had a beautiful study and access to all the museums, universities and places of interest he could want or need; either on his doorstep or within easy transport for travelling, so he was content.

Mother opened the door to me and grabbed me in one of her overacted embraces.

'Darling, lovely to see you.'

'Mind the cakes, Mother.'

'Oh yes. Sorry. Now what brings you here? I thought you were still in France, oh, sorry, silly me—I rang you, didn't I? I was deep in a script and the heroine is in France and that is one of my lines—but this crisis isn't in the play, is it? What do you know about Julie? I've got hold of Portia, she knows nothing and I can't get hold of Francis.'

I'm always amazed at how much my mother can say using only one breath; she never stopped during her explanation of what she'd done and the responses from one of my siblings. I hope her directors and producers realise this ability.

'One thing at a time, Mother. Do you still have Grace coming to help with the housekeeping?'

She nodded her confirmation so after speaking with Grace and asking for coffee, I went to see father who was reading in his study.

'My dear child,' he stood and embraced me, 'how are you? Did the time absent from work help at all?' he held me at arms' length to look at me, 'still a bit weary—or it is something else under the tan? If there is anything I can do to help, you know you only have to ask.'

'Oh Pops.' I said launching myself into his arms again.

'There, there, my dear. We'll talk later if you need to but thank God you're here now. I'm sorry to add to your burden at this time, my dear, but we are worried about our last chick.'

'Pops, we are all grown up chickens and a rooster. You can't keep trying to look after us all.'

'As you will, I hope, find out, my dear, you never stop worrying about your children nor I hope they about you, or at least think about you. Let's go and find your mother and see if you can calm her down; she's been in a great tizzy since the postcard from Julie arrived. She wanted to contact you, but I insisted you were left in peace.'

Fresh coffee made by Grace and Phil's cakes were a perfect antidote to mother's hysteria. I was given the postcard which contained nothing except, as mother had told me, she was going to America for a while. I told them what was in the letter she'd sent to me.

'Well,' said Pops, 'I hope she had enough sense to tell the insurance company; she was pregnant, healthcare in America is not cheap.'

'I doubt even in a highly emotional state she'd risk her and her child's lives by going on an aeroplane to a country where she is unlikely to get the care she needs, in a system she's unfamiliar with. Let me see what I can find out. And, Mother, Phil wants tickets for the first night so it had better get on the stage; just concentrate on your script. I'll get back to you as soon as I've anything to report.'

I kissed them both and told my father I would talk to him sometime. He smiled as he closed the door behind me.

Outside, I thought the most obvious place to start was at Julie's flat. Neither parent had mentioned going there, which I thought they'd have done if they'd been. I couldn't face the journey to Hackney by underground so took a taxi which dropped me outside the modern apartment block. Getting out of the taxi, I saw her at the window and waved. I thought she'd seen me returning my wave before disappearing but it turned out she was acknowledging the grocery delivery man and buzzed him up. I slipped in behind him, joining him in the lift.

'Have you delivered to her before?' I asked.

'Pretty much a regular customer now, at least once a week. Sometimes more often if she's having a visitor. You a friend of hers?'

'Her sister actually.'

'That's nice, here we are. Second door along but I suppose you know, don't you?'

'Yes.' I smiled as the door was opened.

'Yvonne! You're back. Come in.'

As we embraced, I was hardly aware of a small few months' bulge between us before she asked the delivery man to put her order into the kitchen. She signed the chitty he held out to her, he wished us a good day and left, closing the door himself.

'You're looking wonderful and in full bloom of pregnancy. Morning sickness stopped?' I asked.

'Hold me, hold me, hold me, Sis.'

We embraced again before moving into the open plan living room which was immaculately kept with art nouveau paintings and sculptures strategically placed to get the best light to enhance their beauty. She'd chosen a top floor residence with a balcony, which gave a fantastic view over the river.

'Well?' I asked, dispensing with any formalities. 'America? I didn't think so. But why did you not tell me you were pregnant before I went away?'

'You were not, I think the phrase is, "in a good place" and knowing you, you'd have wanted to stay here and look after me. I'm not sure I could have coped with you in your state and you needed time and space to try and sort yourself out. I've had support and managed. Did it help you?'

'Yes. I was calm and ready to move on when I left the big house in France, but quite honestly Julie, since I've been back your bombshell has rather…I don't understand why you had to give up the master's after all your work and your obvious brain, it seems like madness. But,' I paused for a moment, 'surely there were alternatives? Did you even consider an abortion? I imagine such a decision would have been really difficult.'

'No, certainly not. I'm sorry, I seem to have rather mishandled all this. Yes, I did go a bit scatty earlier on in the pregnancy—"hormonal imbalance", I was told by my supervising professor, a real sweetie who seemed to understand even though he looks to be as old as Methuselah! Apparently, he had an awful time with his wife during her first pregnancy. Anyway, once the boy has been born, he says I can go back on the doctorate programme, if I can fix something, which may not be possible.'

'You do realise how much trauma you've caused the parents, don't you? And the rest of the family.'

'Well, actually no! None of the family has contacted me here—or anywhere. Why is it only you who had the sense to come here to see if I'm home?'

'Don't know, my dear. Maybe the oldest and the youngest have some sort of bond. I'm just so glad you're alright. But why on earth did you send the card to the parents saying you were off to America?'

'A stupid thing to do, but I couldn't face mother's theatricals.'

'You left me to do so!'

'I'm sorry, I wasn't thinking I…'

'Joke! Now, have you been having proper antenatal care, are you booked in for a hospital delivery?'

'Yes, yes, yes to all the questions. I'm not going to risk the life of my son by doing anything stupid. But the answers to the unspoken questions you are asking are, yes. I know who the father is; yes, he knows he is; yes, he wants to be involved, but just now he can't be here as he has a big problem to resolve at work before he can come over or I can join him; and yes, he is married.'

My heart sank.

'Julie, you know these married men will never leave their wives for a child from an affair, no matter what they say. The work problem must just be an excuse. What are you thinking about?'

'Well, he isn't free and he's my fantastic husband.' Smiling broadly, she showed me her wedding ring nestling underneath a beautiful engagement one which I'd not noticed. I'd certainly not been expecting this news.

I rested back in the chair and closed my eyes.

'OK,' I said suddenly and stood up, 'get your jacket or coat or something, we're going to see the parents.'

Julie didn't protest, just meekly followed me down the road where we hailed a taxi to take us to our parents' home. I don't know which mother was more relieved about, Julie being well, and safe or the producer having concluded the financial negotiations for the play. She didn't seem at all perturbed Julie was married and soon to make her a grandmother and took herself off to her own private sitting room-cum-guestroom to study her part. Father, on the other hand, took it far more seriously and demanded to know what it was all about.

'I've known him for some time, we first met at uni when I was doing my first degree. We kept in touch on and off and recently we met up at a reunion. He lives abroad but comes over whenever he can and before I was pregnant, I'd go over to him. We'd agreed to get married before the pregnancy was confirmed. When I told him, he was overjoyed and we decided to get married immediately.'

'But why on earth didn't you say anything? I really don't understand how you could do such a thing without involving your family.'

Julie looked at father.

'I'm sorry, Daddy, it all happened so quickly and ...' she paused and turned her gaze to me, 'it was all coming to a head just when, you were so—well, "out of it". I don't think you realise how worried we all were about you. For the last months, before Patrick sent you away, you were acting totally irrationally, nothing anyone said seemed to make sense to you. You really hadn't grieved during the year when you knew Mark was dying and the two years since his death, three years of unrelieved pain, I thought if I'd said anything it would just send you even further...so, I said nothing—to anyone. I'm sorry Daddy, I know how close you are to Yvonne and how you tried to help her—I thought you might tell her.'

I shook my head in disbelief and father just stared at her, then, breaking the awful invading silence asked,

31

'What sort of wedding did you have? Registry Office?' Father's voice was gruff.

'No. We were married in … oh dear … St Mark's.'

I laughed.

'Well, at least you got his blessing then.' I got up and put my hands to her face and kissed her forehead. 'You are a kind, but silly goose. Maybe telling me would have been the news to have brought me back to earth—if I was in the state you infer.'

'You were, believe us, how you managed to keep your job is a miracle,' added Pops, 'obviously, Patrick had had enough.'

I sighed and turned back to Julie.

'Well?'

'You know the vicar, he was brilliant, he seemed to understand our situation and my explanation. I think he had to get some sort of dispensation from those in authority to marry us so quickly. We just had us, him and a couple of university friends as witnesses,' she paused for a moment, 'it was very moving and I'm glad we didn't have a big wedding. For you, Yvonne, yours was special to you, this was special to me. I'm sorry if I've hurt you, Daddy.'

Although he put on an optimistic show in front of Julie, father confided to me later he was more than a little upset at her getting married without telling him or indeed any of us but what hurt him most was, regardless of our closeness, she thought he'd break a confidence which Julie could and should have entrusted to him.

We stayed for the lunch Grace prepared during which Julie told us about her husband saying they were not sure of their future plans but would probably include her moving to France. After the meal, now he knew she was safe, father obviously wanted to get back to his reading so Julie and I left.

Waiting on the pavement while we tried to hail a taxi to take Julie home, she asked,

'Have you been in touch with Mark's parents since you returned?'

'No, I've not really had the chance yet, have I, Julie? But I'll fix to see them before I go back to work. They took his death really hard.'

'I don't think any parent wants to bury their child.'

'Well, just remember that Julie, and don't put Pops through anything similar again. You suddenly disappearing with seemingly no trace really upset him, even though he didn't show it in front of you.'

'Sorry, I was mixed up and not sure what I was doing. It'll be alright when you can all meet Paul and we can be together with the baby. Will you be alright now, Yvonne?'

A taxi stopped and Julie got in.

'I'll be fine, off you go.'

'Bye and thanks for everything.'

'What else are big sisters for? Go on and put your feet up, keep in touch and call me if you need me.'

'My love to Mark's parents when you see them.'

'Thanks, take care now and call me.'

I must see if the car will start, it's been in the garage for a long time now. If it's OK, the long run out to see Mark's parents will be good for the battery.

Later in the evening, I arranged to meet Mark's parents on Monday morning at the church where he was buried in the family plot and, after a couple of protracted phone calls, I rang my father to tell him I'd contacted the rest of the family to assure them Julie was alright. I told him each had taken the news in their own characteristic manner.

'Portia said she knew something "was up" but hadn't been too worried.'

'Nothing much seems to worry her, does it?'

'Francis just said "Okay. Keep me in the loop, Sis."'

'Typical, but I can't see Francis being so brief!'

'No, I had to cut him off. By the way, I am seeing Peter and Georgina on Monday.'

'That's good. Thanks for tracking everyone down, Yvonne. Goodnight.'

Does the "oldest" in other families have to sort their siblings' problems out?

I was glad when, finally falling into bed, I had a little time to think through the day. Then, with my thoughts turning to Ricard, I fell into a deep, comfortable sleep.

§ § §

I'd not planned to do anything on Sunday but when I woke, I thought I'd go to the mid-morning service at the parish church. Returning home, I was thinking about sending Ricard a text thanking him for the pendant and started to formulate the message, searching for the right words, not too eager yet not too cool, when

33

I met a couple of friends, who'd heard I was back and were on their way to visit me. They invited me to go with them for a drink and lunch; I hesitated.

'Well, I have things to do in the flat, you know—back from holiday ironing and such like.'

'Come on, Yvonne, I don't think you have plans for today, apart from the ironing and we aren't going to let you hibernate.'

So, I joined them and abandoned any thoughts of Ricard for the moment. I enjoyed their company and found not only did they help me find my introduction back into socialising, as we met up with other friends too, but I really enjoyed their light banter and company. Such a contrast to the last months and the worries of yesterday. I didn't send a text.

§ § §

I woke refreshed, and decided, after a quick look in my wardrobe, the deep maroon trouser suit and matching boots with a cream blouse would be the correct clothes to wear to meet Mark's parents and fitted what is called "smart casual" and appropriate for lunch at the country club. Over the last few months and the weekend, I'd just used the one black handbag, the condition of which I noticed rather reflected this mild abuse. Sorting through the accumulated detritus, I found a couple of used handkerchiefs, sweet papers, a comb, a couple of tampons, my diary, loose coins and, nestling at the bottom, a small box which I opened and found there a pair of earrings matching the pendant Ricard had given me.

I held one up and looked at my reflection in the hall mirror, the green set off the cream and maroon beautifully and I saw a small glint of green in my hazel eyes. Ricard was right. I put them, then the pendant, on but hesitated, wondering if I should wear them today but somehow it felt alright to do so. I returned to putting things from one bag into another, locked the flat and left town after the heavy traffic through central London had eased.

The journey through the suburbs and onto the A40 wasn't too bad. Mark and I had often alternated between the A40 and the motor way when visiting his parents and found little difference in the journey time, it was mainly to do with the time of day, amount of traffic and our mood. Today I turned onto the motor way and stayed till I exited a few miles before Oxford and navigated through the villages. Mark's family could be traced back in his village for many generations where his father was still regarded, by the well-established families, as a sort of unofficial "Lord of the Manor", which gave him some influence in local affairs.

I left the car in a small parking area and walked through the churchyard. Before going to Mark's grave, I tried the door of the church, as I fancied a moment or two in the quiet, to my disappointment it was locked and I turned away realising the silence, apart from a few birds and the breeze in the trees, in the open air was probably a more natural one. A quote about being near to God in a garden came to my mind and promised myself to look it up sometime. I'd obviously arrived before Mark's parents and sat on a stone bench, erected in memory of one of his ancestors, to wait.

I don't know how long it was before they came or how long I'd been absent with my thoughts, but I jumped when I realised they were standing next to me.

'Oh, sorry, I didn't hear you come. Georgina, Peter it's lovely to see you.' We embraced briefly.

'We didn't mean to startle you, Yvonne, we came across the grass rather than the path. Thank you for bringing those nice flowers, Dear, I've been rather remiss and not brought any.'

Strangely enough, even though I'd been at his grave for several minutes, I'd not noticed the flowers.

'Neither did I, Mark always said flowers were a waste of money as they would only rot, and to give the money to a charity where it could do some good. Remember he requested this for his funeral when we agreed on only the two small arrangements from us?'

Georgina rummaged in her coat pocket for something, if rummaging can be the correct word for her delicate movements, she withdrew a beautifully laundered and perfumed handkerchief to dab her eyes which had started to fill.

Then she said,

'We haven't been over for a couple of weeks or so, but I have to admit I used to bring a small posy so it must have been a friend or one of the Flower Guild members; anyway, it was nice of them.'

'I've managed to get through all the red tape to have his name added to the list of family members already interned here. I'm sorry it has taken so long and afraid because of the rules only his name and dates are permitted.'

'Yes, I understand, Peter. Mark brought me here and explained before he was ill. I told him it was a bit macabre for him to be speaking of this when he was so young and we had, or thought we had, a life together. But it certainly solves the problem of what words are suitable. Some words you see on headstones are a bit weird! Thank you for organising it, is there anything I have …'

'No, nothing, my dear. It's all pretty straightforward from now on.'

Conversation seemed to come to a natural stop as we all looked at the grave with our own thoughts. The hiatus was broken by Peter suggesting we move on to lunch.

'Did you leave your car in the long-awaited carpark, Yvonne?'

'Yes, I was surprised to see it had eventually come about.'

'As you know it had been spoken about for a long time, but until recently nothing was accomplished. It is amazing how many rules and regulations there are to turn a bit of church waste land, which was already used to park cars, into an official church car park. I think the good Lord must despair of his flock at times. Such a waste of time, energy and money.'

'That could have been put to some real charitable use.' We all said together, echoing again one of Mark's favourite phrases, and laughed.

The tension relieved, we drove to the village and the hotel, a former coaching house now renovated to become a pleasant place to stay and explore the Oxfordshire County and for locals, like Mark's family, to appreciate the excellent cuisine. The meal was exceptional with superb wines, a different one with each course and carefully selected from a small but outstanding wine list by, my father-in-law who knew about wines as he'd studied them over the years. I think Mark was right when he said he thought his father had advised the hotel what to buy to make sure his taste was permanently represented.

As I had a long drive home, I drank water and accepted only small measures of wine, refusing any top-ups and declining the offer of a brandy with my coffee. As he and his wife warmed their brandy, swirling it in unison—which I'd seen them do many times, they looked at each other. Georgina gave Peter a small but almost imperceptible nod, which I'd have missed had I not moved my gaze from the gently moving brandy to her face.

'Yvonne, we, well, we…' Peter started and stopped. To my surprise, he started to colour and looked from me to Georgina for help.

I turned from one face to the other, Georgina took my left hand and stroked my wedding and engagements rings, saying,

'Yvonne, we overheard some of what you were saying to Mark or at least over his grave and we both understand there will come a time when you meet someone else. It sounded as if you were almost asking Mark's permission and understanding should this happen. You were also holding that rather lovely pendant while you were talking.'

My hand automatically moved to grasp the pendant and I felt a chill run through my body.

What had I said and how much had they heard?

'We both understand and are sure Mark would too. The only thing we ask is you take your time to be sure. You have had a rough time and then a break to reflect, so please don't forget grief and vulnerability go hand in hand. Give yourself time and be sure before you make any commitment. We are very fond of you and would not want you to act too soon and be hurt.'

'And whatever else you do,' added Peter, 'please keep in touch with us. Talk to us if you would like to but remember, you will always be part of Mark's family, even though he's not here.'

There was nothing I could say immediately, I think we were all too emotionally bound so I just took one of their hands and brought all our four together, then, first one then the other, I lifted them to my lips and kissed them.

'Thank you both.' Was all I could say. We sat quietly for a few moments while they drank their brandies and exchanged more reminiscences which raised a few laughs and helped my departure. I left them at the table and drove home.

Vulnerability again. C'est ça!

Chapter Three

I didn't know what sort of reception I'd receive when I entered the London office four days after my return to England. Office workers, like everyone else, seem to move on and forget people when they are not around, so I was grateful to be welcomed with friendly waves and sincere greetings by those who knew me.

Maybe I'll be alright back in the working environment, although a bit of me hankered for a change in my life.

The report of the project I'd been undertaking when Patrick sent me on leave was on my desk. The job could not have been left for four months but after an initial pang of regret I'd not finished the task, I was gratified to see the client comment was positive and my name had not been removed as project manager. I noted the name of the person who'd completed the task, intending to find her and offer my thanks and congratulations.

It is difficult to pick up someone else's work and requires a lot of diplomacy to unruffle the feathers of an unhappy client. I read the summary and was pleased to see she'd not made any alterations to the approach I'd taken. I'm open to ideas and different ways of looking at the same problem but was delighted to see this hadn't been necessary.

Oh dear, it seems as if it hasn't taken me long to get back into harness.

I'd just finished reading a "Welcome back" note Patrick had left on my desk when Trish, one of the general office juniors, asked if I'd like some coffee, when a voice behind her said,

'Don't bother, Trish, she'll have hers with me.' Patrick stood in the doorway beaming broadly, his arm extended towards his office. 'Come into my office and have coffee.'

I smiled my thanks to Trish and, automatically picking up my pad and pencil, followed Patrick into his office.

Once the door was closed, he pulled me to him quickly and held me tightly, pushing his body against mine.

'Oh God, how I have missed you.' He kissed my neck.

What was going on? What was he doing? This hard, forceful hold on my body physically hurt me.

'Patrick, let go of me. What the hell are you doing?' My voice was sharp but probably no sharper than the situation warranted. He jumped back as if he'd been hit.

'But aren't you glad to see me? Glad to be back? Oh, I'm so sorry, but I've done nothing but think of you all this time. I kept "seeing" you in your office, but that was someone else just finishing off the project. Yvonne, don't you know I love you, I…'

'Don't say that. You can't. Where has this come from?'

'But after Mark's death, you talked to me, expressed your feelings. I thought you were getting close to me, I thought … forgive me, I'm sorry, I've made a mistake. Sit down, have some coffee.'

'Patrick I …'

'No, please don't say anything. I'm sorry, I've obviously made a mistake, please forgive me. Please sit down. Pour us some coffee, please.'

I stood still as Patrick moved rather unsteadily towards his desk and sat behind it.

'Patrick, you do realise I could take out a big sexual harassment grievance against you for those actions, don't you?'

He looked stunned and put his head in his hands.

'You wouldn't. Surely. We've known each other far too long.'

'Known each other? Obviously, we don't know each other at all. I had no idea you had anything but sincere concern for me following Mark's death and these last few awful years—I had no inkling there was anything else. I thought you were, well, in your counselling mode.'

Had I given any indication of…? No, never. And the last time I was in his office and he offered me the leave, had I missed something? He'd held my hand and offered me tissues when I'd cried, we had a small embrace when I left. But no, there was nothing more and I couldn't think of anything I'd said or done to provoke these feelings.

'Perhaps the best thing would be for me to leave.' I started towards the door.

'No, please don't.' Patrick jumped up, intercepted me and took my elbow.

'Why not?' I demanded aggressively, shaking his hand off me. 'After this, you would have to give me a recommendation to another firm.'

'Yes, I know I would and there's no need for implied threats. You wouldn't need a recommendation, you're the best, you'd be swept up immediately. But I need you here, not only on an obviously personal level but the firm needs you. Your reputation is high, clients ask for you. As I say, you are the best project manager around.'

Neither of us said anything, just stared in the silence not knowing what to do. Emotions, different on either side, were running high and an embarrassment dropped heavily between us. I felt a strange feeling come over me as suddenly I realised just how much I regarded Patrick as a father figure, how much I enjoyed my job, enjoyed working in an environment where I was trusted to do a good job, make my own decisions, the freedom to act as I saw fit. In fact, how much I enjoyed working for and with this man.

Had I given out the wrong messages? No! Don't fall into that trap.

I dropped onto the settee where I'd been seated the last time I was here and put my hand on the coffeepot.

'Perhaps, Andrea could bring some more coffee, this is too cold to drink. I need time to think.'

Patrick requested the coffee but stayed behind his desk, looking out of the large panoramic windows till the jugs of coffee were exchanged, then brought the upright chair from the desk and placed it on the opposite side of the coffee table.

'My sister let me have irregular updates on how you were.' His voice was quiet.

'She didn't say anything to me.'

'No, I'd asked her not to. You were supposed to be away from everything here,' he sighed, 'she said you appeared to be more settled after a few days. All the other people loved you—especially the really elderly ones who needed extra help.'

'Perhaps I should change my vocation, but retreat life isn't for me.'

I poured coffee and passed Patrick his, our fingers touched under the saucer.

'Sorry.'

'*C'est ça!*'

'What?'

'Oh, nothing. Just a silly phrase used by…some of the volunteers.'

'Did you get to talk a lot of French?'

'Yes, a lot in the village but most people at Patience's house decided my French is perfect and they wanted to practice their English. But my fluency is still perfect. Why? Is there a "French Connection", if I may make a bad joke, with a possible project?'

'Joke appreciated,' he said without humour, 'yes, there is one actually.'

I waited.

'However, under the existing circumstances, I am obviously not going to tell you what, until you tell me your perspective on continuing to work for this company.' His voice had hardened and had an edge to it.

Still the hard, level-headed businessman.

'Patrick, I'm sorry if you thought I had other feelings for you. I certainly had no idea of yours for me. To be perfectly honest, and this may hurt, I look up to you as a superb boss and rather a father figure—in no way a lover. I appreciate what you have done for me during this difficult time. I've always enjoyed working for your firm—for you and especially with you. Should this, "little interlude", if I may use the phrase, hinder a positive working relationship, we—not me—need to review my future here. The time away you afforded me, has helped greatly with the grieving but, and put this on record if you wish, although I am still vulnerable it is time for me to get back to work. Either here with you or, if you prefer, I can go elsewhere. It is really up to you.'

I stood, waiting for some response from Patrick who'd stayed in his chair.

'I'm sorry I upset you and I'm even more sorry you don't have the same feelings for me as I do for you,' he stood and I expected to be shown the door and asked to clear my desk, some severance money would be paid into my bank account and a recommendation letter prepared by the end of the day. 'I would appreciate it, however, if you would consider continuing to work for this company for now and we could review the situation—should it become necessary. However, in the past,' he continued, 'before this "intermezzo", a much kindlier word I think, we would have had initial discussions about projects over a light lunch. Would you agree to one now?'

I hesitated, wondering if this was too soon, but offered a small smile.

'We ought to be able to talk business as usual.'

A new restaurant had opened in my absence and we ate there. Patrick was obviously known and we had a comfortable table laid for four, but with the extra settings removed gave plenty of space for the opened folder and my spiral pad. Everything would be on the computer but he preferred to use hard copy at an initial discussion of a project. We sat side by side, both aware of our proximity, but kept the conversation concentrated on the project under discussion.

'Where did you say this is centred?' I asked.

'I didn't,' replied Patrick, 'as you are aware, at these lunches we talk in principle, not detail but if you want to know, it's in Toulouse.'

'Where?'

'Toulouse.'

'That's what I thought you'd said.'

'What's wrong with Toulouse?'

'Nothing, Toulouse is quite convenient—for flights and so on,' I added quickly, 'but, with all due respect for your firm's reputation, why do they need us? Toulouse has the "Three Clusters" business park, research centres, universities, public sector agencies. All these establishments work together for innovative ways of economic and scientific development. It's one of the leading places. Why do they need to ask for help elsewhere?'

'Why don't you read the file in detail and see if you get answers to your question? I was approached, they asked for you. I told you, your reputation is spreading.'

'What if I can't see—or do—what they think they are asking for?'

'Oh, come on Yvonne, you know very well, what the client identifies as the problem isn't what it really is, they need to be guided through to the root cause and the solution. What they have said on the paper is often not what is really needed.'

'Alright, I'll have a look and get back to you but before the final decision, I'll go and meet them.'

'Of course, as is our custom. If you still can't see it, then we either say "no" or put in a stupidly enhanced price they're bound to reject!'

'Or they accept, I fail and you have mud on your face!'

I left the restaurant holding the file, full of hope and trepidation. Not only did I anticipate having a project I could get my teeth into but, if my geography is right, Toulouse to Carcassonne is only about 40 minutes and Carcassonne to Lézignan not much further.

Be careful, Yvonne. You are still vulnerable. C'est ça!

§ § §

Patrick wasn't in the office next day. I was concerned and asked Andrea if she knew where he was. She said he was taking a couple of days off to visit an old friend in the Cotswolds who had just been diagnosed with multiple sclerosis. I had an unreasonable spasm of guilt when I heard.

'But I'm so glad you came back when you did, Yvonne.'

'Why?'

'Well, for two reasons. He's been like a bear with a sore head since you've been away. I've had to remind him about appointments, get him to sign contracts on time, at one point I stood over him till he had read someone's project resumé before he signed it and I've been fielding errors in project proposals. One came in with the pricing ridiculously low, the person who'd been asked to price it up had missed off several noughts. If I'd not noticed it and he'd signed it, we'd be in a mess.'

'And if you hadn't noticed it and he had, I wouldn't give much for the operative's future here.'

'Right.'

'Andrea, I …'

'It's OK. I know. He was so distraught after you'd gone home last night, I got him to talk. We sat and had a couple of whiskeys in his office and he told me what had happened.'

'Andrea, I'd never had an inkling about how he felt. I was so wrapped up in myself and my misery. Do you know how long he's had these feelings?'

'I think only since Mark died and certainly more recently when you obviously needed help. He's always admired you and your work,' she paused, 'during our conversation, he admitted in hindsight, his affection for you is really paternal the same way as you view him.'

'I'm glad. I really do like him as a man and as a boss.'

'He does know. Come on, that file won't read itself nor will the monthly stats suddenly appear without someone doing them.'

'Wait a minute, you said two reasons. What's the other one?'

'Well, if you'd not come back till today, I might be having last night's conversation with Patrick this evening and as it's my twenty-fifth wedding

43

anniversary, I don't think my husband would have been too pleased with me for drinking with another man instead of with him!'

'Oh Andrea, many congratulations. Are you going out tonight? Celebrating?'

'No such luck! All the family's coming round so I'll be leaving at lunch time to get everything prepared. If you have nothing better to do, you are very welcome to join us.'

'Thanks. But …'

'I'll leave the invitation open. Any time after seven-thirty if you feel like it; might do you good—better than moping about in your flat.'

'Thanks, I'll think about it.'

We both returned to our work. After reading the file I sent a text. When I received a reply from Ricard, I called Trish to come to me.

Her name suited this retiring, pale-faced, lanky-haired girl who continually wore beige or grey.

'Thanks for coming, Trish. Have you ever done project costings?'

'No Yvonne.'

Am I doing the right thing in offering this diffident youngster a chance to progress?

'Would you like to try?'

Her eyes opened wide.

'Yes please, do you tell me what is needed or do I have to find out for myself?' Her words came tumbling out so fast I had difficulty in understanding her.

'There are several levels to costing projects, Trish. I will start you on the first, basic, level and see how you go. I tell you about my immediate needs in broad terms then you think between the lines. Have you got a pad and pencil? No? Well, sit down and have these.' I opened my desk drawer and took out a fresh spiral notepad and a pencil.

'Right, first and foremost, I'm going to Toulouse for exploratory talks with a company that's been in contact with Patrick. I'll need a flight to Toulouse from Gatwick this Friday, about mid-afternoon if possible, returning mid-afternoon on the following Tuesday. I'll take a taxi from home to Victoria Station and the train to the airport, so cost for a return taxi and an open return for the flight. Then book a room in a good hotel in Toulouse from Friday to Monday. These bookings are for the preliminary discussion with the potential client. If you can do those now Trish, I'd be grateful. And tomorrow I'll go into more depth of what costs I'll need for the whole project, assuming it goes ahead.'

'If you want me to book flights, I'll need the details of your passport, Yvonne.'

Maybe I am right—she's thinking ahead.

'Good point,' I took a card from my bag, 'here's a copy of them, please keep them safe.'

She nodded and stood.

'Thanks for this chance, Yvonne, but…' she hesitated 'how do I go about paying for all these bookings—taxi, train, flights?'

In my excitement at the thought of seeing Ricard, I'd not thought about the need for a finance authorisation form signed by Patrick.

'Wait a minute.'

I managed to catch Andrea as she was locking her desk drawer and explained the situation. She just smiled, opened her drawer again and handed me a signed form.

I remembered, despite our misunderstanding, Patrick had, thankfully, agreed I should go and have an exploratory conversation. I'd tried to be impartial in making this decision but on a personal level, this assignment was too good an opportunity to miss.

'Are you two in cahoots? How come this form is ready and signed?'

'He thought there might be a need for this in his absence. But please, don't take advantage of him. Keep him informed, on both a business and a personal level.'

'I admire him too much to be disrespectful and I like him too much to hurt him.'

I gave the form to Trish and explained the system.

'Oh, when you've made the hotel booking, please email this man, tell him where I'm staying and I'll be at his main offices at ten o'clock on Monday morning for initial discussions.'

She may look quiet, but she is alert to practicalities.

I went back to the file but still couldn't see, from the brief the French company had given, why it really needed any assistance. Nor could I identify anywhere what the problem was. The company appeared to be flourishing and well-funded. One strange factor I'd identified was, although the Board of Directors had agreed to outside assistance, it was clear I would not be meeting any of them, only one of the middle managers, Paul Eschar, and he was to be the main contact. Apparently, he had been the one to initially ask for external support in establishing why, after he'd spent a great deal of time trying to find a reason, the monthly figures did not, in his words "make up to the stuff". I wondered how good his English was and hoped we'd be conversing in French.

Andrea's invitation was very tempting so at eight o'clock in the evening, I turned up to join her and her family to celebrate their quarter century. Although I'd met several of her family, I was astounded how many there were of all generations, including the latest great grandchild just three weeks old. On my way home, I wondered how long Mark and I would have lasted if fate hadn't intervened; I liked to think a good long time.

Come on, time to move on.

I didn't see Patrick again before I took the flight on Friday. He'd decided to extend his visit to his friend. I wondered if this was just a ploy so we didn't have to be in each other's vicinity until his emotions were settled. Trish had received a reply to her email to Paul Eschar saying as he was absent for the weekend and had planned a late start to his day on Monday so he'd meet me at the hotel at ten thirty.

§ § §

During the flight, I couldn't concentrate on the files in my briefcase as I felt the jitters of a youngster on her first date.

Don't be so stupid.

But my heart pounded as I accepted the second glass of sparkling wine from the air hostess.

'Are you alright, Madam?'

'Yes thanks, I'm fine. Thank you.'

Fine, absolutely, fine. C'est ça!

Ricard was waiting for me as I emerged from passport control. It was wonderful to feel his arms around me and his lips on mine. He'd told Marianne he would be away for a few days.

'I gave her no details and as I was in the office when you contacted me, I did not expand so there is no reason she should suspect we are together. Although I have to admit it is a long time since I have disappeared without saying where I was going.'

'Are we a secret, Ricard?' I was a bit alarmed.

'Not as far as I am concerned, Yvonne, but if I had said anything, they would have clamoured to come too or bring you home. You are the topic to start and end every conversation since you left! I think we need a bit of time on our own.'

We took the shuttle to the town centre and picked up a taxi for the last leg of the journey, dropped our bags off at the hotel then, as we'd both been sitting for some time on our journeys decided to walk for a short while through Toulouse arm in arm chatting, easy in each other's company. Ricard updated me on Suzanne's schooling and how Marianne and Sven were. I told him how everyone had welcomed me back into the office with the flowers on my desk and smiles and expressed my surprise at how easy they had made it for me to settle back. Then told him how pleased the freelance worker had been when I tracked her down to thank her, for the work she'd done on the project, I'd had to leave. Apparently, she'd never been thanked before.

'Very kind of you, do you always act so generously? And Patrick? Was he pleased to see you?'

'I certainly try to give credit where it's due but having other contacts in the field is useful.' I decided not to tell Ricard about Patrick's advances, just nodded and said he was extremely pleased I was back.

'We had a talk about the future then, over lunch, discussed the possible contract I am here to investigate. But please, no more about work and the office tonight.'

We retraced our steps to a restaurant not too far from the hotel for an evening meal.

§ § §

We didn't rush to get up on Saturday morning. After a late breakfast we decided the early September sun was welcoming enough to venture out. Most of the carousels had been packed away and the leaves on the trees were beginning to take on their early autumn colours. The wind had a bitter bite to it so we returned to the hotel and settled down in the lounge of the hotel by the modern artificial log fire which gave out heat. We seemed to be the only guests there.

'Tell me a bit about your childhood, Ricard. Your life now seems to be different from how, I suspect, it was on the farm or am I jumping to conclusions?'

'No, you are not. As boys, my brother and I had the full run of the farm. Jules is two years younger than me and we got on well, together. As we grew old enough to be of use around the farm, we were set to work helping. A small farm is very labour-intensive and we learnt the need to pull our weight, but I was not really interested in farming and was more academically inclined than Jules. Although we still had work on the farm and schoolwork to do, mother was insistent we all went to church together on Sundays. The village church is old, very plain and simple, I enjoyed the peacefulness. I remember father protesting he did not have the time due to the amount of work still to do, especially in harvest time, but mother always got her way.

'In our early teens, our brotherly relationship started to be less intense as I studied in preparation for university,' he frowned and shifted his position, 'I think it was then the rift between us really started. Jules resented my education and the fact money was being spent on it while he was being denied things. He continued to work on the farm when I left to further my studies. Perhaps it might have been different if I had gone home more often than I did and probably should have done.

'My parents must have been making sacrifices to support me, the farm did not provide a rich income although it gave a reasonable living. But it was hard graft and I do not know how they managed it financially, as well as affording to send Jules to agricultural college, which they did during my third year. I did ask father, but he was very oblique in his answers and I do not think was telling the whole truth.'

'Is this why there is a rift between you and your parents?'

'Partly.'

'You know Suzanne wants them to invite me to the farm so I can meet your mother and father properly, don't you?'

'Yes.'

'Come on, Ricard, be a bit more forthcoming. If I'm invited, what do I say— refuse and if so on what grounds, or accept and go into a possible minefield? And where does it leave you? Would you go too?' I was silent for a moment then continued, 'Ricard, if you have a problem with your brother, how does this affect your relationship with your parents?'

'Sorry, Yvonne, can we drop it?' He got up and paced to the window and stared out into the gathering gloom.

'If you say so, but the question is going to be there, hovering, you know, like the proverbial elephant, whether I get an invitation or not.' I let the topic drop and asked, 'Where is your brother now? Suzanne didn't mention her uncle during any of our chats about her times at the farm in the summer.'

Ricard let out a frustrated sigh.

'No, he left for Australia when she was about a year old. As far as I know, he is still there and they are welcome to him, I really do not give a damn. I've never heard from him since he went and I do not want to. Whether our parents have I do not know.'

'So, what happened to cause such a rift between you?'

'We had a blazing row, more than a row, in fact.'

I waited silently for Ricard to continue, he seemed to be searching for words.

'After agricultural college, he worked on a couple of large farms gaining more knowledge and expertise before returning to my parents' place. They were pleased to have him back but he'd been thinking about emigrating to Australia for some time and, as I said when Suzanne was about twelve months old, he finally left. He had been talking about it and planning for some time. He had found himself a job on a sheep farm and got all the paperwork and travel arrangements—everything—in place.

'The timing was a surprise and really upset my parents who relied on his help and with his suggested changes to farming methods he had learnt and implemented, the farm was now more productive and gave a good income. The news of his sudden departure, just before harvest was to start, annoyed me as, not only had he let our parents down but also Suzanne—he was her godfather. Technically still is, though I am not sure what sort of role model he is.

'Anyway, because it was coming up to harvest time, he agreed to postpone his departure till it was ended and help the parents, at least one thing to his credit. I went to wish him good luck and it was then we had the argument and he just left—before the harvest was finished leaving my parents in the lurch. I went home, end of story.'

'Does Suzanne know?'

'I have not told her. No reason she should be told and I do not want the past raked over for no reason. Whether the parents have I do not know, but she has never said anything, so unless they have sworn her to secrecy, which I doubt, then no she does not.'

'I'm sorry, Ricard, it's obviously still a raw point.'

He came and sat again.

'Enough! We have too little time this weekend to delve into my emotional hang-ups.'

We sat in silence for some time staring into the fire, both of us with our own thoughts. I moved closer to him and rested my head on his shoulder. His body felt tense and I wondered if there was more to the argument than he'd said, as he relaxed, he put his arm round my shoulder.

'Sorry,' he mumbled as he kissed the top of my head.

This man has a lot of anger holed up inside him. Be careful, Yvonne.

A crowd of noisy tourists arrived at the hotel and invaded the lounge, we excused ourselves and took advantage of the extraordinarily early buffet in the hotel restaurant and opted for our coffee and brandies to be delivered to our room as the restaurant filled up.

§ § §

I was awake and moving around the room early on Sunday morning when Ricard stirred.

'Good morning. I've ordered some coffee.'

'It is a bit early,' he said looking at his watch.

'Not for the eight o'clock mass in the church two streets away. I thought I'd go. Do you want to come?'

'Is it raining?'

'No; what has the weather to do with it?'

'Nothing, I was just giving myself time to think if I can still find my way around the prayer book. It has been a long time.'

'Oh, the years of our mothers' training never fades. You'll have to guide me through it—I'm not Catholic.'

'Well, I will not tell if you do not. Have I got time to shower before I dress?'

When we emerged from the church, the sun was shining. Ricard looked at me with a smile.

'Thanks. That was a good idea. But why?'

'I just felt it was the right thing to do. Maybe we should reintroduce the practice into our own lives.'

The rest of the day and night sped by too fast.

Chapter Four

Monday morning, Ricard left early in a taxi for the train and I returned to bed for a while before having breakfast and waiting for Paul Eschar.

I waited in the foyer until eleven-thirty then, as Paul Eschar had not arrived, I called for a taxi and went to the company's address.

True to their website picture, it was a large, impressive building with glass lifts and open staircases, automatically opening and closing blinds according to the strength of the sunlight. I was looking forward to working in this high-tech environment for a few weeks, but as I announced myself to the receptionist, a man wearing shorts, a t-shirt and trainers without socks suddenly appeared, rather out of breath. He nodded to the receptionist and much to my astonishment quickly guided me out of the building. I started to protest but he urged me forward to his car.

'Please,' he said as he held my elbow and almost dragged me forward, 'please, just come. I am Paul Eschar, I will explain.'

I complied, not having much option apart from screaming, as his hand was firmly on my arm and he seemed very intense. Once seated in the car, which he'd parked right in front of the office building in a "No Parking" area, and seatbelts fixed, he drove off rapidly.

'Hey! Slow down. Nothing can be so bad you want to kill us both!'

'Sorry,' he frowned and slowed down to a comfortable and legal speed as we exited the enormous campus. A short time passed then he spoke, 'I apologise for my lateness, *Madame* Birch, the plane was delayed, and for my clothes, I did not land in time for me to go home and change. When I got to your hotel and found you had left, I just had to get to you quickly.'

I looked down at the strong tanned legs and the rather expensive trainers. There was a mark on the inside of this left ankle.

The remains of a nasty bruise.

'*Monsieur* Eschar, why are we going away from the offices? Where are we going? What is going on?'

'One moment please, *Madame* Birch, I will explain,' he ran a hand through his thick blond hair and thought for a moment, watching the traffic carefully as he continued, 'Some time ago, I asked for an internal review of the accounts department. Figures were just not adding up. My request was denied.'

'Couldn't you just have done it yourself?' I questioned.

'Oh, I did try, but got my knuckles rapped by one of the directors. With the monitoring system we have in place, it was not feasible—as I had found out—because it meant working every evening. It must have been those extra late evening activities that alerted him.'

'I find it strange; if you weren't permitted to audit the work, it's been agreed to let an outsider do so.'

'Yes, I agree, maybe it was because I kept on about it, they finally said if I was still finding inconsistencies after three months, I could put in a request for an external review. But not to use a local or French company. I did some research and on recommendation, I approached your firm and somewhere along the line, your name was mentioned, so I asked for you.'

'I'm flattered, but why me?'

'I do not wish to be rude but I do not know anything about you or your work profile, but you were suggested.'

'Don't apologise, I don't know anything about you either!'

He paused to negotiate a difficult intersection, then continued,

'The day after your arrival had been confirmed, I was told my office and team were to be located elsewhere even though you were coming only for some preliminary discussions. I protested saying it was an insult to a visitor to be suddenly moved to a small rundown office space in the centre of Toulouse which, at the time, I had not even seen.

'Anyway, after my first protest about the office move, I received a phone call, suggesting—well, very strongly advising—I did not resist the move but go along with it. The caller hinted we might find we could work better away from the centre. The voice was familiar, I think it was disguised and I could not quite pinpoint it. So, I had no option but to agree especially as on the Thursday morning when we arrived at the office a couple of security officers told us we could only enter to remove any personal items. Nothing to do with the business was to be touched. I went straight to *Monsieur* Faunier—'

'Who is he?' I interrupted.

'The Finance Director. He said it had been a Board decision and he had no authority to override the instructions, I was furious and told him so, he dismissed me abruptly saying I was to pick up a package at the security desk and to go the address printed on the front and follow the enclosed instructions.'

He was holding the steering wheel so tightly I thought his knuckles must be white under the tan. Then he joined in the un-choreographed hooting from cars around us, whether this was a controlled expression of anger from what he'd told me, or because a learner driver had stalled the engine a couple of times at lights and was holding up the traffic, I couldn't tell but opted for the latter.

'That's not fair, you were a learner once. Relax and tell me more.'
He took his hands off the wheel and stretched, 'Sorry, yes you are right. I went back to the office and told the others, we—'

'Did as you were told and—' I interrupted but didn't finish my sentence as he said,

'Here we are!' and turned into a small carpark. 'The office is not too bad and has a real bonus of this private parking.' After he'd put the car into neutral, pulled on the hand brake and unbuckled his seatbelt, he sighed and said, 'But I am not sure if I am being side-lined; something is wrong and not only with the figures.'

The thought of a small rundown office space in the centre of Toulouse did not enthuse me so I followed him with some foreboding, expecting the worst, but found myself on the first floor of the building in a large, airy, open plan office with views of the town from three sides.

Maybe this won't be such a bad place in which to work, after all.

The large windows had been sensitively double-glazed so there was minimal traffic noise. Placed, rather oddly for an office, in front of the curved triple aspect window, was an antique circular table with five beautifully carved chairs. The spectacular view from here was over a large garden and square.

Monsieur Eschar introduced me to his team members before he disappeared with the overnight bag he'd retrieved from the boot of the car and excused himself, passing into an adjoining room.

By the time he re-emerged, having had a shower and put on a fresh long-sleeved cotton shirt, but still wearing the same shorts and trainers, I'd been offered and accepted coffee and a fresh croissant; found out that Monique Rouse was a graduate in statistics and had a brain for complicated cryptic crosswords; a single mother whose daughter was looked after by her own mother during working hours. She had a habit, whether it was nerves or something she did all the time I didn't know, of putting her well-manicured fingers to her cheek when she spoke. She had a lightness to her voice, as if perpetually expecting something to surprise her.

Shaking hands with Daniel Dacre, the third member of the team, I found myself having to look up as he towered over me. He was a computer "nerd", programmer and electronic contraption wizard and obviously felt at home with all modern devices. He said he'd started out to be a chef and still had connections in the catering trade. I was soon to learn the importance of this latter, seemingly unimportant, piece of information.

'How have you two got on setting this up since I left on Friday morning?' Paul Eschar turned to me. 'Some time ago, before the sudden disruption, I'd booked an extended weekend I really couldn't cancel, so had left them to fix up the office and download the information on the memory sticks in the package.'

On each of their desks were two computers, except for Monique's, which had three. A workstation had been provided for me with one computer but also a printer. All the computers, except the third one on Monique's desk, were wirelessly connected to each other and the printer. This seemed to be an overprovision of equipment.

'We had to set up the computers with the programmes from scratch then followed the instructions in the package and printed out the files, which are old ones from, we think, the date when you started noticing something was wrong.'

'But that is months ago, we will need more up to date information. I cannot understand why the Directors do not want us to find the errors.'

'Paul, it might be nothing more sinister than just a computer glitch.'

'So why did they not want Daniel to work with the computer "boffins"? He could have found out if there was something wrong in the programme, no, there is something dishonest going on and someone does not want us to find it.'

I had the feeling this discussion had gone on before and nothing had been resolved.

'Look, I am just new coming into this and I'm only here for a short time for an exploratory investigation and discussion regarding my possible usefulness. So, as we have, for circumstances obviously beyond anyone's control, lost a lot of the day for work, perhaps you could talk me through the problem and let me look at any evidence you have.' I asked them to start from the beginning and explain in detail.

'I have not seen these printouts for some months so Monique, could you take *Madame* Birch through them. I'll follow you.'

The printouts showed me where the items should cross-reference each other at some point. It certainly was a detailed audit trail. Superficially, there did not appear to be any discrepancies but the small close-knit team were adamant something was amiss but could not see where or how. None of them could see why the figures did not add up. I studied the papers, asked questions, drank coffee.

'But there is nothing here to indicate anything's amiss.' I insisted.

'These printouts are very limiting and only show a snapshot, said Monique.

'And they are old ones too,' added Paul.

'If this is all the available information—or evidence—I can't see I'll be of any use. And why your company has gone to such lengths to stop you—or anyone—looking into their activities is beyond me. So, sorry Paul, seems like a trip back to the airport for me.'

They all looked at me as if I'd just told them the sky was about to fall in.

'*Non, non, non.*' They shouted together.

'We have got this far—which may be nowhere for you—but we have been subjected to all kinds of "cold shouldering" for months. We know there is something wrong; look, *Madame* Birch, we need help. Please do not make a decision just yet.'

'Paul,' I spread my hands indicating the printouts and looked at their three faces, 'look at what we have in front of us, you wanted a fresh pair of eyes; all they seem to prove is the firm's running well, selling well and thriving.'

They looked at each other and sighed. I thought they were capitulating.

Paul nodded to Daniel who left the office, Monique covered, but did not close down her computers. She moved to the sideboard by the antique table and started to lay dinner placings for five people. I was bemused and asked what was going on.

'We all need to eat if we are going to continue to work.' Paul replied.

I looked at my watch and realised it was half past seven. We'd been discussing and searching for clues for hours; obviously, these three were on a mission.

Paul opened a bottle of white wine he'd taken from a cleverly disguised fridge and poured wine into four of the five glasses set on the table as Daniel reappeared with a uniformed waiter from a nearby restaurant. Between them, they carried the contents of an evening meal which they set on the table and the waiter retired. There was a short hiatus then Paul looked at his watch and said,

'Oh, never mind.' And lifted his glass to salute us. As he did so, a man entered the office.

'Oh! Not waiting for me, eh?' his voice was friendly and jocular, 'quite right too. Sorry Paul, it was a bit difficult to leave the office without it seeming to be too obvious. I am glad to see you have dressed for the occasion.'

'Good God!' exclaimed Paul. 'You, sir!'

'And who better than the one who has been watching your backs? Eh! First though, introduce me, a glass of wine and then we will eat.'

Paul regained his composure and poured a glass of wine which he took over to the man.

'*Madame* Birch, may I introduce *Monsieur* Marcel Faunier. *Monsieur* Faunier, this is *Madame* Yvonne Birch.'

The conversation over the meal did nothing to highlight the cause of the problem Paul had identified, but it was obvious Faunier was the "voice" who'd advised Paul not to object to the office move and had also provided all the equipment and venue.

'On the assumption Paul and his team—and presumably you, *Monsieur*— are right about some "foul play", how are you expecting them to trace any untoward happenings from here without direct access to the main system?'

'Yes indeed,' responded Faunier, who produced three memory sticks which he put on the table, pushing one over to Monique saying, 'this one, with the red dot, contains all the authorised codes used in the company for all transactions of any sort, it needs to be downloaded to only one computer and kept read only.' He laid strong emphasis on the last statement. 'You have one standalone as instructed?'

Monique nodded.

'Why that one in particular?' I enquired.

'In case anyone tries to add, alter or subtract a code which has not been authorised. If anyone does try to do so, you'll be able to trace it in the future,' he smiled. 'I really do not know what is going on and it is only due to Paul's vigilance we have got this far.'

'And where is that?'

'Well, actually nowhere! And, in view of this, I suggest the computer used is password-protected and only you four know how to access it.'

'What about you, *Monsieur*?' Enquired Paul.

'No Paul, I will supply you with as much information as I can gather, but we must keep the team small and tight. Let us be honest,' he looked at all of us in turn, 'you do not know if I am one of the bad or good guys, do you?'

'If there are goodies and baddies,' I said, 'and not just a computer glitch.'

'Very true, *Madame.*' Then ignoring the intrusion, he continued speaking, 'Now, the one marked in green,' he passed it to Dominic, 'has the codes of all the computer users and the computer station codes.' He turned to me. 'When employees are engaged, they are told they may use their allocated computer for personal activities as long as they are legal, but made aware their station will be remotely monitored along with everyone else's with periodic checks. Goodness knows there is a lot of guff on as everyone uses their desk computer to email food and Amazon orders and set up birthday parties, but you will be able to differentiate—somehow!' He smiled. 'I'm no technologist, *Madame*, but I can just about download some files to memory sticks.'

'And the yellow one?' Asked Monique, looking at the third memory stick.

'This has all the transactions of the last four months and from 0100 to 1900 today—and shows the codes and corresponding computer stations used during those times. If you need me to try access further back, I will try to do it for you, but remember my station is monitored too and I do not want to be caught till you have solved this riddle,' he must have seen me react to this last statement as he continued, 'it is all above board, *Madame.*'

I nodded.

All a bit "big brother" but if no one had anything to hide, why worry and almost unlimited free internet access is not to be sneezed at.

'Well, I must leave you now, thank you for this wonderful meal, but I must meet some awful acquaintances of my wife's. I managed to excuse myself from the dinner, but I am expected to join them for coffee. I will try to stay longer tomorrow evening and bring an update on the day's activities. Goodnight.'

As we rose, I extended my hand saying,

'Well, I won't see you again then before I return home. I am on the early evening flight out of Toulouse.'

'But surely, you will be staying to see this through?'

'All the agreement we have now is I spend a short time here trying to identify what you need—if I can then feed back to my boss, if he agrees we send you a contract; if you agree the terms, I return.'

'So many "ifs", and have you identified what we need?'

'Quite honestly, with the information I have seen on the printouts, which I understand is old, the answer is "no", but I'm really impressed with the young team here and their commitment, or should I say conviction, something is wrong. But what I can't see is any evidence of wrongdoing, which I think is what you're asking me. Maybe it's just a case of wrong coding; it will take more time to search through the information on the sticks you have brought today, to establish anything.'

'Then look at them, take your return flight, *Madame*, persuade your boss to agree to your returning. Send the contract to Paul and I'll sign it and get you back. I have confidence in this group and don't think they would be so worried if they did not think something is wrong.'

He left, leaving me more bemused about why I'd been brought in to assist when it was obvious, Faunier, as Financial Director, surely had the power to authorise a full investigation and include whichever statutory bodies were relevant.

Or is Faunier involved in a double bluff and playing for time while he and others extricated themselves from… What?

They downloaded the sticks and started to work on them. Again, I asked Paul to explain what I was seeing.

'Every component has a different code. This system tracks when they were ordered, delivered to the warehouse and transferred to the relevant department. Once they have been used or dispatched elsewhere, they are coded appropriately.' He guided me through the system by following one item which was recoded three times as it went from department to department with its relevant cost codes.

'Simple,' he said.

By midnight, I'd had enough and told them to close the computers and we'd start again in the morning. Monique locked the memory sticks in a drawer in her desk, the only one I noticed made of metal and had a lockable drawer and cupboard.

We wished each other a good night and Paul dropped me off at my hotel promising to join me for coffee at the hotel the next morning at seven thirty.

There were a couple of messages waiting for me at reception. One from Ricard wondering why I'd not responded to any of his texted messages, the other from Patrick asking how the day had gone. Although it was nearing one in the morning, I rang Ricard and explained I'd had my phone turned off and I'd only just got back from the office. I was exhausted so we did not talk for long. It was too late to respond to Patrick, so went to bed with Ricard's voice still in my head and nagging thoughts.

Was Faunier involved? Did he have an accomplice? Was this all just an elaborate and expensive "setup"?

§ § §

Paul, dressed more formally in slacks and shirt, joined me in the hotel restaurant as agreed.

'Tell me about your family, may I call you, Paul? As you know, I am Yvonne, do you live in Toulouse or have one of those lovely country houses? Any children?'

'One due soon.' He responded with a smile as he opened the car door for me.

'That's nice, my sister is expecting her first too. Do you want a boy or a girl?'

'We do not mind as long as it is okay. But he will be a boy according to the scans.'

'Same as my sister's. Do you have any brothers and sisters?'

'I do not really know anything about my real family and parents. Apparently, my father died when I was a baby and my mother could not cope so I was adopted. To all intense and purposes, my adoptive parents are my parents and their children my brothers. Why do you ask?'

'No reason, just making a bit of conversation.'

'And you, Yvonne?'

'Recently widowed and maybe just coming to terms with my life again. But unlike you, both my parents are alive and I have two sisters and one brother.'

We entered the office and were greeted by the smell of freshly brewed coffee and the bright eager faces of Monique and Daniel, who parted from each other as we entered and we all exchanged morning greetings.

I wonder if mother was also baby-sitting while Monique was not working. None of your business, so long as they concentrate while they're here.

They'd turned on all the computers ready to work.

'The files are marked "read only", *Madame*, but they can be opened and copied or altered if we need to do so, but not the master code one.'

'Thanks Monique.'

Four hours is a long time to look at the information from the memory stick on screens. Paul came behind me and asked,

'Do you see anything?'

I wish I knew what I was looking for.

'I'll need more time to even start to get my head round all these codes and things. You've obviously been seeing something you did not like. What is it?'

'I just cannot put my finger on it,' he turned away with a loud sigh then asked, 'do you have enough information to take back to persuade your boss you can return to help us?'

'I'm really not sure but I'll do my best. It's certainly intriguing especially in the manner in which you were quite unceremoniously removed from your main office and I'm not sure what to think about the role *Monsieur* Faunier is playing.'

'You mean is he—'

I put up my hand to stop Paul saying any more.

'Let's not speculate or theorise at this stage. At worst, we will be doing him a disservice and at best, we'll be clouding our judgement. We have to work with facts.'

'But there do not seem to be any, which is why we need you to help. You have my email address, please send the contract as soon as you can and come back, we need help if we are going to get to the bottom of this. But if you are going to get the flight, we had better leave soon.'

'OK. Give me a moment.' I ran up and down the codes again.

'Paul, if we work on the assumption of my returning …'

'Oui! Bon.' Once more, three voices in unison.

'An assumption I emphasise, it is not a given, but while I am in England, can you look at different station codes the operatives at specific stations are using and identify sites like Amazon, restaurants and so on, then, using a copy of the file, delete all such transactions. It will be taxing as you may have to use one of your computers to go online, but between you, you may find a quick method of identifying the ones we are not interested in.'

'That will reduce the number of transactions we have to concentrate on,' said Daniel.

'Hopefully and after a time, you may recognise them. But don't work too late each evening; this will be tedious and you'll need to stay alert and do remember to keep your investigations legal. If you crack it before you get the contract, well done and it's been nice knowing you!'

'Yvonne, your flight, we must leave now.'

§

The journey home was uneventful. On the plane I made some rough notes about the experience in the company. I almost forgot to note the sudden change of venue. It did seem all very vague. From Gatwick I got the train to Victoria Station where I thought about asking the taxi driver to take me to Hackney, I wanted to see my sister again but realised it was rather late.

I'll go tomorrow evening.

There was a large bunch of flowers at my flat's door. They looked fresh so can't have been there long. The note, when I extracted it from the cellophane wrapping once I was in the kitchen, said simply, *'Sorry. Please come and see me for coffee and let me know how it went. Patrick.'*

I felt our relationship was going to be alright and back on an even keel. I sorted the post into rough piles and went to bed.

§ § §

I woke late, so rang Andrea and said I'd be in as soon as I possibly could. I was amazed how relatively uncrowded the buses were at this time of the day. Tourists were around, but the different atmosphere from the morning grind was apparent, maybe this is something I could get used to, a less pressurised life without deadlines and projects. I sighed.

Is the grass really greener?

I got off the bus and walked briskly to the office where I found Trish standing in my office, eagerly holding her notepad.

'Well?' She asked.

'All went well, thanks for the organisation.'

'And?' She looked expectant; pencil poised.

'Trish, that's not how it works. I've to discuss my findings with Patrick, he decides whether or not to proceed, if he does, he negotiates with the client before there is any more. As soon as I know, I'll tell you. But you could establish if the cost of the hotel and flights will be the same for the next six months or so—you might even try negotiating for a discount for the hotel.'

'No harm in trying. Let's see if I'm any good at bargaining. If it goes ahead, will you need weekly flights or will you stay there?'

'Probably a mixture of both actually,' I kept my voice as even as I could, 'I'll need to get home to see my sister, especially as she's pregnant and possibly to see my mother's play.'

'Oh.'

'But what you did for this first time was spot on. Thank you.'

Trish smiled and left.

I sat down to write my report and found as many reasons as I could for continuing the project. I did emphasise it seemed as if there was going to be a great deal of checking codes and statistics, rather than my usual management input, but the Financial Director seemed eager to have my involvement. I estimated four weeks' contribution from me but proposed an open-ended contract till the job was done. I added a personal note under "any specific items", identifying a possibility I might need to return to the UK at short notice incurring possible disruption of the work.

I printed two copies and was about to take one to Andrea when the phone rang.

'Hello, yes, OK Andrea, I'll go in.'

Patrick was sitting in his usual place behind the desk. He indicated I should take the upright chair on the opposite side; the formality of this meeting was far more so than normal and was in stark contrast to the start of our last one. I took a seat and asked after his friend.

'Early days yet, but even so very distressing. I've known him, well, all my life, I suppose. It is such a nasty disease.'

'I understand there's some research which is proving to be positive.'

'Yes, he is trying to keep things together and...,' he paused, 'be positive.' He echoed the words quietly to himself.

'Thank you for the flowers, Patrick.'

He sat up and grinned at me.

'Yes. Now, to business, tell me all about this project. Is it worthwhile? What's it about? Are you interested and can you do it?'

I handed him one of the copies I'd brought with me.

'Answers in order of questions. I don't know; I've no idea; yes; I'd like to think so, although it's not my usual area of expertise.'

'Well, you have just given the most useless resumé of a project.' He sat back in his chair and made "temples" with his fingers. 'Tell me what you really think, Yvonne.'

I took him through the document explaining the situation as I saw it, referring to various pages and expanding as necessary and clarifying points when he asked a question. I thought the young team might be too close to the problem and about my concerns about Faunier's possible involvement but concluding it was a challenge for me I'd never encountered before and would like to try and resolve it.

The following silence was most peculiar and only broken by the sound of the traffic outside and wailings of police and ambulance sirens.

'I had a telephone call from *Monsieur* Faunier this morning. He'd not realised you were only there for such a short visit. Some sort of breakdown in communications between this Paul Eschar and him, but he wants you back again. He gave me the impression there's some urgency to getting, whatever it is, sorted. I've made a few notes,' he handed me a paper, 'and I'd like you to add anything else you think to be pertinent.'

It was a formal contract for me to undertake the project. I smiled and said I'd get straight back to him. I was amazed at the amount he'd put to charge the French company and, after making a few additions, with Trish's input, I gave the amended contract to Andrea who shortly showed me a signed one.

'Patrick says you have an email address where I should send this.'

'Oh, it's with the original documents, I'll ask Trish to find it.'

'I don't know what's going on with you, Yvonne, but please be careful.'

Goodness, is it so obvious? Careful girl. You are still vulnerable. C'est ça!

I nodded and thanked her, called for Trish to get Paul's email then gave her the go ahead for the bookings, pointing out I'd need hold luggage this time, not just cabin. Although Faunier wanted me back immediately, Trish couldn't get me a flight till late Friday morning. Even so, as I'd done all I could in the office,

I put my head round Patrick's office door to say I was going home to pack then see my sister and parents before I went away for four weeks, possibly longer.

'As it's about lunchtime, let's eat together first.'

'I need to see Julie and my parents as well as pack, Patrick, I haven't got much time.'

'Have lunch and don't come into the office tomorrow. Give me five minutes.'

While I waited, I sent Ricard a message to say I was returning on Friday and asked if he was available for us to meet at the same hotel in Toulouse that evening. I added I was going to lunch with Patrick then on to see my sister so I may not respond immediately to his return message should he make one.

Lunch was a relaxed affair during which we exchanged news about our families. His sister was well, and she had several people staying and Patrick said he was thinking of going to see her for a few days.

We were sitting opposite each other at the table, when I told him Julie was pregnant and I'd been concerned when I got her note. He reached over for my hand which I withdrew quickly.

'Sorry, I just going to reassure you; she's been looked after, I've been keeping an eye on her making sure she was having proper care.'

'Why didn't you tell someone?'

'For her own reasons, she didn't want anyone to know; she'd sworn me to silence. She came to me initially for some sort of guidance. You two girls seem to get your heads into a bit of a mess.'

'Patrick, she's my sister, she'd been seemingly missing for weeks, my parents have been going…I don't know what, you should've told them, my father at least.'

'I couldn't tell anyone and I doubt an anonymous note saying she was alright and not to worry would have helped them.'

'No,' I agreed, giving him a lopsided smile, 'that would sound rather like the prelude to a blackmail scenario. Thank you for your kindness, Patrick. Do you know who the father is? Has she told you?'

'No, but she did say he's kind and generous and indeed they do intend to marry.'

'Seems like I'm a bit of news ahead of you then, they are married. I'd have thought she'd have had the decency to invite you or at least tell you, I'll read her the riot act. But it seems strange a job should be a barrier though, doesn't it?'

'Unless I know all the facts I try not to speculate or guess, it seems a waste of energy and mental power. Rather like this project you're about to embark on, you went, got me the facts—well, sort of—then I decided. And don't worry, you've seen her and she's fine and I'm sure they'll tell you all about it when the time is right for them.'

'I'll ring her from the office and make her my first port of call this afternoon. Thanks for lunch and again, thank you for everything.'

§

Julie was resting when I arrived at her apartment and accepted the news of my imminent departure calmly. I told her I now knew Patrick had been keeping an eye on her and he'd kept her secret. I once again emphasised the trouble she'd caused the parents.

'Yes, I'm sorry, but I just needed time for the hormones and all the changes to settle. If I need you, I'll call, promise.'

'When do you think I'll get to meet this man of yours?'

'We'll fix it as soon as we can. We're not hiding anything nasty I promise. Let me know when you'll be back again and we'll fix for the family to meet him.'

'Poor man, all of us together? I've already jokingly threatened Ricard with…' I felt the colour rise from my neck to my cheeks and took a handkerchief from my bag and blew my nose.

'Who? Someone in France? I thought you were very keen to get back there. Tell me.'

'Just a casual acquaintance, no-one to get excited about. We were talking about families one day and both trying to outdo each other by seeing who could create the bigger monsters.'

'I don't believe a word of it. But please Sis, be careful. This isn't a sort of reverse rebound after the bad years following Mark's death, is it?'

'It's nothing, Julie, just a chap I met and we've had dinner a couple of times, don't start getting any ideas and don't say anything to the parents, you know how Pops worries and Clementine gets hysterical, mainly due to her playing Lady Macbeth too often! In any case, he's just a friend and I'm going to work in Toulouse on an interesting project.'

'I don't believe you, be careful, you are still at a vulnerable time.'

Vulnerable again!

Before leaving, I made Julie promise to call me, or indeed Patrick, if she needed anything. I rang my father between packing and chatting to friends, inviting myself to dinner the following evening, then went over to see Phillippe and his family to give them an update on Julie. They invited me to stay for supper so it was not till later I picked up Ricard's reply to my message, it was short, almost curt, saying he was tired following a protracted and difficult court hearing and agreeing to meet at the hotel, adding he'd come by train. The tone, or my interpretation of it, worried me. Had I read more into the relationship than was there?

Yes, I was very vulnerable and maybe this was not the right time.

§ § §

I spent most of the next day sorting out domestic things and making sure everything was organised for what would hopefully be a four weeks absence. I saw my elderly neighbour, Mrs Asher, and told her I'd be away and replaced a lightbulb for her.

I went over to my parents for dinner, my mobile buzzed and vibrated as I arrived at their flat, I answered it in the hallway before joining them in the sitting room. It was Ricard.

'Hello!' I answered excitedly.

'Hi! Are you alright?'

'Yes, fine, and you?'

'Fine, see you tomorrow then.'

'Yes. Ricard, is something wrong?'

'No, see you tomorrow.'

He cut the line. I felt something was wrong and a warning rang in my mind.

You are vulnerable, be careful. Who had said this? Marianne, Andrea, Julie, Patrick, Mark's parents—anyone else? Was I running before I could walk?

The visit to my parents was much shorter than I'd anticipated. I went immediately to bed when I was home. Once again, a good sleep was elusive.

§ § §

67

I had time to make two quick calls, one to my parents, the other to Julie and to finish last-minute packing before I got into the taxi to take me to the airport.

Sitting in the waiting area of the executive lounge with a cup of coffee and a book, having checked my luggage in, I was astounded to be greeted by Patrick.

'Hello, I asshumed I'd find you here. Sitting around for flights ish a pain, ishn't it? Come on, have shomething a bit stronger with your coffee.'

'Patrick, what are you doing here?'

'Like you, waiting for a flight. I asshume that iish why you are here. Only minesh been delayeded.'

'Where are you off to? And you sound as if you've already had "something stronger" than coffee.'

'Yesh, tha'sh the trouble with thesh exec plashes. Not 'xactly free, but free flowing. Do you want shomeshing in or with your coffee?'

'Not now, thank you, Patrick, it isn't mid-day yet. What's the matter with you? Why are you here?'

'Plan ish to catch a plane. Yesh, catching a plane—if it ever arrives. I'll jush get myshelf another drink. 'xcush me for a moment.'

Considering the amount of alcohol he must have consumed, he walked amazingly straight to the bar.

'Diagnoshish was…yesh, diagonshish…' he said on his return and sat beside me. 'Sho, I'm going for the cure.'

'Patrick, if you drink any more alcohol, they'll not let you on the plane, no matter where you're going. So, stop drinking. Tell me what flight you're on.'

'To, to…' he stopped.

'To Toulouse?' I asked.

What am I going to do with him in Toulouse? Has Faunier asked him to come over?

'No, you are going to Touloosh, aren't you?'

'Yes, I am going to Toulouse. But Patrick, where are you going?'

'To shee my shishter,' he squinted at me. 'I told you on, when wash it, Tueshday, yesh Tueshday, I was going to see my shishter.'

'It was actually Wednesday and you said you were thinking of doing so, yes, but I didn't get the impression you had arranged anything.'

'Trish ish good, ishn't she? Think I'll see about shome short of training and promotion for her on my return. Good find of yoursh. She got me a flight. A flight to Carcashonne and train all the way to Elne and my shishter.'

Carefully, Patrick put down the glass, the whisky untouched, and stood up steadily and spoke, seemingly suddenly sober.

'My flight's being called. Keep me posted with the project, Yvonne, I'll be back in the office next week. And by the way, whatever is going on, be careful, time is a great healer, but there's an extended period of vulnerability before certainty. Take care of yourself.'

Him too?

I put my hands to my face, covering my nose and mouth as I watched my boss walk away. He did not turn round as he exited the lounge but raised his left hand and waved. I reached for his whisky and sipped it slowly.

Chapter Five

I'd informed the concierge of *Monsieur* Letour's probable arrival and asked for him to be given the second room key; as we'd stayed here before, they were happy with this arrangement. I was coming out of the shower room, wrapping the bath sheet around me, when he arrived.

'Sorry I was not here to greet you,' he smiled, 'but it looks as if I have arrived at just the right time.'

'Mm, I was about to dress.'

'Do not bother now, we have the whole weekend to dress—and undress.' I waited at the foot of the bed for him to come to me. As he removed his coat, he turned abruptly from me, threw his coat onto a chair as he moved to the window where he stopped, looking out.

'Yvonne.'

'You're sounding serious, Ricard.' I realised something was wrong and started to move towards him.

'No,' he must have sensed a movement or saw it reflected in the window as he raised a hand indicating I should stay where I was. I sat on the bed.

I was right, my worst fears were coming true. I've read too much into this relationship. Vulnerable and idiotic.

'Something has been worrying me since the last time you were back and you told me how you were greeted on your return to the office after your time, well, "on retreat". You hesitated for a moment when I asked you how your boss, Patrick, welcomed you, you were almost dismissive of it. How did he greet you?'

I stared at him in disbelief.

'Well, as any boss would greet an employee, I suppose. Why do you ask?' I paused. 'Where's this coming from?'

'Tell me. Tell me exactly how he greeted you.'

I rubbed the ball of my thumb across my lips and closed my eyes, I really didn't want to revisit that encounter and certainly not now, while being naked apart from a damp bath sheet.

'OK, yes, I was a bit—oh I don't know—a little short on the detail, the truth about how Patrick greeted me. It wasn't very pleasant and it was extremely embarrassing for us both.' I looked pleadingly at Ricard's reflection hoping he'd say, "OK. Not to worry", but instead, he turned and shouted.

'Why are you here?'

'Ricard! What do you mean, why am I here?'

What was I feeling? Affronted? Hurt? Insulted? I was here with this man because I wanted to be with him. Surely it could not be more obvious.

Before I spoke out in retaliation, a bit of reason hit me.

If I wanted to make a go of this relationship, tenuous as it seemed at this moment, I'd have to be upfront with him.

'Some things are sometimes best left unsaid, Ricard. I'll tell you what happened, but I'm going to put some clothes on first.' I grabbed what I needed and went back to the shower room and locked the door. I felt ashamed I'd not been upfront with him and realised it had been a big mistake.

'You fool.' I said to the stupid woman I saw in the mirror as I brushed my hair. When I emerged, Ricard had put his coat onto the back of the chair where he'd thrown it and was sitting on the long sofa set in the bay window.

'May I have one?' I nodded to the glass of brandy he'd poured for himself from the minibar. He shrugged. I helped myself then sat on the chair, cradling the glass, feeling the residual heat of his body from his coat on my back.

When I'd finished explaining, I sipped my brandy then went and sat on the sofa. I took a deep breath and extended my hand to Ricard, silently begging him to take it. I tried to convince myself; if he didn't, this would be understandable, after all, the picture I'd painted of Patrick, a true one as far as I was concerned when Ricard and I'd first met, was strangely at odds with this new one.

'I'm sorry, Yvonne, and I apologise, I overreacted. I keep trying to bury a streak of jealousy, I had not meant it to come out and certainly not as aggressively as it did, but when I saw you come out of the shower and thought…I-I just could not stop. I have not felt like this in years and it is tender and elusive; I do not want to lose it.'

'Yes, I know,' I paused, 'I feel the same, but both of us are, as I am constantly being told, still vulnerable. I understand. *C'est ça!*'

'Yes, *C'est ça!*' he smiled.

'Well, that's rather killed the mood, hasn't it?'

'Yes, I am sorry, shall we get our coats and go and see if we can find the last of the children's roundabouts and enjoy a time of innocence with no—'

'—jealousy and, quite understandable, negative thoughts.'

As we walked hand in hand through the streets where the café lights spilled onto the pavement I said,

'Ricard, I think I am in love with you or to be honest, I know I am, but it is too soon to commit. I promise I will always be honest with you, but I don't want to be suffocated.'

He moved me into the shadows of an alleyway and kissed me long and hard, it was lovely and perfectly natural for me to respond in similar fashion.

Over drinks and then a meal, we discussed our plans for the weekend. Our options were wide open, we could do anything we wanted. Again, Ricard seemed tentative in his reaction to most of the ideas I put forward, then asked if I would consider going to Lézignan in the morning and spending time there.

'I'm afraid I let out to Suzanne I was seeing you so you can guess what excitement that caused!'

The thought of spending the weekend in his lovely house was very tempting but before responding to his invitation, I asked,

'Even though you had doubts over my relationship with Patrick, you still mentioned to them you were seeing me?'

'Yes.'

How confusing.

'I find that confusing,' I said.

'Yes, I do too.'

'I'll have to be back here on Sunday night, Ricard, Paul is collecting me at seven thirty Monday morning.'

'OK, the journey is about an hour and a half, Sven can bring us back either Sunday night or you early on Monday. If I ring before we go to bed, he can collect us in the morning.'

'You seem to ask a lot of him, Ricard, how does the relationship with you and Marianne and Sven really work?'

'Works well, but Sven is not family—not yet anyway—and has always been an employee. I will tell you all about him another time, but only with his permission.'

I raised my eyebrow.

'I will not be drawn on the topic of Sven now; as to Marianne, you know she is my sister-in law and I pay her a salary to care for the house, Suzanne and me.'

I raised my eyebrow again, he grinned.

'No! not me! Although there was a brief time when I thought we might get closer but she quickly put a stop to any continuance, so now she looks after the house, Suzanne, my clothes, meals—but not me.'

'I know, she told me.'

Ricard fiddled with the liqueur glass sitting by his now empty coffee cup. It was obvious he wanted to say something but appeared not to know how to start. He attracted the waiter's attention and ordered more coffee for us both having asked if I wanted another one. I waited quietly watching the people walking past the restaurant, pulling their coats around them as the early September breeze made itself known. It seemed as if Ricard like the pedestrians, was gathering some sort of cloak around himself. He acknowledged the waiter who brought the coffee before he spoke.

'As we have found, if we are to have a future, we must have complete honesty between us.'

I must have reacted to his statement.

'Yes, I know, I'm sorry, I cannot tell you about the argument with my parents and Jules.'

'But you expect complete honesty from me.'

'Point taken, but I wanted to clear something else. Suzanne is a lovely child; she can be a bit demanding and headstrong at times. So, things might get difficult in the future. She is already very fond of you so I do not want her to get too close to you if you and I have no future.'

'No pressure?'

He had the grace to blush and took my hand.

'I agree, she's a lovely girl, you and Marianne have done a great job in raising her. Are you worried an outsider, me, for that is what I am, would be a negative influence on her and disrupt what you and Marianne have established?'

'In any situation, the group dynamics change as members come and go. I am conscious she already adores you. I do not want her damaged later.'

'By a group member leaving?'

'In a nutshell, yes. She has, in a very strange way, been almost monitoring me and my relationship with the women I have had to my house both informally and at formal gatherings. She has a particular look when she thinks they are not appropriate—or whatever the word is—she never actually says anything but I feel certain vibes when she is not happy for a relationship to develop.'

'Suzanne is very observant and possibly has a strong influence on how you lead your personal life. She has certainly been monitoring who shares your bed.'

He looked up. 'What has she said?'

'Nothing to worry about; however, she seemed happy I had. But I get your point; we are not teenagers and have to be careful of other people's feelings.'

'Youngsters adapt or so I am told but who can foretell the long-term benefit or damage?'

'Perhaps we're getting a bit too deep into psychology for tonight, Ricard.'

'Yes.' He smiled.

'We need to get to know more about each other and our families before we decide where we go. We need to fix a time for you to meet mine.'

'Will the meeting be scary?'

I shrugged. 'I don't know, how do you feel about ghouls, ghosts and wizards?'

He laughed. 'Come on, they cannot be so bad, are they?'

'You'll never know till you meet them, will you?'

We finished our drinks, paid the bill and wandered back to the hotel where, having checked the time, ten thirty, Ricard rang a sleepy sounding Sven and asked him to pick us up at eight o'clock. I'm sure I heard a, 'Yes sir' from Sven and a groan and exclamation from Marianne.

§ § §

After a night of vigorous then gentle sex, the alarm call we'd booked woke us, we smiled at each other; then, with sudden athleticism, Ricard bolted to the shower shouting,

'Me first!' I joined him so we missed the entrance of the waiter bringing the light room service breakfast we'd ordered.

'*Voila!*' I said when we emerged. 'Breakfast!'

Sven was parking the car as we emerged from the hotel. Suzanne rushed to us, I looked over Suzanne's head and saw Marianne's face and tried to decipher her expression, I smiled and she smiled in return but during the journey, she kept catching my eye in the mirror. I felt she wanted to speak to me urgently and anticipated we would spend some time together over the weekend. I nodded "OK" and she finally relaxed.

The longest part of the journey was to Carcassonne where we stopped, much to Suzanne's disgust, in the old town for coffee and cakes. This was a short stop as Lucille had been left to prepare part of the evening meal and Marianne was anxious to get home in case of any catastrophes. Meanwhile, Suzanne was enjoying the attention she was receiving from Ricard. She sat between us holding his hand and chatting about school and answering our questions.

Lucille had not only carried out all the tasks set by Marianne but had also prepared a light lunch. Marianne was delighted as she could see that what she'd been teaching the girl over the last few months was bearing benefits. I overheard her say to Lucille.

'Congratulations on a wonderful luncheon, Lucille. I had not realised how much you had taken in.'

'A lot goes in, *Madame*, but not a lot comes out till I see an opportunity and take a chance. I hope I have not used too many ingredients and left us short for tonight's meal. I have prepared most of it as you asked.'

'My goodness, you will have me out of a job soon, Lucille,' joked Marianne, Lucille blushed with pleasure but hung her head. 'I will have a look at what you have done and see if we need anything. I am sure we will need some fresh bread so perhaps, Yvonne, would you accompany me and I can show you the *boulangerie*, green grocers and a few other parts of the town?'

'What a lovely idea, thank you, Marianne. I am sure there is far more to the town than the few roads I've seen.'

'Can I come too please?' asked Suzanne.

'As you wish, but you know how bored you get looking at food shops. And maybe I would like to have Yvonne to myself for an hour and I am sure an hour without you will be a welcome break.'

'I would take that as a "no", Suzanne, if I were you.' Said Ricard firmly. Then, seeing the disappointment in her face added with more enthusiasm than I think he felt,

'If you like, we will walk down to the lake and perhaps they can meet us there in an hour or so and have some hot chocolate. I think the stall will still be open, although it is getting near the end of the season. And if we are quick, there might be time to take out one of the rowing boats first.'

The afternoon passed smoothly. Although I thought Marianne wanted to talk to me about the possibility of Ricard and me getting together and posing a load of "what ifs", in fact she genuinely wanted to show me the town. I was introduced to various shopkeepers who greeted me in a warm and friendly manner even though I was aware of a few raised eyebrows and knowing smiles as I shook hands or exchanged the traditional double-cheek kiss.

After Marianne had purchased all she needed, we walked towards the lake. It was during this time, and before Sven caught up with us and took the shopping from Marianne, she did speak again about being careful and vulnerability. She did not labour the point but reiterated what I'd heard from the village shopkeepers and others to whom I'd been introduced this afternoon, namely, Ricard was well respected and no-one wanted him hurt. I responded we were both being careful.

Why, you crafty lady! Parading me in front of people. C'est ça!

Suzanne's cheeks were glowing with cold when we met them as they were getting back from a short boat ride. Even before she'd removed her life jacket, she was chatting brightly telling us all about the wildlife they'd seen.

'The man said to stay close to the edge.'

'And why, Suzanne? Explain the reason.' Said Ricard.

'Even though it is not a big lake, if the wind changes, it can get dangerous out in the middle.'

'And did your *Papa* do as he was told?'

Suzanne's reply expressed her absolute glee,

'Yes, and we got stuck in some weeds.'

'You do not have to tell them everything, Suzanne, be fair, but I did not actually get stuck and if I had not got so close to the edge, you would not have seen the old swan's nest. Did you two have a good time? I see Sven has ended up with the shopping! Hot chocolate, everyone?'

We all agreed and moved to a snack bar converted from an old travellers' caravan which at this time of year concentrated mainly on mugs of hot chocolate. We sat at long wooden trestle tables with other customers. I felt this was an affable, homogenous town and caught Ricard watching me, I looked up and smiled.

On the walk home, Suzanne put her hand in mine, it was cold.

'We'll need to get you warmed up when we get home,' I said.

'Have you had a letter from *Papi* yet? He said he would write inviting you to the farm.'

'Not yet, Suzanne. But you must remember this is a busy time on the farm. He probably hasn't had time to even think about writing. If, and I repeat if, he would like me to visit, I am sure he'll write when he's ready.'

'When do you go home again?'

'I'm not sure, you see I will be working in France for a while. I'll go home every now and then, but I am not sure when the next time will be.'

'There might be a letter there now.'

'Maybe.'

Although there was nothing there Friday morning.

'You do want to visit?'

I looked at her eager upturned face.

'Yes Suzanne, I would be honoured to visit your grandparents. Don't worry, as soon as the letter comes, I will act.' I chose the last verb carefully as I would obviously have to discuss this with Ricard.

The walls of the courtyard had held the heat of the early September sun, and as there was no wind in this secluded place it was decided to eat outside again, possibly the last time this year. We wore warm jackets and blankets were brought out in case they were also needed. The light sensitive lamps secreted cleverly in niches and on pillars came on gradually as the evening drew in giving an adequate light by which to eat our meal. I'd not noticed them the last time I was here, but then the sun was still shining in the courtyard so they'd not been activated. This time I was permitted to help with bringing the cutlery and non-food items to the table, then told to sit with Ricard and enjoy a glass of wine. Suzanne joined us and asked for a little wine too.

'Not yet, young lady, wait until you are a bit older.'

'I thought journalists drink wine.'

'Some do.'

'Well, I am going to be one, so I need to get used to it.'

'Isn't it a bit too soon to think about your career, Suzanne?'

'I need to think about work. *Papa* works hard so he can pay Marianne and Sven and for my schooling and all things for the house. I am lucky to have such a home and family,' she stopped speaking and looked down, 'sorry *Papa*, am I speaking out of turn?'

'No, my dear, you seem to have a mature view of life.'

If a bit advanced for an upcoming ten-year-old child.

She sighed then, looking downcast mixed with the subtle look she had, said, 'Then may I have a glass of wine?'

Ricard's resolve weakened and he mixed some water and wine in a glass and passed it to her. Marianne's face reflected her palpable disapproval of the diluted wine when she and the others arrived with the meal. There is obviously some variance in boundaries between the two of them.

I wonder how a third influence might unbalance the current equation.

On this occasion, Lucille joined us for the meal and ran to and from the house as items were needed. Marianne explained the home where Lucille lived did not provide meals on Saturday evenings.

I realised there would a lot more to a relationship with Ricard than a husband and wife; I would be joining a whole community, quite different from my own family network. Ricard and I would need to talk in depth—maybe before he met my parents and siblings and certainly, before either of us made any permanent commitment.

But I knew I was in love, or did I? Was this just the first time I'd felt for anyone since Mark? I must keep telling myself I am vulnerable. C'est ça!

The evening gently ended with us all taking the remnants of the meal to the kitchen. Lucille went home, Sven and Marianne decided to walk with her to the door of her hostel. Suzanne kissed us both goodnight and, with a reminder from Ricard to clean her teeth, she went happily to bed. To my surprise, Ricard drew me into the kitchen and gave me a cloth while he put on an apron, rolled up his sleeves and started to wash the dishes.

'This is a nice romantic end to the day.' I murmured as I wiped plates.

'Hard labour never hurt anyone,' he replied as he passed me another plate, 'look at it as a trial run for next weekend.'

I nearly dropped the plate I was about to put onto the dresser shelf.

'Why, what's happening next week?'

'I have invited a few of my business acquaintances and friends to meet you, just a small gathering to give you some idea of what you might be letting yourself in for if our relationship should develop, as I hope it will.'

'Getting their approval, you mean.'

'Rather hoping to get yours. A certain amount of entertaining goes with my job and you may not like the people I associate with.'

'I suppose it will have to happen sometime, so why not now before we go too far down the road.'

I'll have to get a dress. I really didn't bring anything suitable for entertaining.

Finally, he handed me the last piece of crockery.

'You will be pleased to hear the glasses are left till the morning.'

'Did you and Charlotte never consider a dishwasher? Not for the crystal, of course.'

'No, not really; we would spend the time chatting about our friends, their odd ideas on life and planning things we wanted to do next day.'

'At the end of our dinner parties, Mark and I were only too happy just to load the things into the machine and let it get on with the job. We also left the good glass till next day and whoever woke first would start on them while waiting for the coffee to percolate. Come to think of it, it was amazing how many Sunday mornings he never woke up first!'

'With any luck, Marianne will be over to do them, she likes the quiet of the morning to herself so we get out of doing the glasses.'

And so, having turned off the lights, we went to bed as we heard the heavy oak side-gate to the courtyard close on our world.

§ § §

There had been no mention of going to church this morning and we all slept late; breakfast evolved into an elaborate affair and extended through the morning to early afternoon, so really represented the lunchtime meal too. Ricard then spent some time in his office, Marianne and Sven took the opportunity of going out by themselves, Suzanne had to do some homework so I relaxed with a book in the courtyard, wearing a thick jumper and wrapped in a couple of blankets. By late afternoon, I was becoming cold; the sun, which had been warm again earlier, had lost its heat.

'Am I interrupting you, Yvonne?' Suzanne's usual exuberance was absent.

'No, my dear, what can I do for you?'

'Would you look at my English essay please? We only had to write a small bit, not a long one like we would in French for history. But I would like it to be right before I hand it in.'

I looked at the three sentences describing a walk in a wood and questioned her as to why she'd used a certain word and tense, then suggested a couple of changes and explained why.

'Suzanne, I'm getting a bit cold now. Do you want to go and rewrite the sentences while I move my things inside and I'll make us some hot chocolate? Meet me in the kitchen when you have finished, but don't rush your writing and remember why you are making the changes.'

Suzanne joined me just as I was mixing the chocolate powder into the hot milk. I put the mugs on the table and sat down indicating for her to sit opposite me.

'Will you go to England before next weekend, Yvonne?'

'No, I told you I don't know when I'll go next. Why do you ask?'

'Well, I thought I could ask *Papi* to write to you here.'

'No, Suzanne, don't pester him, as I said before, he'll write when he has time.'

'When you come and live here, you could teach at the school and be here all the time. Most of the English teachers are students who only come for a year then go back to their own university to study. That is good if we do not like them or they are not good teachers, but when they are nasty, we are pleased.'

'I hope you're not unkind to them if you don't like them.' She looked away.

'Suzanne?' I spoke sternly.

'We try not to, but sometimes they are really horrid. But the only really bad teacher was very old, she did not last long but not because of anything our class did. She was found hitting a boy two grades lower than us. I think our head asked her to leave.'

Probably told, rather than asked, under those circumstances.

'Suzanne, you must not suppose I will come and live here. I think you need to realise both your *Papa* and I have different lives and at this moment I may...'

'Ah! So, this is where you are both hiding. Any hot chocolate for me? May I join you or is this girls' only gathering?'

I jumped up, feigning a sneeze, pushed my chair back rapidly, scraping it across the wooden floor, nearly tipping it over.

'I need a handkerchief, won't be a moment,' I said, 'I wouldn't mind another one, could you fix your own drink? And maybe some more for us—possibly with marshmallows.' I added as an afterthought and left. I was furious; had Ricard really just arrived or had he been listening and made an entrance at a strategic moment to forestall what he thought I might be going to say to Suzanne. Suzanne needed to know I might not be a permanent fixture in their lives and I wanted to put a little warning into her young head. I returned to the kitchen only marginally calmer than when I'd left after rehearsing the arguments I planned to put before Ricard.

'I have looked for marshmallows, Yvonne but cannot find any.' Suzanne pushed a fresh mug of chocolate towards me when I sat in the same chair as before.

'I'm not really fond of them on chocolate anyway, Suzanne, far too sweet. I don't know why I mentioned them.'

'I told *Papa* what we were talking about. He said we would have to wait and see about teaching in the school. But I think it would be a good idea.'

'Ricard, please, we must be open about this.'

'Not now, not yet.'

'Well, when then? I thought you said no lies and we must be honest.'

He sighed and thought for a moment, then put his drink on the table and sat next to Suzanne.

'Alright, but against my better judgement. I suppose now may be as good a time as any. I still think you should not have even started but waited till we had talked further.'

'I hadn't "started" as you call it, but an ideal opportunity presented itself to hint at potential complications.'

We stared at each other, saying nothing. We were both tense with clenched fists.

Suzanne's brow creased and her eyes filled with tears she was trying to hold back as she looked first at her father then me.

'No, no, no, do not fight. *Papa*, I love you both so much, please do not be cross with each other. No, no, no.' She left the kitchen and ran to her room in tears.

'Oh God! What have we done?'

'Well, it was against my better judgement.'

'I'm not going to have an argument of "who's to blame" over this, Ricard.'

'You are right, Yvonne, blame will not resolve this. But it does prove, or at least highlights, we have to be more in tune with each other where issues about Suzanne are concerned.'

'Or perhaps have more confidence in each other about the way and time we approach issues.' I said softly.

'What do we do now?'

'Do you remember what she said? I don't think it's the fact we were disagreeing. I think she's frightened about us having a fight.'

'Why should she think we were going to fight?'

'Probably because we both were so tensed up. It is a fight—or the threat of one—that worried her. Will you trust me to go to her?'

'Yes.'

There was no response to my knock on her door. I opened it and looked in to see Suzanne curled up and asleep. I put a blanket over her and left, leaving the door open.

'She's sleeping.'

'We should think about what to do when she wakes up.'

'Perhaps, we try again—together—without any tension, to explain what we were trying to say just now.'

'You two are looking very glum. Is everything all right or should I not ask?' Marianne entered the kitchen.

'A bit of tension, Marianne, and I am afraid Suzanne is rather upset, she is sleeping. Yvonne and I will take ourselves to the side salon with our drinks for half an hour and leave you to prepare the meal. If Suzanne comes down, please tell her where we are.'

Ricard fixed a couple of gin and tonics and we left her. As we retreated, Sven entered the house.

'What is going on?' I heard him ask Marianne.

'Lovers' tiff, I think.'

If only.

I went to get Suzanne just before Marianne's evening meal was ready. She was beginning to stir and greeted me with a smile.

'How are you feeling?'

'Fine now, thank you.'

'Can you tell me what happened?'

'You were both so angry, with your fists clenched on the table and the dream suddenly came, I do not understand.'

'Nor do I, but I'm sure we'll find the answer. Are you hungry?' She nodded enthusiastically.

'Come on then.'

The meal and rest of the evening was passed congenially with Ricard, Marianne, Sven and Suzanne. All the tension had once more disappeared and we seemed to be back on an even keel. We discussed the coming weekend party and everything appeared to be normal.

Suzanne said goodnight to Sven and kissed Marianne and went to her room to pack her school bag saying she'd see Ricard and me later. After we'd cleared away Sven said,

'Well, tomorrow we have an early start, I will see you at six in the morning, Yvonne, please do not be late. Good night.'

They both left, Ricard locked the door and we went to bed, turning off the lights as we went. I looked in on a sleeping Suzanne. Her school bag packed.

§

Ricard and I were relaxing after he'd moved off me and we were quietly enjoying being together when Suzanne slipped onto the bed on top of the covers and lay between us.

'You do love each other,' she said, 'like a proper, lasting love. I know you will have disagreements, but please do not fight. I love you both. Goodnight.'

She then went back to her own bed. We embraced in a stunned silence. No more was said on the subject that night and we slept.

Chapter Six

Sven was ready with the rear door of the car open for me.

'I'd like to sit in the front with you so we can talk on the way.' I said.

'I never talk when I am driving, *Madame*. Please, …' He indicated for me to sit in the back.

Madame! Formal chauffeur after a weekend together.

He waited for me to get into the back, put a blanket over my knees once I had fastened my seat belt.

'Just till the car warms up,' he said. He started the car and drove me to the hotel in Toulouse in plenty of time for coffee before Paul arrived. I offered Sven coffee, which he politely refused and wished me a good day. On the journey I reflected on what Sven had said, and realised I'd never seen or heard him have a conversation when driving—not even when Marianne sat next to him, and he'd only ever briefly acknowledged Ricard's rare instructions.

The week in the office started as before with the team working on the files provided by *Monsieur* Faunier. They continued to eliminate some of the various extraneous messages as I'd asked them to do while I was away. After about three quarters of an hour Paul stood up, stretched, walked over to the window before returning to look at his two screens again. He then signalled Daniel to join him and following some subdued chat between them, they exchanged a "high five", grinning and saying,

'*Oui!*'

'Hey, is there something going on we all should know about? Do you think you've made a breakthrough, Paul?'

'Yes and no, *Madame* Yvonne,' replied Daniel, 'this has nothing to do with work but this is too good an opportunity to miss. Let me explain, we are members of a group, very informal, who watch out for paedophile activity, not only online but also walking the streets, so when we find suspicious activity, we report it; we certainly didn't expect to find it on our company's files. We must report it, goodness knows what the perpetrator is doing or planning to do.'

'Yvonne, it seems this station user has accessed three different paedophile websites. I think security should be alerted and asked to look into it,' added Paul who'd continued to search through the files while Daniel was talking.

'I agree it should be reported,' I said after a moment for thought, 'if you are sure it's what you suspect, but before you do, let's think through how this might affect our work here. How will the authorities get access to the right station? Won't it show up our monitoring?'

'You remember the whole system is monitored, with the employees' agreement? So, if we are right then whoever it is will obviously think it is a routine or random check. It cannot be traced back here, we are working from copies, not live activities. Just checking online for some, as you suggested.'

'Of course, sorry, I forgot. I understand. But how will you report it? If you ring anyone at the main office, it can be traced to this phone number.'

'Yes, you are right, but we never report from a private line, always anonymously from a bar or restaurant. We will do it from where we are having lunch! Our contact will then inform the authorities.'

'Has this happened before?'

'I have not noticed it before on these files, Yvonne, I certainly was not looking for it and it was only because of your suggestion of eliminating codes and looking on the Internet I saw it. If I may, I will check back on some of the previous files downloaded from memory sticks, now I am aware I might find more and maybe different stations are being used, but the code for the internet site should show up.'

'I appreciate this is important but do remember we are here looking for something else—whatever that turns out to be—but you are obviously not going to concentrate on the job in hand till you have made your anonymous call, use the time between now and lunch to look through back files but then it must be back to work. Monique, can you carry on with our work or are you part of this group too?'

'No, *Madame* Yvonne, I will carry on with you.'

The four of us returned to our computers on two different searches. There followed some time of just clicking computer keys.

'*Madame* Yvonne,' Monique called across the room, 'I've found a code not listed in the master file of codes. I also noticed the "export" amount is the same as the "input" on this code.'

'Impossible.' Despite looking for something else, Paul had heard her.

'Why "impossible"?'

'Because, Yvonne, if an item is bought in for the amount "a", it is recorded as being sold on for "a plus b"; or if it is an internal departmental transfer, it is recorded as "a minus b". Goods never travel around at the same price. The plus represents an enhanced value of the item and the minus a loss, maybe because it has been hanging around as dead money, either due to over ordering or being stored in the wrong department. It is based on the same principle we do not have highly trained mechanics sitting around on the shop floor waiting for work, everything comes in and goes out, processed smoothly.'

'Oh, yes, I see—I think!'

Once again, this highlights my lack of knowledge in this field. Has someone granted Paul leave for outside help just to prove his concerns were wrong? And was I recommended because they knew it was not my field?

'So what does it mean?' Asked Monique.

'Someone is on the fiddle.' Paul said before he and Daniel returned to their search.

'Well, done, Monique,' I said lamely, 'the file covered from 0700 on Thursday till 1830 on Friday, didn't it?'

'Thereabouts, yes.'

'What time did the transaction take place?'

'Hold on, um, sorry, lost the screen.' I heard her clicking the keys then she said, 'At 1800 on Friday. Is that significant?'

'I've no idea. I think we still might be chasing shadows, but it might mean if whoever is introducing new codes wants to do it just before a weekend so he—or she—can carry on over the weekend if necessary.'

I raised my voice and spoke to the three of them.

'Do you know who has access to the master codes?'

'Presumably head of I.T. and probably *Monsieur* Faunier. We are just the end users.'

'Can't be *Monsieur* Faunier.'

'No, he says he does not understand anything beyond filling in a basic spreadsheet and sending emails.'

'People say a lot of things to suit themselves.'

'Anyway, he is helping us.'

'Or himself?'

'Maybe, and all this is a bluff.'

They all had something to say but I cut short the exchanges saying,

'We are not here to start pointing fingers without any evidence. So please, stop speculating.' I felt I'd spoken a little more harshly than I'd intended as they apologised rather like school children. 'I suppose someone, any of the console users, with the knowhow could hack into the system, it need not be someone who has the legitimate right to do so.'

'We'll have to wait for *Monsieur* Faunier tonight before we can check the activities since half past six Friday afternoon.'

'*Madame* Yvonne.'

'Yes Monique?' I looked up and saw her smiling.

'You are not going to like this.'

'Shoot.'

'There is another new code. Input and output the same.'

'Time?'

'1828.'

I sighed.

Checking the time on my watch, I suggested lunch and the sooner they could make their telephone call, the sooner I could get Paul and Daniel back to work. The thought of child abuse was obviously high on their agenda and after an initially subdued but slightly longer lunch than usual, we returned to the computers and files in a more positive mood.

The rest of the afternoon followed the pattern of analysing the latest files on the fobs, the inconsequential stuff deleted from the copies and the tracking of the two new codes.

This was really something outside my understanding. I sat staring into space for a while. Then what Monique had picked up and Paul had explained, suddenly struck me.

Financial, of course it's finance you fool. That's what Paul has been saying all along but couldn't see. There must be other codes over the months with equal in and out figures. Creaming off large or small amounts consistently. Now, as Paul has been asking questions, new codes were being introduced to, maybe,

speed up the action, or maybe increase the amounts before one big transfer out.
We need the company's bank accounts. The link must be there. We can go on
chasing these codes and entries till we exhaust ourselves in a whirlwind, they're
all circular, we need to get out of the box—think sideways.

Despite this thought, I decided we should continue with the same searches for the rest of the day and said nothing. It was tedious but we found more on each day. It was dark outside but with the screens glowing and the intensity of the work none of us had noticed. I got up and turned the lights on and drew the curtains.

'Right, close your computers, we've done enough for today and we're all going boggle-eyed.'

None of them objected. We sat round the table. I continued,

'I've had an idea, derived from what Monique found and Paul explained to me.' I told them my idea.

'How is it happening?'

'I don't know but according to Paul the company is losing money for no apparent reason. Order books are full, the factory is working flat out, good quality components are being purchased at competitive prices. But at the same time, Paul thinks there is a haemorrhage. I think we need to look and see if it is traceable via the bank accounts.'

'It is worth a try; we are not getting anywhere via this route.' Agreed Paul.

'And if the transactions are done late on a Friday, then whoever is doing it has the whole weekend to cover his or her tracks.'

'Can *Monsieur* Faunier get access to the bank accounts?'

Before anyone could answer my question *Monsieur* Faunier entered the office, looking tired and haggard. We all stood in shock looking at his distraught and tired face. He removed his coat and sat quickly.

'*Monsieur—*'

He raised his hand.

'Could I trouble you for a glass of your delicious white wine, Paul?'

When we had glasses of wine before us, we watched his drawn face and waited for what was to come.

'Thank you, and your health!'

We raised our glasses in silent recognition of the toast in expectation of some news.

'Oh! Before I forget,' he put his hand into his jacket pocket, 'here are the fob sticks for Friday until two-thirty today. Only one of each I am afraid, you will have to load them separately, I did not have the time, nor enthusiasm to make copies.' He shook himself, 'I've spent most of the afternoon with the police—the branch dealing with internet grooming and such like.' Both Paul and Daniel stiffened, Monique and I exchanged looks. 'I received an anonymous telephone call about lunch time,' he continued, 'which indicated a certain computer, within our company, was being used for pornographic purposes, in fact, more than one station had been used. You don't happen to know anything about this, do you?'

No one spoke.

'Oh God, not you—'

'Good heavens, no, not me, thank you for your confidence, young man!' He waved away Daniel's gestured apology and managed a wry smile.

'No; *Monsieur* Labaste.'

They were all silent, the uncouth phrase "gobsmacked" came to my mind as I looked at their faces.

'Cannot be him, surely it is a mistake,' Monique was the first to speak.

'The police searched all his computers, his official firm's one, his personal computers, both in his office and home and found what they called "inappropriate" exchanges.'

'His wife will be devastated.'

'Yes, she is, Paul. But not only about the stuff on the computers; it seems he has been...' he stopped and stared at them and shuddered, '...he has been molesting his two daughters.' He passed his now empty glass to Paul who retrieved the bottle from the fridge and topped it up. 'Apparently, he broke down and confessed everything. Although everyone in the administration block knows something is up, they do not know what, so it must go no further than this room. Do you understand?' They all nodded.

'That does include you too, *Madame* Birch.'

'Of course,' I replied, 'but who is he?'

'He was the Head of Human Resources,' replied *Monsieur* Faunier with an emphasis on the past tense.

'Appropriate title; one down, millions more to go.' Mumbled Daniel.

'It is hard, especially when it is "one of our own"; however, it might make it a bit more difficult for me to get the information to you. We still do not want to get discovered, so I may have to use different time frames and computers to do so.'

'*Monsieur* Faunier, it is possible we won't need any more activity downloads at the moment we have sufficient to work on, but could you get a copy of the master code file, just the last six months' additions should be sufficient for now.'

'Yes, that should not be too difficult. I'll bring it tomorrow. Have you found anything yet?'

'Not really, but I think we may have been chasing our tails and need to break out of the circle. I want to try a different approach. May I assume you have access to the company's bank statements? If so, can you let us have at least the last twelve months please.'

'All of them?'

'If possible, yes. Specifically, the current accounts and the deposit accounts which are used for transferring cash to the current ones. There must be investment accounts, but at this stage I don't think we'll need them. And we may need access to the payroll for the bank details of the staff. I don't want to take anything out, I want to see what is going in.'

'Personal information will be more difficult without staff permission.'

'If we can have the bank statements, we may not need them.'

'Good, there are legal obstructions into delving into people's personal finances without good reason.'

'Yes, I appreciate that. But the company's bank statements might negate that need.'

He nodded and finished his wine.

'I will bring them for you tomorrow rather than copying fobs.'

'Thanks, the sooner we can start using them the better. If we can't find anything, then we'll know to search for another hare to chase.'

'Well, I feel as if I've had six rounds in the training ring and I must go and see *Madame* Labaste before I go home. Goodnight.'

Paul helped *Monsieur* Faunier on with his coat and escorted him to the door.

'I assume it was you. Well done, my boy.' He said as he walked from the office.

Paul quietly closed the door and said,

'Well, I'm done for tonight. I'm glad we did not order dinner tonight. I'll drive you to your hotel, Yvonne. Can you two lock up please?'

They nodded. Paul and I did not speak on the drive back till just before I got out of the car; he said,

'*Monsieur* Labaste was such a quiet, charming man, always available for advice. But his girls, I cannot really believe it.'

'You've done your bit, Paul, leave it to the authorities now. Goodnight.'

I had a shower then went to a bistro for a meal. It was warm and friendly and I got chatting to some first-year university students who were eager to practice their English. I was glad to have a diversion and it raised my mood before I went to bed and rang Ricard. He wanted to know if I'd thought any more about our conversation with Suzanne.

'Today's been rather busy, Ricard, quite a lot has happened which has put our personal life out of my mind till now.' He didn't respond. 'Ricard, is everything alright?'

'Yes, just another of Suzanne's moves. I understand she talked about us with Marianne and Sven when she got home from school today. She wants to have a party of her own with her friends to meet you. Apparently, she has told them all about you and how brilliant you are; they are eager to meet you.'

'Ricard, this feels like it's a train with a full head of steam running away from us and we have no brakes.'

'Perhaps it is running away with us and maybe we do not need the brakes.'

'You're supposed to be helping and taking a serious, adult view of all this, not joking.'

'I am not joking.'

'I can see you smiling.'

'Well, so are you. Goodnight, my dear. Sleep well.'

'And you.'

The phone clicked off.

Where does that leave the vulnerability? C'est ça!

§ § §

When Paul joined me at the hotel next morning, it was obvious he wanted to talk about the events of yesterday. I ordered coffee and let him talk for nearly an hour explaining how he and the others had got involved with seeking out sex and pornography abusers and how they felt, if they did find any evidence, duty-bound to do something about it. He emphasised they were not vigilantes who took the law into their own hands but reported what they found. He admitted on one occasion they had reported a mistaken identity, but the situation had, as always, been handled sensitively by the authorities and all was well.

'Just as well, you don't take direct action yourselves.'

'We never do, we just report our suspicions and rarely hear the outcome.' When he finished, he smiled and thanked me for allowing him the opportunity to talk.

'Any time.' I tapped him on his knee and indicated we'd better get to work.

'Are you two alright this morning?' I asked Daniel and Monique when we arrived at the office.

'Yes, thank you, *Madame* Yvonne, although we could not talk about the news to anyone else, we think we have managed to talk it out between ourselves.'

'And Yvonne let me off load this morning, which is why we are a bit late.'

'So, we're all good to go?' I asked. When they'd all said "yes", I carried on.

'I think we need to take a more restricted approach. We need to follow the codes directly connected to the ones that have the same figure in as out. These could possibly come from any computer station rather than just one. So, until we get the master code update, we'll work on the ones we have. Paul, would you look for all entries with one of new codes Monique found and Dominic, do the same with the other. Copy and paste them to a new file for easy reference tomorrow.

'Monique, have you any idea when new codes with the equal figures started to appear? There is no point trawling through all the files again if they have only been added recently.'

'Looking at the master file, there was a spurt of new codes a few months before Paul noticed something was wrong and a slow trickle since then. The system adds them by date so it should be possible to identify the later ones we are interested in and correlate to those with equal in and out figures. We may have more guidance when *Monsieur* Faunier brings the update.'

'Yvonne, rather than Monique looking for possibly more new unlisted codes, would it be worthwhile two of us taking one code and the two another code; the pairs then split the time in half and concentrate on one time span. Then we should get through more days and won't duplicate.' Suggested Paul.

'Sounds good. Let's try and see how far we get. We'll do an hour then break for coffee—no arguments—this is going to be demanding. And it's not a race, be thorough or we'll waste time. Monique, can we have our first code please?'

92

It was well into the early evening by the time *Monsieur* Faunier arrived with the updated information and bank statements I'd requested; we'd also had several coffee breaks and an increasing number of transactions with the same "in" and "out" amounts.

'This,' he said handing over a large ring binder he produced from a solid briefcase, 'contains the last nine months of the equivalent to a current account. Keep it secure. Obviously, the briefcase will not fit into a desk drawer, but perhaps the file can be locked away or,' he hesitated, 'take it with you and keep it overnight.'

'I'd prefer it stayed in the office. Monique, will this fit in the cupboard of your metal desk?'

'Yes, in fact the file could stay in the briefcase as the desk has a lockable cupboard on one side.'

'At the end of your day, lock it inside and give *Madame* Birch the key please.' The tone of his voice forbade any of us questioning his instruction.

'I think it should be locked up now Monique. We have achieved all we can today and I'll start on the accounts tomorrow.'

'*Monsieur* Faunier and *Madame* Yvonne,' I noticed Paul had put the *Madame* in front of my name again, 'I have a personal issue. I know this is not a great time to ask, but I need to leave early on Friday and return to the office about mid-morning on Monday. There is something I cannot do on e-mail or telephone but must do in person. I anticipate we are hopefully about to make a break-through but can I be accommodated?'

Monsieur Faunier looked at me,

'Your call *Madame*.'

I looked at Monique and Daniel.

'What do you two think? It will mean continuing hard work but one person down.'

'One of the things, as head of department, Paul has continually said to us, is family and personal issues are vital and if you are comfortable with them, then you can concentrate on your work. I think, if he needs time to sort something, he should take it.'

Monique nodded in agreement.

Once again, the team spirit.

'I think you have your answer, Paul.'

Paul looked relieved and thanked me and *Monsieur* Faunier formally and nodded to the others.

We closed everything down and had an early night.

Driving back to the hotel, Paul asked,

'Are you not going to tell me what you are looking for?'

'I'd rather leave that till tomorrow. If my hunch is correct, I don't want you to be influenced by my telling you and if I'm wrong, I don't want too much egg on my face! See you tomorrow.'

I ate in the hotel and afterwards fell into conversation with a couple of guests, also English, who were starting out on their married life. Neither had been married before but seemed to have found a deep love in their fifty's.

Ricard and I chatted on the phone for a while before decided sleep was needed. He ended the call first and I held the receiver a while, hoping to hear a bit more of his voice.

§ § §

In the office, I continued, with the others, identifying the relevant transactions. I did just half an hour then, leaving the others to carry on, took the bank statements to see if there were any dates of outgoing transfers coinciding with the dates of the "in and out" transactions I'd identified on my sections of the computer files. I found on several days there were movements of relatively small amounts.

'Paul, could you tell me who these payments are made to?' I offered him the whole transaction sheet, but to prevent him seeing the payment amounts I kept them covered, giving him no guidance to the ones I'd noticed. He ran his finger down the list rattled off the names of companies with which he was familiar, stopping occasionally to say he did not know this one or another.

'Well, there's your answer. I may be wrong, but I think the ones you do not know are the ones we are following on the computer transaction files. The dates tally and if you look at the amount of the debits…' I removed the covering paper and watched his face.

'No, that cannot be right. Our payments are never so small.'

'Small by comparison to most but not insignificant amounts. But if you notice, they have been gradually increasing, not by much, but little by little and more frequently. It will take time to complete the task, but I think quite a tidy sum has been squirreled away over the months.'

'But these codes are only new for the last two months.'

'Yes, and maybe others have been slipped in periodically over the six or eight months or more, even before you became aware of something being wrong. Bring up the day on the first fob *Monsieur* Faunier gave us and see if there are any in and out transactions of the same amount and give me a date.'

'But first, Yvonne, we need to look at the printouts we made from the first fob in the package we were given, they are older.'

He did so.

'April 13th.'

I looked back in the bank account file for the date. A transaction of a small amount correlated.

'But who is the payee?'

'I don't know, the payee is just yet another code! And I don't think, if we have solved the riddle, we are going to know without handing the whole thing over to your Finance Director and possibly the fraud squad—or your equivalent.'

'Have we done it?' Asked Monique.

I nodded. 'At least, I think we have, the payments Paul didn't recognise are, I suspect, the fraudulent ones. Cleverly hidden in all the legitimate transactions.'

We all smiled. In fact, they laughed. I stayed where I was and relaxed as I watched them embrace each other as if they'd just won the million-euro jackpot. We'd possibly made a breakthrough but it might still be quite legitimate. I waited till they'd calmed down before I pointed this out.

'So, what now?' Asked Daniel.

'I honestly think we are at a dead end.'

'But we have come so far, surely we can carry on.'

'Without any formal and legitimate authority, we have gone as far as we can. When *Monsieur* Faunier comes tonight, I think we lay our cards on the table, explain what we have found and leave it to him to decide.'

There was silence; they obviously didn't agree.

'I'm sorry, Paul, Monique, Daniel. You have all worked so hard but unless any of you can see a legal route forward or can suggest something we've missed, you have to congratulate yourselves on getting this far and hand it over. We'll do another half an hour comparing transactions on the bank statements with the file entries we are concerned with. Then we'll put all this to bed for now and turn off the computers. I'm more than happy, when *Monsieur* Faunier comes, for you to put your viewpoints. You never know, maybe he'll see it your way and will want us to carry on.'

They were deflated and in silence cleared up the office space. We'd planned to eat together anticipating working late again so the table was prepared. The waiter came with the food—a large cassoulet which he put on the side over a burner. Paul poured out the wine, we'd all finished our first glass and had nearly finished our second before *Monsieur* Faunier arrived. He looked surprised as he handed the fob with the codes to Monique, then his expression changed to concern. Having accepted his wine, we sat and I let Paul explain the situation and where our differences occurred.

'Well,' he said, 'I am sure we will be able to find an amicable solution to this conundrum, but not on empty stomachs while the cassoulet wafts such wonderful aromas. Shall we eat?'

'You have achieved a result which seems to provide the answer to your question, Paul. I congratulate you all. But if this person is to be stopped then I must agree with *Madame* Birch. You have gone as far as you can legally—I do wonder if your crosschecking activities on the Internet were really permitted.'

The others started to protest. *Monsieur* Faunier sat quietly till they realised he was not going to change his mind.

'This does not mean it is the end of the investigation for you and your team, Paul, but possibly it is for you, *Madame* Birch. However, I strongly urge you all to trust me to follow this through. To this end, I am asking you three,' he turned to his staff, 'to take the next two days off and return here again on Monday, about mid-day and hear what the possible plan could be. I suggest, *Madame* Birch, you discuss the situation with Patrick Court. I'll be in touch when I know more.'

'Are you sure you do not want us to carry on trying to find more of these payments for the rest of this week?' asked Paul.

'No, as *Madame* Birch has said, you will not be able to get much more new information. So, take a break. However, I want to say how grateful I am to you all for the work you have done. I do not know if you are aware of how the company was started many years ago by my two great-grandfathers, making go-carts! Now look at it here in the middle of the aerospace park of Toulouse. I do not want it to be destroyed so, please trust me over the next few days and come back refreshed to start again.

'A toast,' said Dominic, 'to go-carts.' We all raised our glasses.

'Paul, I will drive *Madame* Birch to her hotel, I pass it on my way. May I have the case and folder with the bank statements please?' Monique handed it to *Monsieur* Faunier.

'Try and enjoy this extra free time and I'll see you when I see you,' I said, picking up my handbag and coat and wishing everyone a happy weekend and followed the Finance Director to his car. I had no idea what *Monsieur* Faunier was planning but thought he'd give me some indication as we went to the hotel, but he wouldn't be drawn and only spoke of trivia until he drove into the hotel forecourt.

He opened the passenger door for me, shook my hand and said,

'Thank you for everything. And we will see you again. Goodnight.'

I had expected more but just watched him drive off.

I have no foundation to be concerned, but I hope he is being honest and does not turn out to be a "baddie".

Once again, it was late when I rang Ricard. Without going into details, I told him I had to return home on Monday and asked, before I booked a flight, if Sven could drive me to the airport or should I plan to take the train as I would book the flight depending on the travel options.

'Of course, he will drive you, you did not need to ask.'

'Ricard, I don't ever want to take anything for granted in our relationship as it is now, so of course, I had to ask.'

'Yes alright. Sorry, I understand.'

'I'll go tomorrow from here if it is easier.' I was smiling in anticipation of the response I'd get to this proposal.

'But, but the party, if you go, you will not be here, what am I supposed...' He heard me laughing. 'That is not funny.'

'I'm beginning to learn how to wind you up,' I said, 'and as today has been another up and down one, I'm going to say goodnight. See you on Friday evening.'

Although it was implied when I suggested leaving France the next day, had I deliberately not told Ricard I wasn't working the next two days? Or do I need time to myself? I didn't know. C'est ça!

Sleep was rather elusive but before finally achieving it, I realised with everything going on at work, I'd not had time to shop for a suitable dress for the party.

§ § §

I woke with a start; the telephone was ringing.

'*Madame* Birch, this is the reception. Are you alright, *Madame*?'

'Um, yes, thank you. Why do you ask?'

'Well, on weekdays you have usually had an early breakfast and met with the young man, who is here in reception waiting for you. *Monsieur* Paul Eschar, *Madame*.'

But we are not meeting today.

'He says he needs to see you, *Madame*.'

'Um. Well, alright, could you offer him some coffee and tell him I'll be down soon and ask him if an hour is too long for him to wait, but I'll try to be quicker.'

The receptionist obviously relayed the message and Paul said he'd wait.

'Hi! We're not in the office today, Paul. What do you want?'

'I know, but I had to see you. And as you see, I am not dressed for the office!'

I looked at him and agreed. He was dressed pretty much as he was on the first occasion I'd seen him, shorts, t-shirt and trainers with no socks but this time a fleece around his shoulders. Once again, I noticed the mark on his left ankle.

A long time for a bruise to last.

'I just wanted to say I hope you will come back to help us. I did not get a chance to thank you last night for your support, the others wanted me to say so too. We all hope whatever *Monsieur* Faunier has in mind is going to resolve this problem,' he paused, 'did he say anything to you in the car last night?'

'No. He just enthused about the original go-cart company. The company is dear to his heart, for obvious reasons, then told me he was looking forward to seeing me again.'

'So, no more information or progress than yesterday evening?'

'No sorry, nothing. But from what he said in the office, I think he'll close the investigation as far as I'm concerned.'

'What do you think your boss will say after you've told him?'

'I really don't know, I've never been pulled off a job before, but if Faunier doesn't need me to continue, there isn't a choice.'

'Well, we all hope you will return. But for me this extra time off is a bit of a bonus, I have managed to switch my flight for this morning instead of waiting for tomorrow, so I will make use of the extra two days. Oh, before I forget, this is for you from all of us.' He handed me a sealed envelope and an unexpected hug and left.

'Have a good weekend.'

I assumed the envelope he gave me contained a card of thanks but it was a sheaf of papers and a note to say, "I printed off a couple of sheets from the files to show your boss. They might help in the explanation."

Returning to my room, I emailed Andrea and asked her to book me a couple of hours with Patrick on Monday. Then, rather than doing it myself, I thought I'd see if Trish could get me a flight from Carcassonne on Monday morning. I remembered Patrick had been impressed with her efforts and I wanted to continue to encourage her. I'd left her my passport details in a sealed envelope the last time I was home, so she had those. I showered and changed from the trousers and shirt I'd put on to meet Paul, into a dress before heading out to find something suitable to wear at the party on Saturday.

I wandered from shop to shop, not finding anything I liked. I must have tried on fifty or sixty dresses before I stopped for lunch, then continued afterwards. After several more failures, I bought a dress. The material was man made but resembled silk, the vivid electric blue had caught my eye and when I tried it on, I found the elegant folds of the material fell beautifully, just stopping short of the floor and displayed shafts of green that shot through it. The colour would match my pendant and earrings. I'd been pleased to see the genuine appreciation in the eyes of the assistant. I told her I had no idea how formal or otherwise the gathering was to be, but she said it didn't matter—the dress was perfect for any occasion. She asked me what shoes I was planning to wear and guided me to an elegant and comfortable pair. I expressed my concern about wearing new shoes all evening.

'You should be comfortable in those all night, if necessary, *Madame*, even though they are new.'

They really were comfortable so I decided to risk them. Exhausted but pleased, I went back to the hotel and laid on the bed and slept.

§

I was woken by my mobile phone vibrating. It was a text message from Andrea telling me the appointment with Patrick had been fixed for late Monday and obviously included lunch. Later, my flight ticket arrived from Trish. I acknowledged them both.

What should I do this evening? Perhaps I should have told Ricard I was free as the project was ending. Maybe I should have, but I hadn't.

It was about seven in the evening and I'd no idea what to do. I tidied myself up and went down to the reception and asked if there were any concerts or films nearby this evening. I was pointed to a display of leaflets of various activities currently available, but shortly after I'd started looking at them, the receptionist, Michel, came over and picked up one leaflet.

'This church,' he said, 'is within easy walking distance. I think you and your friend went there one Sunday morning for Eucharist. Tonight, there is a concert of Bach music. It starts at eight. If it is not too presumptuous of me, if you are interested in the concert, *Madame*, may I accompany you to the church? I am one of the violinists but I need a few more minutes till I finish my shift here.'

'Thank you. Yes please,' I replied.

After the concert, I was introduced to so many of the players and their friends I had no chance of remembering their names but I saw one of the students I'd met the other night in the bistro; she remembered me and waved. There was a party to follow the success of the concert. Michel invited me to stay, I declined, thanked him for a wonderful evening and left him to his friends. It had been an exhilarating evening and I told Ricard about the concert when I rang him.

'How did he know about the Sunday service?'

'Sorry, I didn't ask. Maybe he was the presiding priest.'

'I doubt it. See you tomorrow.'

'Oh, Ricard, I'll be finishing early tomorrow; any chance of an earlier pick up? If not, don't worry, I'll wait here as usual. I'd like to bring my big case so would rather not take the train.'

'Just a moment.' I waited while he checked his diary on his phone. 'I do not think so, but I will try unless you are happy for Sven to pick you up on his own.'

'No. I'll wait for you. I'll meet you in the foyer. If Michel is on duty, maybe we could talk to him and ask him about the church spy network searching out non-Catholics!'

'Be careful or they'll lock you up as a secret agent!'
We ended with our usual amorous exchanges and I slept well.

Chapter Seven

Ricard picked me up at the hotel as arranged, Sven was as polite and non-communicative as usual as the perfect chauffeur. How he and Ricard kept the two roles, on one hand chauffer/handyman and the other, the partner to his sister-in-law with whom they shared the table, astounded me. But somehow, they managed it; I was glad to see them both and relieved Ricard had refused Suzanne's wish to come with him. I needed some quiet time alone with him and relaxed fully in the backseat holding his hand, asking questions about the party protocol, what food had been organised and so on.

From what he said this small gathering was far more elaborate than I had been led to believe and suddenly, it became a frightening prospect. I was to be partly hostess on Ricard's arm yet a guest who was to mingle. But also, being introduced as the possible new addition to his life and replacement for Charlotte—as well as being the usurper for anyone else's ambitions to be in his bed. I had already asked Ricard to be careful who he invited.

When we arrived at the house, Suzanne had already gone to bed, so we went up and said goodnight before having a late supper with Marianne and Sven, during which I grilled Marianne to assure myself there were no great pit holes awaiting me the following evening.

'Do not worry, I have personally seen to it and eliminated any vipers, none will be given house room tomorrow night. If any have slipped through my net—you will manage.'

§ § §

Saturday morning was a torrent of furniture moving by Ricard and Sven, a bit of dusting for Suzanne and me, and for Lucille and Marianne—cooking. Ricard had obviously organised parties before and knew just what he wanted and where. As I watched, I wondered if he was always so focussed or if he'd be open to other suggestions. Mark was so flexible and undemanding, we lived as the days came and went, it was going to be a different sort of life to which I was, potentially, being introduced.

The nearest Mark and I had got to a formal gathering, as tonight would be, was when Mark invited his boss for drinks one Christmas Eve when there were also business associates, with whom Mark had to socialise. Otherwise, he entertained clients in restaurants which meant I didn't have to cook, just be supportive.

At eight o'clock, the guests started to arrive and I was introduced. Ricard asked me to receive everyone with him before going to talk to them individually later. There was a delay until the last guests arrived before Ricard indicated to Sven and Lucille to offer wine and soft drinks with canapés. Shortly afterwards, Marianne announced there was a buffet in the dining room, inviting guests to help themselves when they were ready.

All the guests seemed to respond genuinely to my answers to their questions about my life and gave me guidance about life in Lézignan. There were thirty couples present, evenly split between Ricard's friends, who'd known Charlotte, and his business associates and their husbands or wives. It seemed to me they thought it was a *fait á complie* that Ricard and I were a couple. I looked around at all his guests.

I felt guilty, I still haven't broken the news of the project end to Ricard.

My thoughts were interrupted by Suzanne dragging me to the side salon to talk for a while to her godmothers, Giselle and Francine. They were very friendly and assured me if Ricard and I should go ahead and marry, they would continue to be supportive in their roles of godmothers.

As if to confirm this, Giselle looked at Suzanne and said in a serious tone, 'I will pick you up just before eight o'clock tomorrow morning, don't be late.'

'Oh, but Yvonne is only here for one more day, can't I miss it?'

'No! A quarter to eight sharp, on the doorstep.'

'Oh, dear Lord, give this godmother to someone else.' Pleaded Suzanne jokingly.

'She'll be there.' I smiled, wondering if there was an alarm clock in the house.

'I doubt it very much. It will be a first for her and me too, except on my confirmation morning when I was dragged out of bed by my mother. I leave those things to Francine; come on, Suzanne, enough chatter and my glass needs a refill. It is really so lovely to meet you, Yvonne.' She ruffled Suzanne's hair and said,

'Come my dear, you've not told me about your last visit to the farm, how are your grandparents?'

'Oh, they are fine; but I think they work really hard as they take in guests.' They left us holding hands.

I turned to Francine.

'I'm sorry to be blunt, but where do you stand on the godmother scene?'

'I do have a deep faith and I will try to guide Suzanne. I feel strongly, but unlike Giselle, who thinks it is only about an occasional Sunday devotional, when she can be bothered, I think it is more a daily thing and how we lead our lives. I understand you spent some time at the retreat house near Elne.'

'Yes, I had some lovely weeks there.'

'If you are really contemplating marriage with Ricard, I hope you both will be happy. It is a long time since I have seen him be so quiet and content.'

The image of Ricard haring around this morning and agitating about all the preparations flashed through my mind; anyone less quiet and content was difficult to imagine.

'Maybe you will be the influence he needs to bridge the gap between him and his parents,' she smiled and hugged me, '*bon chance*—and I will add— God's blessings.'

'Thanks. What do you know about the rift?'

'Nothing, it all happened very suddenly when his brother left for Australia. Come on, we both need to be sociable and you must meet my delicious husband properly.'

§

Nearing midnight, I passed Ricard the last of the plates and sat down at the table Marianne had insisted on scrubbing before she went across to their flat.

'I hope we'll leave the glasses until tomorrow. I can't do them now.'

'Never do glasses at night.'

'Agreed.'

'Coffee?'

'Please. I really wasn't looking forward to tonight, Ricard, but it—' I didn't finish my sentence as Suzanne came running into the kitchen. She'd not put on her dressing gown nor slippers, her beautiful face was tearstained and surrounded by her hair, which was all over the place. She rushed into my arms and sat on my lap, clinging to me as a baby monkey would hold its mother as she climbed the tree to protect them from danger. I held her tight and tried to reassure her.

'Yvonne, I had it again. This time more, more shouting and fighting, I could feel it.'

'Just a dream, my love, just a dream.'

'No, it is more. More than a dream, it is real. I have seen it. I know I have, sometime, somewhere. I know where but cannot find it.' She squirmed about to look at Ricard. 'I was there, *Papa*.'

'What? I thought you did not have it anymore!' Ricard looked at me holding his daughter whose face was again buried into my shoulder. 'You knew?'

I nodded. 'She told me.'

Holding her close, I put my lips to her tousled hair and gently asked,

'Suzanne, haven't you told your *Papa* about the dream?'

She snuffled into my shoulder, shaking her head gently.

'I gave up, *Papa* did not think it was important.'

Ricard's face paled.

'Suzanne, is this the same one with the fighting?' He asked. 'Who is fighting who?'

'I do not know, I do not know, it is you and not you but it is someone else. I do not know.' Her voice was quiet and supplicant. Then with a sound between a sigh and a sob, she went to sleep in my arms. I tried to lift her but she was too heavy for me. Ricard took her and laid her on her bed and left me to settle her.

When I returned to the kitchen, I smelled fresh coffee. Ricard had his back to me and didn't turn, his shoulders were hunched. From where I stood, he resembled a man in defeat or terror, I couldn't decide which.

I sat again at the scrubbed, now dismal kitchen table and waited. A table which, less than two hours ago, had been surrounded by a few close friends joking and laughing, eating from bowls full of fruit and a selection of cheeses. He shuddered and keeping his back to me, he started, his voice was quiet but full of bitterness.

'As you know, Charlotte died during Suzanne's birth. They did what could be done to save her. Some sort of haemorrhage they could not stop. I was devastated but also delighted as I still had a bit of Charlotte and me, our child. She has all the features of Charlotte except the eyes which are mine and I was so happy to have her. And now I had a new baby to look after. A baby! I realised I had no idea how to look after a baby so, the practical side of me took over and I asked Marianne to help me.

'She had been around quite a bit during the pregnancy, certainly in the latter part when she no longer had her mother to look after. During this time, I think she and Charlotte got very much closer than they had been before. Marianne was devastated at the situation too but had no hesitation in saying yes.' With a strange tone in his voice, Ricard continued, 'My brother, Jules, agreed to be godfather to Suzanne, he was as pleased as Punch to be asked and had met the two friends of Charlotte's I had asked to be godmothers, all three seemed to get on well, together. Jules kept calling her *his little one*. I had never seen him so enamoured with a baby before.'

Ricard stopped and poured some coffee for us both, brought it to the table and sat opposite me. He looked exhausted. I took his hands and waited for him to continue but the kitchen door opened and Marianne entered.

'You two still up? It is late. I hope I am not interrupting but I need some things from the freezer for tomorrow.'

'No, not interrupting anything.' Ricard sighed. 'Come on, Yvonne, enough talk for tonight. Goodnight, Marianne, please lock the door when you go home.'

She gave a questioning look which fluctuated between Ricard and me. Neither of us responded except I mouthed, *C'est ça!* and shrugged my shoulders. We left the coffee on the table.

Ricard had clammed up and wouldn't say anything more. I was learning it was better not to push him so we went to bed in silence leaving many things unasked, unanswered and unsaid. We just held each other closely and slept soundly.

§ § §

When I woke next morning, well after eight o'clock, Suzanne was sleeping peacefully between us, Ricard also asleep.

'So much for early church,' I mumbled to myself as I looked at their faces. *C'est ça!*

I went downstairs to make coffee; Marianne had finished washing and drying the glasses which stood gleaming on the side ready to be replaced in their cupboard.

'Suzanne was not in her own bed this morning.' Marianne said after the morning greeting.

'No, she's up with Ricard.'

'Is she still having those dreams? She has not mentioned them recently.'

'Yes, she had one last night while we were down here. I put her into her bed, but sometime during the night she crept into ours, she's there now. Ricard was rather surprised she was still having the dream—seems he was, at least to Suzanne's mind, rather dismissive of it.'

'Perhaps I should admit to that also. I really thought it was her imagination and it would eventually pass.' Marianne sounded very downbeat.

'Maybe it will.'

Ricard and Suzanne were sitting up in the bed, holding hands, the pillows piled high behind them, Ricard had his right arm round Suzanne's shoulders, it looked as if both had been crying and now, had their eyes closed in restful companionship. My entrance disturbed their peace but they smiled and moved over for me to join them after I'd put the coffee mugs on the side tables.

'We have been talking about the dream and trying to work out what triggers it.'

'Any luck?' I asked; they shook their heads. 'It's pretty obvious surely.'

'What do you mean?'

'For goodness' sake, think about it. Suzanne, what did you talk to Giselle about after you left Francine and me yesterday evening?'

'Lots of things. Why?'

'When you left us, Giselle was asking you to tell her about your last visit—'

'To the farm and she asked about my grandparents. She was really interested and we talked a lot about *Mamie* and *Papi* and she asked about the animals too.'

'And last night, you had the dream. When else have you had it?'

'It seems every time she comes back from the farm.' Said Ricard.

'And every time you won't commit to going to see your parents or talk about them. My Lord, it's so obvious. So obvious it is right in front of your noses.'

'Yes, but I stopped telling *Papa*—'

'Because I dismissed it. I am so sorry, my dear.'

'But I have had it at other times too.'

'When, Suzanne?'

'You are the detective, Yvonne, you will think of something.' Suzanne looked expectantly.

I thought for a bit then nodded.

'When you look in your treasure box.'

'Shall I get it?' She scrambled out of the bedclothes and off the bed at the bottom.

'Seems you know more about my daughter than I do,' Ricard's voice was quiet and sombre, 'you will just have to come and stay. I obviously need help.'

'If you just want a child minder, you can find someone else. You have a perfectly good one downstairs.' There was an edge to my voice I'd not meant to be there.

'You know that is not what I meant, Yvonne. I am sorry. I want you to come and marry me. I love you so much.' He put his hand on my arm which I moved away.

'No, I'm sorry. I think I'm just a bit tired after last night. And as you'll—or more aptly have—found out, I can be a bit snappy if I'm tired.'

'No, there is more to it than tiredness.'

'Mm, talk later.' I responded as Suzanne came back with the parcel in the string bag from her treasure box and laid it on the bed next to Ricard.

'What is that?'

'It is what *Papi* sent you. I tried to give it to you on the station the night Yvonne brought me home then again later. I told Yvonne and she said I should keep it till you asked for it or when the time was right and you would take it. I have not opened it. Yvonne said not to as it is for you.'

Ricard did not reach for, nor touch, the bag, just looked at it.

'I used to take that string bag with me when I went to the village shop to get things for my mother,' he said, 'I am surprised it is still in one piece.'

'Are you going to open it now, *Papa*?'

'No, Suzanne. Would you please put it in the wardrobe drawer?'

'I still say if *Papi* sent me a present, I would open it straightaway. I am going to dress and help tidy downstairs.' She left the bag containing the parcel where it was, flounced off, slamming the bedroom doors behind her.

I sighed.

'I cannot open it, not with her here. I have no idea what it is and what effect it might have on me. Please understand.'

'To understand, I have to know. If we're to have a future…'

'Yes, I know.'

'I'm going to have a shower then join Suzanne and the others; the place needs putting straight before lunch.'

Ricard had gone when I returned from the shower but the bag and its contents still lay where Suzanne had left it. I put it into the drawer and made the bed. Ricard and Sven were replacing the furniture when I went down.

During the time of restoring the room to its normal state, the conversation had been limited and was mainly between Sven and Ricard coordinating the lifts for moving the furniture. Suzanne wandered in and out of the kitchen but said little. When the rooms were straight, I sat down.

'Gin and tonic?' asked Ricard.

'Yes please. Will the others join us?'

'I'll ask,' he went to the kitchen; on returning said,

'They said they would finish preparing the lunch before they come in.'

'OK. You know, your parents aren't getting any younger, Ricard, don't you think whatever it is between you should be sorted out before it's too late? You have a long life ahead of you in which to have regrets if you don't.'

He passed me my drink and stood looking out of the window. The light seemed to be fading as large storm clouds gathered blocking out the wintery sun reflecting perfectly, the mood inside. He flicked on a couple of lights. 'It is complicated and difficult.'

'The longer you leave it, the more difficult it will be.'

'After nearly nine years, a few more months will not hurt.'

'For your sake, I hope it won't.' I paused for a moment and tried to push him a little. 'If there's an invitation to visit the farm waiting for me when I get home, what do I do?'

'Do not cross a bridge until you come to it, just because Suzanne has asked them to invite you, it does not mean they will.'

'You obviously don't know your parents; would you make me another drink please?'

'We will also have ours now please, Ricard.' Added Marianne as she, Sven and Suzanne joined us.

The conversation turned to plans for the courtyard till Suzanne said,

'I am hungry, Marianne, we got the lunch ready; can we eat now?'

'We really ought to or it will run straight into supper time, it is only a light meal so we will eat in the kitchen today and feel a little less formal than yesterday evening.'

Seated in the comfort of the kitchen, we helped ourselves to the various dishes Marianne had prepared and, in an effort, to keep some conversation going, Marianne asked if we'd all enjoyed the party yesterday; there was consensus it had been successful as well as enjoyable and all the guests were suitably charmed by me.

I'd better tell Ricard today. I'm accusing him of holding a secret and I'm doing so.

'I meant to say, Yvonne, the dress really impressed and I have to reinforce I do like your new hairstyle.'

'I knew there was something different but could not put my finger on it, yes, I agree, it really is great.'

'At last, Ricard! I kept making hints but you totally ignored them.'

'I was more concerned in helping you meet people and be relaxed with them.'

'You had all Friday evening and most of Saturday to notice. I'll dye it green next time then maybe you'll pay some attention.'

We all exchanged more banter; Sven was amazing with fast and funny spontaneous repartee; when we'd eaten sufficient, Marianne said,

'Suzanne, I think there was some homework to be done.'

'I did most of it on Friday evening, Marianne, before I had early supper, so there is not much more to do.'

'It will not take too long to finish then, will it?' She urged.

'It is just the English, Yvonne, will you go through it again for me please? I did tell the teacher you had helped me last time.'

'Oh? And what did she say?'

'"Good use of resources"—or something like that. I will bring it down when I have finished.'

'Marianne, why don't you and Sven go and sit down or do whatever you want to? You have both worked so hard and I've not done much, I'll clear up.'

'Thank you, Yvonne,' said Sven smiling, 'come on and no arguing, Marianne.' They left.

'I'll see you later.'

'OK.' I looked at Ricard's receding back, as he went into his office and closed the door firmly.

I'd never been left in the kitchen on my own after a meal and vaguely wondered what Marianne would think if she knew Ricard had not stayed to help me to clear and wash up. But it did save us having to face another argument and gave me time to think. I heard him go upstairs quietly, almost stealthily as if he didn't want me to know. I carried on with the job thinking somehow, I'd have to get him to talk to me; without knowing what was bugging him, I couldn't let our relationship develop and I still had to tell him I might not be returning to Toulouse.

This might be the last day we have together. I'd hate to leave on a sour note but maybe now is the time to make the break before we go any further down the line.

I'd enjoyed the party, especially the latter part with his closest friends talking round the table once the more formal ones had left. I'd relaxed feeling very much part of the group, I could see myself fitting in with his friends and making them mine and working well with Marianne, but now, after our disagreement and Ricard's reluctance to talk, I wasn't sure if it would work.

'You were talking to yourself, Yvonne, do you do it a lot when you are on your own?'

'I've never noticed, but we often don't notice our own habits, do we? Homework?' I asked, pointing to her book. 'Wait till I've wiped the table before you put the book down, I'll finish the dishes before I look at your work.' I dried my hands and used some of Marianne's hand cream before pouring some wine and sitting next to Suzanne.

'Good work, Suzanne, but can you see where you have made the same mistake as last time?'

She looked at the page, twiddling her pencil.

'Why will he not open the parcel? He is ruining everything.'

'He has his reasons, Suzanne, he's his own man and will act how he thinks is right.'

'But you will not stay, will you, if he does not explain?'

'I did try to warn you it might not turn out as you wished; there are lots of questions to be answered before we make a final decision.'

'Well, here is one answer.'

'Will you stop eavesdropping on our conversations, Ricard? You know it only leads to problems.'

'I was not really listening in. I heard the last sentence as I got to the door and would like to tell you something about the contents of the parcel.'

'You opened it? Oh *Papa*, I am so glad.'

'Suzanne, I have told Yvonne, but think you should know.' He summarised his boyhood relationship with Jules and the jealousy arising out of the use of hard-earned money.

'Did you still visit *Papi* and *Mamie* then?'

'Oh yes, but things continued to be difficult between me and my brother.'

Suzanne had been concentrating while Ricard spoke, but now the frown lifted from her brow.

'Then you and your brother were friends again?'

'No, the resentment lasted, though it did ease a bit when you arrived, maybe he felt a bit of compassion when your mother died which is why I asked him to be your godfather. I also hoped I would see more of him enabling us to resolve our differences—which did not fully happen, but this letter and papers explain where the money came from and includes a little surprise about my parents too. It seems they were not married when I was conceived, my mother was only sixteen.'

'So, her parents disowned her?'

'No, Yvonne, quite the opposite; it was my father's father who disowned his son. My father was at college learning estate management and it was on one of his secondments, near where my mother lived, they met. It was my mother's parents who took them both in, gave them a roof over their heads, supported them and paid my father a wage for working on the farm. Not quite what he had planned! Anyway, having developed into a farmer there came a time when my father wanted a farm of his own, because of the inheritance laws, the farm would not go to mother as she had a brother.

'So, with the help of my mother's parents, they bought the farm they have now. Of course, by this time Jules, my brother, had arrived, but what my parents did not know was, although my father's father had no direct contact with his son, he kept in constant communication with my mother's parents who let him know how they were and how they were progressing and sent money, confidentially, to help with the farm purchase and later to see me through my education and then Jules', the fees for the colleges and university were paid directly to the establishments. My parents encouraged us to apply as I said, and I thought they had scraped the money together somehow. But my parents had no idea who the benefactor was for the farm, university and colleges.'

'But why didn't your parents say anything to you before?' I asked.

'Apparently, they were told by my mother's parents, now long dead, not to ask, so he only found out recently when his father died and my father inherited his estate.'

'But you said he'd been disinherited.'

'Apparently, not legally and formally, and obviously he cared about his son.'

'He had a funny way of showing it,' whispered Suzanne.

'Maybe, but do not judge other people too quickly, Suzanne.'

'Sorry, *Papa*.'

'Amongst the papers of explanation, there is a heart-rending letter to my father from his, full of regrets and guilt, putting a lot of it down to pride and how he felt embarrassed. He was a leading solicitor in the town and his reputation would have been tarred by his son's actions.'

'So, are all the documents personal and letters?'

'Actually no. There are several legal ones and a letter from my father asking me to take over the executorship of this father's will. He does not think he can do it.'

'Was it just papers in the parcel then? It felt like some hard things too,' asked Suzanne.

'A few personal items, I'll let you see them one day—but do not push me, understand?'

'Yes *Papa*.'

'Go and finish your homework now, Suzanne.'

'Yes *Papa*.'

I waited for Ricard to speak.

'Another glass? To celebrate the opening of the package?' He selected a bottle of Merlot and carefully uncorked it.

'One step forward I suppose.'

'You do not sound very enthusiastic, what is the matter?'

'They sent the parcel over three weeks ago; what do you think they're thinking? They asked you for help, to do something. But no, in your pride and stubbornness, you refused to open it.'

'OK, I get the message. I was wrong, but…Yvonne, there is another issue I cannot discuss.'

'Can't or won't?'

He took a large mouthful of wine and stared at me.

'There will be a time, but not now, please. I had better go and write to the solicitor who contacted my father and find out more about the estate, it is probably mortgaged up to the hilt and deeply in debt.'

'That's it! Always look on the bright side! Will you act for your father? As you know, solicitors are expensive and you could save him some money and not drain the estate.'

'Yes, to save him expenses, I will do it.'

'You'd better write to your father too.'

'Yes.'

§

I was finishing putting my clothes into my case when Ricard brought me a typewritten letter.

'Do you think this is alright, under the circumstances?'

He'd expressed condolences on the death of his father's father, then continued to say he would act as executor and had written to the other solicitor. He added a couple of lines saying Suzanne was well.

'Well, it's a bit stiff, but what can I say? However, I think it would be much nicer if you hand-wrote the salutation and ending. But up to you.'

'Mmm.'

I looked around the room to see if there were any more of my things lying about and wondered if I'd come back. There was no guarantee I'd go back to Toulouse if I were pulled off the project.

Perhaps, it might be better to be taken off and this emotional interlude would be over. Perhaps it was too soon, perhaps I was too vulnerable. How many warnings had I been given? C'est ça!

Tears I couldn't stop, started to fall followed by a soft deep sobbing. I curled up on the bed and wept myself to sleep.

114

I woke to a gentle touch of a hand on my shoulder, someone had put a light, warm blanket over me at some time while I slept.

'Yvonne,' it was Marianne, 'I thought I had better wake you or you will not sleep through the night; you must be fit for your flight. I have brought you some fresh orange juice, dinner is ready when you want to come down.'

'I must look awful.'

'Wash your face and do your hair, you will look alright.'

'Marianne, what am I going to do?' I felt myself about to cry again.

She held me close.

'I do not know. Only you can make that decision. But be careful what and how you do it and be gentle on yourself and us,' she released me, 'but for now, you must get up and join us, you do not want to eat cold soup, I will be serving it soon.'

I entered the dining room, it was ablaze with candles, small tables had been brought to the room from elsewhere and on each there were candles, as on the mantelpiece; half a dozen three and four branched candlesticks, alight with candles, were placed on the extended dining table, away from our place settings. It was an amazing sight and lit up the faces of the family, light reflected in their eyes as they all stood holding glasses of white wine, even Suzanne had a small one.

I accepted a glass from Ricard who said, 'It is autumn; with everything going on recently, I had forgotten this family tradition. I do not remember how or why it started but it was in existence when I was a child and Charlotte always enjoyed it, so we have carried on, first at my parents and then here. We light candles on this date to help lift the gloom of the autumn evenings and nights and eat in a formal setting. Marianne remembered, which is why we had the light lunch in the kitchen, I thought it a bit strange for Sunday, but accepted her reason for doing so.'

'It looks absolutely fantastic, what a lovely thing to do,' I said and kissed Ricard on the cheek.

He raised his glass. 'To the light shining in the autumn night.'

'To the light shining in the autumn night,' we all repeated.

After we'd eaten and were enjoying coffee, Suzanne was fighting to stay awake so Ricard sent her up to bed saying he would go and say goodnight shortly.

'Marianne, will you come too? Goodnight, Sven. Goodnight, Yvonne,' she said, then left us.

'Ooh dear.' Sven was the only one to express all our thoughts at the harshness of her voice to me.

'Perhaps I should go up and see her now. Finish your coffees and liqueurs.' Ricard left us.

'She had such high hopes,' said Marianne quietly.

'We kept telling her there were problems and it might not end up with us being together.'

'I know, but she is young and idealistic.'

'We have all taken to you, Yvonne, this is not moral blackmail, but there has been a lightness to the house since you landed in our lives.' Sven looked at Marianne and shrugged. 'Well, it is true, do not deny it.'

'Well, maybe the lightness isn't here today, I'm sorry, Sven.'

'The road to true love and so on…' said Marianne as she rose to clear the plates which contained the peelings from our post dessert fruit.

'That, Marianne, is an understatement. Come on, let's clear up. Do we extinguish the candles, we can't leave the room with them still lit?'

'No, traditionally, they have to burn themselves out, as you see they are not tall; obviously, one person has to be in the room all the time. We take it in turns to stack bits in here and take them to the kitchen.'

We did so and when Ricard came downstairs, Marianne went up to say goodnight to Suzanne.

'How is she?' I asked.

'Upset.'

'Sorry.'

'No, no, she is upset because she was rude to you and knows she has hurt you.'

'Oh.'

'I told her she could come down and tell you herself but will not.'

'Why?'

'Embarrassment mainly, I think, but there is also an element of hurt and possibly pride and stubbornness.'

'Well, we know where she gets the last two from, don't we? Sven's on candle watch. Do you want to join him and I'll make a fresh pot of coffee?'

'Thanks. Would you like another liqueur while we watch the candles die?'

'No thanks, I think I still have some left in my glass.'

When Marianne joined us, the coffee was ready and we joined the men who were deep in conversation. We continued to sit at the table enjoying the coffee and each other's company. I'd almost forgotten the trauma of the day and the problem I had to face when Sven asked, 'What time is the flight in the morning?'

'Half past seven, I'm afraid. I need to be there about an hour earlier, but it is not absolutely crucial in business class.'

'We had better be ready to leave at six. Getting out of Lézignan on a Monday morning can take quite a long time. Do you mind if I leave you all now? Goodnight.'

Marianne stayed. 'May I ask what the next move is?'

'First I find out how my sister is, see my parents and then my boss.'

'You know what I am talking about—you two. How are you going to leave or progress your relationship from here?'

'For my part,' started Ricard, 'my feelings for Yvonne have not changed. I love her and would like to marry her and spend the rest of my life with her. I know I have issues, but some are too difficult to just come out with so I ask for time and tolerance. But this might be asking too much and putting excess pressure on a tender situation.'

'And you, Yvonne?'

'My head is telling me to be sensible and work this out logically. There are so many issues to be sorted out, things troubling Ricard he can't—or won't—talk about. I have no idea about my job situation, Ricard's not met my family yet so we've no idea how he'll be accepted; I need to get to the bottom of what my sister is doing and why she didn't tell anyone about the baby and who the father is; I've met Ricard's father briefly but have no indication as to how they will view me,' I stopped for a moment and moved my coffee cup onto the tray in front of me, 'but, after all my head logic, my heart says I love him.'

'So, maybe your initial response was not so flippant and superficial as I thought. You need to go home and sort out some of the practicalities and clear your head, then see if heart is still saying the same thing. Do not be up too late, most of the candles are out so you need not stay much longer. Goodnight.'

We were sitting opposite each other, both staring at the last of the dwindling candles, neither of us speaking. Ricard reached and took my hand.

'Will you ring me from England?'

I nodded.

'And when you have sorted things out and know about your job, will you come again and see us?'

I shrugged, holding back my tears.

'I have no idea.'

'You go on up, I will wait for this last candle then put the tray in the kitchen.' He released my hand and I stood.

When I reached the landing, I noticed Suzanne's door was unusually open, as I was passing, she called my name. She was sitting on her bed wearing her dressing gown and holding her slippers as if about to put them on; going in, I raised my hand to the light switch but she asked me not to turn the light on.

'There is enough light from the landing.'

'Hello.'

'Yvonne, I am so sorry I was rude to you earlier, but the way the talk was going about you not being here, I got so angry. It felt like I had been left and I wanted to hurt you as I felt I was being hurt. I did not mean it. I am so sorry.'

'Thanks for telling me. I didn't hurt you on purpose and I understand you may have wanted to hurt me, now you've explained, it is OK. I think it's all very confusing, not only for you, my dear, but for us too. You have to understand there are a lot of things going on in both your father's and my life to be resolved before we can be sure we are making the right decision.'

'Will you come back?'

'I've told your father I don't know.'

'Do you think I will have the dream tonight, Yvonne?'

'I know we've had a lot of talk about the farm and your grandparents, but I think a step forward has been made and it will not bother you tonight.'

Taking off her dressing gown, she got into bed. I kissed her.

'Goodnight.'

'You do love him, don't you?'

'Yes.'

'Good, he loves you. Goodnight.'

'Goodnight.' I closed her bedroom door and stood outside it for a moment before going to bed myself.

We had gentle prolonged sex. No urgency.

Perhaps this is a gentle farewell. C'est ça!

Chapter Eight

If Suzanne did have the dream during the night, she did not disturb us. By the time I showered and dressed, hot rolls and coffee were ready on the kitchen table, prepared by Marianne. Strangely enough, the atmosphere was, to use Sven's phrase, "light" this morning as if a great weight had been lifted and we all knew it was a matter of time before we were together again, in what arrangement no one knew. There was not a great deal of time for much discussion and after I'd exchanged a quick hug with Marianne, Ricard escorted me to the car in which my suitcases had already been placed. After a brief kiss, he stood back and I settled into the backseat.

'Ring me when you get home.'

I nodded and waved as we drove off through the now familiar oak gates.

§

The seven-thirty flight was earlier than I'd hoped to get, but there were no available seats on the later ones. Once more, I felt strange entering the empty flat but as I'd taken the precaution of leaving the heating on low before I'd left the last time, there was no icy chill to the rooms, for which I was grateful. I picked up the post and put it, unsorted, in the kitchen and sipping coffee rang Andrea to tell her I was *en route* to the office.

I acknowledged the receptionist on the desk who must have been primed to tell Andrea when I arrived because she intercepted me at the lift and took me directly into her own office.

'What's going on, Andrea?'

'One of the outside contractors is using your office again and Patrick didn't want you to feel you were being ousted by walking into someone occupying your office.'

I swallowed. 'OK. No longer my office. No longer a role here?' I looked at Andrea.

'Come off it, Yvonne, if he were going to give you the push, he'd have told you, don't be so defensive. It was my idea to meet you, to save you a potential shock of finding your office occupied. You might be interested to know, by the person who took over your project when you were in Elne, Patrick was so impressed with her, he offered her more work.'

'Sorry Andrea, there are so many strange things about this current project I don't understand and I may have messed up.'

The intercom on Andrea's desk flashed from Patrick's office. She said 'Yes' three times in answer to different questions, picked up a file from her desk and started towards his office. 'Wait here, Yvonne. I won't be a moment.'

What's going on?

I waited for her return.

'Patrick says for you to go straight in. I'll bring coffee shortly.'

Two men rose from the settee where they'd been talking when I entered. I was dumbstruck, *Monsieur* Faunier stood beside Patrick, who came forward and gave me a brief embrace, which I didn't resist.

'You know *Monsieur* Marcel Faunier, of course, Yvonne, so there is no need for introductions.'

'Yes, of course. How nice to see you again, *Monsieur* Faunier, although it's rather a surprise.'

He held out his hand, which I took for a formal handshake, but having taken it, he gave the double-cheek kiss welcome of the French.

'*Madame* Birch, it is a pleasure to see you again.'

I waited for Patrick to say something but he indicated we should all sit and directed us to his desk. Once seated, I removed my report and papers from the folder and waited. I'd not had time to talk to Patrick and apart from my reports to him, he was aware of my oblivion of what I was doing in this project. I looked at him for advice, he gently shook his head and slightly raised his shoulders as he laid both his hands, palms down on to his desk, his fingers splayed out and said, 'As far as I can gather, Yvonne, there was a key turning point in the investigation when *Monsieur* Faunier was alerted to something you said or did, your logic, led to the solving of the problem.'

Monsieur Faunier had clearly been nominated to speak. '*Madame* Birch, it was when you asked to see the company's bank accounts. It was there, open and obvious, money being paid to non-existent creditors, linked to the various false codes you and the team had identified. I had to stop you going further and went to see the bank, they were able to trace the illegal transactions to the originators. A couple of rogue, I am ashamed to say, co-directors and friends, I will rephrase that—former co-directors and former friends—of mine, who have been taking not only money but also technological information from the company.'

'Will your company be able to recuperate the losses?' I asked.

'Possibly the financial ones, but as to the technical developments, I am not sure. We do not usually share or patent-protect them until we are certain of them, as to do so could endanger lives; remember, we build machines to transport people.'

He looked at his watch, at the same time there was a tap on the door. Andrea opened it. 'Excuse me, but the taxi for *Monsieur* Faunier is here.'

'I must leave now if I am to get my flight back, as it is, I will be late for the meeting I'd rearranged with Paul and the rest of the team. I won't invite you to come with me now, *Madame* Birch, but we would welcome you again to say farewell and update you on progress.'

I was totally stunned at the sudden turn of events. Patrick said hardly anything, obviously having talked it all through with *Monsieur* Faunier; the project was over for me. I stood and extended my hand to say goodbye and asked him to give my best wishes to the team, emphasising they had really done all the hard work.

'A good, loyal team,' he said, 'they will be recognised and rewarded, but without your input—ah! who knows what might have happened! Now, don't forget, we expect to hear when you will arrange to meet us in Toulouse. Patrick, goodbye for now, we will talk again.'

Patrick escorted *Monsieur* Faunier to the door and passed him over to Andrea. I stayed and realised all through the previous exposition, I'd increasingly clenched my hands on my papers. I felt a tightness in my shoulders I'd not had for some time and my jaw was so clenched I thought it might break. When Patrick returned to his desk, I waited for him to speak; when he did, I thought his comment rather flippant.

'Well, another happy customer, thanks to you.'

I placed my report and crumpled supporting papers on his desk.

'I still have no idea what—no—I was about to say what the project was about or how the team came to crack it, but it was obviously about industrial espionage and financial theft. And did you know along the way we caught a paedophile?'

'No, Faunier said nothing about that. I hope you didn't do anything inappropriate.'

'No, it was an unexpected discovery by the boys—young men I suppose they are. They reported it in their usual practice and after police investigations, the culprit was found. You know, *Monsieur* Faunier has his work cut out now undertaking one enormous re-appraisal of all their staff and systems.'

Patrick looked at me blankly. 'Why?'

'Because it was the Director of Human Resources, but I don't think I was supposed to say anything, and now these other two directors.'

'Poor Marcel, yes, he has got an uphill job on his hands to ensure the company continues to succeed. Perhaps it is now clear why he wanted outside help and didn't want to use the local facilities. To do so would have alerted everyone to the fact he was concerned about something.'

'And you don't want to wash your dirty linen in public, do you? Well, Patrick, it has certainly been an experience, a very confusing one. But I think *Monsieur* Faunier has a good team and loyal employees in the three I worked with. I am so pleased Paul's intuition and observation bore fruit.'

Patrick stood up. 'Come on, it's past usual lunch time, I hope you don't mind but I've asked Andrea to join us today. She's arranged for Trish to take any messages for her, you've really found a treasure there, Yvonne, thank you.'

'I've not seen her, what are you talking about?'

When we emerged from his office to gather Andrea, Trish was standing beside her dressed in a smart trouser suit and pale pink blouse setting off her dark hair, now trimmed into a becoming "page boy". She was grinning widely.

'Trish, what are you doing now? Look at you!'

'Well, I had to smarten myself up as I am now Andrea's assistant. Well, in fact it is more of a gofer but I am learning so much and she is such a good teacher, like you. Oh Yvonne, I am so thankful you gave me the chance.'

'I'm so thankful you recognised it and took it. It's really all down to you.'

I looked at Patrick. 'Well, don't overwork her or take her for granted.'

'As if!' he smiled.

'Humph!' I responded.

'If I may break up this mutual admiration society,' said Andrea, 'I've booked the Italian place on the corner for lunch today, selfish of me, but as I rarely get taken to lunch on the house and it's hardly worth my while cooking pasta for myself at home, Frank won't eat it, I thought I'd be self-indulgent. Anyway, you look like you need feeding up, Yvonne.'

From habit, both Andrea and I took our notebooks with us, even if lunch appeared to be a social event, the main common denominator between us was work, so it would inevitably be discussed. We ordered our meals and a bottle of wine.

'A toast to the go-cart factory,' I said, raising my glass.

'To the go-cart factory,' they dutifully repeated and drank then asked what exactly we were drinking to.

'It's the company we've just helped to save, of course,' I said and explained the origins.

The pasta was perfect, made on the premises, not bought in. I asked Patrick about the time he'd had with his sister, he said it was what he needed and thanked me for stopping him from drinking the last whisky he'd left in the airport lounge.

'Andrea, have you ever been to Patrick's sister's place?'

'Oh yes, Frank and I have spent several weeks there over the years. Rather like you, we find it so peaceful and there are usually people, especially the old priests and nuns, who just need a bit of help and like to have an audience so they can sit and reminisce as well as give advice. I enjoy the walk to the village too when a break from them is needed!' She smiled with contentment. 'If Frank goes before me—dies I mean—I've considered seeing my days out there.'

'Frank's not ill, is he? He seemed so fit at the anniversary party.'

'A few health problems, nothing imminent, but none of us knows when the reaper will call, do we? And why it's so important to live your life as well and as fulfilled as you can.' She gave me a look I wasn't quite sure how to interpret.

'Patrick, did you know Julie is expecting twins?'

'No, I didn't. Now you are more back into her life, she doesn't need me quite as much as before. I'm really pleased on both accounts.'

'You've been such a support to her, thank you so much but don't think you'll be off the job for too long, we have yet to find out who this husband of hers is.'

'Don't push it, Yvonne, she'll tell you when she's ready.'

'Yes, you are right, Andrea, at times I don't know what I'll do without you.'

'Is there a time you might have to?'

'I'll never relinquish the people I love and respect, Patrick. I'll always need both of you and your guidance and advice.'

'Sounds as if there is something you are not telling us, Yvonne.'

'Can I throw back to you, Andrea, the advice you just gave me about Julie and her husband. I'll tell you when I'm ready and when I know myself. In the meantime, if you look at your watches, we've been here for over two hours, although I've been used to this in France, it is possibly not the norm here and Trish will have a whole pile of messages for you.'

Andrea and I left Patrick to pay the bill. 'Do you realise, Andrea, I've never had lunch with Patrick before when the conversation didn't turn to work, I was not aware of anyone purposely trying to avoid it, have I missed something?'

'I don't think so, he's been concerned about this last project of yours. The messages you sent and conversations you had with him were confusing and concerning.'

'I tried to be positive, but I've been totally baffled and really didn't know what I was doing, it's not surprising he felt the same.'

'And now it's almost finished, I think he wanted to relax with us. You know he and I have a close relationship, don't you?'

'Not…?'

'No, of course not, but we go back years. We almost think the same things which is why he could talk to me so easily about the situation with you when you came back from the time in Elne, not many men could open up as he did.'

'No, I suppose not. But now what? A debrief over coffee in the office?'

'Coffee and debrief in twenty minutes, what else, if anything he has in mind for you this afternoon, I don't know. I need to sort some papers and talk to Trish, go and sit in his office or you might like to see the person using your office.'

'What a brilliant idea.'

The young lady was a little hesitant when I knocked on the door and walked in.

'Hope I'm not interrupting you, but Andrea thought it might be a good idea for me to come and say hello while I'm waiting for Patrick, and for my part I wanted to say in person, what I did in the email, thanks for the superb way you picked up the project I'd had to abandon.'

'I'm glad you did—not had to abandon the project, I mean—but came in. Andrea told me she thought we should meet, but I have to say I was a bit nervous, especially to be found sitting here when you came in if you hadn't been warned of an intruder.'

We shook hands. There was an awkward silence.

'Do you want your office back?' Sharon asked.

'No, of course not, you need a place to work and I'm currently floating, if I come to land, Andrea will sort out office space, I wanted to meet the person on the end of the email.'

'You know it was because of the last project that I got this current one, don't you?'

'It is far more likely it was the standard of your work, but beware, Patrick is a hard taskmaster, he expects the highest standard but is also a fantastic and supportive boss.'

'So I've heard, but you like to give everyone an opportunity, don't you?'

'What do you mean?'

'Look how Trish has grown in confidence since, as I understand it, you offered her the chance to progress. And talk of the devil!'

Trish stood at the open door.

'Patrick is waiting for you, if you'd like to go in, Andrea is already there.'

I joined them and started to move to Patrick's desk as usual for formal meetings, but he indicated the couch where Andrea sat and brought one of the chairs from his desk.

Patrick and I accepted the coffee poured by Andrea then both she and I settled our pencils and notepads ready to take any notes we thought relevant.

There was little more to say on the "Go-Cart" project apart from confirming I would arrange to fix a "closure" meeting with the team, so Patrick changed the subject.

'As you know, we usually look at projects over lunch, but I thought we'd start now, there are six potential projects available.' He outlined three, dismissed two and expanded on the last one.

'This is totally off the wall as far as my company's tested expertise is concerned. But is possibly an opportunity for the knowledge within the company to expand by putting its toe into the water.'

'Using me as a guinea pig, I suppose, with the safety net in place should anything untoward happen?'

'Have more faith in yourself, Yvonne, and in Patrick, he'll never throw you to the wolves.'

'Don't you believe it,' responded Patrick, his face was serious and again I recognised the hard businessman sitting across the table from me.

I nodded in acknowledgement. 'What, if I may ask, is the sixth possibility?'

'It concerns investigating the feasibility of and developing an academy to teach English, initially to school children, age range being from, as far as I can gather, toddlers who are only just beginning to speak their own language to possibly, in the long term to develop into an adult commercial and managerial language institution.'

'Patrick, someone's pulling your leg, there are hundreds of such companies in England and elsewhere with tentacles spreading all over the world doing this. And most academic establishments are organised and controlled by government regulations.'

'According to the outline papers I've been sent, they do not want to use one of the long-established formulas and it is quite possible, as a private entity, to set up such an academy as long as certain educational and legal stipulations are fulfilled. Just to add to the encouragement, they are willing to pay quite a big sum!'

'You're just mercenary.'

'Maybe, yes, OK. But that's what pays your, Andrea's and Trish's salaries as well as another twenty or thirty directly employed by me plus all the costs towards servicing this building. So, don't mock it.'

'Sorry, I wasn't thinking of the wider implications which can of course be extended to their families, their food, housing—'

'And so on,' interjected Andrea, 'yes, we all agree, but can we get back to the subject please, Patrick, before I call this meeting to a close and suggest we reconvene tomorrow at nine-thirty to discuss the details. Trish is waiting to go home.'

'Yes. Yvonne, according to the client, the time scale, which I think is far too conservative, is probably about eighteen months to get everything in place with all the red tape and so on. They are looking to make connections with the local schools within the area so on the micro-management side, there will be timetables and so on to accommodate, taking easily another six months before you can say you have even started to finish. It's a long haul and I don't want to push you, but I thought it might be of interest, and quite frankly, I don't have anyone on my books who could even contemplate this.'

126

'Wow, as you say, a bit out of our…sorry, your usual remits, but it does sound interesting. Can I have a think and maybe investigate online the possibilities and potential problems? Where do I look? Where's the base for this project? Asia? I've never been there.'

And it would be an opportunity to reassess my feelings.

'A bit nearer home, in France again. There's a large town called Lézignan.'

I think I must have said 'yes' or nodded to whatever else Patrick said as it went way over my consciousness, I vaguely heard him outline the broad brush of the contract as usual—'…. where the mayor has got a bee in his bonnet about forming a collegiate establishment between schools, hopefully private and Government ones and he's looking for a neutral person to organise this.

'It's a big job, apparently he—'

'Yvonne!' I felt Andrea's hand on my arm. 'Are you alright?'

'Yes, yes, thank you. It does sound, did you say a meeting at nine-thirty tomorrow morning? Yes, I'll be here.' I had to get out so looked at my watch. 'I promised to meet Julie, goodnight, see you in the morning.' I left the office building and hailed a taxi to take me to the bistro where my meeting with Julie was to take place.

During the journey, I thought through the strange coincidence of this project. How much, if any, was due to Suzanne identifying the need for permanent teachers of English, let alone the personal emotion; the fact I'd recently met and spent quite some time talking with the mayor and his wife at the party; Ricard's obvious influence in the town. Was this a "setup" by Ricard or was I reading non-existent connections into the situation. Both Patrick and Andrea were aware, even before my comment at lunch, there was something in my personal life I needed to sort out, but surely Patrick hadn't been delving into my personal life in Toulouse.

I arrived at the bistro before Julie and was guided to a table which, apparently, she had requested, and served a complimentary glass of white wine which turned out to be beautifully chilled and dry. I rubbed my hands down the back of my neck and across my shoulders trying to release the tension. First Faunier and now this. I'll talk to Julie, find out all about her and leave work behind. The waiter was about to refill my glass.

'Oh, I'm sorry, I didn't realise I was drinking so fast, but no more, thank you, I'll wait for Julie.'

'You obviously have problems on your mind, you are right not to drink too much as they do not disappear in the bottle. Ah! here is your sister, she does not drink now.'

'Maybe one glass of your delicious wine tonight, Miguel, the babies are safe now.'

'Just one, one only,' he poured wine for us both and left us. I stood up and embraced her.

'Boy, they do look after you in this place, don't they?'

'Yes, although it has the reputation of being a so-called "yuppy area", we are all quite normal and look after each other. Once Miguel and his family knew I was pregnant, they have been like mother hens looking after me when I come in and giving me meals to take home. Oh Yvonne, don't look so downhearted, I know if I'd been honest with you, you'd have been here with me, but you weren't, my fault, but now you are.'

'Yes, I am, as far as I can be.'

'What do you mean? Are you off somewhere again? Has the current project finished?'

'Yes, this one is concluded for me, apart from a farewell lunch—hope it will be lunch, as it is a long journey just for a handshake and a kiss on the cheek! But Patrick is talking about others. Scotland, Scunthorpe I think he said and one again in France, which might be a bit far-fetched.'

'Not too far away.'

'No, but let's forget work for now. Tell me how it is you are now having twins when, as far as I can tell, you were not last time I saw you.'

'We were all the time, but one little one was hiding. On the last antenatal visit—oh and Paul was there too, he'd got another day off so came over early, it was wonderful—they heard a second heartbeat, somehow missed before—and then we got a better scan with me moving into different positions and found this little girl kicking her brother. Yvonne, it was so joyous and I was so glad he was with me.'

'How wonderful, so now you expect me to knit both blue and pink bootees!'

'Rather you didn't, it's kind of you to offer but from what I can remember of your knitting in the past, I think I'll pass, maybe we could be looking forward to more useful assistance, how about some "baby grows" and once they are born, perhaps you could think of setting up a savings account for each of them.'

'You are so practical and forward-looking, Julie. I used to despair of your romantic side! But you obviously have one, I'm so happy for all four of you.'

We finished our meals. Julie had a pasta dish but I explained about my lunch and chose the house speciality salad and I ordered a simple sorbet to follow. Julie still had her passion for chocolate ice cream.

'Can you tell me a bit about this Paul? Tall, dark, handsome.'

'Tall, good-looking and blonde.'

'You also said he is French.' I took my chiffon scarf from my neck and draped it over my head and put my fingers to my temples and closed my eyes, then continued, 'He arrived on a flight from Toulouse on Thursday, a day earlier than you expected him, which is why he could join you at the antenatal clinic on Friday. And left, probably Sunday night or possibly an early flight this morning.'

'Bloody hell, Yvonne, have you become a clairvoyant or have you been following me? Tracking my movements? What is this?'

I took my hands down and replaced my scarf. I could not stop myself, but I laughed out aloud, a long and happy laugh. I could not think of a kinder and more appropriate husband for my sister, I just hoped I was right.

'Shh! Stop it. It's not funny. You and daddy used to do this when you thought something was funny and no one else did. Please, Yvonne. Shh.'

Miguel was alarmed at Julie's reaction to my laughing and came over with a look of concern.

'It's alright, Miguel,' I spluttered, 'I just need a moment and some coffee, to tell my sister something.' Once I'd calmed down and Miguel had brought coffee for me and tea for Julie, I asked, 'One more thing, Julie, and please don't take any offense by this question, does Paul happen to have a birthmark on the inside of his left ankle?'

'Yes, how do you know?'

'He does tend to wear shorts and trainers without socks, even in this weather, doesn't he?'

'Well, yes. I've given up worrying he'll get cold he's always done it, says he's comfortable, he told me he got caught out once meeting a client…oh, no…not…'

'Yes, I think so!'

'How long have you known?'

'About half a second ago. It was partly the timing of his arrival for the clinic, the extra day off you said but really when you confirmed his appearance, it fell into place. If, and it is only an if, it's the Paul I've been working with then he's a lovely man and I'll be proud to have him as a brother-in-law. He obviously has integrity and loyalty to keep your secret, but also in his business world; you'll be in safe hands with him.

'I assume you'll be talking to Paul tonight so ask him if what I think is right.'

Miguel waved the bill away and hailed a taxi for me then walked Julie to the end of her road. She really was in an area where everyone looked after each other. I found out, much later, Miguel and his family fed the homeless every night with the food they could not reserve for the next day.

And this in the middle of affluent London.

§

'Hi, Ricard, how are you?'

'I am fine now, thanks.'

'What does "now", mean?'

'When it gets late and you do not ring, I start to worry.'

I looked at my watch. 'Oh, I'm so sorry, Ricard, I didn't realise the time. I've been with my sister talking, now we are back in proper contact, it seems we're unable to stop and we just kept on.'

'How did the meeting with Patrick go? Is the Toulouse project still on the go?'

'No, for me it's over apart for one more visit to say farewell to the team. But after the meeting with Patrick today, I've been wondering how to put this to you, I was proposing leaving it till tomorrow when I have more information, but I need to ask you. Did you set me up to meet the mayor at the party?'

'Yes of course, as with all the other guests at the party, to give you some idea of how your social life might pan out.'

'And what do you know about the mayor's plan for some sort of collegiate enterprise, between the local schools, specifically for teaching the English language.'

'Is he really doing something? I had no idea. I know when it finally got onto the town Council's agenda for discussion it was chucked out again. Thank goodness, at last, someone is doing something. But how do you know? I have not heard anything. Is it on a website somewhere?'

I heard and felt his questions run from excitement about a project he felt sure was needed, to flow into bewilderment as to how I knew.

'Ricard, this is important, really important. So, you have no knowledge of this?'

'No, none. It is brilliant, I have been hoping for some sort of satellite provision here from Toulouse but nothing has come of it. You heard what Suzanne said about the teachers of English in her school and I think it is the same in others, if what you say is possible, it will be great. How do you know?'

'How I know, at this moment, isn't important, in fact it's confidential and I shouldn't have mentioned it even to you, I've probably broken a business confidence, but what's important, Ricard, and please listen to me very carefully, we have not had this conversation. When you are at work tomorrow and you see anyone, anyone at all, I don't care who they are or what influence they have, I repeat we haven't had this conversation. I'll fill you in tomorrow and I'm sorry to have brought a business issue into our personal time. I also have some happy and strange news about my sister—'

'Yvonne,' Ricard stopped me from going on, 'Yvonne, just stop and take a few deep breaths, you are obviously rather wound up about things. I have forgotten the conversation we did not have. Calm down and just tell me you love me.'

'Ricard, I love you.'

'You said you had news about your sister.'

'Yes, they're expecting twins. But it's been a long day and I'm so tired, I can't explain now all I have learned, tomorrow will suffice. I'm going to flop. Goodnight. Love to you and all.'

'Goodnight and love from us all here. Goodnight, sleep tight.'

I held the phone open just in case he said something more. But I heard only the end of the line click.

§ § §

I was surprised how peacefully I'd slept, as I woke vague remembrances of a dream surfaced, in which I was teaching twins, wearing "baby grows", to speak English. I felt refreshed and alert but stayed quietly for a few moments, stretching, pulling my shoulders down and relaxing my body from my toes to my head. I made a decision.

While brewing coffee I realised I'd not looked at yesterday's post, among the circulars there were two personal items. One a card from Georgina and Peter, depicting a spring scene of a beautiful meadow with a stream, bulbs pushing through the grass and snowdrops settling in the hedgerows. Georgina had written, under the printed "Thinking of You", a message to say Mark's name and life dates had been inscribed on the stone in the family plot. She'd signed it with a couple of kisses.

So, is one chapter of my life over? Implying, or reinforcing, what they'd told me the day we met by Mark's grave?

I put the card on the mantlepiece and turned to the other, a letter, addressed in beautiful copper plate. Before opening it, I pondered how a farmer would have this style of lettering, but remembered he'd originally come from a wealthy family and had a high standard of education, obviously he'd been taught to write like this and had continued to do so. Holding the letter opener under the back flap I paused before slitting the vellum, wondering if the request to Ricard to take over the executorship of the will, was a deliberate attempt by his father to get Ricard to make contact. I slit the envelope and read:

"Dear *Madame* Yvonne,

I hope you do not mind the informality of addressing you, but Suzanne always refers to you by your given name. As you know Suzanne has suggested you come and visit us, but quite rightly says as it is our home and not hers, the invitation should be extended from us—but no doubt you can read between the lines!

We both would be delighted if you would come and visit us. Obviously, we do not know your commitments, but could we possibly suggest these dates, near the end of October, early November while Suzanne is on school holidays and she could also come.

Although it is now old, the farmhouse is well-insulated and warm and we have extended over the years, to offer hospitality to holiday makers, so there are plenty of bedrooms if you would wish to stay overnight.

I look forward to meeting you again and thanking you properly for safely delivering Suzanne home in the summer and my wife is wanting to add her thanks.

We look forward to hearing from you.

With many regards, Ramon and Matilde."

He'd written the proposed dates after their names. I read the letter a couple of times; the copper plate was a little difficult to read but it seemed to be a genuine invitation. He didn't mention Ricard or any rift between them, but he was probably aware I knew of it. After a few moments of reflection, I knew I needed to talk to my father.

§ § §

At nine-thirty Patrick expanded on the project which had been proposed by the mayor of Lézignan, *Monsieur* Bassinet. As Patrick explained, I became more interested in exploring a new area and undertaking a project not already started or a problem needing "fixing". It would be demanding and exciting, especially as I knew nothing about the French educational system.

But was my interest developing more because of personal reasons?

As this thought struck me, I decided I had to carry out the resolution I'd made in bed.

'Patrick, I'm sorry to interrupt your flow but there is something I have to tell you before we go any further and maybe I should have said something yesterday. So far, in principle I think the project is interesting and doable but I have to admit, although I am trying very hard to set it aside as we talk, I do have a personal interest in it or at least in Lézignan.'

Patrick looked at me and smiled, then turned to Andrea and nodded. She responded with a "Told you so!" gesture.

'What? You two look like the cats who've not only found the cream but run off with the whole tub.'

Andrea was smiling widely. 'Come on, Yvonne. Tell us all about it—or should I say him? We have surmised there is something important going on in your life as you usually come home for weekends when you are on local or relatively near projects and into the office before you return to it. But the last one…, the main hope I have is you've remembered your vulnerability and not gone, well, I don't know where.'

'And' interjected Patrick as he stood turning away towards the window, 'perhaps, as your employer, I should reprimand you for taking the Toulouse project, or at least not owning up to a personal interest there too. I have a feeling all this started on your way back from Elne when your flight from Carcassonne was cancelled.'

I was so relieved to realise, from the tone in his voice and reflection in the window he was smiling. If he'd been serious, I could have been in deep trouble. I decided to tell them, in broad terms, about my time with Ricard and his family and how things had developed over the weeks. However, I was at pains to reassure them this had not interfered with the work at the Toulouse office. Work was work and social was social.

To clear the air about the upcoming project, I asked Patrick when he'd first been approached by the mayor.

'Oh, about four maybe five weeks ago, in fact he was getting rather edgy about my prevarications as to whether or not I could manage it. I think he was starting to look for another company so, after yesterday's conversation with you two, early this morning I emailed him to accept and said we'd be in touch shortly with an outline plan of how to proceed; he was pleased and I was relieved I'd not lost a contract. Why do you ask?'

'Because I met *Monsieur* Bassinet a few days ago at a social engagement with Ricard. He never mentioned anything, so he probably didn't make the connection with me and your firm. Patrick, I don't mix business with pleasure, but last night I'm afraid I asked Ricard if he knew about this project. He said, and I quote him almost *verbatim* "Thank goodness, at last someone is doing something." As far as I could gather, this has been wanted for some time and it seems that the mayor is activating it privately, not through the council. Ricard knows nothing about it. I did ask if he's set me up a meeting with the mayor, to which he replied "yes, of course, as with all the other guests at the party." I have sworn him to secrecy.'

'So, you've had an introduction to your future social life if you married him.'

'We are a long way from that, Andrea.'

My body moved into a partly defensive and partly comfort position. I looked at Patrick.

Please don't take this away from me. It will be done just as all other projects have been done, accurately and precisely. Reporting back regularly and appropriately.

'Well, we have a professional conundrum, don't we? How do you think the mayor would take to you heading up this project, bearing in mind your current and potential association with this Ricard? They are obviously not only professional but social associates and how would Ricard feel about it?'

'I don't know, but as my priority, regardless of the personal aspect, is you, the firm and to keep your reputation high and unsullied in the business field, I suggest we ask the mayor himself. He would know all the business and social effects if I was allocated to the project.'

'Good call, Yvonne,' said Patrick and pressed the intercom and asked Trish to bring in some coffee then dialled a number, while waiting for the telephone to be answered, he handed the receiver to me. It was on the speaker setting.

'*Bonjour, Monsieur Bassinet, le mayor.*'

'*Bonjour Monsieur. Je suis Yvonne Birch...*'

'Ah Yvonne, how nice to hear from you. How are you? Pardon, but I like to use the English when I can. This is a great surprise. What can I do for you?'

'Charles, I am in Patrick Court's office and we are in a little difficulty. I understand Mr Court sent an email accepting your request to assist in the project to establish the English language consortium in Lézignan, possibly associated with the university in Toulouse.'

'Yes, I am so pleased, it may not be a close link with the university, but that will be decided as the substance gets moved on. Yes,' his voice changed, 'is there now a difficulty? I have worked so hard to get this arranged, please tell me.'

'I think I will pass you over to *Monsieur* Court and he will explain. If it causes you any problem, I will understand.'

'*Ah, c'est ça!*'
'*Ah, oui, c'est ça!*'

Patrick took over the phone and the conversation commenced between the two men. As Patrick had not turned off the speaker, we could follow the exchanges between them. I thought *Monsieur* Bassinet was at first a little confused about the problem of personal relationships and business, then realised he was dealing with the English and sometimes we view things differently. Before they terminated the conversation, having agreed we should continue, with at least investigating the project, *Monsieur* Bassinet asked to speak to me again.

What he said in friendly, second person French, I kept to myself and wished him *au revoir*.

'I assume we were not supposed to understand the parting phrase?' asked Patrick.

'Obviously, but if you did, shame on you.'

Trish came in and spoke quietly to Andrea.

'Excuse me for a moment,' she said and left.

'Has anyone of your family met this Ricard yet?' asked Patrick.

'No, but I want Pops to meet him as soon as possible. If it fits in with the closure meeting in Toulouse with *Monsieur* Faunier and the others, I'd like to make it then if possible. But remember what I said earlier—you, your firm and your reputation come first in work.'

'My dear Yvonne, you know how I feel about you—Andrea and I discussed my inappropriate thoughts and you know I have only tender loving fatherly emotions now. Obviously not quite as intense as your father's, as he is blood, but you know we do have more than just a business relationship. If personal and work issues should come up, just come and we'll talk.'

'Oh Patrick, you've been such a brick on all fronts. I do hope you'll like Ricard as I think he is great. He's so different from Mark, but I think I'm now different too. Of course, I still have a love for Mark, but he is no longer here, I've moved on even Georgina and Peter recognise this, which is really quite remarkable.'

'Try and keep in touch with your roots as you move on, my dear.'

We'd gravitated towards each other during this exchange and were at the end of the desk in a gentle embrace when Andrea entered, we did not move apart in a hurry, there was nothing to hide.

'Patrick, one of the girls in the outside office has taken a nasty fall, she's being taken to hospital, I thought you might like to see her before the ambulance comes.'

'Thanks, who is it and where is she, how did it happen?'

Patrick left in a hurry so I didn't hear the answers to any of those questions, his concern for his staff paramount. I left his office and found Trish.

'Any chance of a temporary desk and computer?' I asked.

'Strange you should ask, Yvonne, come along. Do you want tea, coffee or juices?'

'Any chance of a large gin and tonic?' I joked as she led me into a newly set-up cubicle.

'Anything your heart desires.'

'Doubt you can get him here in two minutes flat.'

'Sorry, miracles take a bit longer for mortals. Give me a bit more notice in future. Now, seriously, what do you need now? I've not been privy to any of the goings on so need some guidance.'

'We are closing down the completed project in Toulouse. And possibly setting up the next one in Lézignan. But for now, please contact Paul Eschar and say I'd like to meet the team for lunch on Thursday, apologise for the short notice, but I would appreciate it. Tell him you need an urgent reply.'

I rang my father.

'Pops, I need to see you urgently. Will you be home this evening?'

'Yes, my dear, do I hear controlled panic in your voice? Come over when you are ready.'

'And, Pops, could you be ready to fly out to France with me tomorrow evening? I will explain when I see you.'

'Yes again, dear, but are you sure you are not acting in haste and you will regret it?'

'That remains to be seen. But could you give me your passport details so I can arrange tickets?'

There was a pause and I heard him open a desk drawer and give me the details.

'Thanks, Pops. I'll see you later and tell you everything.'

Trish returned with an answer from Paul. Thursday suited everyone and they were looking forward to seeing me again. I asked her to reserve two flights for tomorrow late afternoon with open returns and two rooms in the hotel for two nights with a possible extension.

'Make yourself a note about these bookings, Trish, I'll pay for my father's so make sure they are not included in the final invoice. I'll check it with you when the time comes.'

She nodded.

I was very tempted to text Ricard about the project but decided to wait to speak with Patrick before jumping to conclusions, although *Monsieur* Bassinet had no problems with my leading the project and seemed quite pleased to have me, it did not mean Patrick had formally told me I had been allocated. I wondered how the office girl was and caught Andrea as she was returning.

'Apparently she had a fit and hit her head as she fell, the paramedics thought she is possibly an undiagnosed epileptic, which is not too bad as it can be treated, so hopefully she'll be back again soon.'

'I was just going out to get a sandwich. Do you want anything?'

'No thanks, I've brought something with me today. I expect Patrick will want to formally finish the discussion, so please do not be too long.'

'I'll wait then.'

It was not long before Patrick called us back to his office and passed the file, with all the correspondence he'd had with *Monsieur* Bassinet, to me.

'I am not sure if this is any more straightforward than the last job but at least you know what you're aiming for, it's not a bricks and mortar establishment; it's utilising the facilities available and enhancing them, developing the English language teaching within, or as an adjunct to, the structure of the French educational system.'

'What could be easier?' Andrea joked.

I ignored her comment. 'Patrick,' my voice was serious, 'you know there are personal reasons I'd like to be in Lézignan and obviously *Monsieur* Bassinet is aware too. But three things, all of which I keep emphasising are—'

'Me, the firm and my reputation...'

'Don't joke, Patrick, it's important to me.'

'I know, and I thank you.'

'I'd like to go to Toulouse as soon as possible to make closure on the "go-cart" factory before I really start work in Lézignan. In fact, I've started on arrangements for going tomorrow evening and fixing a meeting between Pops and Ricard.'

'Of course, Yvonne, sort out what you need with Andrea and Trish.'

Trish confirmed the flights and hotel bookings in Toulouse. I tried to slow down and thought about how we'd have fixed all this without the Internet.

Don't even bother to go there! We wouldn't. In those days, things moved more slowly. So slow down. Had I been too fast in wanting to get everything fixed? Am I just on a sort of rebound? C'est ça!

I told Andrea I expected to return to the office the following Tuesday but as I was flying tomorrow, I'd stay at home to study the file and pack. I then went to see Pops.

'Your mother's not back from the theatre yet, rehearsals seem to be going on a bit longer these evenings, come into the study. Grace is sorting out supper, I hope you'll stay. Now, what's so urgent it can't wait we have to go flying off tomorrow?'

After about an hour, I'd finished telling Pops everything from my first encounter with Suzanne. At the end, I handed him the letter from Ramon Letour. He too had a little difficulty deciphering the ancient script but having finished, folded the letter neatly and replaced it in the envelope.

'You say you love him?'

I nodded. 'But it is a sort of deeper, possibly less desperate kind of love than I had for Mark. It seems to be a mature one, still full of passion, but at the same time quieter, more demanding and is making me cautious. Am I making sense?'

'Yes, my dear. Cautious yet impetuous, even if it is an oxymoron!'

'Pops—'

'I think I need to meet this Ricard of yours on my own, with you of course, but not with the rest of the family. We don't want to put the chap off, do we?' he grinned.

'I've already hinted at a very strange family, Pops, but I don't think he believed me.'

'But I thought you had a project in Toulouse.'

'No, sorry I thought I'd said, the reason I am going to Toulouse is for me to see the team there and to say farewell, so I thought it might be a good chance for you to meet Ricard, especially as Patrick has now offered me a project in Lézignan, it isn't certain it can be done, as I have to investigate the logistics of it. If it is not feasible, then I will face another complication. But, Pops, what do I do about the invitation to the farm?'

'Nothing for the moment; there is no urgency to reply. But I need to see Ricard and try and find out what is troubling him with his parents, as you have got everything sorted out with flights, I assume I will do so. No more now, my love, your mother's home and not a word of this to her. Currently, rehearsals are going positively and it's best she's not distracted. We have a glass of wine when she gets home, so the timing is spot on!'

'Thanks Pops. I'll see you tomorrow afternoon. Pick me up outside my flat.'

He smiled one of his knowing smiles and went to greet his wife. 'Ah my dear, how did it go? Look, Yvonne has just popped in to say hello.'

'Lovely and in time for wine.' She kissed me absentmindedly on my cheek, I was pleased to see she was calm, rehearsals must be really progressing.

I must remember to broach the subject of first night tickets for Phillippe some time.

§

'Hello, Ricard.'

'Hello, are you alright? Another late night with your sister?'

'No, I was with my parents. I needed to talk to my father and stayed for dinner.'

'Good. What about the school? Has anything been decided?'

'Yes. The Toulouse project has come to an end and I've been given the project to investigate. It does not mean it will go ahead or I'll necessarily be the one to do it. But it does mean I'll be over for a while a bit later when dates are sorted out.'

'What brilliant news to end the day on. Love you.'

'Ricard, before you go, there's something...' I heard a sharp intake of breath.

'I hate that tone in your voice, Yvonne, it always signals trouble. What now?'

'I don't want to put you off, but I've arranged for father to come over with me, could you meet us in Toulouse on Friday.'

'What precipitated this sudden meeting? It is a bit daunting.'

'You said you wanted to meet him and implied sooner the better. Do you want me to cancel?'

'No, no, of course not and I have a few hours to prepare.'

'Don't over-prepare anything, Ricard, he does come at things rather from his own angle.'

'Oh, you are a great comfort!'

'And the letter of invitation has come. So, we'll have to decide what to do. Please don't tell Suzanne though.'

'No, of course not. This call has certainly been packed with information.'

'I might not be able to ring you tomorrow or Thursday, but from what you say about your workload, you probably won't want to be hanging about waiting for late calls, but you'll be here on Friday, won't you?'

'Yes, hopefully about mid-day. Love you, Yvonne.'

He cut the line.

§ § §

I spent the morning sorting the apartment and packing, then made a cup of coffee.

'Hi Julie, hope I'm not disturbing you.'

'No, it's fine, I'm not doing anything particular and enjoying the luxury of a cup of tea in bed and reading while I can, I think things will change in the future.'

'Most likely, did you talk with Paul about my suspicion?'

'Yes, and he thinks it's a strong possibility, but we think it's better not to broach the subject and leave it till he's here.'

'Did he tell you we're meeting tomorrow to close down the project, for me anyway.'

'Yes, so you'll both have to play it by ear.'

'OK, my dear. I'll not mention anything on the family front unless he does. Pity in some ways as Pops will be with me and he could meet both Paul and Ricard on fairly neutral ground for all of them.'

'If it is "my" Paul. And obviously, things with Ricard are far more serious than you told me.'

'Yes, but there are problems. Well, perhaps Paul could talk to me so we can decide and maybe take the opportunity of him and Pops meeting each other.'

'Be careful, Yvonne. I'll talk to Paul when he rings tonight, but as the problem at work is nearly resolved, he'll be more free to sort out his family issues, so it won't be long till it's all in the open. So, don't make any more crises for Paul; if it is him, as I'll need him here soon so will the twins, they are already a handful and they like tuna baguettes. At least I'm into them now even if they aren't.'

'I thought cravings stopped after the third tri-whatever.'

'Don't you believe it! I'm still waiting for the coal crave. Be off now, give my love to Daddy.'

Pops was already standing on the pavement with a taxi when I went down. I checked he had his passport and was told quite rigorously he was not ancient and had his full marbles "thank you"! He also made a most commanding yet polite presence in the airport lounge not only ensuring I had everything but also tending to the needs a couple of elderly spinsters, who were flattered by his attention. I am always astounded how Pops flourishes as the extrovert when mother is not around. "Must never steal another's thunder, my dear," he once said to me when I tentatively asked why he was so quiet in gatherings with mother. Again, my heart swelled with the love I had for him. A couple of drinks for us, a gracious farewell to the spinsters and we set off.

The flight was on time and very calm, Pops charmed the air hostess without being in any way over familiar and congratulated the chief steward on the standard of service by his team. It was my turn to take the back seat and was grateful mother was not with us to inhibit his natural exuberance. I was ready to doze but had to keep up a conversation with an American couple who were giving Pops the third degree on British culture. They'd only been in transit in London and were to return for a three-day visit to England before returning home. We did our best to disabuse them of their planned schedule but I doubt we succeeded. We bade them goodbye as we went through passport control.

The taxi delivered us to the same hotel where I was welcomed warmly and Pops honoured and respected as my father. So much so, he said he felt as if he was an antique and had to be cushioned.

'Enjoy it while you can, Pops, it might wear off,' I joked as I looked around his room and said goodnight at his door after we'd eaten.

It wasn't too late so decided to ring Ricard who sounded tired.

'Just a heavy day preparing for tomorrow.'

'Sorry if I disturbed you. I just wanted to make sure Pops had everything before I came to my room, though, on second thoughts I don't know why I should worry, he's as capable and independent as younger men, I should have thought more about you.'

'Do not worry, I will see you Friday. If you do not mind, I will not talk long now. Love you, sleep well.'

'Yes, and you.'

A quick click and he was gone, which hadn't happened before. He'd often sounded and said he was tired but we'd chatted for some time.

Was something wrong or just tiredness and worry about his cases?

Chapter Nine

Seven-thirty in the morning and the phone woke me from my deep sleep.

'*Bon jour Madame,* I am sorry to disturb you but there is a young man here who says he needs to see you urgently. Can you come down?'

'Can he wait an hour?'

I heard a discussion.

'Half an hour he says, please.'

'OK. Offer him some coffee, I'll be down soon.'

I brushed my teeth, splashed some water onto my face and combed my hair before throwing on yesterday's trousers and jumper. I looked alright, but not ready for a formal meeting.

'I thought I'd better see you before the gathering; it might ease any tension, if there was going to be any.'

'Good morning.'

'Yes, good morning, sorry. I'm not really used to this sort of thing.'

'Well, save me from having to teach you anything, but remember, the small social often seemingly irrelevant graces; gives you time to think out how to react and what to say.'

'And you do it so well!' He smiled.

'So, we agree then?'

'Yes, looks like it, doesn't it? Am I allowed to embrace you or what do we do?'

'I think a family embrace is fully in order.'

It was during this embrace I heard Pops' voice.

'Ah! So, this is the wonderful Ricard, is it? I didn't think he was due till tomorrow.'

'Oh my God.'

'*Oh merde!*'

'Paul!'

'Sorry, but I'd better go.'

'No, remember the social graces.' I turned to my father. 'No, Pops, this isn't Ricard, he won't be here till tomorrow. May I introduce you to one of the young men I've been working with on the project here in Toulouse. Pops, this is Paul Eschar; Paul, this is…'

Did Paul remember Julie's maiden name?

'*Monsieur* Marshall, my father.'

'Enchanted to meet you, sir,' responded Paul, '*Madame* Yvonne has often spoken of you.'

They shook hands, Paul stared at Pops perhaps a little longer than he would normally do when introduced to a stranger.

'Paul just came to confirm I knew where we are to meet.'

'Yes, first in the office where we have been working then to lunch in one of our haunts.'

'Thanks for coming to confirm what I thought, Paul. I'll see you later.'

'Yes, Yvonne, it is good to know our communications are sound,' he took my hand again and was about to leave when he stopped, '*Monsieur,* do you and Yvonne have any engagement or arrangements for tonight? If not, may I offer you a small evening meal at my home?'

Well, if Paul wants to put his head into the lion's den, who am I to stop him?

'This is extremely hospitable of you, young man, but surely rather short notice, especially for your wife.'

I coughed.

'Are you alright, Yvonne? Some water perhaps?'

'No, I'm fine, Paul, thank you.'

'Monsieur, both Yvonne and I will have eaten a large and long lunch, I hope you will do so too, so the lighter evening repast will, hopefully, be sufficient. And I am certain my beautiful wife, who unfortunately cannot be with us, will be more than happy I entertain you.'

Doubtful, Paul!

'Well, if this is French hospitality, young man, who am I to refuse? We thank you very much.'

'Would eight o'clock be convenient for me to arrange a taxi to collect you?'

'Make it eight-thirty please, Paul.'

'Certainly. And now I must go, I have an important farewell meeting at eleven o'clock and preparations to do before then. Until later, *au revoir.'*

'Are you sure there is nothing going on between you and him your Ricard doesn't know about and should?'

'Oh Pops! I work with the lad, well, used to. If circumstances were different, I might have looked at him twice, but most certainly not now.'

'I've been for a walk around. Lovely town.'

'I'm sorry I have to work, well, I think it's almost play actually, perhaps you should have come out today and not last night.'

'Good Lord no! Have you seen the museums they have here and the library let alone the beautiful buildings? I'm not sure how much time I'll have to eat the large lunch the young man was talking about, but I'll do my best to eat well. I can always order sandwiches here if I'm hungry when I return. Hope we get more than a lettuce leaf tonight, but it seemed churlish not to accept.'

'Yes, Pops. Now, have you had breakfast or shall we go in together now and I'll change for my meeting afterwards.'

'Breakfast, good idea.'

§

After we'd eaten, Pops left for a day of exploring all the things Toulouse had to offer him. We arranged to meet in the foyer at eight-fifteen if we didn't see each other beforehand. I showered and dressed and although I didn't need it for an hour, I rang reception and asked them to organise a taxi for me. My mind wandered to this evening.

What was Paul playing at? Was he planning to be upfront with Pops or hide the relationship? How should I play it?

In one way I'd already deceived Pops and I wasn't sure I was prepared to do so all evening. I wondered if I should tell him before we went to Paul's and what if the evening was a disaster. Knowing how streamlined Julie's apartment is, would there be a total contrast? I was beginning to think myself into an apocalyptic scenario when a call from reception cut short my gloom saying my taxi was waiting.

The door to the office was open.

'Monique, Daniel. It's so lovely to see you.' We embraced in turn; it was hard to get away from their clutches.

145

'*Madame* Birch, we are so grateful to you. You have saved us all, the company and so, so many jobs and—'

'No, Monique, you all did the work, maybe I was a catalyst, but you all knew something was wrong and you worked so hard on those files and the data.'

'But you believed, *Madame*. You kept telling us to look here and look there and so on,' added Daniel.

'You know what that's called, don't you? Teamwork. You're a good team and I think *Monsieur* Faunier knows.'

'He does.' Paul entered from the kitchen carrying a tray of champagne flutes. Having seen him earlier, it seemed natural I'd not miss his presence immediately. I reminded myself to be careful how I interacted with him this morning.

'Good morning, Yvonne.'

I couldn't help a broad grin. 'Good morning, Paul. I hope I find you well after all this hard work.'

'Yes, thank you. And you look well, please will you tell us about your discussion with your boss, if it is permitted.'

'Well, I wasn't told not to say anything and I don't think I have any state secrets to impart, but basically I was pulled off the project because you lot were too good. So, thanks, you all have jobs and I don't.'

They all started to make various noises of protest and concern but I stopped them quickly. 'No, no, a joke! Sorry, English humour. In fact, the day I went into the office, I was surprised to find my office occupied by someone else, so I was at a bit of a loss. When I went to see my boss, guess who was sitting in his office! *Monsieur* Faunier himself. I don't know if you've ever had the feeling you've been hung, drawn and quartered, but I did think this was as near to it as I'd get. I gathered there was a lot more going on than we'd realised and *Monsieur* Faunier had stopped our work in time so we did not "mess up" the final exposition of all the fraud going on which needed proper professionals and legal access. Apparently, without our knowing it, we were beginning to act illegally. You probably know as much or more than I do.'

'Well, I am sorry to have put you through such a terrible trauma, *Madame* Birch, your guts spewing all over Patrick's desk would not have been a pretty sight.'

What is it about men, always coming up behind you when you are talking to others!

I turned to see a smiling *Monsieur* Faunier who I approached and embraced a bit more forcibly than perhaps I should have done.

'Is the company safe?' I asked.

'Yes, at least for now. Our reputation is sound, finances in place and as far as we can tell all our innovations are now protected. It is a great relief.'

Whether on purpose or by chance, *Monsieur* Faunier's statement seemed to coincide with a champagne bottle being opened. There followed several toasts, mini-speeches and the exchange of gifts. *Monsieur* Faunier shook my hand and passed me a small box asking me to open it later. Following these formalities, we prepared to adjourn to the restaurant.

'Before we go, Paul and *Monsieur* Faunier, with your permission, if your glasses are full or partly so, may I make one more toast? To the Go-Cart Firm and all who work in and protect her.'

They repeated it.

'Thank you, *Madame*.'

Over lunch, they all talked about their lives and what they were planning to do, their hopes and dreams. Quietly, as I was next to him, I gently quizzed *Monsieur* Faunier about his family life. He was initially a little hesitant but relaxed and told me about the problems with a beautiful wife who had gone from being an extrovert to an introvert and now had been diagnosed as having an Alzheimer's type disease.

'So, were the people you had to meet many evenings after being with us, made up excuses as you had to relieve the carers?'

'Yes, or to make sure the night carer had turned up.'

'I'm so sorry.'

'I think I had my eye off the business for some time due to this. Don't get me wrong, I'm not blaming Isabelle, I still love her deeply, it's not her fault, if anyone is worried about putting blame.'

'There is no fault nor is there blame. It's just what life throws at us. Obviously, I don't know who you have told, and now is not the time, but you, possibly, should share this with someone in the company you can trust, so in the future, if you wish, you may be with her more and be sure the company is in safe hands.'

'You are wise, *Madame* Yvonne.'

'You should talk to my father; he thinks I'm scatty!' I joked.

'And how is your father?' asked Paul.

'Last seen he was fine. He and I have been offered hospitality this evening. Why do you ask?'

'I was just wondering how long secrets should be held or whether other perspectives on a situation might help to, perhaps, prevent an unnecessary confrontation.'

'Your call.'

'What is going on? Are there more problems in my company than I have thought? Have you found more you have not told me?' *Monsieur* Faunier's voice was agitated.

'No *Monsieur*, what Paul has on his mind is how to approach his father-in-law, who he's invited to a meal tonight. Unfortunately, his father-in-law does not know he is his son-in-law.'

'Don't tell just half the story, Yvonne. I am Yvonne's brother-in-law. We only confirmed this earlier today, I had no idea till yesterday.'

No one said anything till *Monsieur* Faunier asked, 'Did you know about the relationship when you invited them for dinner?'

'Err, well, yes.'

Silence surrounded our table like a shroud till everyone, except Paul, laughed. When we had all calmed down, no one had any words of wisdom to offer until *Monsieur* Faunier said, 'Honesty, in this case, Paul, is probably the best policy.' Stifling his laughter before he started again.

'I cannot see what is so funny, none of you has been of any help.'

'I'm wondering if it would be better for Paul to come back to the hotel with me and we face my father together, on neutral ground. Perhaps at this point I should also be honest with you all, while I have been in Toulouse, much of my free time has been spent with someone near here and my father is over here this weekend to meet him—as a potential son-in-law.'

Another silence as they all looked between Paul and me.

'Let me get this clear, you and Paul are not married?' asked Monique.

'Well, yes and no. I'm a widow and Paul is married to my sister, but no one knew—except them, their two witnesses and the priest of course. It has been only by circumstantial evidence I found out who my sister's husband is and only got his confirmation this morning. Paul meeting my father was not planned; it happened by accident. But Paul decided to invite us to his place this evening. Father thinks he's just being a hospitable Frenchman.'

'Well, to retreat now shows a weak backbone and if I was his father-in-law, I'd tell him to go to the devil.'

'Thank you, Sir. If you will excuse me, I must prepare for some visitors. Oh, I might need some time off soon, sir, my wife is about to give birth to twins.'

'Go, go, and once more, thank you all. Daniel, you have the office key, don't you? Please check it is locked then off you both go and I'll see you on Monday. Goodbye. A moment, *Madame* Birch.'

I reseated myself. 'I just wanted to say on a more personal level, especially as you are now aware of my situation with my wife, how much I really appreciate your input into the firm's troubles. I think you have actually saved my company and my gratitude cannot really be expressed other than to say; if there is anything I can do on a personal or professional level to help you, then please do not hesitate to ask.'

'*Monsieur* Faunier, I—'

'Please, time to call me Marcel. If you agree to Yvonne.'

'Yes, thank you. If I need, I will call. And if you need a chat—'

'Then I will call. Now, I suppose we'd better find some transport. Perhaps we could share a taxi to your hotel.'

In the taxi, I opened the parcel Marcel had slipped into my hand earlier. "A small reminder, with my sincere thanks" was engraved on the base of the small silver Go-Cart resting in my hand.

'Thank you.'

I waved him goodbye when he dropped me off. I stood watching the retreating taxi and saw Pops coming towards me.

'Did you have a good day, Pops?'

'Fantastic. This town is wonderful and because of the colour of the brickwork they call it *La Ville Rose*; did you know that? Did you have any time to see any of it while you were here?'

'Not much unfortunately, some bistros, a church, a student's concert and a few merry-go-rounds. But mostly work or away with Ricard.'

'Pity, but you can't do everything. I'm going to order some soup and sandwiches in my room then soak in the bath for an hour. I've time for that, haven't I? And a bottle of good red too, I've a feeling I might need it, as I don't think we'll get much this evening. I'll order one to take with us.'

'You did some shopping?' I indicated the carrier bag he was holding, it looked as if it came from an expensive men's wear shop.

'Yes, I thought I might buy something more casual to wear tonight. And something warm, I'm not sure there will be much heating. I explained the situation to the young assistant and he suggested this outfit. Something I can put on or take off as needs be.'

'Well, enjoy your wine in the bath, but don't drown!' I said as we left the lift together.

'I've been wining in my bath for years and not pegged out yet, my dear—and don't say anything about there being a first time for—'

I cut him off having confirmed we'd meet at eight-fifteen and left him at the door to his room and entered mine. A soak in the bath sounded a good idea, but no more wine, as I'd had sufficient at lunchtime.

Only two, I reflected. Strange for me but I don't seem to fancy it.

§

I didn't notice the man who entered the hotel's front entrance and walk past me and nod, 'Good evening.' I replied in English too but continued to watch the lift from where I expected Pops to emerge. I looked at my watch, nearly eight-thirty.

'Your taxi, *Monsieur*,' the receptionist called to the person behind me.

'Thank you. Shall we go, Yvonne?'

I twisted my head then stood.

'Like it?' He slowly turned around for me to see his new clothes.

'Pops, you don't like roll-necked jumpers, but it really suits you. And the scarf, sets off the light beige. Are those new trousers and sneakers too? Sneakers Pops! I must say you look like a million dollars with that jacket.'

'Not too young for me? I just went outside for a little walk to be sure no one laughed at me.'

'No, not too young. Pops, you look great.'

'Right, let's go and starve and freeze in this young man's place. I've got the wine.'

During the taxi ride, which was longer than Paul had indicated when he'd told me how far out of town he lived, Pops said, 'You know, the shop assistants here are so fantastic. They seem to know what we need just by a brief explanation of our quandary.'

150

'I had the same, well, similar situation, over a dress I needed for a party at Ricard's. The girl seemed to know what I needed and her advice was spot on.'

'Well, I think a lot of it's the way they wear it. When the scarf was suggested, I was very reluctant and thought he was joking but he insisted I try it. As I put it on, his face fell, he readjusted it and "*Voila!*", as he said, a totally different look.'

'It looks good on you.'

I was grateful for the small talk as silence would have been intolerable. We arrived at a rather forbidding block of flats and the taxi driver came with us to the lift for Paul's flat, saying the layout was a bit of a rabbit warren and we might get lost. Leaving us at the lift, he said he'd called Paul to say we were on our way up and he'd return later when Paul telephoned. Paul was standing at the open door to welcome us.

'Please come in, welcome, I am so pleased you could come, Yvonne, Mr Marshall.'

'It's good of you to invite us, young man. I hope giving you this is in order,' Pops offered the bottle, 'it's something we do in England, but possibly not appropriate here?'

Paul responded to the question, as he accepted the bottle of wine, it was appropriate, most acceptable but possibly not necessary.

Knowing Julie's taste and streamlined apartment, I was a bit concerned her husband had totally different ideas. I imagined, with no basis apart from his dress code, his place would be a mix between Bohemia and student rooms. Father had no prior knowledge of the man but had obviously developed some domestic ideas for himself.

I stood amazed for a moment and felt father's recognition too, possibly our silence could have been interpreted as rudeness; but apart from the specific artefacts and pictures, I was transported to Julie's apartment.

'I apologise for my rudeness, young man, but this place reminds me very much of my daughter's apartment. You must use the same designers.'

'Yes sir, we do, they are called Julie and Paul. They are—'

'I think I'm beginning to get the picture,' interrupted Pops, 'perhaps now is the appropriate time to offer me a large brandy from the cellar cupboard which, if I am not mistaken, is over there,' he pointed.

'If I may suggest, with sincere respect, some excellent white wine while we talk, some food with more wine and the large brandies to follow. We possibly have a lot to get through this evening.'

I could see Pops getting rather agitated and his mood was verging on anger, he'd come here in good faith for a pleasant evening with a sociable young man, strange though the invitation had been. Now he was faced with a sense of duplicity he'd not anticipated.

'Please Pops, sit down. We'll explain, it's only been within the last few hours that Paul, Julie and I had any idea, let alone confirmation, they were married to each other. Honestly, Pops, and it was not my call to tell you earlier.'

'Perhaps I should have said something this morning, *Monsieur* Marshall, but as Yvonne and I had only just—'

'Alright.' Pops' voice was harsh and firm, but I recognised the humour behind it. He was obviously going to give Paul a grilling. 'Let's do as you suggest. Some good, cold, dry white wine to start.'

While Paul was in the kitchen, I said, 'Please Pops, be careful, be gentle.'

'If he's robust enough to get through what Mark did, then he's OK.'

'Too late if he doesn't pass your test then, they're married, besotted and expecting their first babies, your first grandchildren. So be careful, don't push too hard.'

For most of the evening, I watched quietly as the two of them sized each other up over the initial white wine; an excellent three-course meal with red wine; followed by coffee and brandy, which I declined. The two men bantered, exchanged ideas and philosophies, disagreed on a few points but agreed on most—specifically, they would meet again very soon. Pops suggested meeting tomorrow.

'That would be good for me, sir, in the morning. I have a flight to see Julie late afternoon. Perhaps I could meet you for coffee about eleven and we could also have lunch together before my flight. Then I'll be able to tell her about our meetings,' he paused, 'and perhaps your final verdict. But now, I'll ring for the taxi to take you back to the hotel.'

Pops turned to me. 'And at what time am I to meet your young man tomorrow? Will I have time to talk more with Paul first?'

'Yes Pops. Ricard won't be with us till late afternoon or maybe early evening. If he is earlier, then we could all get together.'

My father's face dropped. 'Joke!' I said. I turned to Paul and asked, 'Will you be in your usual travelling gear tomorrow? No harm if you are, but best to warn Pops now so he doesn't disown you.'

'Yes, I find it so comfortable. Ah, there is Jamie, the taxi driver, he is my brother.'

After our farewells, we settled into Jamie's taxi and I explained to Pops what to expect from Paul's dress tomorrow.

'Very strange, is that all?'

'I think it depends on the weather and his mood.'

Before I left him at his room door, Pops asked, 'Yvonne, are you feeling alright?'

'Fine thanks, yes. Why?'

'You weren't drinking much wine tonight.'

'I had plenty at lunch time and was content with the white this evening.'

'As long as you are sure.'

'Yes, promise, goodnight. Sleep well, Pops.'

I'd changed into my nightwear when there was a knock on my door. I wrapped the hotel's thick gown around me and answered it. The night clerk was there holding a note.

'I am sorry I missed you coming in, *Madame* Birch, but I thought you might need this. The message came in about nine. I hope it is not bad news.'

'Thank you for bringing it up, Michel. I'll let you know if I need any help. How does night duty fit in with your studies?'

'Quite good some weeks, not too good others, *Madame. Bonsoir.* '

'*Merci et bien tôt.* '

The note was a message from Marcel:

Thank you so very much, Yvonne. Business or personal, anything I can do, please ask. Sincere regards. Marcel.

I rang Ricard and after the usual greetings and my apologies for lateness, I asked, 'What time did you say you'd be here?'

'Probably about mid-day. Why?'

'Slight change of plan this end if you don't mind. I'll fill you in as best I can tomorrow, too complicated now. You remember the restaurant by the cathedral where we ate on our first time together in Toulouse. On the corner opposite the cathedral?'

'Very well indeed, it had the strange mixture of paintings on the walls, possibly inappropriate for such proximity to the holy place.'

'Yes, you've got the one, could you meet me there and not the hotel? I need to talk to you and I am hoping Pops will be otherwise engaged till about three. I'll fix to meet him about five or six.'

'It all sounds very mysterious, my love. Is everything alright?'

'Yes, just a few more developments I'd not expected, I'll tell all tomorrow, but now I must go. But before I do, how did the case go?'

'It did not, more complications which took all day and half the evening, so, we go into round two next week. But that is not your worry nor mine for the weekend. Pity I cannot tell Sven to have an extra hour in bed though.'

'Why not?'

'Yvonne, look at the time. I will have to wake him up to tell him! And Marianne has to get up for Suzanne and so on. The sooner you are living here and we can get into a reasonable style of living, the better.'

'Don't take too much for granted, Ricard. There's Father to meet and a lot to sort out yet! I'll see you tomorrow. Night and I do love you.'

'Good night and sleep well. All my love.'

I lay awake thinking over the day's events; sleep must have come at some time.

§ § §

The dim morning light was seeping through the windows onto my face. I'd forgotten to draw the curtains before I went to bed. I can't stand the room supplied coffee, so rang, and asked for some to be sent up with some croissants. As I'd ordered and staff had pass keys, I'd no need to get out of bed to let the waiter in on the knock and call of "Room Service", but what I'd not expected was the breakfast nor the waiter who brought it.

'Ricard! What are you doing, why did you wake up Sven, so unkind, oh, Ricard—' The rest of my burbling was hidden in the body of the man who smothered me with his kisses and prevented me from saying or doing anything. We lay holding each other, he fully clothed and me still under the covers.

'Coffee smells good,' I said. 'I'd like it hot, so please get off me and pour some. And I think there is more food than just the croissants I ordered.'

He shifted.

'My apologies, *Madame*, if I disturbed your morning rising. Shall I go?'

154

'Just give me some food, Ricard. You obviously need some as you must have left home at some stupid hour. Have you made sure Sven has some food and somewhere to rest before he drives back to Lézignan? I assume he'll be taking you back at some time?'

He raised a plate silently asking if I wanted some food.

'Yes, some of the bacon and all the rest. I'm hungry. Thanks.'

He'd passed me a plateful of food and served himself. I stayed on the bed and he sat on the seat by the window. We concentrated on eating. I couldn't understand why I was so hungry after all the food I'd had yesterday.

'Now, tell me by what right you have to come barging into my room uninvited at this hour of the morning.'

'No right at all.'

'Is that it?'

'Well, yes. In the starkness of the question, there is really no further answer I can give.'

'What's the time?'

'About half past six.'

'So, at what time did you drag Sven from his bed to be ready to bring you here to harass the kitchen staff at this hotel to provide food for you, hours before they are usually cooking. You are quite unbelievable.'

'Well, yes and no. After you rang last night, I checked the train timetable and booked a taxi to take me to the station. I then rang the hotel and explained who I was, who you were and asked if it would be possible to have breakfast taken up to your room when you ordered your coffee and croissant. So, I did not disturb Sven, I left him a note.'

'What did you say the time was?'

'Probably about—who cares? Have you finished eating? I'll put the trolley outside.'

§

Later, I rang my father's room, there was no reply so I called reception and was told he'd gone out and had left a message, saying he'd meet me at six o'clock this evening in the foyer.

I put the phone down and looked at Ricard. 'I assume you have the basics for meeting my father this evening and an overnight stay or do we have to go shopping?'

'I think I'll need to use some of your toothpaste, but the rest is at reception, I'll call for it when needed.'

'Good.'

Ricard and I spent the morning mostly in bed. In between a certain amount of sexual activity, we talked about our families. I told him how Paul had engineered the meeting with Pops which led on to talking about Ricard's imminent meeting with him. About mid-day we showered and went into town to have lunch. The sun was doing its best to clear the gloom in the sky as we started to walk from the hotel, looking at the early sprouting Christmas decorations.

'Have you had any thoughts about what is going to happen for Christmas? Flights to and from France and England are going to be limited and subject to cancellation.'

'I think we have time before we need to think about that. Maybe we should wait at least till we meet Pops and you both see your reactions to each other.'

Distancing himself from me, Ricard asked, 'If he disapproves, will you have to choose between your family and me?'

I smiled and kissed him. 'Ricard, my love, as you know full well, it's not just about you and Pops, but also about you and your parents and what's going on and my invitation to the farm. Please understand, I need to know.'

'OK, I'm sorry, I shouldn't be pushing you.'

'And there's Suzanne wanting to know what's going on and am I coming back, and I can't give her answers until I get some.'

He sighed and took my hand as he pushed open the door to an inviting looking restaurant, similar to ones I'd been eating in with Paul and the team.

'This looks a nice place to eat,' he said as we entered and looked for a table.

My heart stopped. 'Can we go somewhere else please?'

'Why? What's wrong with here, and after our activities this morning, I am hungry. Sorry if that insults you, my dear.'

'It's far from an insult, it's a sort of compliment, but I think it might be better…'

Ricard did not hear the pleading in my voice and followed the waiter to the table situated near one occupied by Pops and Paul. Before we got there, I asked

156

if there was not another table in another area; apparently, there was not and Ricard again disregarded my request we go elsewhere to eat.

'Everywhere else is going to be busy too, Yvonne, we are probably lucky to get a table here.'

I could have walked out but didn't. I caught Paul's eye and shook my head, he acknowledged this and returned to his conversation with Pops. Because of the table arrangement, Pops and Ricard had their backs to each other; even so, I could not relax and spent time just holding the menu, but not taking in what the waiter was saying about the dish of the day. After what seemed like an hour but was probably less than a minute, a waiter offered the credit card console to Paul. Leaving a tip, Paul stood behind Pops acting as a visual block between him and me; simultaneously, I let my napkin slip to the floor and bent to retrieve it.

'Yvonne, are you alright? I'm sorry if I insisted and you really did want to go somewhere else—'

'No, no it's fine, I'm alright.' At least I was now Pops and Paul had left. I saw Paul walk on the side next to the restaurant window, he'd lifted his flight bag onto his shoulder to further block my father's line of vision to me. I felt sure the meeting between them had gone well and Paul would have a positive report for Julie. I wondered what, if anything, he'd say to Julie about the man he'd seen with me.

'Ricard, I er, just wasn't prepared to see my father sitting at a table here.'

'Where? Why didn't you say something?' Ricard twisted in his seat to look around.

'No, they've gone now.'

'They? Who? Yvonne?'

'Ricard, trust me, I was just not prepared for a surprise encounter between you and Pops, I don't think it would've been the right time considering he was with his new son-in-law, Julie's husband; they'd only met yesterday.'

I explained the situation.

'Maybe you are right but a hint would have been nice, so I could have at least seen him.'

'And given you an advantage for this evening, which wouldn't be fair!' I joked. 'But seriously, to have everyone meeting each other spontaneously would not have been a good idea. Too much to be taken in and too many explanations in a possibly too short a time. Paul is off to get his flight and Pops probably needs a short rest, he was planning to take Paul to the art galleries this morning.'

The *plat du jour* arrived for both of us. I certainly didn't remember ordering it in my anxious state, but Ricard reassured me I had done so. We both enjoyed the rabbit casserole followed by a green salad then apricot tart, rounding off the meal with coffee. Ricard drank the small carafe of wine included in the price, I declined and had water.

'Come on, let's walk a bit and look in some of the shops. Marianne has been dropping hints I should start thinking of Christmas gifts, maybe you'll be able to make suggestions.'

'What a good idea. I might find something a bit out of the ordinary for mother and maybe the twins too. Nothing too big as I've only got cabin luggage this time.'

We spent a pleasant time looking around shops once they had reopened after the lunchtime siesta. In one Ricard asked, holding a wooden box, 'What about this? It would be an improvement on the old tin box Suzanne uses for her special things, don't you think?'

I took it and fingered the carved relief depicting a farm scene, I turned it over, on the base was the name of a person and a village—Ortaffa.

'I'm not sure it would be appropriate.'

'Why not?'

I returned the box to his hands.

'Didn't you see the carvings and what's on the base? It might cause her more harm now, perhaps it would be more appropriate, after my visit to your parents and when I have the answers.'

'You do keep pushing the visit to my parents.'

'Ricard, don't sound so angry; they are obviously keen for me to visit and probably expect to see you too. You know it will have to happen sometime if we're going to be together. Let's get the meeting with Pops over then discuss it again, he's expecting to raise it somehow, so please don't back off when it comes up.'

'Yvonne, I do not know what to do.'

'It's simple. Tell me.'

He shook his head.

'Well, put the box down for now and let's get back to the hotel. We'll surely work something out. Come on.' I took his arm and slipped mine through it. We walked slowly to the hotel.

Passing one of the bars, he asked, 'Shall we have a drink before we go back? We've probably got time.'

I felt he was stalling and maybe wanted to talk a bit more before meeting my father.

'OK, but not too long, I want to change and I'll just have an orange juice.'

'Well?' I asked once we were seated, my juice and his Pernot set before us with a jug of water.

'Nothing, I just felt like another few minutes with you before we went to the hotel. But I will admit I am more nervous about this evening's meeting than I thought I would be. Maybe the impromptu lunch time meeting would have been better for us all.'

'Whether we agree or disagree, I can't turn the clock back, I made the decision.'

'My dear, I've not asked this before, but do Mark's family have any indication about our relationship and possible life together? It is only—what?— just over two years since they buried their son.'

I was taken aback by this question and I was shocked too because I realised, I'd not thought about Mark for some time.

'Yes.'

'And?'

'They understand.'

Ricard sighed, finished his drink and said, 'Shall we go?'

§

Collecting my door-key, I was given a message taken from the pigeon-hole. It was from father apologising for the late change in plan and instead of meeting us in the hotel foyer, as he'd indicated earlier, he would meet us at a restaurant a couple of doors from the hotel as near to eight as he could. The table was booked for seven but could we please be there by half past or it might be given to others. I told Ricard what the message was.'

'Obviously, something has caught his attention. I told you he was unpredictable and a bit spontaneous.'

'And obviously a Francophile, to be so flexible,' he responded.

'Is there a dress code for *Chez Maxime*,' I asked the receptionist, 'or doesn't it matter?'

She screwed up her face and looked at both Ricard and me and said, as delicately as she could, 'I think a little more formal, *Madame* Birch, than you are currently wearing, but not, as I think you say in England, the tiaras.'

'Thanks,' I looked at her name badge, I'd not seen her before, 'Brigitte. We'll go and change.'

She smiled and nodded then added, '*Madame* Birch, I have been told the sole is out of this world, if you like fish, it is expensive and I have never eaten it. I only go there as a waitress, and as it is cooked to order, I never have a chance!'

'Thanks for the price warning! I'll let you know if anyone has the sole.'

We went upstairs where we found Ricard's luggage had been delivered and a suit and shirt laid out on the bed.

'Forward planning,' he said as I took out a simple chiffon dress from the wardrobe hoping it would be dressy enough. 'Come on, you know there is little dress code now. I expect we'll find people wearing torn jeans.'

'They are becoming the fashion.'

Unpredictable as father might be, to move a six o'clock meeting to eight with a table booking for seven and a different venue was not like him. I wondered what he was planning. We arrived at *Chez Maxime* within the timeframe asked by father and were shown to our table and provided with previously ordered wine. We were dressed appropriately and there was not a torn jean in sight! We sat quietly waiting for Pops, generally looking around when I noticed a couple were being guided to the table. For the second time today, I was dumbfounded. My parents were coming towards us.

'Ricard, it seems—' I started to say but had no time to finish before mother grasped me and set off into one of her long diatribes about the flight and the traffic and nearly missing Pops at the airport. Meantime, Pops had taken Ricard by the hand and was shaking it in a friendly and welcoming manner. Once we'd managed to calm mother down, she and Ricard were introduced. Apart from saying, 'How do you do', as they shook hands, mother said nothing more to Ricard and sat down. A waiter poured wine into the two fresh glasses and topped up Ricard's before, sensibly, retreating again.

Pops came around and gave me a hug.

'Sorry about this sudden change of plan but it fitted in well with your mother's rehearsals.'

'And when did you start to arrange this? You know she can upset everything. You were supposed to meet Ricard on his own.' I hissed.

'As soon as I saw the breakfast trolley outside your room this morning. All a bit of a rush I must admit, but that girl Trish in your office is marvellous, she got everything fixed up so quickly. I'd decided I could not meet Ricard on my own after all, so got your mother over too.'

We seated ourselves.

'So, tell me, young man, what is it you are wanting and expecting from my daughter?' Mother looked straight at Ricard.

He may have been a little surprised at the forthrightness of the slightly ungrammatically phrased question, and from its source, but he did not show it.

'*Madame* Marshall, our introduction was rather fast, so I would appreciate it, if you would tell me how you would like me to address you.'

'Perhaps for the moment, *Madame* Marshall would be appropriate.'

I saw from the corner of my eyes Pops raise his eyes to the ceiling, perhaps wishing he'd not suggested her coming over after all, but I kept my gaze on mother and recognised the sparring spirit in her face.

'*C'est ça!*' said Ricard looking briefly at me. '*Alors, Madame* Marshall, I wish to take your daughter further into my family, to love her, to honour her, to cherish her, to argue with her, to make babies with her, to—'

'Stop, enough, can you provide for her financially without her having to work? And when you die, will she be well provided for? I know the inheritance laws in France differ from those in the UK?'

'Pops! Stop this aggressive conversation; what are you doing, Clementine?'

'It is alright, Yvonne,' Ricard stopped me, 'these are important questions and I can give positive responses to *Madame* Marshall. Firstly, *Madame* Marshall, if Yvonne wishes to be an independent woman and follow her own career, I will not stand in her way, but yes, I can provide for her without her having to work if she prefers. As to the second question, *Madame* Marshall, yes, there are differences in our country's approach, but be assured I will have made necessary and appropriate arrangements for Yvonne before my demise comes about.'

No one on the table said anything. A waiter hovered, anticipating we were about to order, but no one moved until mother said, 'Well, that is all fine then. You may call me Clementine and I hope I may call you Ricard.'

'Thank you, Clementine.'

We relaxed and the relieved waiter brought the menus. We ordered and ate and talked. Ricard explained his current household and Pops and mother expanded on our family and discussed Julie's situation as far as we knew it. Pops,

Ricard and I kept diverting the conversation from the issue of Ricard's parents whenever mother tried to raise it. Somehow, we all knew this was better discussed without mother, once she was safely on a plane back to the UK, early the next day in time for her rehearsal. We said our farewells to her before we retired, Mother giving Ricard one of her most theatrical embraces, before she indicated to Pops to open the door to their room, which he did with an appropriate flourish.

'An amazing woman,' said Ricard as he closed the door to our room.

'I'm sorry I couldn't warn you, but I didn't know she'd be here.'

'You did say to be ready for something exotic when I met her.'

'Yes, I did, but you should have been given some warning. I was surprised how quiet Pops was even though he's especially careful not to overshadow her in any public situation.'

'Oh well, I think your mother is quite happy about you and your financial future with me.'

'You now need to meet with Pops on his own.'

'Yes.' Ricard took off his clothes and went into the shower.

I was in bed and asleep, unaware of his damp body joining me, but that state of ignorance didn't last long.

Chapter Ten

We met Pops at eleven o'clock in the hotel lounge after breakfast. Ricard and I had eaten in the restaurant but Mother's plane had been delayed so Pops had something delivered to his room on returning from the airport.

'Tell me about your parents, Ricard, and why you have, or appear to have, a difference of opinion with them.'

Ricard was stunned at the directness of my father's approach and took a while to gather his thoughts; realising Ricard needed time to think, Pops continued, 'You do realise some transparency on this is essential for Yvonne to be fully committed to you, don't you? For my part, I would not be happy to see her married to you without her understanding. To have secrets within a family is not good, tensions are always present and can put too much pressure on any relationship.'

Ricard nodded.

'I have neither visited nor been in direct contact with my parents for years. Not until I had to after finally opening the package.'

'The package?' asked Pops.

Ricard explained how he had responded to his father's request for help with the inheritance. Then looked around the lounge to ensure we were alone, sat forward in his chair and continued, 'For years both before and after we were married, Charlotte and I spent the summer months at my parents, the last time I had to return earlier than usual for work, although she wanted to come with me my parents persuaded Charlotte to stay on for a while longer. She not only loved working on the farm but there was still a lot to do, even though my brother was working there and two itinerant labourers my father employed during the season.

'Charlotte was fantastic at guiding the horses while harrowing. One evening it seems one of them was spooked, she tripped and got caught in the traces and took a bad fall into the equipment and must have got dragged along a bit because she was terribly bruised. She told my parents what had happened and decided to come home to rest.'

A waiter entered and asked if we would like some coffee, Pops looked at his watch, nodded and ordered a glass of brandy for each of us.

'Not for me Pops, just the coffee.'

Ricard spoke again, 'I had another reason to go home; after three years of marriage, Charlotte still hadn't conceived a child, we both were keen to have a baby and I wondered if I was at "fault". I'd already made an appointment to discuss this with our doctor following which I gave a sperm sample. But then Charlotte arrived home earlier than I'd expected and told me about the accident, she was obviously in need of care. She kept saying she was sorry; her moods fluctuated, I just put them down to feeling a bit sorry for herself. Then of course, after five weeks of her being home, these were easily explained when she said she'd been to the doctor and she was pregnant.

'Of course, her mood swings were understandable, Suzanne was growing inside her. Charlotte kept saying she was sorry. I told her there was nothing to apologise for, some women just had a bad time during pregnancy and to wait for the joy we would have with the baby. But I blame my parents for the hard pregnancy and the difficult birth and her death. I am certain the fall over the traces was the root cause of it all.'

'So, you blame your parents for keeping Charlotte on the farm?'

Ricard nodded in response to my father's question.

'And you have held this feeling—this grudge—ever since?'

Another nod. 'But I did visit them with Suzanne until she was about nine or ten months old, then I could not any more without challenging them. So, I stopped.'

'Have you ever tried to discuss this with them?'

This time Ricard shook his head.

'Then I strongly suggest you do so. At least explain to them your feelings, perhaps they too have consciences about it, and maybe an exchange of feelings would bridge the gap. And you now have at least a reason to visit, surely some of the documents regarding your father's inheritance will require his signature?'

'No, my father has given me full powers and my grandfather's solicitor has accepted this.'

'But,' persisted Pops, 'there'll have to be some discussion between you about the estate's affairs when the inheritance is completed.'

'That is a possibility, I had not thought so far ahead. We are still in early correspondence and I am not clear how big or small the estate is.'

'When you do have to talk, you'll go in with what seems to me to be a lot of hate and you'll act totally inappropriately with aggression, and all the years of resentment will burst over into more hostility, leaving you and your parents in a worse state than you are now.'

'Pops!' I'd never heard his voice so strong and antagonistic to someone he'd only recently met.

He ignored me, keeping his face concentrated on Ricard who, having held Pops' gaze for a while, put his head into his hands and said, 'Yes, sir. But I think it is likely to happen on any meeting.'

The waiter brought the coffee and brandy, as we sipped our drinks, Pops continued, 'Perhaps not, if you take the opportunity currently on offer.'

'What is that, sir?'

There was silence. Pops looked at me.

Of course.

'My invitation to visit them?' I asked.

'Quite so,' responded Pops.

'Between you two and Suzanne, it looks like I am cornered into action.' Ricard gave a wry grin.

'The invitation is not to you actually, is it?' Pointed out my father for a second time.

'Well, I'm not going without him, Pops.'

'Of course not, my dear, but now we know the reason, may I suggest a response to Ricard's parents accepting the invitation should be sooner rather than later.'

I looked up to see Sven hovering in the lounge doorway.

'Ricard, Sven is here.'

'Oh, my goodness. I forgot, I said I would call him if I did not need him to collect me.' He turned to my father. 'If last night had turned out to be a total disaster, Sven was to collect me. But if all were well, I would call to cancel him and I forgot to do so. I do hope last night and today have not been as such.'

'As long as you can fix this problem, all, so far, is well,' Pops answered.

'Ricard, now Sven is here, why don't we all go to Lézignan? Pops can meet the rest of the family and I can change our flights for us to return from Carcassonne instead. How does that sound, Pops?'

Neither of them took much persuasion. Ricard rang Marianne and asked her to prepare for our arrival. Hopefully, Sven did not realise his trip had almost been a wasted journey; if he had, he showed no indication. I sat in the front seat and dozed while Pops and Ricard talked all the way home.

Home—again, I'd used the word. Yes. C'est ça!

Marianne welcomed me with hugs and my father with the utmost respect, showing him to his room ensuring he had everything he needed. Suzanne was not around and I missed her.

'She'll be down in a minute,' said Marianne when she returned from settling father in. 'I think she is feeling a little shy at meeting your father. Somehow Ricard has given her the impression he is a bit of a tyrant, maybe she overheard some of your conversations about him.'

'It's possible I can be, when necessary, *Madame*.'

We both turned at his voice.

'*Monsieur*, I think not. Yes, a sensible stern man for sure and if I may say so, some humour but forever fair, not a tyrant feature in you.'

Joining us, Sven introduced himself to Pops who took the changed relationship in his stride. He'd already congratulated the chauffeur on his driving ability when Sven had opened the car door for him and made no reference to it again here.

'Shall we go in?' Ricard took my hand and the others followed into the living room where Marianne had already laid the ingredients for the pre-meal drinks.

'Ricard, I am concerned about Suzanne, where is she?'

'Hiding from the tyrant apparently.'

'What have you said to her?'

'I only said I was going to meet your father.'

'Yvonne, how have you described me to Suzanne? Obviously, Ricard's parents are not ogres. So, perhaps to her, I am the intruder, the nasty bogey man who has come to upset everything,' after a pause, 'maybe that is also how you saw me, Ricard?'

No one moved for a moment. Marianne broke the silence, '*Monsieur* Marshall—'

'Clive, if you will allow me to address you as Marianne, with Sven's permission, of course.' Sven nodded and Marianne agreed. 'Perhaps,' continued father, 'if you would take me to her room or wherever she is hiding,' he started backing to the curtains hanging at the windows, 'we could have a friendly

166

introduction with this elusive spirit and I could let her know I have no desire to upset the family, and I believe tyrants have to be fought and confronted, not run away from.' He stopped abruptly then pulled the curtain back and knelt down with more agility than I had seen for some time to expose a surprised and excited Suzanne, who threw herself into his wide opens arms as she had done so many times with me.

'*Papi-Pops*,' she whispered into his shoulder, 'you've come to save my *Papi.*'

'Or your *père*,' he replied.

She released herself from his arms and came and hugged me.

I noticed Sven go and assist father to his feet and guide him to a chair. Pops patted Sven on the shoulder, smiled and nodded in response to a question I didn't hear as Sven's back was to me; soon after, Pops had accepted a gin and tonic, Sven dispensed drinks for us all.

Over dinner, which Marianne said would be taken in the kitchen as it had been quite short notice, the conversation was mainly concerned with everyday life at Lézignan, in London and touched on Christmas. But Pops was not going to let the visit to Ricard's parents be dropped.

'Oh good! You've got the invitation, when can we go? Soon? Please, Yvonne.'

Ricard turned to Marianne.

'You know the situation there. How soon could a visit be arranged?'

'At this time of year, things are only just beginning to quieten down on the farm and they may still have paying visitors but it could be easily set up with a phone call. You could go tomorrow morning and be back in the evening.'

'By that, I assume you infer I go on my own.'

'Of course, I assumed you wanted to sort out the estate, nothing more, just business or else why the rush?'

Suzanne was about to speak, but Pops who was sitting next to her, now re-categorised from tyrant to friend and protector, stopped her.

'No, Marianne. I think, if I may speak on behalf of Ricard and Yvonne, following our earlier discussions at the hotel, what is needed is a full family visit with everyone,' he looked around the table and repeated, 'yes, everyone. I, too, would like to be included.'

'In which case, with all the arrangements to be made by Ricard's parents, the earliest would be Friday night, Clive. However, I apologise, I did not consider Yvonne's work and your commitments.'

'Well, at least it could be sorted in a short time if needed.'

'*Oui*!' shouted Suzanne. '*Oui! Oui! Oui!*'

'*Non, non, non*,' Pops reverse parroted, 'we need to take this step by step, my dear, but the invitation, it seems I have to remind you again, is to Yvonne and indicates the All Saints' school holiday is a suitable time for them when perhaps Suzanne could go too.'

'And if we are all to go, they will need ample time to prepare, not only the physical arrangements but also get their minds to the fact of meeting Ricard.'

'Yes, Marianne, there is a possibility when I suggest him coming, they may not want him,' I commented.

It was very enticing for us all to get over enthusiastic planning the visit but Sven, who had been his usual quiet self, said, 'Enough for tonight, there are many issues to consider, it is late and we need to plan when we are clear-headed. I suggest we talk tomorrow.' He looked at Pops for guidance, who nodded.

'Sven has offered good advice; we will try to work something out tomorrow. Right Suzanne, off to bed now,' said Ricard.

'Will you come and kiss me goodnight, Yvonne?'

'Yes, Suzanne, a bit later.'

'And clean your teeth,' called Marianne to the disappearing child.

Marianne and I sent the men to the sitting room with more coffee and drinks while we cleared the meal then joined them for another hour and chatted.

'I'm going to excuse myself, I think if I stay up much longer, I'll nod off, such a rude thing to do. Goodnight and thank you, Ricard, for our talk today and your hospitality.'

'Perhaps you would like to go by Suzanne to say goodnight; breakfast any time from 7 a.m.,' said Marianne.

Ricard stood to shake Pops' hand but was enveloped in his arms. Pops turned. 'Goodnight, Yvonne.'

'Night Pops,' I returned.

Suzanne was sleeping by the time Ricard and I went to bed, so we said a silent "goodnight" to her.

It was wonderful to be here.

As I came out of our bedroom, I saw Pops was already halfway down the stairs, I let him go on and followed slowly, stopping at the bend in the staircase and watched him enter the kitchen.

'Oh Marianne, I apologise for my dress, I didn't realise anyone would be down just yet. I came to make a cup of tea,' he offered a tea bag as evidence.

'Clive, an apology is not necessary. On a Sunday morning, we all come down at different times. I am an early bird—but I admit partly to ensure the crystal glasses do not get smashed in some enthusiastic effort to beat me to washing them! Thanks for the tea bag, but we have also enjoyed the occasional cup of tea for many years, though I have to say coffee is very much nicer and for dress, what better on a Sunday morning?'

He looked at his bare feet protruding from the dressing gown he was wearing.

'I found this hanging on the bathroom door. I hope it's alright to wear it or will someone else need it?'

'No, you are welcome; it belongs to Ricard's father, he brought it back by mistake the last time he visited them.'

'So, it's been hanging there for some time?'

'Yes.'

Marianne passed his tea across the table and they both sat.

'Thank you. Marianne, Ricard has told me a little about what is troubling him with regard to his parents but without asking you to break any confidences, which I'd never do, can you spread any light on the situation?'

'I'm afraid not, Clive, not because he has told me in anything in confidence, which as you say I would not break, but purely because I do not know. He has not told me anything. I know he had a big argument with his brother following which the relationship stopped. Please do not quote me but I do not think his father or mother have any idea what is at the bottom of the issue Ricard has with them.'

'Well, sometime and somehow, it will all have to be revealed if Yvonne is going to fully commit to him.'

'Yes, she is a strong lady. What are her brother and sisters like?'

'I'm not sure I'm able to describe the rest of them in sufficient detail to do them justice, Marianne. As a father, you'll have to understand I accept them—and their quirks. Ah! That's a nice sound.' He looked up to the kitchen window.

'What?'

'Church bells.'

'How stupid of me, sometimes they are so much part of the day I do not hear them, which is bad especially as I am to have our marriage blessed there after the civil service. That is the seven o'clock call, it is rare for any of us to attend the early service, but we do try to go to the eight o'clock.'

'How far away is the church?'

'Not far, *Papi-Pops*, just around the corner, can I come with you?'

Suzanne, still in her dressing gown, had whizzed past me with a quick 'Good morning, Yvonne' and joined them. The three were drinking tea and coffee when Ricard came and joined me.

'Eavesdropping? I thought you disapproved.'

'I wasn't—'

He stopped my protest by putting his hand on my shoulder and guided me into the kitchen to join the others. We were all in our dressing gowns.

'Wow, are we all after coffee before church this morning? May we have some?'

'I will have to make some more, the pot's empty.'

'Do not get up, Marianne. I will do it.' Ricard moved around the kitchen efficiently making the coffee. 'Are any of you coming to church this morning?'

'I was just telling *Papi-Pops* I will help him through the service.'

'How kind of you, Suzanne.' Ricard's sarcasm was wasted on Suzanne. 'You had better get dressed if you are going to do so. There is no pressure, Clive, but Yvonne and I will be going.' Ricard looked at me, although there had been no discussion on the subject. I nodded.

'I'm looking forward to my instruction,' Pops replied, smiling at Suzanne, 'what time do you like to leave?'

'At about a quarter to eight gives us plenty of time to get there and sit quietly before the service, but ten to is time enough if you prefer.'

'Quarter to it is. Thanks for the tea and chat, Marianne, I will go and dress.'

Marianne and I walked to the church together; she was saying how quickly Suzanne had taken to Pops.

'Someone else who has to be careful not to break her young heart then.'

'Yes, Yvonne, we have all taken to him.'

'I'm sorry, Marianne, I hope you understand I need to know about this feud with his parents.'

170

'I do and I too would like to find out the root of it, it is not comfortable being the go-between.'

'*C'est ça!*'

I may have misinterpreted the expression on the presiding priest's face when the six of us turned up for the service, even though Marianne and Sven had to make an appearance on a regular basis now. The service was not difficult to follow as, in custom with several churches, there was a prepared handout to use if we wanted one. Although encouraged by the others, neither Pops nor I received communion. By the time the service was over and all the congregation had shaken hands with the priest on leaving, introductions made to friends, greetings exchanged and waiting while Marianne and Sven had a long talk with the priest, it was nearing ten thirty before we sat down at the kitchen table to eat a large, late and welcome breakfast.

'Is that going to cause any problems, Ricard, should you and Yvonne eventually marry?' Pops asked.

'What are you referring to, Clive?'

'You can't ignore your religious upbringing and neither can Yvonne. Paul and Julie may soon have to face the same quandary, they had, as far as I can gather, a marriage following the Church of England rules even though Paul is Roman Catholic. Will they choose in which faith to bring up their children or will they not bother with any?'

'It all seems so stupid to me, today we all prayed to the same God and used many of the same prayers, especially the Lord's Prayer, even the Eucharistic section is almost identical.'

'Yes Yvonne, but there are deep-rooted different theological perspectives.'

'I know, Pops, but even so—'

'You do realise,' interrupted Sven, 'I am adopting the Catholic faith to marry Marianne and have a blessing in church.'

'It must be hard to give up one faith for another.'

'I have never been a very devout Muslim, Clive, and as Yvonne has intimated, all religions of the accepted and conventional kind do seem to have the same root originally. I regret religious intolerance and am happy to embrace Catholicism, especially if it makes Marianne and her family happy.'

There was a strange and peaceful silence round the now very messed up breakfast table.

'I obviously have a lot to learn as I really do not understand much of what you have just talked about, but perhaps we should all just say thank you for our food this morning to whichever god we would like.' Suzanne stood and left the kitchen with the parting shot of, 'I have homework to finish.'

Before anyone else left the table, Sven spoke again, 'Yvonne, I know you have asked Ricard about my history and he has refused to tell you, for which I am grateful, but you might like to know a bit. I had some trouble when I arrived in France, you see I came as an illegal immigrant, I spent quite a long time managing to get work in seasonal jobs where no one bothered who you were or where you came from, most of it was poorly paid, cash in hand.

'Somehow, one night, this was quite a few years ago, I ended up in Lézignan wandering the streets looking for somewhere to bed down, in a corner or on a park bench, when I saw,' he stopped and looked at Ricard who nodded slightly, 'a man staggering around. He was well-dressed but obviously inebriated. A couple of youths were following him, I watched the three of them, then the young men started to attack the drunk. I was angry that anyone so vulnerable should be attacked and bullied so I went to fend off the attackers.

'By this time, one of them had got the man's wallet and was running away with it. "Why," I thought, "should he have it when I need it?" I followed and got it off him, it was full of cash and cards. The second attacker had gone and I was very tempted to disappear too, but through all my hard times, I had never been a thief and I returned to help—'

'Me,' said Ricard. 'I was in a bad state after Charlotte died and often lost control. I was lucky that night, I had a guardian angel watching over me.'

'Maybe, but with my recent history of limited cash, it was very tempting to leave you in the gutter and flee with your wallet.'

'But you did not.'

'No. I helped you back here where you offered me a bed in the garage for the night and in the morning we talked. Perhaps we could say the rest is history, but it would skim over the hard work Ricard has done on my behalf. Sleeping in the garage, I kept my nose clean and held down several jobs Ricard found for me. I took a drivers and mechanics course, funded initially by Ricard. He has stuck his neck out for me and was acting against the law by not reporting me, foolhardy when you think of his job, but he has been able to help and support me in applying for and being granted permanent residency. The day you first arrived,

Yvonne, I'd been in court with Marianne and Ricard again to argue my case for citizenship.'

So that is the half-conversation I heard.

'I thought it strange no one had gone to collect Suzanne from her grandparents, I did wonder.'

'Yes, we were all in court.'

'Thank you for telling me, Sven.' After a thought, I asked, 'Where are you from originally, Sven? Do you still have family there?'

'Ethiopia is where I was born. I am Ethiopian—soon to be French. I do not think any of my family are alive now, we were all in refugee camps.'

'But—'

'But my name? Sven.'

'Yes.'

'I do not really know, but I remember my mother often speaking about Sweden. Whether she had ever lived there or it was just a dream I do not know. I think, for me, it is now time to close that chapter, I have a life here.' He took Marianne's hand which she freely gave.

Obviously, it was to be the end of the topic. Well, at least I knew there was no secret there, he'd been open and honest. I liked the man, both his family friendship and his professionalism.

I took a deep breath and changed the subject.

'We need to make a decision about the visit to the farm. Although both the first and second weekend of the holidays are suggested, I think the first weekend would be better, that still gives three weeks. It should be my decision, after all the invitation is to me and I'm asked to bring Suzanne, and you all could be viewed as interlopers!' I smiled.

'You would not really go without me?' asked Ricard.

I just looked at him and raised my eyebrows.

'Knowing that look,' said Pops, 'it means she probably would. But doing so might not resolve the problem we're faced with.'

'First weekend it is then. If all goes well, Suzanne could possibly stay on a while.'

'If you and your parents can talk, whatever the outcome, I'll be happier knowing.'

'It may not be a very polite exchange, Yvonne.'

'I hope you won't embarrass anyone, especially yourself, to do so won't be of any use to anyone,' said Pops.

Ricard nodded before asking, 'Do you need any help with the reply letter?'

'Thank you for offering, but no, Ricard. I'll take my time mulling it over and get it off tomorrow. It might come as a bit of a shock to your parents, but I have a feeling they will welcome everyone visiting.'

'You seem so sure you know my parents.'

'Is there anything I shouldn't say to Ramon and Matilde in the acceptance letter, Marianne?'

'I do not think so. If I were you, I would not go into too much detail. Just thank them, tell them the date you have chosen, who is coming and we will arrive on the Saturday about mid-morning.' The time was more of a question to Sven than a statement to me.

'Yes,' he nodded, 'if you and Clive arrive at Carcassonne on the Friday evening, we could leave about eight on Saturday morning. Small overnight bags should be sufficient luggage which will fit easily into the boot of the car. You do not want to be squashed in the car with large cases.'

'Fine, thanks Sven, I'll book the flights as soon as I can and let Ricard know our arrival time.'

We said our farewells, Suzanne and Marianne stayed at home. As before, at the passport control, Ricard walked away with just a wave, not looking back.

As we boarded, I must have smiled.

'What does the smile mean?'

'I was thinking back to a few weeks ago, this is where the flight—didn't happen. If the flight back from my time in Elne hadn't been cancelled, we wouldn't be here now.'

Would that have been better?

After we'd settled into our seats and the cabin crew had checked other passengers were buckled up so we could take off, father greeted the hostess like a lost friend and asked for two large gin and tonics.

'Pops, can I just have tonic. I had enough wine at lunch time.' He nodded and gave the order. These were delivered just before take-off with the request, 'Please keep your trays upright. Thank you.'

'She's taking a risk,' I said.

'Not in business class, it's supposed to be one of our perks,' Pops said.

'Perks are supposed to be free! I overheard you give an evasive answer to Marianne about your children. What do you make of us?'

'Well, as far as I know, Portia is as happy as she ever is working as a stage manager for one of the theatres up north.'

'Hmm, she really wanted to act though, didn't she? How's Francis' career going?'

'I think he's making a name for himself. He's had a couple of papers published and I think he's been guest speaker at some police conferences.'

'And the other two?'

Pops stopped to order another drink. I didn't want one.

'Julie is fine, she'll get something sorted out with her husband soon and they will settle to life in France or England or some sort of commuting. I hope she'll arrange something with her supervising professor, though how they think they'll manage with two babies I don't know. And as to the other one, I think she has a brilliant career but her personal life has hit the bumpers.'

I started to cry. Perhaps this last month had just been a total fantasy and I'd wake up soon to the reality around me.

Stupid, insensitive, vulnerable. Oui, C'est ça!

Pops said nothing, just held my hand for a while as I cried then passed me a clean handkerchief, an action I'd seen so many times over the years, the handkerchief being passed to all my siblings at one time or another, he always seemed to have one when it was needed.

'I'm so sorry, Pops, I've been so selfish, so self-centred. It feels as if I've not really been on this planet.'

'It looks as if you are about to land again, my love, and it might be with a big bump.'

'You mean my relationship with Ricard and what I feel may not be real? It's just a rebound or a fantasy? Am I making him into some sort of saviour, a figment of my imagination?'

'No, he seems, to me to be a genuine man, kind and considerate with a view that the world should be fair, even if it means bending the rules sometimes. But he's too cagey about his relationship with his parents which does concern me, I think there is more than he is saying.'

'Hopefully, to be sorted out in October. You'll come, won't you? Or do you think I should reply saying it's too soon to visit the farm?'

'What will be the point of postponing? If you're to pursue this relationship you won't progress it if you don't visit and try to find a reason. If the relationship then falls apart you will have tried. Unless, of course, you find you don't love him and it has just been an aberration.'

'Caused by temporary insanity?'

'Who knows?'

'Thanks! I'll let you have the hankie back some time.'

Once we were on the ground and were able to use our phones, I texted Ricard to say we had landed safely and I'd not ring him tonight as I'd go in to see mother and it would be late by the time I got home.

'Wise move,' said my father who'd looked over my shoulder, 'and without sticking my nose in where it's not wanted, you might also consider having a complete break from communicating. Tell him you need a little time to think things through.'

I didn't go in to see mother as the taxi route to their apartment passes mine, so Pops dropped me off first and waved as he went home.

I got into bed acknowledging I'd a lot to think about and probably some bridges to build between me and my siblings, if not bridges, then at least a lot of catching up to do, but decided to take a lead from Scarlett O'Hara and leave it till tomorrow.

§ § §

On waking, I once again, realised how supportive Patrick was being especially in allowing me even more time off, such as today. He'd obviously seen me jumping from pillar to post in a frenzy and why his protective feelings towards me, had been manifested in another way. Was he now possibly, in his manner, trying to protect me from going off course? And Julie, had she seen a much deeper stress than I was conscious of feeling and couldn't find a tactic to intervene to prevent more hurt? On reflection, I concluded, all communication between me and my three siblings had ground to a halt recently. Although we were probably not able to meet up very often because of our various employments, we were usually in touch one way or the other at least once a fortnight. Perhaps they had all tried to help me earlier and I'd not been receptive to their advances.

I thought about father's suggestion of a moratorium on contact with Ricard, but if the visit to his parents' farm was to happen during the All Saints' school recess, I wasn't sure how practical the suggestion was, even so, I would reply to Ramon and Matilde accepting the invitation for three weekends ahead for the whole family, including my father. But of one thing I was certain, I was not going back and forth to Lézignan until the farm visit weekend. I had far too much to do during the time I had free and none of it would be resolved or achieved in one day. Nor was lying in bed going to progress anything.

Refreshed after a shower and coffee, I settled down to write to Ramon and Matilde. My first draft was far too long and had gone into lengthy explanations of everyone's thoughts and ideas, I ended with a simple acceptance for the first weekend of the holiday, asking, if it was convenient to them for everyone, including my father, to come. I added, hoping I was not overstepping the mark of friendship, I appreciated there might be some tension, but I hoped this visit might be a step towards bringing back previous affection between son and parents.

I left the letter on the table and went to the local shop for some fresh fruit and cheese, on my return I reread it, placed it in an envelope and took it to the post office. As I left it with the post-mistress, I sent off a small prayer. All I could do now was wait.

C'est ça!

Next stop was the expensive boutique card shop where I purchased several beautiful and rather eccentric cards and some postage stamps. I bought a bunch of flowers and went to see Julie.

After the usual greetings and thanks for the flowers, we settled down with mugs of coffee. Julie didn't push me but realised I needed to talk and gently assisted me to express my deep confusion as to where my mind may have possibly been over the last few months.

'Was I totally out of control?' I asked.

'Well, you certainly were not the Yvonne, my big sister, I'd always known and depended on. You were either over-indulging others or weeping or sharp—nearing on aggression. But recently, after your time in the retreat in France, you seem to have calmed down again. I hope all this secrecy and uncertainty over Paul hasn't been in your way.'

'I suppose it was on my mind, but now it's all out in the open, you're happy, I'm no longer worried and I'm here to help you if you need me. At least for the next few months anyway.'

I told Julie about the possible contract in Lézignan and without going into all the details about Ricard and his parents told her this was a stumbling block in progressing our relationship.

'It seems to me, Yvonne, you're not sure which is the horse and which the cart.'

'What do you mean?'

'Surely, if the relationship between you and Ricard doesn't go ahead then you'll not want the job in Lézignan?'

I looked at Julie in shock, realising I'd had the two issues in two watertight compartments, but of course, they were totally entwined.

My mind must really be elsewhere.

'Yes, that could be awkward. I seem to have lost all my analytical and logical skills. I hadn't put the two together, I'd got them in separate compartments.'

'And now you're in a mess.'

'I certainly am. In enthusiasm, when I heard where it was to be based, I told Patrick I'd do the project and he's confirmed his acceptance with the French man involved. In fact, I spoke to him too, the day Patrick and he confirmed we'd proceed. I'm supposed to be developing a plan of action.'

'Is Patrick aware Ricard is the connection you have with the town?'

'Yes, but he doesn't know about the family problem.'

'And without some resolution, you can't go ahead with either the project or the relationship.'

'What a dismal-looking future.'

'Any idea when the family problem might be sorted out? From the outside looking in, it must be the first thing to sort out, then you'll know more certainly how you feel emotionally and everything else will fall into place.'

'I'm waiting for a reply to a letter I've only just posted to Ricard's parents. But, assuming the date it alright for them, it won't be for about another three weeks.'

'That is a long time to be working on a project without saying anything to Patrick.'

'Patrick will go spiral!'

'Wouldn't it be better for you to tell him upfront?'

I certainly had no idea how I was to tell Patrick but dreaded his reaction.

'When do you expect Paul to come over again, Julie?' I decided it was time to change the topic.

'Now the pressure's off at work, thanks a great deal to you, I understand, he's negotiated half days on Fridays and Mondays till the babies are born with an occasional whole Friday off if I can arrange an antenatal visit for him to attend, the mid-wives are being very accommodating. Then nearer the delivery date, he'll come over and stay for a while. I'm glad I met him before you did, he keeps going on about how great you are and he's a high opinion of Daddy.'

'Do you want a gathering of the family one weekend when Paul's over so he can meet as many of us as possible? I have a feeling I'm going to have time to organise something if you'd like me to.'

'Strange you should ask because Paul and I discussed this last night and we decided it would be a good idea. And I was wondering if you could take the lead for me. Two reasons really, one I do run out of energy easily these days but also I thought if either Portia or Francis were a bit "miffed" by your strange behaviour, it might be a bridge-building exercise, as you are doing it for me.'

'That's so thoughtful of you, Julie, thanks. I'm honoured to do it for you and now it's quite possible I'll have a lot of time on my hands. Yes, I'd love to do it. Thanks, and you never know it might just be the thing to stop me being so self-centred.'

'Except for these last few months, Yvonne, you've never put yourself first. You've always been at everyone else's beck and call; your recent behaviour is what surprised us. Anyway, thanks Yvonne. I was going to ask you even if you didn't have much time.'

And how much free time I'll now have isn't certain.

'Paul and I would like everyone to meet here over the fourth weekend in October if possible or the first one in November, it should give everyone enough notice to arrange their work and so on and be far enough from the birth so I'll be OK.'

I looked at my diary, glad I'd insisted on the meeting at the farm being at the start of the school holiday and not the end.

'A weekend day? From what little I gathered briefly from Pops on the plane, but not really knowing, it may be the Sunday would possibly suit Portia best and likewise Francis; as most laboratories don't work over the weekends, but of course, it would depend on whether or not he was called in for any police work, I understand he is still involved with them.'

'We can always send out an SOS to all criminals not to work on the Sunday we specify!'

'Perhaps not, but with enough notice he can fix not to be on call.'

'Anyway, you have given me a wonderful reason to communicating with the family, thanks. I knew the cards I bought this morning would come in use! I'd planned to use them as ice breakers, but now they'll have a dual purpose. I'll keep you informed then we'll talk about what food and drinks you want.'

'I think I'll ask Miguel and his family to cater. They can also help serving and so on and still be part of the gathering, they seem to be pretty much part of the family.'

'Right, do you want me to do anything before I leave you? Make more coffee, get lunch or anything else?'

'No thanks, I'm fine. Let me know how you get on with Patrick and the family.'

We kissed and I took the bus back home.

At least I had one job to do.

I decided an email to both my siblings would be the first step, outlining my understanding of their reactions to my contacting them if I'd seemed distant and non-responsive recently. And I'd been charged by Julie to organise a family get-together to meet Paul. I gave them the two weekend dates suggested by Julie, emphasising the first one would be preferable, but she would go with the majority. I ended by saying I'd be writing more fully to them individually. I pressed the send button and hoped I'd get some positive responses.

§

'Hello Yvonne.'

Pops picked up the phone on the third ring.

'You were quick, is everything alright?'

'Yes dear, your mother has just settled down for a short rest before another rehearsal. Seems things are "hotting-up" as she calls it, which I think means tempers are fraying.'

'Usually happens at some time in a production—I often wonder if she is the common denominator!'

180

'Harsh words, my dear, possibly true. But not this time, apparently the director keeps changing the directions. What can I do for you, my dear?'

'Julie has given me some occupational therapy if Patrick throws me out.'

'Is he likely to do so?'

'Well, as Julie pointed out this morning, what's the point of the job if no Ricard?'

'Ah! It did cross my mind but thought there might be a way around. But she's most likely right. You're seeing Patrick tomorrow, aren't you?'

'Yes, and I'm not looking forward to his response when I try to explain the complication. But Julie's asked me to fix a family gathering when Paul is over.' I told him the optional dates which he wrote down. 'I'll let you know which one is suitable for most people when I've heard from the others and hope you are both free.'

We said goodbye, with him wishing me good luck for tomorrow's meeting.

My mind moved to my financial situation so I checked my bank and savings accounts in preparation for the worst event. My salary had always been generous, I was mortgage free as Mark and I had managed to buy the flat, so I knew if Patrick decided to "dispense with my services", I'd be alright financially for a while and appreciated I was in a much happier state than a great number of others.

Having decided there was nothing I could do short term on the money side, I sat down to write the cards to my siblings. When I'd bought them, I'd done so randomly with no individual in mind. I laid them out on the table and chose two which reflected each of their interests. I'm not really into omens, but I thought this might be a positive one. I wrote to both referring to a specific incident which only applied to them. I found apologising and remembering cathartic.

Was I being self-centred and selfish again? Releasing me from my guilt? No, it was to return to the true bonding we had all learned from our parents.

Although I now had the rest of the mountain to climb, starting tomorrow, I felt I was beginning to land, and maybe not with such a bump as Pops had envisaged.

When I'd finished writing and addressing the cards, I put them in my bag ready to take to the post the next day and feeling happier about the future relationship with my relatives, if not Patrick, went to bed.

Chapter Eleven

I dropped my coat and bag in my office space then entered Andrea's office.

'You're looking good this morning, Yvonne.'

I was greeted by Andrea who, to my eyes, was, as ever, immaculately turned out.

'Thanks, I suppose that's a backhanded compliment. Good morning.'

Although I said nothing, I'd taken a little longer in my self-presentation this morning and last night I'd spent time ensuring my nails and hands were in a good condition, I felt today rather as I did when I first came for an interview with Patrick, although then he'd head hunted me. I was not sure how successful this interview was going to be.

'No, you always look good, but there is a special something about you today.'

'Does Patrick have a few minutes free to see me, Andrea?'

'It's tight, he's on a telephone conference now till ten, another one at eleven, then he's out all afternoon. Can you come back at ten fifteen, I'll have done the post and reviewed his diary by then, I'm sure he'll see you if he can. Is your desk area alright? If you need anything just ask Trish and I've put a few references on your desk that might be worth looking at from the French legal point of view.'

'Thanks.' I returned to my newly created work area and looked at the references Andrea had provided, one of the office girls brought me a cup of coffee, I smiled my thanks and turned on my computer, logged on to the Internet and stared at the screen watching the various wallpaper images but not taking them in.

§ § §

'You wanted to see me?'

I jolted back to the present, I'd been far away, I've no idea where, the screen pictures still continued to change as they had when I'd turned the computer on, nothing on the desk had been touched and the cup of coffee now lay cold where it had been placed. I looked up.

'Yes please. If it's not inconvenient and you have a moment.'

'You'd better come into my office. You sound serious and we may need a bit more privacy than this rather open office space affords.'

I followed Patrick into his office and sat formally at his desk.

'Well? When you're ready, I haven't got all day even though my last conference did finish earlier than expected.'

'Sorry, yes. Patrick, the Lézignan contract…I'm not sure I can do it after all.'

'Well, you must give me an extremely good reason why not, Yvonne. You eagerly accepted it. You were here when we cleared it with *Monsieur* Bassinet. In fact, you spoke to him and had some sort of personal interaction with him. Why the change of mind? Are you still not well enough to work? Do you want more leave?'

'No Patrick, or yes. Listen, I don't want more leave, but there's a slight…' I explained the situation I found myself in with Ricard, father's involvement and the proposed visit to Ricard's parents farm to try and resolve the matter.

He sat in silence his elbows on his desk and his chin resting on his folded hands until I'd finished, his face expressionless. He then leaned back in his chair with a quiet sigh and put his hands together. I stared at him saying nothing and wishing he would. I tried to gauge his reaction but he gave no indication what he was thinking, it was like looking at a blank wall.

'I'll get my things. Thanks for everything you have done for me, I'm sorry to have let you down after all your support and confidence.' I'd reached the office door and was holding the handle.

'Where do you think you're going, Yvonne?'

I shrugged. I'd no idea. I couldn't expect a reference now and there'd be many questions if I applied to join another company. My first move would be to sign on, to at least get my insurance stamps credited, but I really knew nothing about being unemployed. Maybe I could go freelance.

'You do not just walk out of my office.'

I turned but stayed where I was, he said nothing for a while till he'd resumed his position of elbows on the desk but, instead of resting his chin on his hands he linked his fingers together and looked over the top of them.

'Since when have you started to walk from a problem? Eh? We, or you, obviously have a work situation. It's also clear it has been created by you. So, as it is your mess, I expect you to come up with a solution.'

I opened my mouth and started to reiterate my concern for his firm, for him and—when he stopped me.

'Well, if you are so concerned, sort it out. Think laterally, think out of the box. I expect you tomorrow in here at ten thirty with a solution. On your way through Andrea's office, ask her to diary our appointment.'

I was obviously now being told to leave his office. His voice was firm but he didn't appear to be angry, but maybe he was restraining himself, I wasn't sure if I was picking up vibes of disappointment and frustration and if I had, was it about the situation or my apparent defeatist attitude?

Andrea entered the appointment in her large desk diary. I sat at my desk. After a minute, I checked the contents of the desk drawer, none of my usual pieces of stationery was there. Of course not, this was a new work area and hadn't been provisioned yet or personalised by the collection of idiosyncratic items preferred by the occupant, so I got up to start making the desk my own. I suddenly felt more positive and welcomed the challenge I'd just been thrown. Instead of calling for Trish, I went to the stationery cupboard and selected what I needed. I moved my computer to one side and started work as I used to do in the early days when given a new project.

Back to your comfort zone. Simple project management at its basics.

§

'May I join you for coffee, Yvonne?' Andrea stood at the door with two mugs of coffee.

'Of course, nice idea.' I looked at my watch. I'd not realised how much time had passed.

'How's it going?'

'Slowly. I'm not sure where to start, but it isn't as if there's an easy way out of this one. Has Patrick told you?'

'Yes, but I'm sure you'll find a solution to the problem.'

'Problems,' I sighed, then remembered what Julie had said and turned it into the basis for an idea.

'Well, let's talk about something else for the moment, how's Julie's pregnancy progressing? Still going well?'

'Yes, thank you. Oh Andrea, I'm not sure if I've told you all about her husband.'

'A secret one is as far as I have gathered.'

'He was, yes but…' I explained the situation and the plan for the family gathering I'd been asked to collate. At the end, I told her about my discussion with Julie, my relationship with my brother and sister and my recent messages to them. She was pleased with the news, then getting up, she picked up the mugs and wished me luck with the project proposal.

'I'll need it.' I returned to the thought I'd had earlier over coffee. I had to run the work and personal problems side by side, putting in the pivotal points and solutions to follow from them. And another obvious thing I realised I was missing was a skills profile for another project leader if needed—for whatever reason.

Idiot. Always expect the unexpected and have a contingency plan. That's what Patrick was saying.

So, ruler and pencil in hand, I started on a timeline, plotting dates and critical incidents. By mid-afternoon I had roughed out a plan and went out to buy a sandwich which I ate at my desk. I spent the rest of the afternoon and well into the evening, after everyone else had left, writing it up and entering it into the software programme Patrick liked, to check I'd not double-booked or misplaced an action. Paper and pencil still served true! I saved it on my computer and left the printing for the morning. I was let out of the building by the night security guard who doubled up as the evening cleaner. I'd not seen him for quite some time and was delighted he and his wife had at last got their own house.

'It's only small, but it is a start.'

'I'm glad to hear good news, Jöel. Is there much work to do on it?'

'Oh yes, we have plans for it but we want to live in it for a while and really decide the best way to develop it. So many people jump in and commit themselves to something without thinking it all through.'

'Oh yes Jöel, I can certainly relate to that! Goodnight.'

For the third night in succession, I didn't ring Ricard and there was no message from him. As I got into bed, I wondered if Pops had contacted him and told him it might be a good idea if we didn't communicate daily but also wondered if there was something wrong from Ricard's perspective. As I settled to sleep, I realised I missed our nightly talks and waiting for another word from him before he disconnected the line.

§ § §

I took two copies of my project plan into Patrick's office at precisely ten thirty. Both were in the formal plastic covered folders, clear front sheet displaying the topic, author and date. I placed his copy on the desk positioned so he did not have to turn it round. He did not touch it or attempt to read it.

'Thank you, Yvonne, a very adequate and informed project plan, it will need costing, I assume?'

'Phase one has been costed, Patrick, you see on page…' I turned to the page on my copy.

'Yes, I am sure it is, thank you.'

I was stunned. 'And,' I continued, 'an outline of costs for the options for phase two together with a—'

Again, he cut me short. 'Thank you, Yvonne. I am sure you have some work to do, I certainly have.'

'Yes, Patrick.' I left his office in amazement wondering, if and when, he'd read the document. I hadn't put a secure key on the file but thought he wouldn't do such a thing it would have been rather under-hand and not his style, we'd always worked on trust—even if I'd slipped up a bit recently. But more likely, I thought on reflection, he had enough confidence and faith in my abilities to turn this around. I metaphorically kicked myself for not coming up with the plan before I saw Patrick. Even so, I felt better in myself.

I started work. Later in the day, having received the document with Patrick's signature, I asked Trish to go through the process of getting a financial code and to stand by for requests for flights to Carcassonne in about ten days' time.

'I'll get you the code today, Yvonne, but I am taking some leave next week so unless you want to trust your passport details to someone else, I'll need to book them soon.'

'Thanks for letting me know, Trish. I'll let you know tomorrow. I have a couple of things to confirm before you book.'

She left smiling returning later with the form stamped with the project number saying she was going home and suggested I did too. I agreed, saved my work and closed the machine. The signed document I put in the desk drawer and locked it.

I decided to make a detour to see Pops. I needed to tell him what had happened in the office and to ask him about his possible intervention on the communication between me and Ricard. He was complimentary about the project outcome and denied having any involvement in the silence by Ricard even though he agreed he'd suggested it to me.

'But I thought you were going to tell him you were planning not to communicate regularly.'

'Perhaps I should have done,' I conceded, 'but I must ring him tonight in view of the face-to-face meeting I hope to make with *Monsieur* Bassinet. This is part of the first stage in the project for the school and if I didn't tell Ricard I was in town, it might be a bit awkward if he found out.'

'You might also think about you and Ricard talking on neutral ground.'

'You mean I should stay in a hotel rather than in his house.'

'Correct,' he affirmed my understanding, 'and not involve any of the rest of the family, keep it low key for a while. Are you planning to stay over a weekend at this stage?'

'Probably not, I just need to get some basic information from *Monsieur* Bassinet which will be easier to do together rather than on the telephone or internet, face-to-face questions and answers often lead on to other issues and possibilities. And I need to spend time in the office, as well as looking after the arrangements for Julie's get together, and remember we'll be away one weekend in October too.'

'Busy month for you then.'

'Seems so. Thanks for the talk again, Pops.'

§

At home, I sorted my handbag. It usually accumulates things during the day. The cards were still there. *I must post them tomorrow.* I carried on throwing out rubbish and replacing things I needed. One item stared me in the face.

Oh my God.

I checked my diary.

Missed a month. But he'd been careful to use… Don't panic.

I didn't ring Ricard. The *Bassinet* news would have to wait. And I didn't sleep well.

§ § §

I timed leaving for work to coincide with the chemist's opening. I put the test in my bag, the instructions said for the most accurate result, I'd have to wait until the next morning to try it. The cards I dropped into a letterbox.

Concentrating on the job was hard but I managed to arrange to meet with *Monsieur* Bassinet the following Wednesday morning; asked Trish to fix me a flight to Carcassonne for Tuesday afternoon with an open return; a room in the Lézignan hotel, for a flexible stay, in the same chain she'd used in Toulouse.

The rest of the day was spent on further research and contacting the people forwarded by *Monsieur* Bassinet, who turned out to be the principals of two of the local schools, both of whom sounded enthusiastic on their replies.

§

On a visit to Julie, at the end of my working day, I told her Francis had replied to my email—the first week in October suited him. I was still waiting to hear from Portia; some of their friends had accepted and others regretfully declined, though wished her all happiness.

She was obviously pleased with the positive responses and said she and Paul would go and see Miguel over the weekend to book him and discuss the food and wine. I felt relieved she was taking on this part of the preparations and involving Paul. I promised to let her know Portia's response as soon as I got it. I updated her on how the meeting with Patrick had gone.

'I'm not surprised you sorted it out, you just needed a bit of a push and somehow Patrick has a knack of doing that. Which reminds me, would you please extend the invitation to him as well, on my behalf.'

'Of course, a good idea, he's been so much part of your life—and mine—recently. I'm sure he'll accept.'

My answer phone light was flashing when I eventually got home. I left it, removed my coat, poured a glass of soda water, after a sip left the glass in the kitchen and put the pregnancy test in the bathroom before returning to the phone.

What I heard when I pressed the play button was both heart-warming and gratifying.

'Fantastic to get your email, Von.' As soon as I heard my name, I knew it was Portia as no-one else contracted my name. 'Of course I'll come, looking forward to seeing you all and meeting this mystery man of Julie's, my dearest sister, there's no need to do any sort of apologising, we were all so worried about you, you have always been the one we came to, all of us, you were always the big sister we could rely on, and it was so hard not to get close to you and help, look, now you are back, is there any chance of you making a trip to Leeds this weekend?

'I know you are probably busy now you're back from France but I do want to see you and hear all your news, if you're free this weekend, any chance of you coming up to Leeds? I can't get away now the opera is in full swing but I can get you a ticket for the Saturday night, we can spend most of Saturday and all Sunday together, call me, phone is better than email, in haste, cast just coming back from mid-morning break. Love you. Please come.'

It seemed as if she had said all this in one breath, so like mother! Portia had always wanted to be an actress, but somehow the acting opportunities never presented themselves. I planned to accept her invitation and would be able to see how happy or otherwise she was in her role with the prestigious company she worked for.

I checked my watch and decided now wasn't a good time to ring, she would be coordinating the performance so checked the train timetable online. A train on Friday evening would get me to Leeds, I guessed, when the performance should have finished so Portia would be able to either meet me at the station or be home if I arrived by taxi. I'd need to get the train back on Sunday evening but we'd have some of Saturday and most of Sunday together. I booked the tickets.

I drank the water slowly while I cooked my evening meal then relaxed with a book before I rang Ricard. He was obviously delighted to hear from me and didn't question why I'd not been in touch nor did I question him. I explained I had to meet *Monsieur* Bassinet on Wednesday and would arrive in Lézignan on Tuesday evening.

'Will you want to meet up, Yvonne?'

'Yes, but I think it's better if I stay in the hotel and not at your home.' He said nothing but I could almost hear his mind whirling. 'Also, I think it's best the rest of the family isn't involved.'

'Will we have dinner in the evening?'

'That would be nice, does Charles Bassinet know we have this problem? I've not told him anything and I'd prefer he didn't at this point.'

'Not to my knowledge, Yvonne, I think as far as he is concerned, everything is fine between us. Which, in fact, I think it is.'

'Ricard, you know very well, resolving, or at least identifying, the problem between you and your parents is key to allowing our relationship to proceed. Please don't belittle it, I'm so afraid it's something we might not get over.'

'So, you do love me!'

'Of course, I do, but I can't commit fully without this being resolved.'

'I'll tell Marianne I have a working dinner.'

'Will she accept that?'

'Of course, I do have them every so often, so I see no reason why not and I do not have to answer to her for my actions. Do you envisage my staying with you overnight?'

'Maybe, we'll see, you're well-known in the town and I don't know how your reputation—or mine—will be affected.'

Ricard laughed. 'This is France, my love, we are not so strung up as you lot.'

I decided to ignore this comment and said I'd see him on Tuesday at the hotel.

'Goodnight, Yvonne.' He clicked the line off immediately.

I spent the time before ringing Portia getting changed for bed, so wrapped in my dressing gown, about eleven thirty, I called Portia. She'd just got in from the performance and was still on a high and was pleased to have something to settle her mind. She agreed with my proposed train plan but said to meet her at her flat in case she got caught up at the theatre. She said her neighbour had a key and could let me in if necessary. When I replaced the receiver, I realised I'd caught her excitement and felt alive, almost light-headed. Relief came over me as I realised how much I was now back with my family. I felt happy, a sensation I'd not been aware of for quite some time. Sleep came surprisingly quickly and easily.

§ § §

190

I woke early. I waited a moment as I opened the sealed test packet. I'd already read the instructions several times and followed them precisely and waited for the result.

I sighed with mixed emotions.

Oh! C'est ça!

After a cup of coffee, I put together everything I thought I'd need for the weekend in Leeds—something presentable for the opera on Saturday evening, my jogging gear, a clean blouse, a jumper and all the usual basic stuff should suffice as the trouser suit I was wearing would be acceptable the rest of the time. I managed to get through a great deal of work and gleaned a lot more information. I caught Patrick as he was leaving the office and gave him the invitation from Julie, he was delighted to accept.

Late in the afternoon, Sharon knocked on my office door.

'Have you got a moment, Yvonne?'

'Sure, come in.'

Sharon explained the problem she had with her project; we talked through some areas for half an hour. She ended, 'He's a total control freak, I can't get him to budge.'

'I wonder if Patrick saw this coming.'

'In that case, I've failed.'

'No, not if you've covered everything. It might be Patrick knows something, he's been around a bit and is very astute. Is there anyone in the company above this man you have to report to?'

'No, the contract is clear, the firm's managing director wanted me to report only to Patrick.'

'Maybe the time has come to do so. Is your report written up?'

'Nearly, I need to go through it again as some parts are not clear.'

'I suggest you make an appointment with Patrick and tidy it up. There comes a time when you have to stop.'

'Thanks for listening.'

'My pleasure, that's what colleagues do!'

'Do you fancy a drink? There's the Italian wine bar around the corner, with us both being out of the office so much we've not had the opportunity to talk.'

'What a good idea, I've got a bit of time to kill before my train. I'll just say good night to Andrea, shall I tell her you're off too?'

'Yes please, oh no, I'd better come and make the appointment before I go.'

§

I toyed with my Saint Clements as Sharon explained she has a daughter, Lucy. Sharon and her mother jointly own the house where they live and share all the bills. Her mother has a pension so is financially independent but looks after Lucy while Sharon works. In exchange for all the childcare Sharon pays for "extras" and their holidays.

'This works out well; gives me quite a bit of freedom from the work point of view, though I don't really want to work away like you do.'

'Seems like a perfect setup for you both, and Lucy, of course. How does discipline work with Lucy?'

'We're lucky there because both of us have the same strong ideas on how children should behave. Don't get me wrong, we have plenty of fun and games but, for example, at mealtimes there are no phones, bedtime procedure is fairly strict as is homework.'

'But there must be times when you and your mother disagree.'

'Yes. In those circumstances, whoever has made the decision gets the other's supports—at the time—and we discuss it later. Sometimes the decision is reversed.'

'Surely, Lucy must find that confusing?'

'So far, so good. It might become more of a problem as she reaches her teens and the less compliant phase of her life. Why are you so interested?'

I smiled, thinking of Ricard and Marianne and how they respected each other's decisions.

'Sorry, I didn't mean to pry but I find it interesting how different people handle these things. I suppose it's the same within marriages, a lot of give and take.'

'Yes, but I think it is basically respect for the other person, openness and trust.'

'Is it an intrusion to ask about Lucy's father?'

'Oh, he went off when he found out I was pregnant. We're better off without him.'

A warning bell sounded in my head.

'You may be right. I'd better be off to the station. Thanks for the drink, have a good weekend and good luck with Patrick.'

'And you, and thanks for your help.'

The train was crowded, all seats occupied and a fair smattering of some rather over tired and fractious children, so it was hardly a peaceful trip. Even so I found I'd dozed off at one stage and was roused by the ticket inspector. I showed her the ticket on my phone and remembered the last time I'd been woken from a snooze on the train, seemingly years ago yet it was barely six weeks. I thought about the people I'd met and grown close to in the time as well as the many acquaintances and wondered if all our lives were destined to be further entwined.

§

It was only three flights of stairs but as I had my case, I decided to take the lift to Portia's floor. She was not home when I arrived so I decided to ask her neighbour as she'd said. The door to her neighbour's flat was opened, to my surprise by a man, not a woman as I'd anticipated.

He was much taller than me, his deeply tanned face had crows' feet lines around his dark brown eyes, gained, probably, from long period out of doors screwing them up, especially in the strong sunlight. He was wearing a pure white singlet over a muscular torso which I assumed was as tanned as his arms and his hand, which he extended in greeting. It felt hard and gnarled as it enclosed my hand when I shook it.

I was stunned, it couldn't be.

'G'day, you must be Portia's sister, she is expecting you. Let me get the key to her flat, unless you'd care for a drink here, while you wait for her. She shouldn't be long, she's usually back by eleven-thirty at the latest.'

'Err, thank you for the invitation, but I'd rather just go into Portia's flat if you don't think me rude.' I didn't want to be in an enclosed area with this man to whom I had taken an instant dislike and a possibly well-founded fear.

'Of course not. You are probably a bit pooped after a day's graft and long journey. Just a sec, the key's in the kitchen.'

I watched him almost lope along the hallway and disappear into the kitchen reappearing again, dangling a key in one hand and extending the other to the sitting room.

'You sure you wouldn't like to come in for a bevy before you hunker down?'

'Yes, I am sure, thank you for your kind invitation. I am, as you say, rather tired.'

He brushed, unnecessarily close, past me as he went to open the door to Portia's flat. He dropped the key which landed near my feet, I stooped to pick it up, he came so close as I returned it to him, I had to back from him, he paused for a moment before turning the inserted key in the lock and pushing the door open. Then, instead of standing away for me to enter, he leaned against the door jamb half blocking my entry. I waited for him to move.

'Thank you for unlocking the door, now if you'd excuse me, I'd just like to go in.'

'Of course, sorry.' He moved from the doorway towards me, extending his hand for my wheelie case.

'Thank you, I can manage, it's not heavy.'

'You're a strong, independent "Sheila". I hope to see more of you over the weekend.' He'd taken a step closer and towered over me, his action, tone of voice and the look on his face seemed to be stripping me bare inferring it was not just social interaction he was talking about seeing. 'Portia hasn't talked much about her family, so maybe you'll be a bit more forthcoming.'

Everything he said and did, repulsed me, and had double meanings, no doubt some psychiatrist would say it was all in my mind, but this was a blatant sexual attack.

I heard the lift door open and Portia got out.

'So sorry not to be here, Von, got caught up, the tabs got stuck again.' She hugged me. 'Oh, you've met Jules, have you been here long?'

'No, just long enough to get the door opened for me.'

'Do you want to come in, Jules, quick drink before bed?'

'Portia, I'm really tired,' I cut in before Jules could reply, 'can we just call it a day for now, please?'

'Of course, sorry. You don't mind, do you, Jules? Catch you tomorrow?'

'Of course not. Your sis has already said she is ready for bed,' he looked straight at me and smirked again, 'G'd night.'

We were about to go into the flat when a man came bounding up the stairs.

'Oh Portia, I'm so sorry. Have you been waiting long?' He turned to me and extended his hand. 'I'm John, I am so sorry, I told Portia I'd be here for you. I'd hoped to be back before you arrived. I didn't mean for you to be standing outside.'

'Never mind, all well now. Goodnight, John.'

'Goodnight, Portia, Von,' He smiled and went through the still open door into his own flat.

'Nice guy?' I asked.

'John, yes.'

'The other one?'

'He hasn't been around long. John does Airbnb so doesn't have people for extended periods. Probably time for him to move on now.'

'The sooner the better I'd have thought. He's a creep.'

'Oh!'

'Sorry Portia, he came on to me while we were waiting and I certainly don't want anything to upset this weekend. It's so wonderful to see you and for you to invite me so quickly after you got the email. It means a lot to me.'

'Good, now, do you want a drink while we talk or would you really rather get to bed?'

'Well, you probably need an unwind period, so let's chat for a while, you have a wine, have you got some soda water? I'm rather thirsty.'

Although we talked till one and I was tired, I found it difficult to sleep. I'd recognised features of both Ricard and his father in Jules' face. And there was also a definite French accent below the Australian one. I had to find out to be sure, without divulging anything, if this man was who I thought he was. I felt frightened.

§ § §

We both woke early and, still in nightclothes and dressing gowns over bowls of cereal and glasses of freshly squeezed orange juice, we discussed how we'd spend the day. Portia had to go to the theatre about ten o'clock, I said I'd accompany her. We would then have some time to catch up further on what we'd been doing before she returned to the theatre for the evening performance.

'Jules isn't coming, is he?'

'Not to my knowledge, he's not said anything to me and John rarely socialises with his paying guests. He expects them to entertain themselves. Why have you taken such a dislike to him, Von?'

'There's something about the way he was with me before you got here last night. Maybe it was just the forthrightness of the Australian character I didn't like.'

'Oh well. You get ready while I clear these things then we'll head out. Do you mind a walk? It'll take about twenty minutes but I find if I don't walk to the theatre at least once a day I get too lazy, mind you it is usually quicker than the bus with the traffic.'

'No, fine, I packed sneakers in anticipation.'

As we left the flat, Jules came out of John's door. My heart sank but then thought I might be able to get some information if I was careful and not too pushy.

'G'day, my beauts! Are you walking my way?

'Which way would that be?' I asked.

'Well, you got me there! I'm going whichever way to suit you. I'm very accommodating!'

'Come on then.' I set off at a good speed down the stairs and out through the entrance lobby. 'Do I turn left or right?' I shouted over my shoulder to Portia.

'Cross the road and go right then first left then take the underpass.'

'Have you got something you have to do in a hurry, Von?' Jules asked as he came up beside me.

'Not really, but if I'm out for a walk, I like to walk not saunter. If it's too fast for you, I'll jog on the spot while you get your breath. You're alright with this speed, aren't you, Portia?'

'Fine by me. Seems like you're an outdoor man, Jules, you must be fit enough for this.'

'Sure thing, but we can't really talk when we are going so fast and dodging other people.'

I set off again. 'What do you want to talk about?'

'Well, you for a start. Where do you live, what do you do, what are your hobbies; apart from Portia, do you have any other family and most important are you married?'

'That's all very forward and intrusive, are you always so direct? Why would you want to know all that anyway? I assume you're only here for a short while if you're doing Airbnb, before you go back home.'

'Well, I'm planning to visit my parents, where I grew up, then I'll decide whether to go back to Oz or not.'

'Where's your real home then? Not Australia?'

We'd stopped at some traffic lights where Portia and I were jogging on the spot. I was surprised to see Jules had stopped to get his breath back he was obviously not as fit as he looked.

'No, I am French, I left France about eight years ago and decided it's time I visited the parents and see my goddaughter.'

'That should be nice for them.' I managed a smile as the lights changed and we walked across the road avoiding pedestrians coming towards us.

'Maybe, maybe not, we will see.'

'You don't sound sure, I hope it goes well. Which part of France is home?'

'It's a small village in the south, not far from the Spanish border, Ortaffa, do you know that area?'

'No...'

Concentrate, just a coincidence.

'...the only thing I remember reading about is the story of a Swiss Hospital set up to help the refugees escaping from Spain during the revolution.'

'Yes, it's quite famous and not far from my village.'

'We're here; stop walking, we did it in fourteen minutes, that was quite a sprint. Do you want to come in or do you both want to carry on and I'll catch up later?'

'No, I'll come in and see how it's all set up before the show, thanks. See you later, Jules.' I followed Portia into the theatre quickly, not giving Jules a chance to respond.

'That was a bit abrupt, Von, you really don't like him, do you? And what's with all the questions?'

'Just interested. A man back from Australia to see his family, quite romantic. I wonder if he plans to see the goddaughter's mother too!'

'You've got a vivid imagination, Von. He's probably just a bit homesick. Australia's a long way from France.'

Portia took me onto the stage and introduced me to two stagehands who were trying to fix the mechanism for the tabs—or stage curtains as I would have called them. I left the three of them discussing the best approach to resolve the matter for at least tonight's performance and sat in the front row and thought seriously about Jules. What he'd told me was too much of a coincidence for this man not to be Ricard's brother. What, of course, I'd not asked, was his surname? No one had used it, perhaps I could ask John later. After about an hour of discussion and many failed attempts at closing then opening the tabs, they finally achieved several successful runs and we left.

'Where to?' I asked.

'I know I shouldn't answer a question with a question, but what do you like to do about eating? There's a gathering backstage after the show this evening then on to a restaurant so we shouldn't need to bother about any supper, so the question is do you want to eat an early lunch and have a sandwich before the theatre; or have a coffee and pastry now and have a late lunch. We should leave for the theatre again about six-thirty and go by taxi—or earlier if you want to walk, not jog.'

'Taxi please, I don't fancy walking in the heels I've brought with me for tonight. And as it's not far off mid-day, I vote we skip the pastry and go straight for lunch. By the time we find somewhere nice and have ordered, it will be well into lunch time. Where do you suggest we go, considering we are dressed as we are?'

'Von, this is Leeds on a Saturday morning. We go where everyone goes, dressed as they like—the docklands waterfront.'

'Of course, silly me! I assume we jog to build up an appetite?'

'Not sure how much of an appetite you can build up in about five to six minutes. But yes, we'll jog.'

'Portia, if you see Jules, if it's such a popular place, I don't want to eat with him, please make some excuse about just being sisterly time together,' she looked at me, 'please. I promise I will tell you, but not just yet.'

The waterfront of the docklands area was indeed busy. The weather was unseasonally warm and tables had been put outside, we were lucky to get one of those. We had a superb lunch, without wine as Portia said she preferred not to drink mid-day; I was happy to forego it. Although I was not totally forthcoming about my relationship with Ricard, I admitted there was a possible man on the horizon; emphasising it was still only a possibility.

'I'm so glad you can come to Julie's gathering; all the family will be there.'

'Come on, we'd better shift. I don't think I am going to jog the return journey; my lunch deserves a more leisurely walk.'

I paid the bill on my card and Portia left a generous tip in cash. The route back took in a small park and a different shopping area. It struck me this is a great city in which to live and work.

§

Jules was standing outside Portia's flat when we arrived back.

''Allo ladies, did you have a good morning? Nice city of yours. Sorry I've to leave it without having had the pleasure of a drink with you, but my host has given me my marching orders. Seems I've outstayed my welcome, so tomorrow I'm hitch-hiking my way to Scotland.'

'Hitching! I wish you luck and hope you enjoy the company of the people who offer you lifts.' said Portia putting her key into the lock.

'I've found most people to be very friendly—so far.'

'Well, I think we are a pretty friendly bunch on the whole, but I must admit I don't like picking up hikers anymore. Any plans for what you are going to do in Scotland?' I asked, moving to the door.

'Yea, some mates of mine are there, they came over a bit before me and I said I'd join them to try out the whisky tours, a bit of fun before a more sober visit to Stratford on Avon. I did some farming there before I went to Australia while I was on a course and told the people I worked with I was coming over; they have invited me to stay for a while. Mind you, the old man was partial to a beer or two, I hope he hasn't changed.'

'You seem to be cramming in a lot on this visit, will you be going to London or is that too tame?'

'Not at all, Portia, half of Australia's in London. I won't be without a few people to talk to there.'

'Well, I hope you have as good a time in Britain, as you are planning, Jules.'

'But not as good a time as I could have. It would be so much better if I could get to know you, Von. Come on, how about a drink and a chat, eh?'

'No thanks, Jules. Have a safe journey.' I followed Portia into the flat feeling Jules' eyes on my back. He gave me the shivers, but I wondered when he planned to go to France, perhaps I'd made a mistake and should go for a drink with him after all. I turned back to him.

'You know what, Jules, I will, but it will be just a quick friendly drink at the bar round the corner, the one we passed this morning. Just a friendly drink as Portia and I have to get ready to go out.'

His face brightened up as if he'd won and he swaggered again.

'Sure, just a friendly drink, nothing more.' He just couldn't help smirking.

'Okay, if you are sure. Thanks Jules; coming, Portia?'

But the look on his face, which was one of barely hidden anger, obviously signalled he'd wanted me on my own; we trooped down to the bar.

'Jules,' I said as we sat with our drinks, 'I'm sorry if I've offended you by not responding to your repartee and overtures, rather brash though I found them, but you see, I'm still in mourning and not really used to being out in male company yet. I thought if I told you, you wouldn't think badly of me or feel so slighted, as I think you are.' I looked down and brought out a handkerchief from my joggers and dabbed my eyes. The last time I used it was on the plane with Pops when I was bawling my eyes out.

I'll have to launder it again.

'Oh God, Von. I'm sorry, I am so sorry. I'd no idea. And yes, I am a bit brash, I used not to be, but I changed and roughing it in the outback hasn't given me any...' he searched for a word.

'Finesse?' offered Portia.

Jules scowled at her as she put her hand on mine and made "there—there" type noises.

'Anyway, I thought you'd better know so you didn't think I was just being standoffish.' I sniffed, wiped my eyes and nose and stuffed the handkerchief back into my pocket. I looked up brightly but trying to keep the "weeping widow" picture. 'So, tell us about your family in France. When do you hope to see them?'

'After Scotland, a quick visit to Stratford as I said, a good week or so in London, then I'll hitch down to the south of France. I won't rush, I'll stop at another farm I worked at to say "hello". I'll go slowly and arrive somewhere about the twentieth, that will still give me time to get back to Paris for my return flight to Sydney.'

'Eight years is a long time to be gone, you all must be excited about your visit.'

'Well, I haven't contacted them yet, I thought I would surprise them, to be honest, I don't know how the meeting will go as, when I left, we had had a row and I walked out.'

'Oh Jules, that is so tragic. I'm so sorry.' Portia put her hand on the back of his, he withdrew it rapidly.

'Sorry.'

'Don't know why I told you that,' he snapped, 'none of your damned business anyway. Thanks for your reluctant company. Perhaps, Von, you should get yourself out into a man's company and have a good f***; would do you good, get you unwound. Goodbye.'

We watched him go.

'What is going on, Von? One minute you don't want to be in his company, the next you are accepting invitation for a drink and now you have really upset the poor man. Yes, okay, he's a bit smarmy and rough, but at least he recognised that and apologised—well, sort of. But what on earth was the last broadside about?'

'Portia, I promise I will tell you sometime, it will not be tomorrow or the next day but I promise I will. I'm sorry, but I think I have some information and I'm not quite sure what to do with it. I have to be careful.'

'Okay, but don't leave me in the dark for too long.'

'No longer than necessary. Come on, drink up or we'll be rushing our showers before we go out.'

We took another ten minutes enjoying each other's company sipping the wine which certainly tasted more pleasant now we were on our own and hadn't paid for it, which was a bonus, it was really too delicious to abandon.

John must have heard us coming up because he came out of his flat as the lift arrived.

'What have you done to Jules? He came storming up swearing like billy-o about you two, paid the balance he owed me and stormed out again saying he hoped Scotland was friendlier than Leeds.'

'I think I hit a raw nerve,' I said.

'It wasn't you, Von, he needn't have said anything.'

'Whatever, I hope he doesn't give you a bad review on Airbnb, John.'

'I'm not worried if he does, I'm pretty much fed up with Airbnb and think I'll just get a lodger, much simpler. What time do you two want to go? Shall we all go together? I know Von and I'll be a bit early, but the bar will be open, won't it?'

'If not, I'll get you something. Half past six suit you?'

'Fine thanks.'

He turned to go but stopped when Portia said, 'John, please don't take this the wrong way, you know I'm more than grateful you have a key to my flat for emergencies and so on, but I was a bit surprised to find Jules had opened it yesterday evening.'

'What? How can he have done? I've got the key on my ring,' he pulled a bunch from his pocket, 'see, here it is. I never leave it in the flat and if I did, I'd never ask anyone to open your door.'

'Then how did he open the door?' They both looked at me.

After a thought, I recounted the incident of the key being dropped and landing so far from the door I'd had to pick it up.

'The key he pretended to use was a decoy. He must have thrown it on purpose, then used a credit card to flip the lock while I was distracted.'

'Are you missing anything, Portia? Von? He might have gone in at other times.'

Portia and I left John for a few minutes to look in her flat, neither of us thought anything was missing. I racked my brain to remember if I'd brought anything with me to connect me with Ricard or his parents but assured myself there was nothing and as I always carry my mobile, he couldn't have had access to any communications.

'What about your property, John?' asked Portia when he re-joined us.

'So far, I've not missed anything, the trouble is though, you often don't miss things till you need them. Just because someone can get into a building using a card doesn't mean they are criminals—does it?'

'Why else would they have the knowledge or need to do it?'

'John, you do take references for your guests, don't you?'

'Yes, you bet. I think I usually ask for more than many people do.'

'And he obviously checked out alright, what surname did he give you? He only introduced himself as Jules.'

'A strange one for an Australian, but I think he said he was of French descent, so I don't know why I should think it strange; that country, like ours, is multicultural, but something along the lines of Leetor, just a moment, I'll look it up, I only checked it once in his passport.' He got out his phone and started scrolling through emails.

'How about Letour?' I asked.

'That's it, yes, have a look,' he handed me his phone and I saw a photo of the passport, 'how did you know the surname?'

'Just a hunch. John, would you forward that picture to me?'

John frowned at me and I saw he was going to object.

'What do you want it for? Surely you've not fallen for him and want a picture to remind yourself of him.' Portia grinned.

I ignored her and addressed John.

'It's something personal, John. I think, if I may have it, it will stop a great deal of hurt and potential harm, it might also give some hope for a reconciliation of a divided family.' I paused. 'It's important, John.'

'OK. But promise me you'll delete it as soon as possible. I have it for a transparent reason and promised to clear it once he left—as I do all my guests.'

I promised and gave him my email address; shortly afterwards, my phone vibrated and I checked the screen.

'Thank you, it won't be on my phone any longer than needed, I won't forward it to anyone and I'll let you know when it's been deleted.'

'And if it was of any use?'

I nodded and watched him delete the photograph from his phone. 'Goodness, the time; I need a shower, see you at six-thirty.'

As she shut the flat door, Portia said, 'You're going to have to tell me, Von. How did you know his name? What's going on? Are you in any trouble?'

'Portia, please believe me, my dear, I promise to tell you as soon as I can, but not just now. Let's get ready for the opera, you mustn't be late, they can't get on the stage without you and even if I could tell you, it will take much longer than we have time for now.'

§

The opera was magnificent; after meeting the cast backstage, we moved on to the restaurant which was set out in a much more informal manner than I'd expected, long scrubbed wooden benches and tables reminding me of a tourist "traditional village evening" I'd experienced with Mark in Bulgaria.

Outside her flat, I gave John a goodnight hug, took Portia's key which she'd retrieved from her bag and left them together in the hallway.

'Your diplomacy was noted but not necessary, Von,' said Portia as she poured a glass of wine for herself and tonic for me, 'it's not going anywhere along the romantic scale, we're only exceedingly good friends. You haven't signed "the pledge", have you?' You didn't drink any wine this evening.'

'No, I did rather overindulge when I was in Toulouse so thought I'd give it a rest for a week or so, it won't last long! And Portia,' she looked expectantly, 'I just wanted to tell you how much this weekend has meant for me from the relaxation point of view and how grateful I am for your invitation.'

'Well, we still have tomorrow. If the weather's good, I'll show you more of Leeds and we can enjoy the time together, or do I hear a "but" coming?'

'Only a partial one, but by coming here and maybe it was fate, I think I have met someone who is related to the—'

'—man you are attracted to!' she finished my sentence.

'Yes, but it's rather a tricky situation which is why I'd rather not go into it all this weekend. I really do need to talk to a couple of people and let them know what I think, I know. But rather than leave you totally in the dark, I owed you a bit of an explanation.'

'Well, thanks for describing a little bit, Von. Like you, I didn't really like the man even before you took to upsetting him, I really hope something good comes out of this and doesn't mean you'll have to get an earlier train tomorrow, you're not planning to, are you?'

'Certainly not. I'm at your disposal till the evening train, as agreed.'

'That's more of a relief than you can imagine, I've a full day planned for you so we'd better get to bed.

§ § §

The day was full of activities and meeting Portia's friends. She accompanied me to the station in the evening and waved, as we did as children, till we were out of sight of each other.

§

Returning to the apartment was not as traumatic as it had been recently, the heating left on low had kept it warm. I picked up the post from the deliveries on Friday and Saturday and saw an envelope with the now familiar copper plate writing, I put it and the others on the side in the kitchen before unpacking my case then changing into my night clothes. I poured a glass of soda water and took it to the sitting room with the letter. Once again, I took Mark's letter opener and slit open the envelope. I carefully read the reply from Ramon and Matilde which was the positive response I'd expected. I went to bed wondering what to do with my new information.

Chapter Twelve

A bad night's disturbed sleep did nothing to solve my quandary. I felt sure the man I'd met in Leeds was Ramon's second son, there were far too many similarities for me to believe otherwise. Whatever Ricard was keeping from me about his relationship with his parents and brother, I'd not gathered in Leeds; perhaps I should've been friendlier and developed a semi-relationship with the man and found out more.

Well, you missed the chance.

I went into the office but found it hard to concentrate, the words displayed on the computer screen made no sense as the various strands to the project kept getting jumbled. I knew I would be wasting time till I took steps. I hesitated before ringing Ricard, neither of us encouraged communicating during office hours, business and personal were not supposed to intrude upon each other—but if he couldn't talk, he'd either say so or not answer his phone.

'Yvonne, is something wrong?'

'I'm sorry to ring during the day, Ricard, but have you got a moment to talk?'

'Yes, of course, what is it? Is everything alright?'

'Something has come up I can't fully explain on the phone but I think I've some information I need to clear with you in person,' I took a breath, 'and then you may agree we need to share with your parents.'

Ricard was silent for a moment. 'You have asked if we could go and visit on—um, I can't remember when.'

'Yes, they have agreed, the letter came over the weekend, but I think we need to see them before the school holiday weekend. Would it be possible for you to be out of the office either Thursday or Friday this week? As you know, I am arriving in Lézignan on Tuesday evening, I have to meet with Charles Bassinet on Wednesday but can arrange to be free either Thursday or Friday.'

I heard him flick through his desk diary, like me he kept a hard copy, as well as one on his mobile. 'Yes, either day, I can re-jig my appointments if needed, or pass them on to a colleague. Yvonne, this sounds all very cloak and dagger stuff.'

'Ricard, I'll tell you more when I see you, I might be quite wrong but I can't say anything more now. By the way, how long are French passports valid for?'

'Usually about ten years, I've just had mine renewed.'

'See you at the hotel tomorrow evening, bye. Love you.' I clicked off the connection before he could ask any more.

Even though I felt marginally more settled having spoken to Ricard and alerted him, I still found concentrating hard so, after another couple of abortive hours trying to understand the overall financial set up, realising it varied from school to school so would need in-depth discussion with each institution, I closed my computer and told Andrea I was going home to pack.

'Are you alright?'

'Not really. Something rather unbalanced me over the weekend and I'm wasting time on the computer.'

'Do you want to talk?'

I thought about it but declined her offer.

'It's all a bit complicated, but hopefully things will become clearer over the coming week, then I'll be back on track again.'

'You didn't row with Portia, did you?'

'No, indeed not, we had a fantastic weekend, a wonderful time,' I rattled off all the things we'd done and people I'd met—except Jules, 'it was relaxing and stimulating.'

'OK. Well, remember I'm here if you change your mind.'

'Thanks Andrea.'

I packed clothes for a few weeks, did some ironing and ran the duster and vacuum cleaner over the flat. I thought about responding to Ramon's letter but decided not to, in case we went to the farm when I could tell them in person.

And if we do, things might alter all over again.

§ § §

'I didn't expect you in today, Yvonne.'

'I'm not off until the afternoon flight. I had hoped to see Sharon and after yesterday's conversation, to thank you again and to confirm I'll not be back in the office for some time. When I spoke with you and Patrick, before the weekend,

I realised most of what I said was prearranged anyway but thought I'd better confirm with you today. I'll be seeing *Monsieur* Bassinet tomorrow then either Thursday or Friday I'll try to sort out my problem, to save flying back just for the weekend I'll stay in Lézignan, it will be my base for the next week or two. And if you remember, the following weekend I was supposed to be flying over with Pops, so he'll travel on his own.'

'Yvonne, I don't think Patrick meant you had to tell me all your movements.'

'Probably not, but as I'd got my diary mixed up, in my head at least, I thought I'd touch base with you. Is Sharon in with Patrick now?'

'Yes, she seemed a bit wound up though.'

'We talked about her project on Friday afternoon before we went for a drink together, from what she told me, I think she'll be fine, but she was worried.'

'Do you want me to tell her you were looking for her?'

'That's a difficult one, isn't it? I don't want her to think I'm interfering but at the same time I'd like to see her as I'm concerned, especially if she needs someone to offload on.'

The intercom from Patrick's office interrupted our conversation.

'Yes Patrick?'

'Could you arrange coffee for two please, Andrea?'

'Certainly.'

'Oh, do you have another box of tissues, mine's run out.'

'I'm sure I can find one.'

'Is that good or bad?' I asked when she'd disconnected.

'Well, he often likes coffee at odd times and he has the start of a cold, so I really can't say if the tissues are for him or her.'

I returned to my office; after fifteen minutes, Trish came and said, 'Patrick wants to see you, Yvonne.'

Now what have I done?

I picked up my pad and pencil.

Sharon was sitting by Patrick's desk; he turned from looking out of the window as I entered.

'Good morning, Yvonne, I wanted to say your advice to Sharon was, as far as I can gather, impartial and non-directive, you both behaved in a manner in which I hope my employees would do, supportive and collegiate, thank you both.' He turned to Sharon. 'The project I gave you was a nasty one with your hands rather tied, you were right to ask Yvonne's advice, but more importantly you recorded every single interview and gained the cooperation of the majority of people and everyone's signature to the notes you took, as you'd been asked. Your attention to detail is superb and I anticipate, when I talk to the director who commissioned this project, the system you suggested and tried to initiate will be implemented but without the blockage.'

'So, I've been instrumental in someone losing his job?'

'Sharon, we are not responsible for the fallout from our work and the people concerned usually adapt. In this case, perhaps early retirement on a reasonable pension will be the outcome.'

'Actually, redundancy on full pay and pension would be the correct and legal outcome.,' Responded Sharon harshly as she left Patrick's office, closing the door more firmly than necessary.

'I think you might have just lost a good project manager.'

'Good lord, I hope not; she's good, such an understanding analytical brain.'

'And empathy for those who might be in the firing line, no joke intended,' I added.

'It happens sometimes.'

'I know, but she's upset.'

I grabbed Andrea's arm as I went through her office to find Sharon who was, predictably, packing her personal things into her bag. She looked at Andrea and said, 'Please look after the plant.'

'What's going on?'

'Sharon, please don't just walk out of here, think about what you're doing.'

'Yes, Yvonne, I'm the one who gets people sacked, great reputation.'

'No, you're the one who facilitates a good company get rid of the dross—with compassion and support. That man won't get slung out with nothing; what you said to Patrick as you left will go back to the managing director who will treat him appropriately, a proper discreet retirement or redundancy package, as you said. This is another thing to put into your kitbag and something to remember to put in your future project conclusions, namely a good, face-saving way out for the people who may have to be "let go".'

Sharon stopped her frantic bag packing and looked at me, I realised I was still holding Andrea's arm, she released it from my grip.

'Sharon, I don't know what happened in there but if Patrick thought you were not, in any way, up to doing a project and didn't want you on his team, he would have told you so—word for word—believe me, I've heard him do so, he's a hard-biting businessman, so if you want to stay and work with and for him, go back in there and have it out with him.'

'Kill or cure.'

We watched Sharon knock on Patrick's office door and enter before she got a response.

'And underneath the harsh business exterior is the most compassionate man I've ever known.' Andrea reflected aloud my thoughts as we walked back to her office.

Sharon looked at me and smiled as she and Patrick emerged from his office.

'It's all well,' she said.

'And all manner of things shall be well.' I responded as I tried to remember the proper quote and where it comes from.

'Yes, hopefully, Patrick has told me to take the rest of the week off with pay, then come back on Monday to discuss some other projects he has been asked to facilitate.'

'Have your break, find out the details of those on offer, take the time you need before you decide. And Sharon, can you wait till I have decided whether or not I can do the one I'm investigating now, before you agree anything with Patrick, please.'

She looked at me quizzically.

'Sorry, I can't tell you my reasons just now, but there is a possibility I won't be seeing it through. How good is your French?'

'Not bad, I read French language and literature at university alongside statistics, my mother's first language is French so we converse in French and we're bringing Lucy up bilingual, so I'd say it's good.'

'That's great! I must go now or I'll miss the plane. Enjoy your break.'

I'd left my luggage at reception and the concierge helped me load it into a taxi.

§

The journey to Lézignan was uneventful; as promised, Ricard was waiting for me. While checking into the hotel, I realised it would not be easy to explain everything in public, so ordered food from the room-service menu as Ricard was impatient to know what I had to say. I freshened up while waiting for the meal to be delivered then described, while we ate, every interaction and exchange with the man in Leeds. Ricard thought it possible the man was his brother; when I showed him the picture of the passport, he was convinced.

'So, what do we do?'

'I think you go to see your parents on either Thursday or Friday and tell them.'

'I can't just turn up unannounced.'

'No, I agree, but your father's inheritance gives you the perfect reason to go, tell him, for you to proceed further, you need to talk through some details, say something has come up needing his attention before the planned weekend.'

'Well, that's true even if not completely in context.'

'Take the papers with you in case there might be an opportunity to discuss them. As you've not had any direct contact with your parents for such a long time, I suggest you ask Marianne to ring them tomorrow and ask which day would be suitable for them.'

'You're coming too, aren't you?'

'Yes, but don't say anything about me, only you know I'm here, don't tell the others, which is why I think it would be better for you to drive and not Sven.'

'He won't say anything.'

'Marianne's very aware of people's moods, Ricard; if he tries to keep a secret from her, she'll know something's up.'

'You are probably right; I could drop Suzanne off at school then come and get you.'

'Where are you supposed to be now?'

'Working late then dinner with a colleague.'

I looked at my watch. 'Well, you'd better go then.'

'I am sure I will have to work late again tomorrow evening!'

'Yes, most likely, especially as you will be out of the office one day. Let me know tomorrow which day we're going to see your parents.'

We kissed and he started a familiar move.

'No Ricard, not tonight, you must go home.'

I unpacked my cases, after he'd reluctantly left, put my phone and laptop on to charge before having a shower and getting into bed.

I was thinking, as I dropped off to sleep, how strange it was to be so near and yet how far apart the few yards to his house made it seem, or was I kidding myself and the problem was not the physical distance but still the barrier of the emotional one.

C'est ça!

§ § §

Charles Bassinet greeted me warmly in the accepted two cheek kiss, apologising he didn't have as much time as he'd hoped to talk with me; but the meeting, which lasted well over half an hour, was very productive.

'Now, let me hand you over to my personal assistant, Vivienne, who will be able to help you with anything you need. I tend to be rather in and out of the office but she will know where to find me if you need to see me.'

Vivienne was a tall smartly dressed woman wearing her auburn hair in a chignon. It constantly amazed me how the women still dressed faultlessly while there existed a trend for men to don informal, although obviously expensive, clothes as her boss had. Her smile was broad and genuinely welcoming.

'At last, I meet the lady everyone is talking about. Welcome Yvonne—I may call you Yvonne, may I not?'

I was taken aback by this greeting. 'Who is talking about me?'

'Several of my acquaintances who met you at *Monsieur* Letour's house a little while ago.'

'Oh!'

'Do not worry, everyone is so pleased, it is time he found a lovely lady to share his life with. Come, let me show you the, rather small I am afraid, office I have had prepared for you. Although I anticipate you will probably be out a fair amount, I thought you would like a business type surrounding for your work and research rather than working in your hotel room, which should be a more restful place to relax.' She raised an eyebrow and I felt myself blushing.

Then I had an awful thought. 'Vivienne, how many people know I'm here now? Apart from you and *Monsieur* Bassinet?'

'I do not know, I assume *Monsieur* Letour does, so his family probably do, as you say, me and *Monsieur*, but who else I do not know. Have you been in touch with any of the people *Monsieur* suggested you meet? If so, they will probably realise you are expected.'

'No, I haven't made any appointments as I have to do something—personal—tomorrow or Friday, so I didn't fix any appointments until I knew which day I would be free. Vivienne, has *Monsieur* Bassinet gone out yet? I need

211

to ask him not to tell anyone I'm here yet. Please, it's important, in a couple of days, it won't matter, but just for now it does, I'm sorry I can't explain.'

I waited in the small office while Vivienne went to catch her boss and relay my message. The brightness of the room and small vase of flowers, an obviously feminine touch of welcome, did nothing to relieve my tension until she returned.

'He looked a bit bemused, but said his lips were sealed till you tell him otherwise. Are you really here to do this school or are you a secret agent undercover?' Her voice was partly joking yet conspiratorial.

'The former, I assure you, though the week before last someone questioned whether I was a spy—that too was a joke.'

'Well, whatever it is, I hope you sort it out. Now, to business, the Internet connection is good and the code is on the desk. If you want anything, please ask but first, let me introduce you to the owner of the café we use for our coffee, you do not have to use them but they can bring it over to you if you want it here, just ask them to credit it to the office account.'

Vivienne showed me the "facilities" as we went to the café, where I followed her lead and picked up a coffee and pastry before returning to set up the computer I'd been provided with.

'Thank you so much for your welcome and understanding, Vivienne, and for the beautiful flowers on my desk.'

She gave me her winning smile, again saying I was more than welcome and reiterated I should be sure to ask for anything I needed.

I transferred the information I'd gleaned, on how the education system is organised, quality controlled and financed, from my laptop to the computer then started to review it again so, after three hours and more coffee I decided my head couldn't absorb any more and went for a walk. Following Vivienne's directions, I went to the Tourist Office where I obtained a couple of maps, having made sure, with the guidance of the assistant, several roads in which the schools where my contacts worked, were clearly marked. I also picked up copies of current bus, metro and train timetables as I would need those. Even though I knew it would be closed, I walked to the nearest school to see what the exterior looked like. I walked along the road and realised I must have passed the school as the road ended in a park; retracing my steps I found a small plaque set in the wall of a building stating its function and the director's name, no wonder I had missed it.

I arrived back at the office to find Vivienne about to lock up.

'Sorry, have I kept you waiting?'

'I should have said, you will have to stick to my arrival and leaving times, Yvonne, I cannot let you have the codes, it is to do with insurance.'

'I understand, so if I'm late, please lock up, don't wait for me. I'll just get my laptop and if I'm not in tomorrow, please don't worry.'

We parted at the office door, going in opposite directions.

§ § §

I was anxious to know from Ricard the outcome of Marianne's phone call to his parents. 'So, what did your parents say?' I asked once we had kissed on his arrival at the hotel.

'They said to go tomorrow; apparently, my father was not surprised I need to talk about the inheritance, but was getting a bit concerned as the package had been with me for some time before I had contacted him. Marianne said she had hedged a bit about why this was.'

'Did she make any comment herself?'

'She was a bit inquisitive as to why I wanted to go this week when we are booked to go next weekend. I told her I had found a complication which might not be appropriate to discuss with Suzanne and your father around. All a bit flimsy I suppose, but the best I could think of without a full lie.'

'Let's hope we can sort something out tomorrow. Are we eating or do you want to get back?'

'Shall we eat a bit later? I am hungry for something else.'

I found myself enveloped in his arms.

§

Later, we showered and Ricard left me in the foyer after we'd eaten in the hotel restaurant, saying, 'I'll pick you up at a quarter to nine.'

§ § §

The roads were clear once we were out of Lézignan and between other large towns we passed through. The French scenery between the urban areas was developing beautiful autumnal colours. The number of small to medium-sized lorries increased as we the entered Corbiere and Rousillion regions.

'Grapes are still being harvested; a number of small growers form a co-operative for producing the local wines. My father used to send his grapes to one.'

Although the sun had been working valiantly to escape from behind its jail of cloud during our journey, as we got closer to Ricard's parent's farm, in the village of Ortaffa, nestling in the lower Pyrenees, it broke through and shone on the snow-capped peaks of the mountains and the distinctive shape of the Canigou.

There was no snow up there last time I was here.

Ricard must have seen my gaze and followed it.

'*Papom* took me up there once, long ago.'

'Who's *Papom*?'

'Goodness, I have not thought of him like that for years. It is what I called my father as a child.' Ricard was silent for a moment, lost in his own thoughts. 'Not at this time of year though, far too dangerous even though we were fit, the mountains are only safe for those who live there or know them and the weather intimately.'

'Some people had to brave them when they escaped from Spain though.'

'Yes, years ago. Did you go to the "Suisse Hospital" when you were down here at the "retreat"?

'No, someone mentioned it, but Patience didn't think it would be a good idea for me to visit then. Have you?'

'No. I think the restoration of the building was in progress when I left and obviously there has not been a recent opportunity.'

'Have you thought how you're going to approach your parents and the potential identity of the man I met?'

'No and not from the want of trying, but I honestly do not think there is any doubt it is Jules.'

Ricard turned off the road through some new looking farm gates, the track did not have the usual rutted surface I'd anticipated, although not perfect, it was reasonably smooth.

'Wow!' Ricard stopped at the end of the track in front of a small farmhouse. 'It has not changed.'

'Did you expect it to have done so?'

'Well, yes. Marianne said they had made alterations to accommodate paying guests, but it does not look as if they have. The barn looks as if it has had some care, but I cannot see much else different.'

'Are you alright?'

Ricard had suddenly lost a lot of colour. I turned my head to where he was looking, the old oak door to the farmhouse now stood open, waiting there was a woman wearing a 1940's wrapround overall, covering a pale blue woollen dress, and comfortable looking flat shoes. The expression on her round face was one of welcome.

'Come on, you can't sit in the car now you've got this far.' I got out of the car and went towards the woman. Seen at close quarters, her skin was silky though gently tanned, presumably from long hours working outside. Her smile creased her smooth skin into lines of delight and exposed a set of her own teeth, a little uneven but strong. I took both her extended hands in mine and found the firm grip reassuring.

'You must be Yvonne, we were not expecting you, Marianne said nothing about Ricard bringing you. We were not expecting you till next weekend.'

'No, *Madame*, Marianne didn't know I was coming.'

'Oh! Well never mind, you are welcome, Yvonne.' Her voice held an element of concern. 'Come, come on in and it is Matilde, not *Madame*, as you know.'

She turned her attention to Ricard who had got out of the car and was standing behind me.

'Hello Ricard.'

'*Mamon.*'

Chapter Thirteen

Neither of them moved but I saw Matilde's eyes turn as Ramon approached across the yard. He was wearing his work clothes, they appeared to be the same jacket and trousers he was wearing when I first saw him, his only acknowledgment to the change in season was a light weight scarf wrapped around his neck. Ricard changed his position to face him but neither man advanced. There was a hiatus, almost a standoff between them till Ramon took a step forward and extended a hand in welcome. As their hands touched, what I expected to be a handshake turned into a strong embrace, initiated by Ramon as he pulled his son into his arms. Ricard responded and they both clapped each other on the back.

'*Papom.*'

I let out a sigh of relief, not realising I'd been holding my breath and Matilde's intake of breath sounded loud as she rapidly moved to her son, after their embrace, she turned sharply, wiping tears from her eyes with the hem of her overall saying, 'Well, it has been a long time, what brings you here now? Not of your own volition, I am sure.'

'Matilde, do not ruin this visit before it is started,' her husband begged, 'let the boy get his feet over the thresh hold before you start nagging him. Get the coffee on and I expect we could all do with a cognac with it. Yvonne, it is a pleasure to see you again though it is a surprise. I hope it does not mean next weekend is to be cancelled, we are both looking forward to seeing Suzanne and the others and of course, your father.'

'I sincerely hope it won't be.' I smiled and accepted the coffee and brandy set out in front of me together with a few crisp homemade biscuits.

Ramon looked at me over his coffee cup, resting it down again he said,

'What is wrong?'

'*Papom*,' Ricard again used the childhood name for his father which I saw made his father smile, 'we think we might have a problem over next weekend.'

'Oh no, what is it?'

'I will let Yvonne explain but I have to say I agree with her.'

Ramon and Matilde turned to me expectantly, once more I saw the likeness in the three men.

'Forgive me if I start right from the beginning, it will be easier for me to explain and possibly for you to see the links.' I related everything, as I'd done to Ricard on Tuesday evening, telling them of the places the man planned to visit but omitting the outline time schedule. I stopped and drew my phone from my bag, selected the photograph and handed it to Ramon. He did not react or say anything just passed it to Matilde who gasped and put her hand to her mouth.

'Obviously, the man I saw was a little older than the one in the passport photograph.'

'Yes, yes, but what has this to do with your visit next weekend?'

'According to his travel plans, which I didn't tell you in as much detail as he told me, he anticipates arriving here on Sunday week.'

'Has he been in touch with you at all, *Papom*, since he left?'

'No, not a word. Matilde, has he contacted you and you have not told me?'

'No Ramon, we have never had secrets and I hope we never shall.' She got up from the table and started to make fresh coffee.

'You agree it is Jules then?' Ricard asked.

'Yes,' said Ramon, 'yes, it will be good to see him after all this time—as it is to see you, Ricard.'

'How dare you say that—after what you have done? After what you know? You will welcome him back?' Ricard was on his feet scraping the wooden chair across the flag stoned floor.

'What are you shouting about, Ricard? What are you saying?'

Ramon was now on his feet too and Matilde stood stock still by the cooker holding the coffee pot.

'You may have no secrets between yourselves, but you kept one from me for over ten years. You behave like this and expect me to be in the same place as him next week? How dare you?'

'Ricard, this is not the way, go outside and cool off, let me talk to Ramon and Matilde.'

He stormed out swearing extremely uncouth anti-paternal, maternal and fraternal oaths and sentiments.

'What has got into him, Yvonne? What is he on about? Do you know?'

'Not all of it, Ramon, the whole story he will not tell me but from the disjointed and half stories he has tried to tell me, I think it is possible he blames you two for something; he won't tell me fully, but possibly he blames you for Charlotte staying on her last summer when she had the accident with the farm equipment.'

'That does not make sense, Charlotte wanted to stay.'

'Yes, but underneath I get the impression, because she had the accident, he thinks her strength was affected, which had some effect on her dying when Suzanne was born. But I have a feeling, something stronger than a feeling, there is more to come.'

'He is being ridiculous,' Matilde came to the table and sat down, 'he was distraught after her death, but he still came to see us, brought Suzanne with him. And why after visiting so many times should he suddenly blame us? He came to say goodbye to his brother before he went to Australia, of course we did not see much of Suzanne for a long while afterwards, till Marianne managed to persuade Ricard to let her bring our granddaughter.'

Grief can make you do some strange things even if on the inside you think you are behaving normally.

'No guilt on our part and I cannot see how the accident would have affected the birth; if it had been a contributing factor, there would have been severe problems during the pregnancy.'

'It did not.' We'd not heard Ricard come back and we had no idea how much of the conversation he'd heard, he walked over and refilled his brandy glass and drank some quickly.

'Then what are you so angry about, son? We do not understand.'

'You do not understand? He must have told you and you kept quiet. No guilt? Ha!' He finished his brandy and reached for the bottle again.

Ramon intercepted him and poured a small amount into Ricard's glass.

'I suggest you sit down and tell us, as calmly as you can, what it is you are so cross with us about.' Ramon's firm voice, although quiet, was a mixture of hurt and aggression.

'Right—and at the end, you tell me I have no right to be enraged with you.' Ricard spat the words out. Gripping his glass, he started slowly.

'You remember I was cross with Jules for what I saw as abandoning you both and going to Australia?' He looked at both his parents who nodded in response to the question. 'Even so, as you know, during his last few months I visited frequently and obviously brought Suzanne with me; on the evening before he was due to leave, I came with Marianne and Suzanne to wish him luck. After we had eaten in the evening, I went outside to talk to him and say a final brotherly farewell. He was bedding down the milk cows in the barn, the weather was too cold to leave them out.

'Before he closed the barn door he turned, to this day I do not know how much was due to the light shining from the oil lamp hanging in the barn or hate mixed with triumph, but I had never seen such glowing distain on anyone's face before or since.'

Ricard stopped and sipped his brandy. 'But he sneered and I remember the exact words he used. "Got the sister too now, have you? You may be alright at getting it up, but you are not man enough to get a child. Three years of marriage! What have you been doing? Shooting blanks? One time with me, okay very reluctantly, she fought like a tiger as hard as she could, but I had her and bingo! Suzanne!"' Ricard stopped and gulped down the last of his brandy.

Matilde put her hands to her face. I couldn't move and Ramon stared at his son in horror. After a moment, Ricard continued, 'It took me a moment to realise what he was saying. Then I just saw red and thrashed out, he was physically stronger than me, but I was more agile and able to land punches more accurately. Eventually, he went down and I kicked and kicked till I heard *Papom's* voice shout, "Stop it, Ricard, you will kill him." The way I was feeling, I did not care if I did, I gave Jules one more heavy kick in the ribs and walked away from him.'

'Not only from Jules, but you walked away from us as well.'

'Hardly surprising under the circumstances, I think you'll agree. Protecting Jules for years, not saying anything over the last ten years.' He reached for the bottle again, but before he touched it, I passed him my untouched glass.

'But we had no idea, Ricard. Charlotte said nothing when we asked about the state she was in and her dishevelled clothes, nothing about being raped, she said she had got tangled up in the harness and harrow, even joked about losing her concentration as she was thinking about you, missing you...' his voice petered out.

'Same story she told me.'

'Dear Lord, no wonder you hate us. You really thought he had told us what he had done? And you think he is Suzanne's father?'

Ricard looked at his parents with tears cascading down his face, he just nodded.

'It must have taken a while for her to get over that before having sex with you, but she did and you two made Suzanne.'

Ricard stretched across the table and took his mother's hand.

'No *Mamon*. Yes, of course, we had sex but you were not listening to what Jules said. He was right whether he knew it or not.'

'What do you mean, son? I do not understand. On your own admission, you both continued making love.'

'You are right but before any of this, I was worried Charlotte had not conceived during our three years of marriage, I saw a doctor and gave a sperm sample. When she told me she was pregnant, it never occurred to me I had not fathered Suzanne so I did not follow up with the doctor. But after the encounter with Jules, I returned to the doctor to see the result of the sperm sample I had given several months before.

'As Jules so crudely said, I had "been shooting blanks". It was Jules who, with Charlotte, made Suzanne.' He stopped for a moment then putting great emphasis into his voice continued, 'But it does not make her any less my daughter. If he thinks he is coming down here and taking her from me, he has another big think coming.'

'He would not, would he?' Matilde's voice was full of horror and fear.

'It's possibly on his mind, he emphasised the word "daughter" when he told me he was planning to see his "goddaughter".'

'That will not happen.' Ramon's voice was quiet yet echoed through the room.

Simple domestic tasks filled the following silence, everyone addressed their own deep thoughts.

What about me, Lord? Now what do I do?

I moved the used cups to the sink, washed and dried them and replaced them on the table. Ramon refilled his and Ricard's brandy glasses and offered me another which I declined as did Matilde, who said matter-of-factly,

'Do not drink too much, the cassoulet is just about ready.'

I wasn't sure food was on anyone's mind.

Ricard stood up and took my hand, excusing us from his parents and led me outside where he held me close.

'What a waste of years, what a waste, they had no idea.' He sobbed into my shoulder.

'I don't think so much was supposed to come out today, it must have been really hard for you. For all of you, in fact.'

He pulled back and looked at me, trying to control his tears and fears, he asked, 'Well, now you know, has the problem preventing you from marrying me been cleared up?'

I nodded. 'Possibly.'

'But your face and voice tell me it has created another.'

I nodded.

'What now? You said not knowing was the blockage to us getting married. Will you marry me?'

'I would, Ricard, but—'

'But? You no longer love me enough? Changed your mind?'

'None of those, but I cannot accept without telling you I'm pregnant.'

'But I have always used those awful sheaths, even though I thought I did not need to.'

'That's what I thought, but you didn't, not the first time.'

'But what about my sample report?'

'You have several choices,' I checked them off on my fingers, 'your sample got mixed up with someone else's or the reports did and you were never sterile in the first place; maybe you are one of the few who actually regain their fertility; or this is a miraculous conception; or I am experiencing a phantom pregnancy, which is doubtful as the test was positive; or, finally, …you think I've been unfaithful to you over the time we've known each other.'

With his jealousy over Patrick, can he think this?

I waited.

'No, I would never think that, Yvonne. Kiss me, I never thought this would happen to me.'

'Again, Ricard. Happened again. Ricard, there is every possibility Suzanne is your blood daughter and Charlotte didn't conceive when she was raped by Jules, but when you and Charlotte were together either before, during or after the holiday at the farm.'

'I wish I could know for certain, but my feelings towards Suzanne will never change. So, now will you marry me?'

'Are you sure you don't want to go and see the doctor again first?'

'I am sure I do not. Will you?'

'Yes please.'

We clung to each other, initially not kissing, just holding tight and close but then the inevitable deep penetrating kiss started.

'I wish we could go to bed.' He whispered.

'Later.'

'Are you two coming up for air sometime? Your mother is serving food and if you do not eat it, I will be having it every meal for a week.' Ramon's gentle voice roused us from our private world.

'Ricard, it's early days in the pregnancy, only about six weeks, so it's early days and things can still go wrong, so please, let's say nothing yet, a bit later when I'm further on.'

'I wondered why you were not drinking so much. Please, can we get married soon?'

'Yes, I don't want to look too obvious as I walk down the aisle!'

'*Mamon, Papom*, there is something wonderful we have to tell you, Yvonne has agreed to marry me, now she knows the reason for my not contacting you.'

'I am also glad to know the reason, sorry, not the reason, but why you took the attitude you did, knowing does put it into context.' Ramon clung to his son then continued. 'A triple celebration—the truth, reconciliation and marriage—honoured with good honest local wine. What more could anyone want?'

Nothing now. It all feels right.

The wine was poured.

'Please raise your glasses. To my beautiful bride-to-be.'

There followed more handshakes, kisses and hugs and a couple more toasts before the meal was put on the table. We sat and Matilde said grace before serving us. I was surprised to realise how hungry I was and watched, with relief, the others were eating too.

'I don't think either Ricard or I had expected the meeting today to have turned out as it has. I'm sorry it was so traumatic for you all. So, the original reason for my father to come next weekend has rather evaporated.'

'We hope he will still come; I have been looking forward so much to seeing you again and when you asked if your father could come too, we were pleased. Now this awful misunderstanding has been resolved and with your news, we can all move on.'

'To the future,' said Ricard and we all raised our glasses in acknowledgement.

'When is the wedding to be? Please give us plenty of notice, you realise not only is this still a working farm but as you may have heard from Marianne and Suzanne, we also take in guests, especially during the summer.'

'It will be soon, as we can't see any point in waiting too long now the big problem has been resolved.'

'Where do you sleep your visitors, *Mamon*? You don't seem to have done any building on the farmhouse.'

'My goodness, of course, you have only been in the kitchen since you arrived, as you see we have modernised it and kept the farmhouse effect. Guests really enjoy it and often sit around the table talking for hours after eating. Come and see the accommodation, we found an excellent architect who designed and then supervised the building of six rooms all with en-suite facilities. It is cleverly camouflaged to look like the old barn buildings and joined to the farmhouse by a short corridor.

This simple description didn't prepare me or Ricard for the attached building we finally reached. To access it, we walked from the kitchen into the original small hallway.

'This part of the house,' said Ramon, 'apart from the kitchen which you've seen, has not been altered, nor the upstairs.'

Off the hallway we entered a large sitting room where we stopped. I felt it had retained the wonderful happy family feeling which must have existed despite the arguments during their sons' teenage years.

'This has hardly changed, *Papom*, still the same old couches, bookshelves, pictures,' Ricard opened one of the doors of the low level fitted cupboards, 'my goodness, you still have our old toys! And some books too.'

'Suzanne plays with them and we have reading sessions in the evenings when she is here.'

'Like we used to do, *Mamon*?'

'Yes, holidays are no reason why she should not keep up her reading and learning.'

'As you always told us too. I remember Jules fidgeted during the reading sessions clutching one of his toy tractors or such like, I thought...' he stopped, 'never mind.'

'Come through here, Yvonne.' Matilde had pulled back a heavy curtain hung on a pole across a square archway exposing a second room furnished as a dining room. A little light came through from the sitting room but the evening darkness gave none through the large picture window, almost filling the length of one wall. She walked to the window in front of which were a couple of comfortable armchairs facing outwards.

'There is a wide panoramic view over the countryside from here, you cannot see it very well now of course, but there is a patio out there which is lovely in the summer and we often sit here, inside, and read by the window in the Spring and Autumn evenings when it is a bit too cold to sit outside.'

She turned to the small old oak table in the centre of the room, which to me seemed too miniscule for the room and was dominated by the heavy carved sideboard. Four chairs were placed round it and several more set back against the walls.

'We will extend the table and eat in here next weekend, we do not use it much now. The doors,' she pointed to the arch, 'were taken away some years ago when the boys were small, so they and their friends could run around more freely when the weather was too bad to play outside.'

'They can go back again if you would like them, Matilde, they are wrapped securely in one of the outhouses.'

'Maybe, one day, Ramon, they would certainly reduce the draft.'

We retraced out steps and the curtains were pulled across again.

'Those rooms may not have changed much but the farm office has altered a great deal, *Papom*.' Ricard had crossed the hallway to a room on the opposite side which was furnished with modern desks on which stood two computers and a printer; shelves around the room were filled with box files and ring binders all neatly labelled in copper plate print, indicating their contents—tax returns in year order; insurances for the farm; equipment; domestic; buildings; contents and so on. Another section was devoted to the holiday accommodation business—advertising; returns; bookings; menus; the list seemed endless.

Ricard turned to his father and spoke quietly yet firmly clenching then stretching his fingers in an action I'd seen him do before when he was having some difficulty in expressing an emotion. I wondered what was troubling him now.

'It was all a farce.'

'What was, son?'

'You, needing my help with the inheritance, you are perfectly capable of dealing with it yourself.'

There was no hesitation in Ramon's response.

'Capable yes, but time-wise, short. The original letter, as you would have noticed, came just before the peak of the season for both the farm and the tourists, it sat in the "pending" tray for some time as I did not have time, so thought you could help. I have to admit I had hoped it would also save me some solicitor's fees.'

'Your speech sounded as if you were prepared and had it ready to give when you thought I was coming on my own to discuss it.'

'Would I have got away with it if we had not sorted out what you really came to see us about?'

'The situation would not have arisen as I would not have come had it not been for the other matter. The inheritance was only an excuse.'

'Well, you were deceitful in giving your reason for coming and not telling us Yvonne was coming too.'

'For goodness' sake, you two, do not start an argument over nothing. Does it really matter now? Come on and let me show you the rooms.' Matilde brokered a possible pointless disagreement.

The men shook their heads at each other and smiled. Ramon seemed to me to have become less hunched, more upright thus taller since they were again together.

'I will get the papers later, they are in the car.' Ricard put his hand on his father's shoulder as we walked through to see the guests' accommodation.

We were shown how the six rooms are approached from outside, into a communal area provided with shelves marked with the room number where guests were asked to leave their walking boots and hooks similarly marked where heavy outdoor wear could be hung. Then into a smaller central area containing a domestic fridge, a kettle and coffee making machine, off which were the rooms.

'We had thought about making it totally self-catering but taking advice about the problems of hygiene and human nature we decided to provide *table d'hôte*, we serve in the kitchen,' Explained Ramon.

'That must be an enormous amount of work on top of the farm.'

'Yes, but Matilde employs a couple of girls from the village for the rooms and sometimes to help with the food preparation. We only take prior bookings so know how many people will be here and for how long. We advertise mainly for walkers and hikers who are out most of the time and at the end of the day the last thing they want to do is cook, so it really works well.'

Matilde joined in, 'Also, I wanted to ensure people ate the local food in the local style which I like to show off, it is a good use of my time in the winter as I can get a lot of basic preparation done and freeze it.'

The rooms were furnished comfortably with beds to be joined or separated for double or single use, a couple of easy chairs, a small desk, an upright chair, and ample clothes hanging space.

'I plan for you all to be in here next weekend, we could not afford to extend the old house as well as build this, so the bathroom arrangements would be difficult to manage with eight people. But I expect Suzanne will want to use the room she usually has—your old room, Ricard.'

'We will be fine in here next weekend, thank you,' I said.

'You are welcome to come and go via the kitchen at the front unless you prefer the back, of course.'

'Depending on what happens,' said Ricard, 'we might need a bolt hole. Should we start thinking about any sort of action plan? Will you put him up if he does come? I do not want him anywhere near Suzanne, so it may be a case of rethinking about where we all sleep—or even us leaving if he stays.'

'Talking of staying, it is very dark now and the country roads are not much fun—especially if you have not driven them recently—let alone the alcohol still in your veins—can you two stay tonight or do you have to get back? As you see, we have plenty of accommodation!'

Matilde's voice had an urgency, now her son was back with her, she didn't want to lose any time with him. I wondered if she dreaded he might distance himself again after a confrontation with his brother.

Ricard turned to me and said, 'Your call, Yvonne. I cleared my diary for tomorrow and told Marianne to expect me or not.'

I hesitated.

How do I explain another day out from work? Patrick would understand, would Monsieur Bassinet?

'For goodness' sake, Yvonne, what is there to consider? I cannot drive nor can you, you are not listed on the car's insurance.' Ricard's voice penetrated my thoughts. He had obviously caught up his mother's yearning.

'A toothbrush?' I answered.

'Ever the romantic, obviously,' said Ramon.

226

'I will get the papers and parcel.' Ricard went out to the car.

'I must go and see to the cows. Excuse me.'

'May I come with you, Ramon?'

'Of course, there is a thick coat at the front door and several pairs of boots, one of which should fit you. Come.'

I followed him out to the field where the cows stood by the gate waiting patiently. We stood silently together for a while.

'Are you bringing them in for the night?'

'Ah, no, not yet, they stay out till it gets too cold, several weeks yet. And now a sad time to remember.'

'Sorry, I didn't mean to raise it again.'

'No, no, it is good it is now out in the open but more importantly, we have Ricard back again.'

'So why did you come to see the cows?'

'I just needed to get some air and time to think.'

'I'm sorry, you should have refused my request to come with you.'

'No problem, but why did you ask to come?'

'The same reason as you. Thank you. I'll leave you now.'

He patted a cow who snorted.

'I will come in shortly. Just a few more minutes. Beautiful air and sufficient time for thoughts.'

'You smell of fresh air and cows.' Ricard embraced me as I returned to the kitchen.

'And you smell of garlic.'

'*Mamon* has had me hard at work helping her prepare the meal. She does not believe I can do anything in the kitchen.'

I watched them both for a while putting together the various ingredients.

'Is this the preparation Marianne makes for the meals we eat? Does she do this every day?'

'I think so, most days anyway. At the moment she has Lucille to help, of course, as she is teaching her.'

My heart sank. Did Ricard expect me to do the same when we were married?

I decided to ask the question.

'Did Charlotte do this too? Is this what you expect of me?'

I've never heard such a hearty laugh emanate from Ricard which was shortly joined by Matilde. Ramon entered the kitchen and somehow between their guffaws they explained their laughter, immediately Ramon joined in too. I was suitably reassured, slaving over a hot stove was not required as part of the marriage contract. Apparently, Charlotte hadn't the culinary skills of her sister.

Now he was not having to drive, Ricard enjoyed some more wine with his parents which I felt they were all rather wanting after today's exposures. We ate in the kitchen and once the meal was cleared, moved to the dining room and settled at the table on which, before his culinary duties, Ricard had laid out the documents and letters Ramon had received from the solicitor. In the centre of the table, he'd placed the bag, with its remaining contents, two fresh wine glasses and a bottle of wine.

Referring to various documents as he went, Ricard briefly outlined what the papers in front of us showed, which was a not insubstantial inheritance consisting of a chateau and estate, several other houses, the large family house, a couple of factories and a significant amount of money in various forms of cash, bonds, shares and so on.

'I will need to get expert advice on inheritance law and taxes due *Papom*, which will be an expense I cannot avoid, but my understanding is that, as you are the only son and there are no other surviving relatives you will be the sole beneficiary. But I think we are talking several zeros. It will take some time to finally sort it out.'

'And in the meantime?'

'In the meantime, it might be advisable for someone to go and look at the factories with a view to seeing whether they are viable and what they are doing; check up on the houses and look at the investments and make sure they are favourable, ethical and legitimate.'

'So, I could be a millionaire, or until further exploration into the assets and the tax, I could be back to where I am now.'

'Yup!' smiled Ricard, 'except, my lord Baron, you also inherit the title of a long vanished semi-nobility when land was given in exchange for allegiance to the local lord. Whether the lands you inherit are part of the original estate I do not know; of course, the title is of no practical use now, but, strangely enough, there is something in the old baronial documents which caught my interest. Please bear with me.'

He put the two fresh glasses in front of Ramon and Matilde and asked Ramon to pour a small amount of wine into his glass; after he'd done so he instructed Matilde to put her fingers over her glass; turning again to his father he said, 'Now pour some wine into *Mamon*'s glass.' Ramon did as he was asked then stopped, realising he was pouring wine onto Matilde's fingers.

'Now *Papom*, lick the wine from her fingers.' He did so.

They both looked with bemusement at their son who turned to me.

'Do you remember?'

I nodded. 'So, it was an old family tradition all along.'

'I remember now,' said Ramon, 'my father told me this happened when he proposed to my mother, as a child I thought nothing of it, just silly old people getting too romantic for their age.'

'As far as I have been able to gather, according to the records, you are supposed to drink the wine down in one gulp, which is why the measure had to be small.' They did so and Ramon refilled their glasses.

'There are accounts of this happening over the centuries in this Baron's family, descendent after descendant. But more to the point is this,' once again he paused, pulled the bag towards him and removed a box which he opened, 'the engagement ring your father gave your mother and the wedding rings they exchanged. They are old, having been passed from generation to generation through the male line—bar one—till now.' Ricard passed them one by one to his father.

Ramon turned to Matilde holding the engagement ring in an offering. She shook her head. 'I am happy with the one I have, thank you.'

I noticed there was no engagement ring on her finger.

Ramon nodded and put the ring down. He picked up the wedding ring and offered this. Again, she shook her head.

'I am more than happy with the one I have. Thank you.' She smoothed the brass curtain ring around her finger. She then picked up the ring in front of her and offered it to Ramon who did exactly as his wife did—another brass curtain ring.

'I think we will continue the tradition of the rings passing down the male line, thank you.' He put the rings back into the box and moved it gently across the table to Ricard.

'They are very old, *Papom*, I've had them checked out.'

'Good, then use them as you wish, I give them to you.'

Ricard accepted the box and extracted the engagement ring.

'Well? I acknowledged your acceptance earlier, but there was no ring. Will you accept this ring as a representation of my love for you for ever?'

'Thank you, Ricard, but you remember I still wear the rings I exchanged with Mark. Am I able to wear both?'

'In answer, I have to ask you another question. Will you ever forget Mark?'

'Well, in return, I have to ask you a similar one. Will you ever forget Charlotte?'

Matilde's voice broke the silence when neither of us responded to the other.

'Neither of you will be able, nor should you be able, to forget previous loves, previous lives, by some strange incidences, through grief and a cancelled flight you two met, you are together and in love. Take the chance, what have you to lose?'

'A lot if I don't accept the ring,' I said, 'his love, his family and a happy future.'

Ricard put the ring on the ring finger of my right hand, kissed it and smiled whispering, 'We will sort out the rings later.'

The following kiss was long and sweet and clapped by Matilde and Ramon.

'Matilde, may I ask where your engagement ring is?'

She pulled a locket on a long chain from her dress. Inside, behind a glass cover, was the remains of a ring made from twisted grasses.

'It is a bit fragile now, so I keep it in here. For years it sat in an envelope until we could afford the locket.'

I could say nothing, just watched her calm face looking at her husband, their hands touching.

We sat and talked for a while before Ramon said, it was all very well and good, for the office workers to sleep in late, but his cows expected him at five thirty. He bid us all a goodnight and went to bed. Matilde found us some toiletries from the stock she kept for holidaymakers who, she had found, often needed to replenish their supplies, then followed her husband to bed.

Eventually, we slept.

Chapter Fourteen

Ricard and I emerged from the room about eight o'clock. Ramon had finished the milking and had returned the cows to the field. He joined us from his office as we passed the door on our way to the kitchen where Matilde greeted us warmly. We sat down to a breakfast of slices of home cured ham, eggs, freshly baked bread and strawberry jam made by Ramon—apparently his speciality—served with the traditional large cups of café au lait. Fresh fruit rounded off the meal.

'Do you want to take back sorting out your inheritance, *Papom*? We now know why you asked me to do it, but you are more than capable and perhaps you would prefer to.'

'No, but thank you. If you are happy to continue with it I would be grateful, it does sound as if it could be quite an undertaking and anyway the papers have been signed giving you full authority, leave things as they are.'

'Alright, if you are sure,' Ricard nodded, 'these places will have to be visited sometime. I will get reports and copies of the financial situations from the people in charge of the factories. Your father's house has been shut down so should be visited urgently.'

'Can we get next weekend out of the way before we start planning anything. Neither I nor your mother slept much last night, we are quite concerned about Jules possibly turning up unannounced—at least we have some sort of warning though.'

'Should we cancel coming after all? I know it will be a disappointment, but at least there will be no chance of him meeting Suzanne or Ricard having a fight with Jules.'

'I think, Yvonne, my parents will need some support next weekend, whether he comes or not, so we need to stick to the visit. There is a chance he will not turn up, his plans were vague and he also might think it better not to come after such a long time.'

'He was pretty focussed on his god-daughter when he spoke of her.'

'Why would he think of coming here though if he wanted to see her?' asked Ricard.

'It cannot be to ask us for your address, you were in your current house when he left, and remember, neither he nor Charlotte had said anything about what had occurred nor had you after the fight. So presumably, as far as he is concerned, there is no argument between him and us.'

'Which there was not until we heard what you said yesterday. I put his silence down to just not bothering to keep in touch.'

'On the other hand, *Mamon*, he could think I told you and maybe he has been feeling guilty and thought you would not want to be reminded.'

'Then why, for goodness' sake, come now? I do not understand.' Matilde almost screamed and went into floods of tears. 'I am frightened of what might happen.'

'The unknown is always a fear, my dear.' Ramon went to his wife and put a comforting arm around her.

'Apart from mounting a guard at the end of the track, I cannot see we can do anything until we see if he actually comes. Can you, *Papom*?'

'No. I think the main thing will be for everyone to hold on to their tempers, preventing any more fighting.'

'My father is quite good at diffusing situations but he will have to know the reason for your misunderstanding over the years, before he comes.'

'Of course, he must be told, it would be wrong to keep him ignorant of this, and without him knowing it will be difficult for him to intercede if needed. He might also be able to protect Suzanne better if he knows.'

'But *Papom*, Suzanne must not be told, I do not want her ever to think I am not her father.'

'Ricard, you know she will always think of you as her father, she adores you. She is not stupid and is very sensitive to atmospheres, it might be better, at some point she does know—in fact, if Jules comes, she might well sense there is something more going on, than just a long-lost brother coming back.'

'Yvonne, I will do whatever I can to protect her from knowing, she must not be told directly and if she is—then I and only I will do so,' Ricard banged his fist on the table, causing the crockery to clatter and one cup to fall over, 'do you all understand?'

A stunned silence followed this unexpected emotional outburst. We all murmured assent then Ramon said,

'Ricard, that is exactly the sort of reaction we cannot afford to happen next weekend, especially in front of Suzanne. Do you understand?'

'Yes, of course. I apologise to you all. I love her so much I do not want her to be hurt.'

'Come on, son, a walk in the fresh air before you two go, stretch your legs before the journey.'

The two men, reunited after so many years through a terrible misunderstanding, walked out of the house, once an estranged place, now home again.

I helped Matilde clear away the breakfast things.

'I'll go and put the bed straight for next weekend, Ricard and I can use the same room, so no need for any linen change—unless you have guests.'

'No, not next week. If we have a late booking, we can use the other rooms, thank you. We will have another coffee before you leave.'

This was, I understood, a statement not a question. When I returned from the room, Matilde and I sat at the table, coffee in front of us.

'He is looking well, now the strain of yesterday's discussions has worn off. It is so good to have him back, as he said yesterday, such a waste of years. But at least we have heard a bit about what he has been doing and how he is, from Marianne on her visits with Suzanne, I am so grateful she kept on at Ricard to let her come, she is such a joy and we have been blessed with her company and watching her grow.'

I said nothing, waiting for the inevitable questions which came next.

'Have you considered the effect it will have on Marianne when you marry and move in permanently? She has been with Ricard for nearly ten years now, what sort of relationship do you think you will have?'

'Yes, I've thought hard and long. My main area of concern is not my relationship with Marianne, but how the relationship between three of us and Suzanne will be managed. I already see the odd occasion when Ricard will permit Suzanne to do something which, from the expression on her face, Marianne disapproves. I have certainly not had any need or felt it to be my place to interfere directly with any of the behaviour or discipline issues. She is usually so well-behaved and mature, I don't see there will be any problems—maybe later, when she is a bit older and wants to be independent, things might change. I think it is something to be aware of and go carefully.'

Was I parroting Sharon?

'Yes, there are always different views even between husband and wife and their own children. Just be careful of yourself.'

'I will. I think all relationships will change when we are married and again when Sven and Marianne are married, so we'll all need to be aware of the shifts.'

'I am so glad to have met you at last, Suzanne has written such lovely letters about you and Ramon was singing your praises about how you met and so on. I do not think they got it quite right though.'

I looked at her in horror; what was wrong?

'Do not look so worried, my dear. They understated your looks, love and sensible approach. Welcome to the family, Yvonne.' She leant close and hugged me.

We left the farm late morning confirming we would arrive about mid-morning the following Saturday. We still had no plan of action as none of us could think of one. Ricard didn't go into any detail about what he and his father talked about while they were outside but I knew it was a good discussion and he was at peace with his parents. But one thing they had agreed on was not only my father, but also Marianne and Sven should be told about the rape.

'We can tell Pops on the Friday evening returning from the airport, we won't take Suzanne. But it's going to be difficult to tell the others with Suzanne in and out of the rooms and there's no guarantee she won't come down in the evening or at any time even if we think she's asleep.'

'Yes, I have been thinking, would you be happy to tell Marianne? Go out together sometime this weekend—obviously without Suzanne?'

'If you don't mind my telling her.'

'It will be a great relief actually.'

'OK, I'll try to find a suitable time and excuse. As no-one was expecting me, I presume nothing special has been arranged and it is to be a quiet weekend at home.'

'Yes, thank goodness. I am pretty washed out after all the expended emotion.'

'I think your parents were pretty shaken up about the cause of the estrangement.'

'Shall we collect your case from the hotel and let them know you will be back on Monday? Or do you want to bring everything and cancel the hotel?'

'Well, as I'll be with you over the weekend it would be a bit daft to stay in the hotel, wouldn't it? Except of course, I can then meet Marianne without Suzanne knowing I'm here this weekend. The booking is flexible so it can be either way.'

'I would prefer you to come home, I think we need to tell them about the engagement tonight.'

'Ricard, won't they think it strange I've agreed to marry you if we don't tell them what the argument was between you and your parents?'

'I think, for tonight, we can just say it has been resolved. Suzanne will be overjoyed and Marianne and Sven will know better than to probe.'

'Alright, but I want to hear everyone else's news first. So, wait till everyone has settled down and I've unpacked. Maybe when we have our aperitifs if it seems the right time, but not about the baby.'

'No, we have agreed, not until you are ready.'

§

I cleared the room and bill at the hotel and we drove home.

I still get a buzz from calling his house "home".

Marianne and Sven greeted me warmly; obviously, my presence was not a surprise to them but made out to Suzanne that it was.

'I bet you knew all the time she was in Lézignan and she is staying for the whole week. Can we have some of my friends in to meet her please, *Papa?*'

'We still must not jump to any conclusions, Suzanne,' Marianne said sharply, 'nothing has been decided yet.'

Neither I nor Ricard said anything against her statement but agreed with Marianne a party just now was not going to happen. Suzanne was disappointed but realised there was no point in arguing and pointedly went to her room, saying she was going to read, banging her door behind her.

'Come on, I'll take your cases upstairs,' Ricard started and was joined by Sven, 'they can go in the guest room you used for now, Yvonne, there is free wardrobe space in there.'

'Thanks, I'll come and unpack shortly; hopefully, my clothes won't need ironing if I hang them quickly. I'm sorry about the short notice, Marianne, I hope I've not messed up any plans you had for the weekend.'

'Not at all, and do not be daft, you are more than welcome. Did Ricard sort out the business with his father? How was he welcomed?'

'I think he'll want to tell you all about it. Obviously, the greeting was rather formal and fraught, but suffice it to say, they parted on good terms.'

I'll have to contrive something for tomorrow. Maybe a shopping trip, I am sure I need to buy something Suzanne could not possibly be interested in.

The perfect excuse arose later in the evening when, having unpacked my cases, I needed to press a badly crumpled skirt. The iron and ironing board in the utility room were old and unsafe, they obviously needed replacing.

'Marianne, would you be insulted if I asked if we could go tomorrow and buy new ones to replace these?'

'Insulted? Of course not, they have needed to be replaced for months and I have never got around to doing it. You know how you get used to something without really seeing it, leave your skirt and we can go to town tomorrow.'

'You will need to go to the out-of-town store, it has a much wider selection than the local one and ironing boards are awkward to carry, it will be much easier in the car, I will take you. I need to get a few things too.'

'Thank you, Sven, an excellent idea,' said Ricard, 'you can give them support and guidance.' He added.

Marianne finished preparing the evening meal while I laid the table.

Ricard organised champagne for the aperitif and Marianne helped him bring in the filled glasses and some orange juice to the living room where Sven and I were chatting. Ricard then went to the bottom of the stairs and called,

'Suzanne, would you come down here for a moment please. Leave your homework or book for a moment and come here.'

'Have I done something wrong, *Papa*?'

As she entered the living room, he replied, 'I do not know, have you? Stomping off was not very polite. But now I have something to say and I will start by saying I want no interruptions. First thing, I went with Yvonne to see my parents, I am not going to tell you what happened or what our argument was about, but we have resolved our differences and so, at last, Yvonne has agreed to marry me.'

Sven took the floor.

'Thank goodness, so now can we raise our glasses to you both before this loses the fizz? Congratulations. To the bride and groom.'

Smiles and hugs and handshakes and chatter followed. When things calmed down a bit and glasses topped up, Ricard spoke again,

'I think that was an interruption!'

'Sorry, I thought you had finished.'

'*Papa*, Yvonne, such wonderful news so now you will come and stay here, Yvonne. Will you come and teach in my school? And can I have my friends in to meet you now please?'

'Suzanne, I presume I will live here, though I will still be working which might mean going away, so teaching at the school is not on the agenda now and you have already been told by Marianne and your father—no parties at the moment.'

'Alright, can I take this to my room and read till dinner is ready, *Papa*?' She indicated the glass containing orange juice and a dash of champagne.

'If you would like to do so, yes.'

Saying thank you, she left us.

We chatted for a bit longer before Marianne suggested we ate.

'If I had known it was a special occasion, I would have done a better meal, I will make up for it another night. I am so happy for you both, congratulations. Would you call Suzanne please, Ricard?'

During the meal, Suzanne seemed rather preoccupied.

'Are you alright, Suzanne? You seem quiet.'

'Yes, thank you, Yvonne, and I am so happy for you both I think I am going to burst.'

She said nothing more during the meal and excused herself from the table while we were having coffee.

'What's wrong?'

'Disappointment at not having a party, she has been waiting and hoping for so long to introduce you to her friends.'

'Surely it is rather an overreaction to not having a party.'

'Maybe, Ricard, but I cannot think of anything else it might be,' Marianne offered, 'we all react in different ways and maybe her hopes have been dashed more strongly than we realise. She will be alright tomorrow.'

§ § §

Before setting off in the morning, Marianne said,

'There is a new café near the hardware store I have heard good reports of, perhaps we could give it a try while we are out.'

'Have fun. If you find the café has good food and you want to stay out for lunch, I am sure Suzanne and I can find something in the fridge.'

'I expect we will be back, Ricard, but if not, please do not eat the pâté I made for dinner.'

After buying the board and iron and a few other household items Marianne needed or fancied trying, we went to the café she'd mentioned. I searched for a table set apart from the centre of the room and found an alcove with some easy chairs and a low table. Sven gave the coffee order when the waitress came.

'Thank you, Sven.' I smiled up at him.

'OK Yvonne, what is bothering you? I saw your face relax when Ricard encouraged Sven to bring us, something about support and guidance. Is this about yesterday and his parents?'

'Yes. We decided it is important you both know about the estrangement and a new situation. Some of this is very painful and must not reach Suzanne's ears, but the good news is the friction between Ricard and his parents is over.'

I proceeded to tell them what Ricard had explained to us yesterday. Marianne was shocked.

'My poor child,' she said, 'my poor dear sister, she never said anything. What a weight to carry all on her own.'

Then Marianne groaned and started to rock back and forth. Sven moved closer to her and put his arms around her in an unusual display of emotion in public.

'Calm down, my love.'

Marianne continued to rock and tears started to cascade like a cataract down her face. It seemed like a torrent she could not stop. A concerned waitress came over to see if she could help. Sven ordered a cognac and continued to hold Marianne until she became more composed. He passed her the brandy which she sipped and stared at me through red swollen eyes.

'I thought it had stopped with me. I should have known, but even though no one had said anything, it was as clear as clear. I should have known, I suppose I did really, but refused to believe it, even though the evidence of the curse was there. I should have said something.'

I waited, saying nothing. I'd been told she'd become extremely close to her sister during the time she'd helped, near the end of the pregnancy, and realised this news must have been a terrible shock.

But what on earth was she talking about? What should have stopped?

'I'm sorry, Marianne, perhaps I should have prepared you a little before telling you the news, but I have no idea what you're talking about.'

'Give me a moment. So why...,' she asked through gulps for air, '...was there the separation between Ricard and his parents?'

'He thought they knew what had happened and they were protecting Jules. But they knew nothing.' I continued to relay the conversations of the Thursday.

Marianne drank her coffee and sipped more brandy.

'I think I have to tell you this now, especially as one problem has been resolved and you and Ricard are engaged. I need to tell you before you marry as it may have repercussions later and you might be upset and say I should have told you. Especially in view of the information you have just told us.'

'Marianne, what is it?'

Marianne looked at Sven who nodded and held her hand. 'Have you ever heard of the "Curse of the Dubois Family"?'

I shook my head. 'Should I have done?'

'No, no reason why you should. I don't know if this was happening before Rachel Dubois, but I imagine it was, for more generations than I like to think, but certainly the last four when Rachel Dubois, the product of rape herself, married. She and her husband had a girl but he died and Rachel remarried, the new husband raped his stepdaughter; she in turn had a daughter who married, had a girl and the history repeated itself time and time again. You are probably getting the picture, young girls, generation after generation abused and giving birth to a girl for the same thing to happen. I thought the curse had now come to an end.' She looked up.

'It didn't happen to you too, did it?' I asked.

She nodded.

'Yes, a friend of my parents was staying with us, one afternoon my parents had to go out urgently, leaving me in his care. He did what we now know is the usual, told me my parents would not believe me if I said anything but would take his word and throw me out. By the time I found I was pregnant, he was well gone. I told my parents what had happened; they were horrified to have so misjudged the man. I was not even sixteen, too young to cope on my own. My parents were supportive and mother and I disappeared from our village for a few months returning after the birth. After a lot of consideration, it was decided the female baby—yes, I had twins—would be brought up by my parents, as my sister—"surprise blessings late in their lives" they told people, but they could not afford to keep the boy as well. After a lot of heart searching, it was decided he had to go for adoption. We settled down, my parents caring for me and bringing up my so-called "sister"—Charlotte.'

'You mean…?'

Marianne looked pale when she had finished and nodded giving me a wan smile.

'You see? It is a curse in the bloodline. Now Charlotte has been raped.'

'You said something about evidence, you saw something,' I probed.

She lifted the hem of her skirt. I saw something I recognised.

'Every child born down this line by rape has had this birthmark on their leg. My mother, me, both Charlotte and my boy and Suzanne has it. It is a curse mark.'

'I still say it is just a birthmark, inherited by genetics down the bloodline,' said Sven, 'it is not a curse.'

'What happened to your father, Marianne?'

'He and mother had long lives, they were so happy; I do not think my mother ever really got over his death, even though he was a good eighty-nine at the end of his life. When I met Fredrick Göest, despite our age difference I fell in love with him, he was so like my father, it was probably why I was attracted to him.'

'You didn't have any more children?'

'No, my body was damaged, I could not have any more. Before I agreed to marry him, I told Fredrick the history, he understood and said he was too old to cope with a young family anyway, we were well-suited and happy for the short time we had together.'

'After he died, you cared for your mother—Charlotte's grandmother. At the start of your story you said, in view of what you told me, I should know in case of repercussions in the future. What do you envisage?'

'Suzanne has expressed an interest in her family history. Now Ricard and his parents are reconciled, I am sure she will want to research his side, she has had the sense not to do so recently, what if she decides to investigate Charlotte's side, it will be difficult as there are many gaps or distortions in the records, but some documents are available.'

'What's the problem if she does?'

'If she does, she will see I have lied to her all her life, as I did to Charlotte.'

'But you have been there all her life, looking after your granddaughter.'

'But not as her grandmother! As her aunt! And what about Charlotte? All her too short a life to her, my mother was her mother, not me! I was her sister!'

'Marianne, you have been there with nothing but love for them both and everyone close to you as well.' Sven tried to console his fiancée again.

Marianne shook her head.

'How are we going to protect Suzanne? Regardless of what you say, the curse carries on.' She gave a big sigh and closed her eyes. 'Thank you for listening.'

Well, Ricard, you were wrong about Marianne, she certainly had a secret.

'I need a couple of minutes to absorb all this, Marianne, thank you for confiding in me.

Oh Lord, could Paul be her son?

I decided now was not the time to raise this possibility as I still had to impart the news of Jules' imminent arrival, which I did as gently as I could, having first prepared them for another piece of shock news.

'Surely we will not be going next weekend then?'

'As we don't know where he is, we can't stop him and we agreed with Matilde and Ramon we would go as planned. We doubt he'll try anything with us all there. Ricard's biggest concern is Suzanne.'

'What is she to be told? She knows she has an uncle who is her godfather who left years ago, she never asks after him as far as I know. But why does he want to come back now if no-one has heard from or about him since he left?'

'Marianne, I have a strong sense, in view of what you have told me and the situation we find ourselves in, you need to tell Ricard about your family history.'

'Furthermore,' added Sven, 'if you are worried about Suzanne's reaction if she uncovers your family tree, surely you should be equally, if not more, concerned about the effect it might have on Ricard and all of our relationships. I support Yvonne on this point.'

'Alright. I will do so during the week. But I will have to make sure Suzanne is at school.'

We sat without talking for a while. The waitress asked if we were ordering lunch, hinting we either ate or left as the space would be needed for those having lunch. Sven accepted the proffered menu cards and asked her to return in a few minutes with some wine.

241

'What do you think? Something light to eat?'

We agreed and ordered.

§

'Do you want to have the first use of the new iron and board, Marianne, or shall I do my bits?'

'You carry on. If you have the energy there are a couple of shirts hanging too. I'm going to see if Ricard has a moment or two to talk or at least listen, I think I want to get it over with now rather than wait till next week. Sven, will you come with me please?'

They knocked on Ricard's study door and went in. I interrupted Suzanne who was doing her homework and chatted at her bedroom door about what she and Ricard had been doing while we'd been out. She wasn't very forthcoming so I didn't pursue the matter.

'Have you got any ironing, Suzanne? I'm just going to do a few bits.'

'No, I think Marianne has done all my stuff, thank you. Who will do it when you live here?'

'Don't worry, it's one of several things we'll all have to talk about and decide. Meanwhile, Marianne oversees everything she always has and I'll just do as I'm asked. There's time to sort these things out.'

'When will your wedding be?'

'We haven't decided a date yet but soon, I hope.'

'I must get back to my homework and book.'

'OK. I'll do my ironing.' I left her with a frown on my face.

I find ironing is a good time for some thinking. Once again Suzanne had asked some relevant questions echoing Matilde's of yesterday. I hoped Marianne liked ironing as it was one of many domestic duties I don't.

Be honest, there are none you do like.

I put the old board and iron by the coat rack in the hall to be disposed of later and to make room for the new ones. I was passing Ricard's office door taking my ironing upstairs when Sven came out.

'Just making some coffee,' he said as he passed me.

Ricard followed him.

'Will you dump those and join us? Please bring some glasses and brandy.'

'What about Suzanne? She'll think it strange we are all in your office together.'

'Just tell her where we are and we do not want to be disturbed. OK?' He turned and went back into his office closing the door firmly. I did as I was asked.

'OK,' was all Suzanne said, as if this was a daily occurrence.

Sven and I arrived at the office door together, I managed my tray along my forearm and opened the door after tapping. Ricard was speaking,

'...saved the embarrassment if you'd told me then.'

'But there was no reason to do so then. All I had to do was to make sure you realised there was no possible hope of a romantic or physical relationship between us—which I did.'

'Yes, yes, of course, Marianne, I am sorry, you have acted exactly as you should. I was out of order then; forgive me.'

'You were lonely, grieving and out of your depth with a baby. You did not know my situation; no forgiveness is needed.'

'Is Suzanne alright?'

'Yes, Marianne, she was reading and just took the fact we are talking as a perfectly normal thing for us to do.'

'I hate having secrets.'

I looked at Ricard, almost unable to believe what he'd just said, the others looked up too.

'Consider what it nearly did to us, Yvonne, and what a waste of years for my parents and me.'

'Now you know the secret I have carried for some time. Sven has known since we started to get close. I am not sure if I should tell Suzanne and if so, is it possible without telling her the whole story—not about her mother and Jules, of course, just stop at me, Charlotte and the boy.'

What do I do about Paul? Should I say anything now? Raise false hopes he is the other half to the twin? What if he doesn't really want to know and he was just making conversation?

'No. I don't think it's the right time just yet.'

'Why not, Yvonne? If things blow up next weekend, it would be terrible if she hears it during an argument.' posed Marianne.

'Who is going to raise it? Jules won't say about you not being Charlotte's sister, he doesn't know, he thinks you are sisters.'

'Of course.' She sighed.

'We just have to keep her away from Jules at any cost.'

'The only way we can be one hundred percent sure is not going or not taking her next weekend.'

'Can you see her meekly agreeing to such an arrangement, Sven?'

'Of course not.'

'There have been enough unspoken truths already which have caused a lot of harm,' Marianne's voice was full of sadness, 'I think I should tell her about me and face the next problem as it arises.'

'Please Marianne, leave it for now. We need to digest all the information we have received and consider the possible implications. There has been a lot of news and emotion today, I think we need to sleep on it and mull it over for a couple of days then talk further.'

'I agree with Yvonne, it sounds like good advice.'

Sven held Marianne's hands. 'We know it is your relationship and it has been troubling you, even more so since we heard from Ricard about what Jules said and your fear of Suzanne hearing the whole story. Perhaps she is a little young now; let us do as Yvonne suggests and put our heads together again on Tuesday evening.'

Marianne nodded. 'I agree. I think I am too emotionally drained to think straight now. I am going to take my brandy and sit in the lounge, may I have a top up please, Yvonne. Thank you all for listening.'

I followed Marianne to the lounge with the tray of brandy and glasses, Suzanne was there spread out on the couch reading a novel, she shifted her position when we entered and patted the seat beside her indicating Marianne to sit there.

I saw Ricard and Sven pass to the kitchen and followed them.

'Are you alright, Ricard?'

'Yes, I think so. Sven and I had a talk. But there is, as you said, a lot to take in.'

'May I use your office and the landline please Ricard. I'd like to make a call to my sister to make sure she's alright and the battery on my mobile's low.'

'Of course, are you worried about her?'

'Not really, just wanted to check.'

'Sven and I are going to fix some sort of dinner. The hors d'oeuvre is ready so we will not starve!'

'That's good of you both. Marianne is exhausted. She's dozing next to Suzanne.'

I rang Julie. She was surprised to hear from me and even more surprised when I asked to speak to Paul. I asked him if what he'd said, weeks ago in general conversations to and from work, before we knew of our family relationship, about investigating his birth mother was true.

'Yes, very much so. As I think I said, trying to trace her was something I planned to do. Yvonne, why are you asking this? Why are you asking now?'

'Paul, I have met a woman who has the same birthmark as you. She says when she had her twins, a girl and boy, she was living with her parents and for various reasons they could not afford to look after two babies, so the girl was kept and the boy put for adoption,' I heard a deep intake of breath, 'sorry to have sounded so harsh, but there were good reasons. Her daughter had the same birthmark as does her grandchild.'

'Do you think it could be her?'

'I don't know, it might all be circumstantial but from what she says, I think there's a strong possibility. But before I say anything to the woman, I thought I'd approach you to see if you think it's worth taking what's probably a great risk, for both of you. I don't want to raise any false hopes in her, she has had enough heart ache, and I don't want you to raise your hopes, only for them to be dashed, if there's nothing in these circumstances.'

'Your instinct has served you well in the past, Yvonne. If this woman would be willing to risk meeting up, then so would I. What are you suggesting?'

'From your point of view, now I've raised the issue, I doubt if much would be gained by delaying too long. Obviously, I will have to find out if this woman would also like to take the risk and if she does, I don't think she would want to wait.'

'As soon as possible. How about next Tuesday or Wednesday?'

'Don't be too eager, Paul, this might not be her, she may not want to meet you and if you meet, you both might be disappointed.'

'It will confirm—or eliminate—one person—then maybe it will give me the impetus to follow through my search.'

'Alright, I will give you half an hour to reconsider. Paul, ring me back immediately or within the next half an hour if you change your mind or I'll contact her.'

'I do not think you will hear from me and I hope to hear from you. Do you want to talk to Julie again?'

'No, I've had her news and no doubt you'll want to talk to her. Bye, I'll be in touch.'

I relaxed into Ricard's comfortable office chair and closed my eyes, hoping I'd done the right thing. I didn't want another uncle popping up unexpectedly for Suzanne if Marianne did go ahead and explain her situation. Someone knocked on the door rousing me from my deliberations and Suzanne put her head in.

'You are all so sleepy this evening, early to bed for you all.'

'You may well be right tonight, Suzanne. Is Marianne alright?'

'Yes, she has gone over to their flat to brush her hair and wash her face ready for dinner. Well, *Papa* says it is more of a supper in the kitchen tonight. He wondered if you had finished your telephone call.'

'Yes, finished. If Marianne is washing her face and brushing her hair, perhaps I'd better do the same. Where's your father?'

'In the sitting room.'

I went to see Ricard briefly before going upstairs.

§

The supper, prepared by the two men, was enthusiastically received by everyone and Marianne rejoiced,

'So, I'll have one evening off from now on, perhaps we should set up a rota of cooking!'

Both Ricard and Sven thought otherwise and decided the meal was not as good as they had anticipated, even though they ate everything they'd prepared and had second portions. During the rest of the meal, the adults were quiet and rather unusually restrained. Suzanne was quiet but managed to say she was looking forward to showing me around the farm next weekend. All in all, it was a rather down-beat meal.

Before we had coffee, Suzanne said, 'I want to try and finish this book tonight. If you do not mind, I will go and get ready for bed and read upstairs. Marianne, please come and say goodnight before you go home.'

'Of course, I will, it must be a good book for you to want to read so much, you were doing so for a lot of the afternoon.'

'Yes, it is good. Goodnight, Sven, see you tomorrow.'

'Yes Suzanne. Goodnight.' Sven stood and opened the kitchen door for her to leave.

'Bit strange.' Ricard said once the door had been closed again.

'She is obviously aware there is something troubling us all and is waiting for some explanation.'

'It's our problem, not hers.'

'You are wrong, Ricard, I think it concerns her too.' Marianne stood.

'What I do not understand, Marianne, is why you did not tell Charlotte at our wedding. Surely you had the opportunity—or even before when you and your mother knew we were engaged.'

'Mother and I were tempted and did discuss it then, but finally we decided not to do so. I cannot remember all our reasons, but basically, I think we decided it would be rather putting a dampener on your celebrations. Then time went by and with mother's illness and death and then Charlotte's pregnancy, there never seemed to be the right time. But now I know about how she was attacked I think this is an appropriate time to tell Suzanne.'

'Marianne, you agreed to wait till next week until we have had time to think this through and consider all the ramifications both good and bad.' Sven had remained at the door and now looked as if he was guarding it to prevent his soon to be wife from leaving to join Suzanne in her room.

'Oh, very well, we will sort out this lot,' she indicated the remains of the meal, 'and take coffee in the lounge. I need to check what I need for tomorrow's meals.'

We were all grateful for something to do, so while Marianne made her arrangements for the next few meals, we three cleared and washed up, then moved to the lounge for coffee.

After a short while, I rose and closed the door between the hall and the lounge.

'Are you in a draught there, Yvonne? Perhaps we ought to keep a note of all these extra points about the house, I think I have lived here for so long I do not notice its quirks.'

'No, not now, maybe there will be one later as the year gets older and colder and I notice the different wind angles. There are, possibly, one or two improvements to make it a little more comfortable.'

'Mmm, I have probably let it get a bit—'

'No, Ricard, if there is anything I think might need changing at any time, I'll make a suggestion, we'll discuss it and then we'll decide. I only closed the door because I wanted to be sure if Suzanne should come downstairs, she won't hear our conversation.'

'What is it, Yvonne? You have been quiet since you called your sister, is everything alright with her?'

'Yes, thanks, she is fine, what I have to say doesn't directly concern her, though I am sure she will be affected.' I related how I'd met Paul through work and what I knew of him. 'I hadn't planned to say anything till much later, but because of Marianne's news today and the potential of telling Suzanne soon, I decided I had to do something.'

I turned to Marianne. 'Paul has the same birthday as Charlotte and the same birthmark as you and Suzanne, you said Charlotte had it too. He would like to find his birth mother, it may all be my speculation and circumstantial evidence, but there are several similarities in your stories so I think, there's a reasonable possibility you are his mother.'

'And what has this to do with the phone call to your sister?'

'Marianne, Paul is my brother-in-law, Julie's husband. We only found out at the end of last week. I spoke to him this evening specifically to ask if he was telling me the truth about wanting to meet his birth mother, and did he want to take the risk of meeting "someone" I'd met who might be her. I emphasised I may be mistaken. I told him not to raise his hopes as I had no idea if "this someone" would want to take the risk too.'

'And does he want to take the risk? I am not really sure how our meeting will prove anything one way or the other.'

'Well, maybe he will have some of your features or maybe look like Charlotte in some ways. I suppose, we could ask for DNA testing before any introductions are made. Or maybe you would rather not even—'

'Oh no, I think it would be good to meet him. At least, if neither of us think we are related, we would have eliminated the possibility and hopefully no harm done.'

'He sounded almost relieved the decision to take a first step to trace his natural mother has been taken for him.'

'What do you suggest is the next move? Have you made any suggestions to him?'

I shared Paul's eagerness to meet possibly on Tuesday or Wednesday evening.

'I think Wednesday would be good.'

'Are you sure, Marianne? That is a very quick response, do you want to think about it further? I do not want you to be hurt any more than you have been.'

'Yes, Sven, I am sure. Now a carrot has been dangled, it will not go away and will only gnaw into me if I do not meet him.'

'I'll call Paul again, he wanted to know if you were willing to meet him. I'll sort out the venue tomorrow.'

I re-joined the others in the lounge in time to find they'd agreed, as indicated by Suzanne to me before dinner, an early night was called for. Marianne went to say goodnight to Suzanne then she and Sven went home. Ricard and I made some fresh coffee and sat in the kitchen.

'Quite a day for revelations.'

'Yes. I sincerely hope there are no more hidden life stories. I'm finding it all quite exhausting.'

'I doubt any of it would have been exposed if your flight from Carcassonne had not been cancelled.' Ricard smiled and took my hand fingering my rings.

'Would that have been better? Do you think it will adversely affect Suzanne? How will Marianne be if they dislike each other and want no further communication? Perhaps I shouldn't have said anything.'

'We will have to wait for the answers to the last two questions, there will be a great deal of emotion whatever the conclusion and we can only be supportive. But as to the first one, most of the outcomes are good. I think Marianne is relieved to have been able to unburden herself from a secret she has held for so long, good as far as I am concerned, you have been the catalyst to bringing me and my parents back together and can you doubt we and the baby are not good?'

'I suppose you're right. I think next week's going to be hard for us all, not only Wednesday but also the build up to the weekend. Will you go and see the doctor to find out about your specimen results?'

'Yes, but we can do no more tonight, bed for us. Tomorrow we will offer all our problems to someone who will help us through everything.'

As we finally relaxed resting in each other's arms after mutual arousal and satisfaction, I mumbled, 'make sure I am up in time tomorrow.'

I received no response, the gentle sound of his breathing told me Ricard was already asleep.

Chapter Fifteen

The service seemed to hold a great deal more significance for me today. It was very much orientated to problem solving and I found it reassuring we are not on our own when we have to make decisions. Walking back from the church I asked Ricard, 'Have you had any time, or indeed room in your brain, among everything we have found out recently, about how you are going to tackle the issue of visits to your father's new properties?'

'I cannot say I have in the last few hours but I have concluded I will have to employ someone to go and make assessments of them all. The question is, basically, who to employ and fully trust their evaluations and judgements.'

'Would you trust me to do it?'

Ricard stopped suddenly. 'Yes, of course I would. What a great idea, but you cannot do it as you will be working. You will not have any more time than I have.'

'I've been thinking, Ricard, there might be a way, but it will mean you'll have to pay all expenses and,' I hesitated, 'pay me a salary or I'll become a kept woman. I would prefer a business arrangement.'

'I cannot see how you could do it with the project you have with Patrick and Charles.'

'If they would both agree, I've already put into the project plan an outline of how it could continue without causing anyone any problems without me as the lead. It will also offer employment to someone who will ensure everything would be done to a high standard. It will need some discussions to find out a couple of things to make the outline plan concrete.'

'As I said, I have not really been able to give the issue a great deal of thought, I doubt another few more days will make much difference. And certainly I, and I am sure father, would be delighted for you to take it on.'

'Good. Let's leave it there for the moment, I'll try and work something out this week, but even if they agree it might take some time to finally action it.'

'Understood. Are you sure your family does not have any secrets? After all, Julie kept her marriage and pregnancy a secret from everyone…' he paused, '…except Patrick.'

'That's a very loaded statement, Ricard. I've never had any interest in looking into my family history further than my parents' parents all of whom I knew before they died. So, please, don't start on any dead-end chases. Not everyone has skeletons in their cupboards, if there's anything you or indeed I, should know we can start by asking Pops at the weekend. But quite honestly, I think we've quite enough to cope with without you creating fantasies about people—especially Patrick and me, which is really what you are saying, isn't it? Patrick is a friend of my father and the family and my employer. Can't you understand?' I walked off furious and hurt.

Is this really the way to go? We seem so far apart at times. Today he trusts me one moment and not the next.

My mobile was fully charged by the time we arrived back at the house, I went straight to Ricard's office to search for hotels in the new town area of Carcassonne, the second one I tried was able to give me three bedrooms for Wednesday night, I made a reservation then rang Paul at Julie's flat.

'We will be there at about six in the evening. Marianne, her fiancé and me. OK?'

'Yes, thanks.'

'It may not work out, Paul, be prepared.'

'You sound a bit down, are you alright?'

'Yes,' I lied, 'all this has been a bit of a strain on everyone this end with other things going on too. See you on Wednesday.'

At least I had done something constructive and managed to calm down a little too.

I left his office and went to the living room where I told Marianne I'd fixed a hotel in Carcassonne for Wednesday night, not realising Suzanne was there with Marianne and Sven.

'Oh, are we all going—?'

She didn't get a chance to finish her question as Sven interrupted, his voice was sterner than I'd ever heard before, to me he'd always seemed a gentle person.

'No Suzanne, you will stay here with your father. Marianne has something very personal to do, you remember when you have very personal things you do not like to talk about—like I did—until it is the right time? So now, Marianne has something to do for herself; do not ask.'

I realised he was protecting Marianne from having to give any explanations and me for my stupidity, I admired him. Suzanne looked shocked, obviously Sven had never spoken to her like that before.

'Sven, I—'

'Come, Suzanne.'

I took her by the hand up to her room where she cried into my arms.

'What have I done wrong?'

'Nothing, my dear, perhaps you have been rather indulged and been involved in all discussions, now you are having to face up to the fact people you love have many problems not of your concern. Believe me, you will be told when things do concern you.'

Her tear-stained face looked up at me. 'But I love Marianne and Sven, he has never been so sharp with me, what is it?'

'As I said, if it affects you, you will be told.'

She seemed to relax in my arms a little. 'Can we still go to *Papi's* this weekend?'

I too relaxed, smiled and chuckled as I held this child-cum-woman realising she had gone back to looking forward to concrete issues as opposed to potential problems but I knew, she like me, would not be happy without the full answers.

'Do you want to come down now with me or come later?'

Suzanne waited a moment. 'Could I stay here and you can say I have to read my book?'

'You could, but I never thought of you not facing up to issues.'

'I will come down and apologise.'

'Before you go down, what do you think you're apologising for?'

'I do not know, I was not rude, I just wanted to go with you all.'

'Exactly, as I said, maybe it's not your fault, you've always been involved in everything, now you must realise there are things you can't be included in.'

'I do not need to apologise?'

'I think, not for being rude, but about expecting to be involved in everything. Splash some water on your face, brush your hair and come down, you can come up later and finish your homework.'

'I have done it, but I have got another good book.'

I returned to join the others. 'I'm sorry, my mistake, I was bit wound up and just blurted it out, I'd forgotten Suzanne could be in the room.'

'Is she alright?'

'Yes, Sven, she realises she can't be included in everything, she'll be down in a minute.'

'I did not mean to be so sharp with her but—' He stopped as Suzanne came in.

'I understand, Sven. I am sorry for expecting to go everywhere with you and Marianne.' Suzanne went over to Sven and hugged him.

'Come on then, there is time, before we eat, for a game of Monopoly.'

We all groaned.

'Does no one like it?'

'No, Sven, horrible game, can we play Draughts?'

'OK.'

The rest of the morning was spent quietly flicking through the newspapers we'd bought on our way back from church. There was little conversation, just a few comments being passed between Sven and Suzanne.

Marianne fixed a few pre-lunch nibbles and the makings for aperitifs which Ricard mixed and dispensed, I declined. I felt the tension high between Ricard and me, neither of us made any attempt at reconciliation following the earlier disagreement.

'Where would you like me to lay the table for lunch, Marianne?'

'The dining room please. Not only Sunday, but a special meal too, a celebration for your engagement, thank you, Yvonne.'

Let's hope it is not premature and wasted.

After lunch, which was really appreciated by us all, despite some lingering tension from all quarters, Sven and Marianne went to their flat as I'd offered to clear up. Ricard joined me.

'I will wash,' he said.

'Fine.'

I carried on clearing the table before I turned to wiping the plates and cutlery.

'This is ridiculous, Yvonne. I apologise for raising Patrick again and I know he is nothing to you except as you say.'

'I get the feeling you are always looking for something that's not there, not really believing me. Are you regretting asking me to marry you? If you are, then say so now and let's cut our losses.'

'No, of course not, I love you so much it hurts.'

'Well, you'll have to curb the jealousy and trust me, perhaps we are both emotionally overwrought because of the things we have learnt recently, maybe we need some time apart.'

'After all we have been through? Do you really think that is the answer? Hardly practical now anyway, please do not go away, please...' He put his arms round me and kissed me. I didn't resist, I knew what he meant when he said this love hurts. After a while, he released me and we finished the clearing up.

'Perhaps we should go for a walk with Suzanne. There's another half hour's light out there. I'll ask her.'

'No thanks. I would like to carry on reading my book in my room.'

'Are you sure? There is still a bit of sunshine.'

'No, you go if you want to.'

'Do you want to...?'

'No thank you, Yvonne, I want to read the book, it is exciting.'

'OK. We'll read the papers then.'

When I told him of her response, Ricard sighed, 'What is wrong with Suzanne?'

'I don't know, I thought she understood about Wednesday.'

We sat quietly reading till Marianne said from the doorway,

'I think I will attend evening prayers tonight; I will not be long but there is a cold meal prepared in the kitchen for anyone who wants to eat before I return.'

I followed Marianne and asked if I might go with her. We walked most of the way in companionable silence in the October wind which had turned cold.

'I am glad you told me of your suspicions about Paul, it was right of you to do so, even though it was possibly a shock too many in two days. Would you have mentioned it if I had not told you my history?'

'I don't know but probably at some stage. I think it would've been too difficult for me to keep it to myself for all time and I imagine at some stage you'd meet him and notice the birthmark, then where would our relationship be? Yes, I think I would've told you at some juncture before you two met.'

We entered the church both now with our own thoughts.

§ § §

Returning home, Ricard poured an aperitif for the others, Suzanne and I had orange juice. While we were clearing away after the meal Suzanne went to bed, then Sven and Marianne went to their own apartment, Ricard and I sat quietly till we too decided to retire.

'Are you alright now, Ricard?'

'Yes, Yvonne, it will not happen again, well, not in the same context anyway.'

'I hope I will never give you any cause to feel jealousy, Ricard, we need to get more into the habit of telling each other how we feel before things blow up.'

There was no doubt about how each of us felt about the other once we were in bed.

§ § §

Setting off for work in Lézignan from Ricard's house was quite unusual for me but it felt comfortable to do so. Suzanne however was still unnaturally quiet although she denied anything was wrong.

When I reached the office, Vivienne greeted me in a friendly manner and obviously wanted to know where I'd been for the last two days and the weekend.

'I rang your hotel to see if you were alright, they said you had checked out on Friday evening.'

'Yes, as I told you and *Monsieur* Bassinet, I had some personal issues to sort out. They took a little longer than anticipated so I decided to leave the hotel rather than charging extra to the project account.'

'As you wish, but you were seen with *Monsieur* Letour and his family at church on Sunday.'

'OK. Vivienne, I was with them, happy now? But nothing is sealed and dried!'

She smiled. 'Must be very nearly so—no one has ever spent such a long time with him and his family since his wife died. Be careful, but good luck, it is said he is still very vulnerable.'

Me too and fragile. C'est ça!

'Yes, shall we go across the road for coffee at eleven?'

She agreed and I went to my office and started writing up the outline of where I'd got to in the project, which was not really far, I had to think how to put to Patrick, the optional plan would now be needed. About ten o'clock, I rang the London office and asked to speak to Sharon, she was obviously surprised, not only to be receiving a call but also to find a voice addressing her in French asking if she'd decided on any of the projects Patrick had shown her. I could almost hear her mind getting into gear as she responded.

'Hold on a minute,' her colloquialism was perfect, 'who are you? What do you want? What do you know about the projects currently being pursued by Patrick Court's firm? I am not prepared to talk to you. Goodbye.'

Just before she put the phone down, I called, 'Sharon! Sorry, it's me, Yvonne. I'm ringing from France. I'm sorry, but I needed to be sure—'

'—my French is as good as I said it is.' There was a silence.

'Yes, I'm sorry, I think it's far better than mine.'

'What is it you want? I have a meeting with Patrick any minute now so I'm looking for alternative work while I wait.'

'Have you looked at all the possible projects?'

'Yes, but none of them is feasible with my home commitments nor interesting enough to disrupt them, unless I really have to do so.'

'Sharon, my personal circumstances have changed and I'd like to get out of the project I'm doing. There's nothing wrong with the project and I think it's workable for you. Depending on how you'd want to organise it, there's leeway in how it's handled. Patrick knows there's a possibility I might drop out so he won't be over surprised and I've already given an alternative means forward in my original proposal should I need to. I think you'll be able to take over, I've done some research but not set up any meetings with people, so now is the time for someone else to take over. I think you'll be interested and if you say yes to Patrick, could you be ready to fly over tonight? I'll meet you at Carcassonne airport.'

'Yvonne, are you alright? What's happened?'

'Only good things, thanks for asking; could you be ready to fly tonight with enough clothes for three or four days?'

'In theory yes, but no promises till I talk to Patrick and find out what it's about and of course, my mother.'

'I think this is a time to make a speedy decision about the job. From what you've told me, your mother and Lucy will fall in with whatever plans you make.

On a personal basis, I think the hours can be flexible, a point which is already in my original proposal.'

'What do I do next? You've got me intrigued.'

'I'll talk to Patrick and hopefully get his agreement. If I can get him now, don't be surprised if he wants to see you immediately. Whatever happens, I'll talk to you soon, can you put me back to switch please?'

I was put through to Andrea.

'Andrea, could I to speak to Patrick urgently.'

'Oh, good morning, Yvonne. How are you today? Has the week gone well? Did you have a good weekend? I—'

'I'm so sorry, Andrea, good morning, how are you and Frank? As always, your antennae are working well! Yes, I am a bit wound up after the events of the weekend, but they are all positive. Now, if possible, may I talk with Patrick?'

'He said he was expecting you to call and to put you through as soon as you did.'

'How did he know I'd call?'

'I don't know but he sounded a bit annoyed, I'll put you through and you can ask him yourself.'

After the preliminaries of greetings and asking after each other's welfare I asked why he had expected me to ring him today.

'Well,' I imagined his fingers poised like a church steeple, elbows resting on his desk with the phone on speaker mode, '*Monsieur* Bassinet rang me late on Friday asking if your apparent "disappearance" was normal and if the project was really going ahead or should he seek another company. I assume you are in the office now?'

'Yes. I have seen his secretary but not him, I don't think he's arrived yet.'

I couldn't explain to Patrick about how my situation now stood with regard to Ricard and his family but asked him to trust me and appreciate I needed to withdraw from the project. I added I thought Sharon would be perfect for the role.

'I suppose I was expecting this, your optional approach was sound, otherwise I would not have agreed to you starting out in the first place. The problem we have now, of course is to find a suitable person with the command of French and skills to fit the bill and hope my persuasive skills are sufficient to get *Monsieur* Bassinet to agree.'

'Patrick, didn't you hear what I said? Sharon is perfect for the job, her French is better than mine and she's already proved herself to you. If you could show her the project which I think she could do with her hands tied behind her back— in a different meaning from the last one—and also manage her personal life. Please contact *Monsieur* Bassinet and ask if he is agreeable. I've heard him come in, so you might be able to catch him before he goes out again.'

I did what I could on my computer to get things ready for Sharon or who ever came to take my place and, after an initially rather awkward meeting with Charles Bassinet in his office during the afternoon, I met Sharon at Carcassonne airport late in the evening. Sven had driven me and it was well after eleven in the dark October evening, by the time we booked her into the hotel, where I'd reserved a room for three nights. I made sure she was alright and promised to pick her up at eight forty-five in the morning.

As usual Sven had not spoken while in chauffeur mode but once we'd arrived home, he told me Suzanne had returned home from school with a letter addressed to Ricard, she'd dropped it on the kitchen table and gone straight up to her room without saying anything. Because he'd left again, almost immediately, to collect me, he'd no idea what it was about.

'I thought you ought to know before you go in, I will not come in if you do not mind.'

'Of course not, thank you for the driving and thanks for telling me. Looks like Marianne is at your home—the lights are on.'

'Yes, maybe the letter contains something just for her father—and maybe you—to sort out.'

'Thanks again, Sven, I'll be ready at eight thirty tomorrow, good night.'

I entered the house, most of which was in darkness, but a low light came from the lounge where I found Ricard on the sofa with Suzanne resting in his arms, both asleep. I decided not to disturb them, assuming they'd wake up later feeling cold and go to their beds.

§ § §

I was wrong. I woke to find Ricard hadn't come to bed. I pulled on my dressing gown and looked in Suzanne's room, she was not there and the bed undisturbed. I checked my watch, we all should be up and having showers and

259

dressing by now. I found them both almost as I'd left them when I'd gone to bed. Marianne was quietly working in the kitchen preparing breakfast.

'What's happened?'

She shrugged her shoulders.

'When Ricard read the letter…Sven told you of the letter?' I nodded, 'he went upstairs to Suzanne, Sven had already gone to get you for the airport, I waited for an hour, but nothing happened, it was eerily quiet, I heard them speaking in low voices. As they did not come down, I decided to prepare some food and leave it for them in case they wanted it later, then I went home leaving the landing and lounge lights on but turned off all the others. They must have eaten as the plates were neatly piled on the side when I came in this morning.'

'The kitchen was in darkness when I got home, I didn't look in the kitchen and only the lounge light was still on.'

'Good morning,' Ricard said as father and daughter, looking rather dishevelled but smiling, came to the kitchen.

'Good morning, would you like the usual breakfast or an omelette before you go to work?'

'No omelette, thank you, Marianne, usual breakfast please. Suzanne and I are taking the day off so, when you are ready, Yvonne, Sven can drive you to the office. Sorry Marianne, we might be a bit under your feet today, unless you and Sven want to take the car and go off somewhere together.'

There was obviously no explanation forthcoming from either of them even though I waited for a few moments, looking enquiringly at Ricard.

'Well, I'm going to have a shower. I've to meet a colleague this morning. I'll get a taxi back home when I'm ready—I don't know what time, so enjoy your day.' I went to get dressed for the office and met Sven at the car as arranged, neither of us spoke on the short journey to town.

Leaving the house, once again I had a gnawing concern my relationship with Ricard was not solid, he'd not said anything about the contents of the letter or his and Suzanne's strange behaviour, nor come up to see me while I dressed. Was this going to be another barrier between us? Although I'd asked Patrick to pass the project over to Sharon for a different reason, I was glad I'd done so as it seemed as if I might be leaving Lézignan anyway.

C'est ça!

I pulled myself up short.

260

I'm behaving like Suzanne. Do I expect to be involved in everything concerning Ricard and his daughter? Am I experiencing feelings of jealousy and being kept outside? Quite possibly, but I also feel angry.

Sharon had slept badly and was now concerned she'd made a mistake in accepting the project.

'It all happened so fast, Patrick was enthusiastic, but possibly because he didn't want to lose the contract. Mother was supportive and encouraged me to accept, she even started to pack my case while I rang the school asking to see Lucy before I flew. She took the news in her stride, as youngsters do, she has plans to spend weekends over here! But today, I'm not so sure. I've yet to meet *Monsieur* Bassinet, what if he doesn't like me or thinks I can't do it?'

We talked over coffee in the hotel lobby.

'None of the clients know our capabilities, Sharon, it's Patrick who has confidence in you and he assures his clients our expertise, experience and personality are appropriate. This is a fantastic opportunity and if *Monsieur* Bassinet hadn't been convinced, he wouldn't have agreed to the change-over. Come on, finish your coffee.'

Vivienne welcomed Sharon warmly and took us to the office where she'd arranged the furniture to accommodate a second chair.

'It will be a bit squashed for two people but I expect, as before, you will be out more than in.'

'If *Monsieur* Bassinet agrees, I'll be taking over the project from Yvonne, so there'll only be me in here.'

The coolness with which I had been received by Charles Bassinet on Monday had evaporated. The conversation between Sharon and him went smoothly, she had far more questions than I'd posed which obviously made an impression, they explored further options on the way to proceed.

'I am given to understand by *Monsieur* Court, this project in education is a little different from the ones he has accepted in the past, this, I think is good, as it does not bind you to any previously conceived ideas and methodology.'

'Basic project management will apply, *Monsieur*, but yes in a new area and having discussed it with you, I'm sure it's achievable.'

'That is good to hear, now I must get on, as you must.'

Sharon left the meeting in a more positive frame of mind, we spent time with Vivienne who went through how the office ran and of course, the essential coffee! They discussed various issues before Sharon and I sat down and I went briefly through the files I'd already loaded onto the computer. Leaving her to decide what she'd transfer to her laptop at a later date. I handed over the list of contacts I'd been given having highlighted the ones with whom I'd been in contact.

'I'll try and get a couple of appointments this week. I hope you'll come with me it'll be easier to explain the change of personnel if we are together.'

'Of course, but I don't want to hamper your discussions. One request though, if you fix a meeting for tomorrow, could it be in the morning? I must be free to leave by four, do you really need me?'

'Oh yes, please hang about for a while although I'm more confident now than this morning, I'd like your support. It's strange, but I'm having the same feeling as the last time I took over your project.'

'A good feeling, I hope.'

'Oh, yes. Thanks for your confidence.'

'Fancy a walk around town?'

'I'll make a couple of phone calls first.'

§ § §

Vivienne joined us for coffee before we walked, pretty much the same route as I had on my first time, picking up maps.

'What about tonight? Would you like some company or are you fed up with me?'

'Not at all, Yvonne, your company would be great, but surely you have to get back?'

'I told them I didn't know what time I'd be home, I'm at your disposal.'

'Then why not a glass of wine here?'

We entered a Bistro and ordered wine for Sharon and I chose a soft drink, she made no comment on this and took the map she'd picked up earlier out of her bag.

'I'd like to look for rented accommodation, hotels are alright but I'll get bored and would like to make a room more homely and find more enjoyable modes of spending my evenings. As far as I can gather, you didn't need to worry.'

I smiled.

Well, she's settled. Now it's back to my flat in London with my baby.

'Excuse me, *Señoras*, but I overheard you are looking for a room to rent, if it is for one person, there is a large room available in my parents' house, our family home. His last lodger left two weeks ago and the room has been redecorated, I wonder if you would be interested in having a look at it.'

Sharon spread out her map and asked where the house was.

'Well, José,' Sharon looked at his name badge, 'it's just for one and I see no harm in having a look.'

After being introduced to José's father, Pedro José Perez, who owned the Bistro and had the room to rent, it was agreed Sharon and I would go and see the house on Thursday evening. The need for mutual references was agreed and details exchanged, we stayed there and ate a delicious Catalonian meal after which we walked back to the hotel and Sharon waited with me until the taxi arrived.

What will I find when I get "home"? The word sounds more like a bell of doom now.

The taxi pulled up by the oak gate, I paid and entered the drive by the side gate. The solar lights around the courtyard glowed dimly giving sufficient light to navigate to the house door. There were no lights on in Sven and Marianne's flat.

The hall light was on in the main house; as I entered, Ricard came out of the sitting room smiling as he came to embrace and kiss me.

I pushed him away.

'I was beginning to get worried, you are late.'

'I said I didn't know what time I'd be back. I had to spend some time with Sharon.'

'Is everything alright?'

'I don't know, is it?'

'As far as I am concerned, yes. Did you have a good day? How was your colleague?'

'Yes, thank you, a good day and she's well too. And you?'

'Very pleasant, thank you. Would you like something to eat? Marianne left something in the fridge for you.'

'No, thank you, I've eaten.'

'A glass of wine or a brandy nightcap?'

Why not? I only had one with my meal at the Bistro.

'A Merlot would be nice, thank you.'

'I will bring it into the sitting room if, you would care to go in.'

Shit, he's using his charm like the first night we met, hold fast till he tells you.

There was something different about the room layout, almost the same, but slightly different. I sat on the settee.

Just your mood, it's all the same.

'Here you are.'

I accepted the proffered glass, Ricard sat next to me and put his hand on my knee, I moved to one of the easy chairs.

'Yvonne, what is wrong?'

'If you don't know, then—'

'Ah! Suzanne and me having time together! Do not tell me you are having a little tantrum!'

'I hardly think it's a little tantrum! The girl comes home from school in some sort of distress or mood with a letter, the contents of which you don't share with me, you stay up all night sleeping on the couch then take a day off without a word. No! I'm not having a little tantrum—I'm having an angry rage, a bloody big tantrum. Don't you think we've enough problems without you cutting me out? Have I got to beg and ask for an explanation? Do I have to do all the work to get this relationship on any sort of equal and sure footing? Is any of it worth it?'

'Wow, wow, wow, slow down a bit, I am sorry, I have obviously handled it badly.'

'Badly? I should say so.'

'OK, very wrongly then. I was going to tell you this evening, but you were out and perhaps with your mood, it would be better to leave it till tomorrow evening.'

'Oh! Great, so we won't be talking till at least Thursday, because, unless you've forgotten, you're staying home with Suzanne tomorrow evening while I go with Marianne and Sven to meet Paul. And you expect me to carry on without knowing what's going on? Tell me why I should be bothering? And the weekend visit? Will it still go ahead? Don't you think I deserve some answers?'

I got up and went to the kitchen to refill my glass which I'd gradually drained during my rampage, Ricard came behind me, retrieving the bottle then turning me round, he enfolded me in his arms holding me tight. I tried to get out of his grasp, but he held on even more firmly restricting my movements.

'Stop fighting and listen. I have been totally selfish and unthinking, I apologise. Now, about Suzanne and the letter from the school. Apparently, she has been very disruptive recently, it seems her head has been all over the place and her behaviour totally out of character. They have tried to find out what is wrong, both by directly questioning Suzanne but also by asking her friends. As far as they are concerned—apart from distancing themselves from her—they know nothing. Yesterday, she was extremely rude to a member of staff. In his letter, the head apologised for not putting their concerns in writing before, but assumed I was getting the phone calls and I was dealing with it. But yesterday, she was really out of order and he demanded she stay home and I try to find out what is troubling her.'

'But she's been fine at home,' I mumbled into his shirt, I could not move. 'she's not said anything about troubles, has she?'

'No, but if we think back over the recent past, she has been quieter than usual. All the book reading, mini tantrums and isolating herself. I asked her last night to tell me about the books, the stories, she could not remember anything about them; usually, she can relate almost word for word.'

'Could you let me breathe a little, please?' He released his hold fractionally. 'I don't understand why the school didn't contact you earlier.'

'I rang today asking the same question, they have rung several times but there has been a cock-up which I won't bore you with, partly their fault and partly the answerphone.'

I was beginning to feel calm again and started to make a move to release myself from his hold but decided to stay where I was.

Be honest, you need time to compose yourself after that outburst of jealous rage.

'What did Suzanne have to say about her behaviour?'

'She's been getting worked up about the weekend. She says she spoke to *Papom* and picked up some sort of vibe something might happen, she cannot understand why your father is coming, she has been having the dream more often and she is worried about what she calls "all our secret conferences"; why

Marianne is going to Carcassonne and to top it all, she is worried about the future when we are married and if you have babies, she thinks you will die.'

'You didn't tell...?'

'No, do not worry. So, the only means she could cope was to lash out at everyone and everything.'

'Everyone except the people she felt, hopefully still feels, closest to. With us, she just went into her shell. Poor child, she must have felt completely lost.'

'Abandoned, is the word she used. But today, talking, it eventually all came out, she expressed such happiness at some things then went into sort of dark places. A lot of tears as well as a great deal of laughter.'

I extricated myself and we sat at the table.

'Why didn't you tell me this morning?'

'There was little to tell you. Most of this came out today, last night she just clammed up and got me to talk about Charlotte.'

I looked up.

'Have you told her about Jules and her?'

'No, maybe the time will come, but I said nothing and hinted at nothing. Just explained the joy Charlotte had at the farm and how much my parents and I loved her. She did a lot of crying, so did I, she then asked about you and me and why we were having problems. I could not tell her, because I have been so blind as to not see how much of a strong and guiding force you have been. Until you came out with it tonight.'

'Badly expressed and in temper, touched with a bit of jealousy maybe. Not the most efficient approach to resolve our problems. I'm sorry. How is she now? Will she go to school tomorrow or are you two staying at home again?'

'She is calm and relieved to have it all off her chest and she has promised to talk to us in future about any problems. I asked her if she wanted another day off, but she said she needed to go back and apologise to everyone. She said you had taught her putting things off was not good, remember the incident with Sven?'

I nodded.

'Then she asked if she could have a few close friends back here after school, hoping, of course, they wanted to come, to make amends for her behaviour towards them. I rang the parents of those she mentioned and explained, both they and the girls agreed. So, while you are having a great time in Carcassonne, I will be here.'

'Equally enjoying yourself, as some of the parents are bound to want to come and chaperone their little darlings.'

'Yes, I did invite them too. It will be a chance to get to know some of them.'

'Thanks for holding me; it could all have gone badly if you hadn't. You've organised the sitting room between you, what about refreshments? Are you ordering in or dumping a load of quick catering on Marianne in the morning?'

'I suggest you never mention the former to Marianne if you value your life! I've written a note under Suzanne's instructions. It is a pity you will not be here; remember she wanted a party to show you off.'

'We'll fix something as soon as possible to meet both the children and their parents but it seems there is a different purpose for tomorrow's gathering. I'm sorry, I can't cancel tomorrow.'

'No, it is important for you to go. Maybe organising the food for the party will help Marianne keep her mind off the evening meeting.'

'Nothing like labouring over a hot stove to take your mind off things. Which leads me to a question. What do you know about *Señor* Pedro José Perez and his family?'

'I do not see the connection but lovely people, large Catelonian family...' Ricard continued to tell me what I already knew, ending with, 'I often give a reference for them when a new lodger is considering taking the spare room. Why do you ask?'

'And Charles Bassinet's involvement?'

'I think he gave them a loan to set up the business several years ago. Perez has probably paid it off by now, certainly the small one I gave has been. Again, why do you ask?'

I explained about Sharon and our evening.'

'So, the good news is, your colleague is definitely taking over the project? After the weekend, we will have to start thinking of how to manage the visits to gauge *Papom's* inheritance.'

Ricard offered me the bottle; I shook my head.

'Perhaps I shouldn't have had the last one, but I needed it.'

'Which reminds me, I've not seen you to talk to properly, until this evening—you were right, the sperm reports got mixed up. I am and always have been fully active.'

'Then why so long for you and Charlotte and so fast for me?'

267

'I asked the doctor, he said there could be almost any reason, time of the cycle, the woman's fertility, the energy—even good sperm have to swim on each occasion. But he also said, sometimes it just takes longer—a sort of potluck!'

'So, as I said, there's every chance Suzanne is yours anyway.'

'Let's not think about that now. I'm ready for bed.'

We turned the lights off as we went upstairs. Suzanne's door was slightly ajar and she was fast asleep.

After a while so were we, satiated and wrapped in each other's arms.

Chapter Sixteen

'What time did we go to sleep?' I woke as Ricard brought me a cup of tea at seven.

'Later than we should have done, but never mind. They say making up is wonderful.'

'You're wonderful, making up or not. Thanks for the tea.'

'The kitchen is a bit like an industrial area. I think breakfast is available but it might be self-service.'

'Have you or Suzanne told Marianne what you told me?'

'A shortened version and with apologies from Suzanne about the unexpected extra work.'

Sven drove us all to our various workplaces. Suzanne was as chatty as her normal self, obviously yesterday had been cathartic for her. In her bag she had letters of apology to the staff member and head, as well as invitations to her friends for the afterschool gathering. Although she'd spoken to her friends on the telephone, she wanted to give them the invitations and apologise in person.

I joined Sharon for her first appointment feeling my presence rather unnecessary after explaining the change of personnel. My mind kept wandering to the evening meeting between Marianne and Paul, so after lunch I excused myself from Sharon, collected my computer and went home to pack an overnight bag.

Marianne was not in the house when I arrived. I assumed, correctly as it turned out, she was in her own home preparing for the overnight stay and her meeting with Paul. There was an open note on the kitchen table for Ricard about food for the party and stating she would not be returning to the house this afternoon before leaving for Carcassonne, but she and Sven would meet me at the gate at half past four.

I had a hankering for a cup of tea and was drinking this when I heard the car drive up and Suzanne running up the steps in her usual happy manner.

At least she seems to be on an even keel again.

'Oh Yvonne, I wish you could be here tonight to meet my friends, I do so want to introduce you to them.'

'Maybe soon we can have a daytime party and all your friends and parents can come. I'm looking forward to meeting them.'

'I am so sorry about my bad behaviour. *Papa* said he told you about it,' she looked down at her hands and I felt she was about to cry. 'I should have talked to you. I know you would have understood. But I felt so…' She stopped. I took her in my arms.

'There are times when it seems impossible to talk, but providentially there comes a time when it can all come out, the time for you was with your *Papa*. Always remember, we're all here for you—and each other.'

She stifled a sob and grinned. "The Three Musketeers! All for one and one for all?" But there are more than three of us.'

'No matter, it still stands, just change the numbers. Now, you must get ready for your party. Marianne has left instructions about the food and drinks and I must pack a bag for tonight.'

'Is it still a secret?'

'Yes, it is. Now, off you go and get ready, your guests will soon be here and if you're anything like me, I'm hours behind and still have lots to do before they arrive.'

'I love you.'

'And I you; now shoo.'

Ricard entered the house and I heard the car being driven down the courtyard. As he embraced me, he said, 'Sven says Marianne is really uptight about the meeting tonight and wonders if the meeting should be postponed.'

'Too late, Paul will be on his way. Having got this far, it must happen sometime and it might as well be now as it's arranged. She's obviously expecting to go, even if a bit reluctantly. She's every right to be nervous, they both know I might be quite wrong and they know the risk too.'

'With conscious awareness, yes, but I wonder if the emotional stress is just coming into play.'

'And probably affecting Paul too, to call it off will be devastating for him, and if I may say, for Marianne too.'

We heard Sven coming up the front steps and enter the hall.

'Are you ready, Yvonne? Marianne is wanting to go as soon as we can, I think her nerve is about to break. After she had seen to Suzanne's party refreshments, she spent the rest of this afternoon searching through more of old suitcases and papers for something, then just as I was going to collect Suzanne and Ricard, she said she was coming back to the house. She says she found it in Ricard's study. I do not know what she found, she will not tell me, but she put it in her bag to take with her; so as soon as you are ready, can we go?'

'Of course. It won't take me long to put my things into a bag. I'll meet you at the gate in twenty minutes.'

Ricard came upstairs with me and watched as I put a few things into my overnight bag.

'Very professionally done.' He joked.

'Years of training. Take care of your daughter and her friends. See you tomorrow. Ricard, what can you have had in your study Marianne was looking for?'

'I do not know. I will have to go and see if anything is missing. But I do not have anything of Marianne's now. She took everything belonging to her when she and Sven moved to the flat.'

'Well, no time now my dear. We can sort it all out later.'

We kissed, as I passed Suzanne's room, I shouted, 'Bye, have fun.'

'You too!' was her reply.

Fun! You just don't know what is about to explode. Then neither do I.

Marianne and I sat in the back of the car, periodically she sighed then took my hand and squeezed, letting it go a few seconds later. On one of these occasions, I asked, 'Do you want to talk?'

She shook her head. We drove in silence then Marianne said, 'What if he is not my son?'

For a moment, I had no answer then twisted the question back to her.

'Maybe he's thinking "What if she is not my mother?" Surely, it's at least worth a try. If I were with him and not you, I think my answer to him would be the same.'

'Maybe you are right.'

'It's been so long for both of you, Marianne, perhaps I've made a mistake in even suggesting this. But I couldn't marry Ricard and have Paul as my brother-in-law without knowing.'

For the first time in the journey, Marianne turned to look at me directly.

271

'So, this is all about you? Not me and my relationship with Charlotte and my possible son? How can I have been so stupid as to open up to you? Sven, please take me back.'

The anger in her voice shot through me like a lightning bolt.

I'd never thought my action could be interpreted in any other way than trying to help two people get together again. No, not for myself. Although I suppose the way I had just expressed it could be interpreted as an element of selfishness.

Sven pulled off the road into a picnic area.

'Please Sven, we must go on…'

He got out of the car, ignoring me, and opened the door, summoning Marianne out and indicating I should stay where I was. A few minutes later, we were on our way to Carcassonne again. I said nothing nor did Marianne, but later, she tentatively put her hand on mine.

'I am sorry, Yvonne, I was unfair.'

I responded with a smile and we both relaxed.

The hotel was modern and impersonal. I wondered if I'd chosen the right sort of place but reflected this was probably the atmosphere for a difficult meeting. Cold, no emotion, undistinguished. If there was any relationship or emotion between Paul and Marianne, then it could still materialise here.

I told the reception clerk I'd reserved three rooms and asked for the latest time I could cancel the booking. Paul had not arrived, I ordered coffee for the three of us and sat where I could see the hotel entrance. We said extraordinarily little waiting for Paul to arrive which he did five minutes before the agreed meeting time. He looked around the lobby and waved to me.

I stood to go and greet him, turning to Marianne and Sven. 'Here he is.'

Paul and I embraced but I was aware he was watching the two people still sitting. As we approached, Marianne and Sven stood. Sven smiled and extended his hand to greet Paul, but Marianne kept her eyes down to the ground—well, not quite the ground. Paul was dressed as I'd first met him in a t-shirt, shorts and trainers without socks. Marianne was searching his left ankle. Then she looked up at his face and he smiled.

'Charlotte!' she said quietly. 'Look Sven, it is Charlotte's smile. You see?'

'Marianne, I did not know her, she was dead before I met you.'

'Oh, of course, yes she was. Well, he has Charlotte's smile.'

Paul looked rather uncomfortable during this exchange, so I decided, rather unnecessarily, to introduce them.

'Marianne, this is Paul; Paul, this is Marianne.'

'Yes, thank you, Yvonne,' said Marianne not taking her eyes off Paul who smiled again.

'And this,' I continued, 'is Sven. He and Marianne are soon to be married. But I think I told you before.'

'Yes, Yvonne, you did. Can we sit over there? Perhaps it will be a little more private than where you were all sitting when I arrived.'

Paul indicated a group of chairs. He and Marianne positioned themselves so they could continue to examine each other easily. Paul broke the silence which had now settled on us by saying, 'Yvonne has mentioned this,' pointing to his birthmark, 'she said you have a similar one.'

'Yes, to her it indicated there might be a connection between us. The birthmark also appeared on my mother, my daughter and my granddaughter.'

Marianne lifted her skirt sufficiently to expose her left ankle. The birthmarks, now seen together, were almost identical, perhaps just the shape and age of the ankles causing a slight pattern alteration.

I was about to say something when Sven put his hand on my arm to still me. Paul took a deep breath.

'Look, okay, we have a birthmark, but does it really mean anything? We have nothing else to go on, it is circumstantial but I am willing to share with you the little I know about my time as a baby, some of it might fit. So, as we agreed to meet, shall we get on with it?'

He showed no emotion and I thought I saw Marianne sag a little after her hopes had been raised; he cleared his throat. 'When I was five, the couple I called *Mama* and *Papa*—and still do when I see them—told me I was adopted, so although then I did not understand the meaning, I have known pretty much all my life these lovely people are not my natural parents. The way I feel about them, and they about me will not change whatever the outcome of this meeting. At the time, they gave me an envelope and said I was to keep it very safe as one day I might want to use it.'

Paul rummaged in his bag and extracted a large envelope from which he took some papers and passed one of them to Marianne; when she'd finished looking at it, he gave her another.

Marianne read it quietly then put her hand to her face and started to cry, tears falling down her cheeks.

Tears of despair? All her hopes dashed.

'Copies of my birth certificate and adoption papers,' Paul said in response to the questions on Sven's and my faces while Marianne wept. 'Until Yvonne came up with the idea, she had found someone who might be my blood mother, I had forgotten about the envelope. Obviously,' he said with a wry grin, 'I have always kept it.'

'I'm so sorry, Marianne, I shouldn't have interfered, it was just a birthmark I saw after all. Perhaps you were right in the car, I was just being selfish.'

Ignoring me, Marianne removed her trembling hands from her face and reached out to Paul.

'Oh, my dear, I…'

Before accepting Marianne's offer of her hands in what I thought was an act of condolence, Paul again dug into his bag and pulled out another envelope which, with no words, he passed to her. Seeing this, she burst into uncontrollable tears. Paul stood and moved to her, she let him take her arms to help her up, then they moved together, their bodies dissolved into a fierce embrace which lasted and lasted. Eventually, they gently relinquished their grasps and stood looking at each other; when they sat again, it was side by side. Marianne had creased the envelope and contents.

'You do not really need to read it.'

'No, but I would like to, do you mind?'

Paul shook his head, Marianne pulled out a paper and flattened it out on her knee.

Sven indicated to me we should leave them together. I was about to protest but his expression was so insistent, I followed his lead to the bar where he ordered coffee to be taken to Marianne and Paul.

'Sven?'

'It is alright, Yvonne, your hunch has paid off. I saw the name on the last envelope. *For François Charles*. It was written in Marianne's handwriting.'

'Who is François Charles?'

With the look on his face often used to offer patience to a troublesome child, Sven explained, 'Paul; the name she had him christened, his adoptive parents changed his name. The note said, "From his ever-loving mother and sister Charlotte. May the Lord always keep you safe. Until we meet again."'

'Pretty conclusive then?'

Sven nodded. We sat in silence, both with our own thoughts. Mine went initially to Julie and the twins she and Paul, or François Charles, were about to have, then wandered around the different relationships and secrets people have.

After a while drinking soda water, I said, 'Sven, I'm hungry. I need to eat. Should I go and see if they're alright?'

'I agree, sustenance would be a good idea. But let me go and see them.'

He returned a few minutes later saying Marianne and Paul were talking and had a bottle of wine on their table as well as the now empty coffee cups and they too were ready to eat, so he had booked a table to eat in an hour.

'I'll go and confirm the room bookings and pick up my key, you'll all have to register.'

'Fine. I will get the bags and bring them up. I will knock on your door when I have them.'

Before going up, I had a quick look at Marianne and Paul talking, then ordered a glass of wine to be delivered to my room.

The first knock was Sven delivering my bag, he handed it to me, smiling.

'See you in an hour—or just under.'

'Thanks for the bag. See you at dinner.'

The next knock was the waiter with the wine which I sipped before ringing Ricard.

'How are things going?' I asked.

'Not too bad, so far. I think I need a lot more physical support for this sort of party, not only your good wishes. The guests are starting to depart, so I had better go and will ring you back in a few minutes. Sorry, I must go.' The phone went dead.

I unpacked my bag and started to spruce myself up for dinner but decided I felt rather messy and decided on a shower. I was wearing the bathrobe and sipping the wine when a knock came on my door. When I opened it, without waiting to be invited in, Paul pushed past me, shutting the door behind him and took me in his arms.

Oh God, please not a repeat of Patrick.

I pushed him off and tightening the robe, moved backwards.

'Sorry Yvonne, I did not mean to startle you but it is brilliant, well done, thank you. We are both so sure, it all seems so logical, the birth certificate, the envelope—and look—this was in another envelope, with my christening certificate, she gave another one to my sister. Apparently, she has been looking for the one she gave to my twin and found it,' he showed me a silver crucifix and turned it over, his name was engraved, 'the one Marianne has is the same with my sister's name engraved, it seems to be true—Marianne is my blood mother. It makes no change in how I feel about my adoptive parents and brothers, but I think—we think—we know—this is right. We need more time to really get to know each other and the families, but there is time now we have met. Thank you.'

I've seen a similar crucifix hanging somewhere.

I racked my brain, then realised, it was when I was ringing Julie from Ricard's office over the weekend. It was hanging on the photograph of Charlotte on his desk. I wondered if it was still there or if it was the crucifix Marianne was looking for and eventually found this afternoon.

'Yvonne, are you OK? You have not said anything.'

'Yes Paul, I'm fine and I'm really happy for you and Marianne.'

'I hear a "but", Yvonne. What is your hesitation? After all, you started this hare running—like you did at work?'

'We didn't have time to talk downstairs before you met Marianne, but did you speak to your adoptive parents and the rest of your family as you said you would?'

'I had a long serious talk with my parents. They were fully supportive, but obviously a little hesitant, I tried to reassure them of my feelings towards them and that they will not change if the woman I met turned out to be my blood mother. I think I reassured them. As to my brothers, they are all happy with whatever happens, they are all my family.'

'I'm glad—for all of you. Wow, how to get a sudden extended family in one easy meeting.' I paused. 'I hate to put a damper on your happiness and be a bit down to earth, but may I point out we are eating in the hotel and…' I looked at his bare legs and t-shirt.

'Oh, do not worry. Clothes have been sorted, courtesy of the hotel. I will look respectable in the dining room.'

'As this has really worked out so well, I wouldn't really care if you turned up naked.'

He opened his eyes wide. 'I think Marianne might though!'

'And Julie might not be too pleased! OK, see you at dinner.' I smiled as I saw him out.

Thank God his exuberance was no more than true happiness, nothing more. Perhaps, I am being oversensitive.

My phone rang.

'Hello Ricard, I can't talk long, we're just going down to eat, but will you do something for me now?'

'Of course, if I can. What is it?'

'Are you in your office?'

'Yup. Suzanne is still trying to clear up, I must go and help her but what is it you want me to do?'

'Please look at the photograph of Charlotte on your desk.'

'Oh, my dear, I hope you do not mind it still being there.'

'No, of course not; we've spoken about this before but is there anything missing from it?'

'What?'

'Is there anything missing?'

Silence, then, 'Yes, Charlotte's crucifix and chain have gone. Are they what Marianne was looking for? Why did she just not ask? Is there any significance in them?'

'It does seem to have been the clincher, I'll ring you later, I don't know what time the evening will end.'

'It sounds as if you will need to talk, ring any time.'

'Must go, bye.'

I left for the restaurant.

§§§

Having finished my meal and agreed a time to meet in the morning, I left the three of them talking and rang Ricard. He was pleased the meeting had gone well, but I didn't give many details as we agreed Marianne should be the one to tell him. He gave me a brief rundown of the party but again, by mutual consent, decided Suzanne should tell us all about it on her return from school the next day.

'Have you enjoyed having time on your own with her, Ricard?'

There was a slight pause before he replied in the affirmative.

'I think one also needs the stimulus of adults too, if some of the parents had not been at the party, I think I would have found it difficult, but the one-to-one time we had recently, although rather forced on us, has been great. Maybe I have been a bit too wrapped up in myself and my concerns to have given her sufficient attention.'

'There have been several issues around recently to distract all of us, so perhaps not only you but Marianne and I are also guilty. It's a good lesson to learn and hopefully, we'll reap the benefit in the future.'

'Quite the philosopher tonight then! Has Marianne said anything about how and when she will explain the visit to Suzanne?'

'Not to me, but I doubt she'll leave it too long.'

'I hope she does it before we go to my parents on Saturday. What time does your father arrive Friday?'

'He lands at six thirty.'

'Good, I will come with you and we can explain the situation regarding Jules as far as we can, on the journey home.'

'Suzanne is bound to ask to come along, don't you think it would be better to let her do so? Another trip to Carcassonne without her, especially as it's only to pick-up Pops might seem a bit strange and unfair, especially after what's happened recently. We can talk when she's in bed.'

'Maybe you are right. We have both had long days, so I will bid you good night. I love you, Yvonne.'

'I'm glad, as I love you too. Goodnight and sleep well.'

'Goodnight.'

I waited to hear the telephone receiver replaced in its cradle.

§ § §

We checked out of the hotel after a prolonged breakfast. Marianne and Paul seemed convinced they were mother and son and parted reluctantly. Paul now had to go and talk to his adoptive parents and siblings again as well as Julie. We climbed into our respective cars for the journeys to our homes.

I still think of Ricard and Lézignan as home. And it seemed to be getting nearer as a reality.

'Why didn't you ask Ricard for the crucifix?' I asked Marianne at one point while we were travelling.

'I was not looking for it specifically, I was just looking for anything amongst my cases which might have some connection, it was only yesterday, just before you came back from work, I suddenly realised what it was and where I had seen it. I was too wound up by the time Ricard got back to think about telling him. I suppose I am a thief now; it was not mine to take.'

'I doubt Ricard will see you as such, but he did ask me why you'd not just asked for it, I think maybe he would've preferred you to have done so. But he'd not noticed it was missing until I asked him if it was on Charlotte's photograph, I had to push him to look for a missing item; maybe if I hadn't, he would not have noticed and you could have put it back.'

'I will replace it, openly, no more secrets.' She pulled it out of her bag and sat back into the seat, looking exhausted.

Perhaps the events of the last few days were suddenly hitting her. It must have been utterly traumatic, telling me about Ricard, the story of her life and then meeting with a stranger in the hope it would be her son. She sighed and closed her eyes, probably wanting some peace and to gather her thoughts before she had to relate everything to Ricard and, most probably, include Suzanne. Marianne sighed again. I thought it was one of calm, of a satisfaction but touched with exhaustion. However, I was shattered by her next utterance.

'Why did you have to come into our lives? We were all quiet and settled in our safe ways. Everything has changed since you came.'

There did not seem to be any bitterness in her voice; even so, I was astounded she should be resentful.

I had no reply to offer but felt a trembling of anger gently stirring.

'It is just as well you did though,' she continued, taking my hands and then, turning towards me gently touched my face, 'if you had not come bursting in that late summer evening, my supposedly outward calm would have continued to burn up inside me, churning and worrying and searching and beseeching. I do not know who sent you to us, I know you are not a god or prophet, you are, like the rest of us, a human being looking for happiness. Thank you.'

My emotions suddenly took another route. My anger dissipated as quickly as it had arisen.

'I didn't "burst in", I was picked up on a railway platform and unwittingly dragged into your lives by a total stranger.'

'As Marianne says, just as well, for all of us that you did.' Sven momentarily broke his own driving rule and was then silent again for the rest of the journey.

We arrived back in Lézignan in plenty of time for Sven to drop me at *Monsieur* Bassinet's offices and Marianne at home before collecting Suzanne and later Ricard. Sharon hadn't returned from her appointments so, with Vivienne who seemed to have some free time, I went to the café for a coffee.

'Do you know if Sharon has asked *Monsieur* Bassinet about a reference for *Señor* Perez?'

'I suppose there is no harm in telling you, I wrote it this morning—well, printed off a fresh copy for him to sign. He has no qualms in recommending them. He has helped them out in the business and quite often eats at their bistro. Sharon also forwarded an e-mail from your boss with a reference for her she wanted me to print, they are both on her desk. I have been to the Perez house, it is quite…' she hesitated, searching for an appropriate word '…lively, I should say describes it well. It is a real family home where all the lodgers have been happy. There is family life if you want it and seclusion if preferred, but totally quiet it is not!'

'Well, it's up to Sharon, we're off to see the house, room and people this evening. Come on, we'd better get back your boss will sack mine for my wasting your working time!'

'I do enough overtime and extracurricular duties for *Monsieur* Bassinet so half an hour out of the office cementing good relationships is not going to worry him.'

'Extracurricular?' I asked.

'Nothing untoward! Organising his parties, ordering the food and wine, checking his wife is happy with the arrangements, keeping her informed of his diary movements. All above board, I assure you.'

'And do you get invited to these parties?'

'Of course, with my partner. Officially as guests, but in practice I am there to smooth any problems. I expect to see you at some of them too.'

We returned to the office as Sharon was putting down her laptop. She picked up the two envelopes.

'Oh good, you're here. Are you ready to head off to the bistro? How did the evening go? Let's talk as we walk.'

We bade Vivienne goodnight. *Señor* Perez was waiting for us.

'We will get the bus this evening then you will know where to get off, especially in the winter months when the walk is not so pleasant as in the summer.'

After a short journey we alighted from the bus and followed him to his house which was situated a few steps further along the road. It stood in its own grounds approached by a curved drive guarded by strong stone columns. It was symmetrically designed with a central front door over which was a porch with ground floor windows on either side. Three windows on the first, second and third floors were arranged in perfect harmony, lights shone through some of them.

'Wow, this is some house.'

'Yes, it really is, *Señora*, it is as deep as it is wide perfectly designed. But come inside and meet the family, I hope you are both alright for time, my family likes to chat so please, do not think this will be a very brief visit.'

Sharon looked at me, aware I had just returned from, what I told her was a difficult family meeting.

'I'm fine, Sharon, in fact, a diversion is probably a good idea and I would like to satisfy my curiosity about the inside of the house and its occupants.'

We passed in front of *Señor* Perez as we entered his home. After nearly two hours loving the family's friendship, seeing the available room and facilities, I declined the offer of an evening meal with the Perez family and left Sharon with them to enjoy their company and sort out the details of the rental agreement.

§

When I arrived home, Suzanne had already related the news about her party to Marianne and Sven but rewound the tape and started again for my benefit. She retold every detail saying how much Marianne's food had been appreciated, explained Ricard's role in the proceedings and how he had interacted with all her friends and their parents. She sounded both pleased yet surprised at the way he had relaxed and joined in the games.

'He seemed to be having more fun than anyone else!' was her comment when describing the game of charades, 'but he chose the most awfully hard books when it was his turn to act; only the parents had heard of them.'

'I had to involve them too, all you youngsters were getting the answers before any of us.'

'You must've got one though or you wouldn't have had a turn.'

'Oh, he did, Yvonne, but only because I did the book I had been reading during the week. The one you gave me, Yvonne.'

'That was a bit unfair though, wasn't it? Surely none of the others would have known it.'

'Well, it gave *Papa* a chance.' Suzanne grinned and continued to talk, remembering several episodes she'd forgotten to tell the first time until suddenly she stopped. 'I am sorry, I haven't stopped talking, but it was such fun. Thank you, Marianne, for all the food and thank you, *Papa*, again for letting me have the party. Everyone really enjoyed it and look,' she pulled out some envelopes from her school bag, 'so many "thank you" notes.' She spread them on the kitchen table, where we were sitting, offering them to us to read.

When we had finished with them, Suzanne collected the letters together, picked up her bag and prepared to take it to her room.

'Would you like to hear about our trip to Carcassonne, Suzanne?' Marianne had started to place crockery on the table.

'Yes please, but I did not know if you would be telling me, it all seemed a big secret.'

'Yes, it was and it is a little difficult to explain. You might as well know; I nearly did not go.'

'In fact, she wanted me to turn the car around and come back before we got there.'

'If it was something so frightening, why did you want to go in the first place?'

'Perhaps, when I explain, you will understand, go and put your school things in your room while I finish setting the meal. I will talk while we eat or it will get too late and you will be tired in the morning. Oh, do you have any homework tonight?'

'No, no more for this term, we break up tomorrow lunch time.'

During the time it took Marianne to explain to Suzanne her history and the build up to yesterday's meeting with Paul, no-one interrupted her narrative.

'Well, there you have it.' Marianne concluded. Sven put his arm around her shoulders and hugged her, whispering something to which she responded with a smile and a nod.

'May I?' Sven asked Ricard, who nodded in agreement. Sven rose and got another glass from the cupboard.

'Add some water for Suzanne.'

'Oh, *Mamie-Marianne*, this is a special occasion. It is not every day I lose an aunt and get another *Mamie* and an *Oncle!*'

'Even so, you are to have only half a glass of diluted wine, you have school tomorrow.'

'I thought grandparents were supposed to indulge their grandchildren.' Suzanne pouted, looking at Ricard but realised from the slight shake of his head, this time, Marianne would have his support.

'I'll join Suzanne in diluted wine please, Sven. I had a glass at the Perez house earlier.'

How will this now openly confessed relationship alter the dynamics of the household? Perhaps Marianne had been right—why had I entered their lives? Nothing you can do about it now, Yvonne, whether you stay or leave.

Marianne passed Ricard the item she'd been holding, concealed in her clenched hand.

'I am sorry I did not ask you for it.'

Ricard accepted the chain and crucifix, left the kitchen and returned shortly afterwards without it. He looked at me and we exchanged smiles.

It, and they, will always be there. C'est ça!

Having poured the wine and before he sat again, Sven said, 'A toast. To families and honesty.'

It was a quiet repetition from us all.

Suzanne asked, 'Will you be another *Papi*, Sven?'

'I will think about it. Goodnight.'

She went to bed and Ricard and I sent Marianne and Sven to their flat. We cleared the dishes and did the washing up before falling into bed.

'What relationship is Suzanne to Paul and Julie's twins?'

There was no response from Ricard.

Cousins, I suppose, and soon a half-sister or brother. And probably none of this would have come out without a baggage handlers' strike. C'est ça!

Chapter Seventeen

I went with Ricard and Suzanne in the morning, although they had to work, my time in the office was more social and concerned the final hand over of the project to Sharon. She'd really been on her own most of the time recently anyway.

She'd had a very productive couple of days and was returning to London on the four o'clock flight. In retrospect I should have suggested she take a later flight and we could have offered to take her to the airport. This was now an obsolete thought so did not mention it but stored it up for possible use in the future. She was pleased with the progress she'd made and had been met with nothing but enthusiasm about the potential English language school.

Her first week report to Patrick was half written in her head. The only negative aspect of the assignment was she missed Lucy, even though they'd spoken and seen each other every morning and evening on Skype. She was excited about her evening with the Perez family and had agreed to take the room.

'You saw how big the room is and the en-suite is great. The family is so welcoming and there is ample room for an extra bed in my room for Lucy and, if she comes when I am working, such as school holidays, she'll be well looked after, they said mother could have the guest room if she wanted to come too.'

I was relieved Sharon was so positive and felt confident she'd do a good job. I said a temporary goodbye to Vivienne and Charles Bassinet as I didn't expect to be back unless Sharon called for me, but we did anticipate seeing each other socially in the future. I left and took a taxi home.

§

Suzanne was excited as we set off to collect Pops.
'I have so much to tell him.'

'It is not your place to say anything about Marianne and what she has told you, it is for her to decide what to say and when, so, you just stick to your own news.' Ricard's voice was flat and authoritative. Suzanne nodded.

'Yes *Papa*, I will tell him about my bad behaviour at school,' she hesitated, 'and why,' she added the latter with a bit of defiance which Ricard ignored, 'and the party and I will tell him more about my *Papi's* farm we are going to tomorrow.'

'If you tell him everything about it then we needn't go. He won't have any surprises and we can just spend the weekend quietly at home. After all the excitement and travelling I've done this week, I'd welcome a few days of peace.'

'No Yvonne, we must go, everyone will be so disappointed if we do not go. And you promised to arrange a visit during my school break. I promise I will not say another word.'

'Well, miracles do happen,' muttered Ricard.

'Are you alright, Ricard?'

'Yes, I am fine, as you say it has been a rather informative and active week. I am looking forward to seeing your father again and introducing him to my parents.'

On the return journey, Ricard sat in the front of the car with Sven, not a word passed between them except the unnecessary, initial instruction to drive once all our seatbelts were fastened. Suzanne told Pops about school, the party and the plans for the Christmas show which she'd not shared with us. She hadn't been cast in any of the characters but said she was more than happy to be working backstage.

'There's far more to putting on a production than just the final acting, all roles are important,' said Pops, 'I remember doing almost anything when I was at school and helping when Yvonne's mother started out in small theatres. I was stage manager for some of the plays, but the most nerve-wracking function I found was being prompt, especially when the actors missed lines—sometimes pages with vital clues in them—and they had, somehow to get back and include them at a later time, without repeating everything. Oh, how they would dig themselves great big holes!' Pops laughed, 'but it played havoc with my nerves.'

'You said Clementine often got them out of the mess though.'

'Yes, she still does, I think she learns practically everyone's parts, so she knows what has been skipped and manages to include it in her speeches, amazing how she does it.'

'Perhaps I will not volunteer for that role then.' Suzanne had taken this information seriously.

'Oh, give it a try at least once, you never know, you might enjoy it. You're probably made of sturdier stuff than I am.'

§

Suzanne was reluctant to go to bed, even though it was late after we'd finished the evening meal, but Ricard was insistent as we had an early start in the morning. She unenthusiastically agreed to go and pack her bag for the weekend and to call downstairs when she was ready for Marianne to go and say goodnight. She gave Pops a big hug before leaving us in the sitting room with our post meal drinks and said she would say good night to Ricard and me when we came up.

'I hope you will be asleep by then, I do not want you bleary-eyed and crotchety from tiredness tomorrow.'

'Oh no, *Papa*. I will be awake and ready before any of you.' So, with her ebullient enthusiasm for the next day, she left us.

Deferring to Marianne, Ricard let her explain, without going fully into all the history, her relationship with Paul and Charlotte and so how all our families are connected.

Pops got up from his chair and moved to the table where Marianne had placed the brandy and other bottles, he lifted one and silently asked Ricard for permission to pour himself another; this duly granted, he turned to face us.

'Thank you, Marianne, for telling me. I'd some inkling from Julie there was going to be an interesting piece of information awaiting me when I arrived this weekend, I'm glad we've got it out in the open before the visit to Ricard's parents. Well, Marianne, Sven and Ricard, I don't know whether to welcome you all to our extended family or whether you should be welcoming us to yours!'

'How about a mutual welcome?' Sven raised his glass and we acknowledged each other.

'However,' Pops resumed his seat, 'as Suzanne is obviously party to this information, she did refer to you, Marianne, as *Mamie-Marianne* or something similar at one point earlier this evening, I surmise, late though it is, there is more you wish to tell me and why Suzanne was sent to bed with such firmness.'

286

At this point, Marianne responded to Suzanne's call indicating her bag was packed and she was ready to get into bed.

'You carry on, I know what you will tell Clive, I will be back to join in the decision of how we go ahead with the potential meeting.'

Ricard nodded in agreement as Marianne left the room, closing the door behind her.

'Clive, the original request for you to come this weekend to visit my parents was, as you know, to act as a sort of referee about the problem and misunderstanding between me and my parents, which is now resolved. However, a potentially greater problem has arisen.'

'And this has to do with the stranger Yvonne met in Leeds?' asked Pops.

'Yes.' Ricard explained the outcome of our last week's meeting with his parents, resolving their differences yet raising the issue of Suzanne's parentage, 'which,' he emphasised, 'has no bearing on how I feel about her, she is my daughter and I will not let this klutz get even near to her. And I do not want Suzanne to know.'

'Never?' asked Pops quietly.

'No, not yet at any rate, not just yet. One day maybe, but why should she even want to know? She is my daughter and now we know there is a strong possibility she is my blood, why raise the question in her mind?'

Marianne had joined us again and had been sitting quietly listening to the two men talk.

'I too wonder if she should be told, possibly before Sunday, in the safety of your parents' home, with her family near her. A gentle explanation might be preferable to rough and raw—and possibly fuming—outbursts from you and Jules.'

'If, and I emphasise if, he is really coming to try and see Suzanne, wouldn't it be better she was prepared?'

'As you say, "If". You are not one hundred percent sure, are you, Yvonne? And, if it is a different reason, why should the girl be upset by knowing I am possibly not her blood father and how she was conceived? I am her father in all and every other way and always will be, he cannot take her away from me.'

Suzanne burst into the room in her nightgown, tears streaming down her face.

'Yvonne, Yvonne, I had it again. Worse this time. The fighting, it is *Papa* but not him, someone else, I do not know who it is.'

I grasped the frightened girl in my arms as she threw herself onto my lap, clinging tightly, she turned her tearstained face to Ricard.

'It is you, but it is not you. Oh, *Papa*, I wish it would stop. I have had it so many times recently. When will it stop?' She then sobbed hard and pressed into me. After a while, she calmed down, and as before, she went back to sleep. Ricard took her from my arms and carried her to her bed and left me to settle her covers. I sat with her for a few minutes before returning downstairs.

It's strange how these dreams come, exhaust her and then let her sleep again.

As I returned to the sitting room, I heard the end of Pops' input into their conversation.

'…but of course, I'm not a child psychiatrist.'

Marianne was pouring coffee.

'No, Clive, she is not to know—not till I am sure it is the right time. She is my daughter and I ask you all, in fact tell you all, not to say anything until I agree.'

'Alright. But we have got no further on how you think Sunday, if it is Sunday this man arrives, is to be handled. Do we all lock ourselves in the house until he leaves? Which might not be for several days, for all you know he might have taken the stopover in Paris to renew his passport, so he could miss his flight and camp out for years, keeping us all hostage till he gets what he wants.'

'A bit over dramatic, Pops.' I smiled and suggested we all think of a possible way to handle Jules, should he arrive. No one had any practical suggestions, but some of the mad cap ideas had us all laughing which was good to relieve the tension before going to bed. Finally, we agreed to play it by ear and hope our joint antennae were synchronised when the time came. We also assured Ricard, none of us would say anything to Suzanne unless he said to do so.

§ § §

I turned in bed on waking, expecting to see Ricard, but was greeted by Suzanne's face. Over her tousled hair, I could see the back of Ricard's head. They were both still fast asleep even though the low October light was starting to push through the gap between the curtains, and the smell of coffee and freshly baked croissants, was emanating from downstairs. I slipped out of bed, picked up my robe and went down.

'In your bed again last night.'

'Yes, good morning, Marianne. I don't know what time she came, but obviously she needed some reassurance and I don't know if she disturbed Ricard, but I was not, but they are both still sleeping.'

'Sven is giving the hire car a final check and I have packed some food for the journey. We will find somewhere to stop for a coffee break before we are due to arrive.'

'What a lovely idea.' I felt the conversation was rather restrained and asked what was wrong.

'Oh, I do not know. It is probably just being aware we cannot talk openly and easily about what is on our minds. I respect Ricard's view but cannot but think he is wrong.'

'I agree, but we must try and relax and have a good time. For my part, starting with some coffee and delicious warm croissants. You must have been up at the crack of dawn to prepare these. Has Pops been down yet?'

'No, strangely enough, you had better knock on his door too.'

After I'd eaten, I took a second cup of coffee upstairs and to wake up the sleepers. We were going to be late leaving if they didn't get up soon. Pops was coming out of his room and we met on the landing, exchanged morning kisses.

'Lovely coffee and food downstairs. Did you sleep well? Are you packed and ready to go?'

'Good, no and yes in that order. I'll see you later dear. Yvonne,' he sighed, 'I thought your siblings were a problem, but this is a step above any of them!' he grinned and went down for breakfast.

Eventually, we were all settled in the larger car Sven had persuaded Ricard to hire so the six of us could travel more comfortably. Several blankets, which were welcome when we stopped for a break at a picnic spot on our way, had been placed with the basket of snacks and coffee in the boot. Although the sun was shining, it didn't give out much heat and did little to take the edge off the October breeze.

§

Ramon extended both hands to Pops as he introduced himself and offered a heartfelt welcome as he did so; Matilde welcomed him with a hug and the double cheek kiss. They then turned their attention to the rest of the family, Suzanne holding back until everyone else had been greeted when she made up for her unusual retiring manner and commandeered her paternal grandmother's attention.

Ramon, after we had enjoyed coffee and sweet meats sitting around the kitchen table, took Pops for a walk around the farm. I stood watching them from the window, they started off in high spirits, laughing and joking. When they reached the gate to the field of cows where Ramon and I had stood last week, they, like us, leaned against the top rail. After a while, it appeared the conversation had turned to more serious matters with Ramon gesticulating in his manner which, after a time I noticed, to my amusement Pops was copying. I imagined they were talking about all the information gathered about the expected visit by Jules.

Suddenly, Ramon seemed to freeze and stared pointedly at Pops, shaking his head, both men turned towards the house but did not make a move to come towards it. Ramon shook his head again and put one hand to his brow and the other on the gate, seemingly to support himself. Pops waved at me.

'Ricard, I think we should go and see if Ramon is alright.'

'I assumed you knew, Ramon.' we heard Pops say as we approached the two men. Ramon shook his head.

'God, there are so many hidden parts of our pasts, I had no idea, she has never even hinted. Does Suzanne know?'

'Yes, Ramon, Marianne told her.'

Matilde and Suzanne came racing up to us, looking anxious, Marianne and Sven, I noticed, had stayed behind watching from the window. It took a while for the news to be assimilated by Matilde who turned from the group and walked back to the kitchen where she embraced Marianne, they disappeared from our view and Sven joined us in the yard.

'It is alright, *Papi*, please do not worry, I will still love you and *Mamie* and I still have Marianne, whether she is *ma Mamie* or *ma Tante*.'

'It takes a bit of getting used to, Suzanne.' Ramon ruffled the girl's hair.

'Are you alright, *Monsieur* Ramon?' Sven offered Ramon his arm.

'Yes, thank you, my boy, let us go and see if there is any lunch. I could also do with a cognac if we are to face the next onslaught.'

'What onslaught is the next, *Papi*?'

Oh Lord, Ramon has forgotten we've agreed to say nothing to Suzanne.

'Just a phrase used after a bit of a shock, Suzanne, come on, let the men go ahead. You could say we have had the assault on our reasonably comfortable lives with the news of Paul and Marianne, and even the news about the school Christmas show we knew nothing about, until yesterday, I expect you've volunteered your father and me to do some jobs to help, I wonder when you were going to tell us! Come on, show me a bit more of the farm before lunch, where are the horses kept?'

'Stabled.'

'Yes, sorry, stabled.'

We walked to the barn where two large horses stood quietly. I looked around at the farm machinery, ploughs and other hefty equipment, visualising Charlotte managing the heavy gear needed to harness up these four-legged workers. She must have been extraordinarily strong, much stronger than the few pictures I'd seen of her indicated. Suzanne leant over the stall side and patted the animals, they snorted in what I thought was an affectionate manner.

'Do you ever get on their backs, to ride them, Suzanne?'

'Once or twice, with *Papi* walking with me, it is extremely high up and I am not sure if Troy liked me on his back though, he seemed a bit unsettled by it,' Troy moved restlessly and hoofed the ground as Suzanne put her hand out saying, 'this one with the light mane, Angus, seemed not to worry so much but they are really work horses, sometimes I ride behind *Papi* on him when he puts them out in the field, but Troy does not like me on him so *Papi* lets him follow or leads him.'

I stared at the horses.

I wonder if it had been Troy out with Charlotte and my mind started to imagine the alternative scenes.

'Would you like a ride on one of them?'

With an animal of his size and the trappings of a plough, the bruises and cuts could easily be excused as an accidental trip and fall.

'Are you alright, Yvonne? You have gone a funny colour.'

'What? Yes, absolutely fine, my dear, I don't think I've brought any suitable trousers to wear even if Ramon would take me on one of them. Come on, the others are probably ready for aperitifs before lunch, I know I'm ready for a drink.'

'Me too!' she grinned.

Ramon and Matilde were fully composed by the time Suzanne and I joined everyone in the sitting room where the conversation was on general issues and Ricard was dispensing drinks. After lunch, the weather suddenly turned extremely inclement and no one felt like battling the wind for a further tour of the farm so it was deferred until another time. We spent the afternoon in companionable, extended family discussions and activities.

Ramon and Pops set up the chessboard and became engrossed in the game. It was not till late in the evening, after we had eaten and Suzanne in bed, there was a chance to talk further on the impending visit by Jules. But apart from Ramon staying home in the morning, neither he nor Matilde had come up with any further suggestions as how the day should be handled. The main issue, however, was Suzanne should be protected as far as possible from being alone in Jules' presence and gaining the knowledge of her possible blood father.

§ § §

The church seemed too large for the small congregation which consisted of the local population, some second homeowners taking advantage of the school holiday to ensure their properties were safe for the winter months and a few holiday makers, mostly British and Spanish, enjoying the final autumn sunshine.

Sitting between us, Suzanne nudged her father's arm. '*Papa, Monsieur* Jacques is sitting there. Should I tell him *Papi* is waiting at home for him?'

'What do you mean, Suzanne?'

'When I asked *Papi* if he was coming to church this morning, he said "no because someone had to stay on the farm this morning" but I said "why, as nothing happens on a Sunday morning" then he said, "well, I have to wait to see my neighbour, he said he would do the evening milking for me " so I said "will it be *Monsieur* Jacques who comes over sometimes for supper when I have stayed with you?" and he said "yes, he said he would come sometime this morning to see me." But he is sitting in church, shall I tell him?'

'No, dear, do not disturb him, now is not the right time, is it? They probably did not fix an exact time, but just said in the morning. He will probably go on his way home.'

After the service, Ricard excused himself from our group and spoke to *Monsieur* Jacques who looked a little surprised to be approached. After a

292

moment, he recognised Ricard and shook hands warmly and although, with initial reluctance, he agreed to the urgent request to see Ramon on his way home.

'It is exceedingly difficult to explain just now, *Monsieur*, but it is really important. Perhaps you would care to walk with me—ahead of the rest of my family.'

We spent an enjoyable hour in *Monsieur* Jacques' company. Although a trifle bemused as to why he had to visit Ramon, he had the sense or intuition not to probe. We sat in the dining room looking out of the windows across the fields. The view was as majestic as Matilde had indicated and complemented by several glasses the local wine. Suzanne played happily with the games from the cupboard in the adjoining room, inevitably setting out the chessboard just before *Monsieur* Jacques took his leave.

'It was lovely to see you again, Suzanne, will you be staying with your grandparents for the holiday?'

'I am not sure yet, *Monsieur* Jacques, I would like to stay.' She looked at Ramon and Matilde who said they would see.

'Well, if you do, I hope to see you sometime,' *Monsieur* Jacques moved on quickly, 'and it was a pleasure to see you again, Ricard, and to meet you, *Madame*,' he turned to Pops, 'a great pleasure to make your acquaintance, *Monsieur*, I hope we meet again.' He bade Marianne and Sven a friendly farewell and kissed Matilde at the kitchen door. Ramon escorted him across the yard and the two men walked down the track side by side and out of sight.

'Can I stay, *Papa*?'

'I think we will decide that later, Suzanne, as you said we have not discussed it yet and your grandparents may have a busy week with visitors and end of year farm jobs to do.'

Suzanne frowned and was about to say something but obviously thought better of it; instead, she turned to Pops.

'Do you think we have time for a game of chess before lunch, *Papi-Pops*?'

'The start of one at least, but whether there'll be time to finish it I don't know. You're beginning to think a little more before making a move, so the games take longer. But let's start. I'll just refill my glass.'

Sven and Ricard returned to the chairs by the window with the papers while Marianne and I joined Matilde in the kitchen to help prepare the mid-day meal.

'Yvonne,' Ramon entered the kitchen, 'I understand you want to borrow some trousers and go for a ride on one of the plough horses.'

I laughed.

'I have never been on a horse in my life and I don't think getting on one the size of those beasts would be a particularly good start. Where on earth did you get that idea?'

'Something to do with how you reacted when you were out with Suzanne yesterday afternoon.'

'Oh, in the barn before lunch, my mind was imagining the scene when…,' I stopped, thinking it redundant to put into words the thoughts on all our minds, 'she doesn't miss much, does she?'

'No, and I wonder if she is aware of the tension under all our behaviour— well, not all, but a lot of it.'

'She is sensitive to these things, but maybe she just thinks it is because we are all together and Clive is here. It is a vastly different gathering from those we are used to. Add to this she knows some of the information we have accumulated over the last few days and hours, it is enough to alter anyone's behaviour.'

No-one disputed Marianne's analysis. I trusted she was right and certainly Suzanne's mind was well occupied trying to beat Pops at a game of which he was a master.

'Do you want me to set the table in here or the dining room, Matilde?'

'The dining room please, Yvonne, it is used so seldom I want to serve both meals there today. And it will be more pleasant as we are a large family group.'

§

After a delicious lunch Matilde, reluctantly at first, accepted my offer to see to the kitchen while she went and sat with Ramon, Marianne and Pops. I dragooned Suzanne into helping me while Ricard and Sven took themselves off for a walk. With paying guests, Matilde and Ramon had sensibly installed a dishwasher and I found Suzanne was logical in the way she packed the crockery and cutlery. Her lively chatter helped pass the time. I still found it strange there was not one in the house in Lézignan and mooted this to Suzanne.

'I think you will have a battle on your hands, Yvonne. Neither *Papa* nor Marianne want one. And just think, you would not have such close times to just talk. As *Papa* says, it will not do itself, so why not use the time and talk, sometimes, having something to do with your hands helps if you have something difficult to talk about', she took the glass I'd washed by hand and rinsed, 'like

294

now,' she continued, 'I cannot remember where I was, but I heard someone talking about an elephant hiding in the room, I know we were not at a zoo, but wherever I was, no one wanted to talk about the elephant, I looked everywhere but I could not see it. Yvonne, I think there is one here. I am getting scared.'

I dropped the dishcloth I was using and held her by her shoulders at arms' length and looked in her face.

'Suzanne, there is nothing to be scared of, we will never let anything happen to you as long as we can prevent it.'

'But there is something going on, Yvonne.'

'Come on, enough washing up, if washing up is going to set your imagination running, I'll definitely have a dishwasher.'

'Not if I have anything to say about it!' Ricard entered the kitchen followed by Sven, bringing in the fresh smell of autumn air.

'See, I told you so, Yvonne. But I am going to leave you two to discuss it,' she turned at the door leading to the comfortable living room, 'and the unseen animal.'

'Do not tell me she is on about a dog again, how many times have I said—'

'No, Ricard, she hasn't mentioned a dog, she wants to know what the elephant is.'

Ricard looked bemused, wrinkling his face in question.

'She knows what an elephant is.'

Sven sighed, 'Well, should she be told before the explosion?'

'There might not be one, Sven.'

'I agree, Yvonne, there might not, but if there is, would she be better prepared if she knew?'

'And a waste if there is not.'

'You know she will be aware of something and be worried.'

'Pardon my stupidity, what are you two talking about?'

'Suzanne is starkly aware something is going on, Ricard. She's obviously picked up vibes from us all, she wants to know what's going on.'

'No!' Ricard left the kitchen and I heard him go along the corridor to the rooms.

I turned to follow.

'Leave him for a bit, Yvonne, it is his decision, we must support him. If we do not, then there can no longer be trust between us all.'

'And what about the trust Suzanne has in us?'

'She knows we all will do our best to protect her. If later she decides what we did was not right, or could have been handled better, then she will say.'

'And we will be responsible for the fallout.'

'But for now, it has to be a united front with Ricard.'

'OK. I'll finish in here you go and join the others. I'll be through in a minute.' I leaned against the sink knowing Sven was right. I'd no more idea how to handle the unknown than the others.

§ § §

Everyone, except Ricard, had moved to the living room into the comfortable couches and large armchairs, the open log fire had been lit and a warm glow enveloped the room with the heavy curtains drawn against the encroaching night. Sven had taken over the challenge of the chess board, now laid up as draughts and he was winning against Suzanne whose face was full of concentration and an element of bewilderment. When the game was over, Pops took Suzanne's place and thoroughly beat Sven.

'How very ungentlemanly of you, Clive.'

'Well, I cannot have you beating Suzanne in three games without some sort of a challenge.'

'OK. Best of three?' Pops won all three. They shook hands and grinned.

Ricard joined us, bringing in some cold air on his clothes.

'Been outside?' asked Pops.

'Yes, just a little fresh air and exercise before another great meal. I will get too fat if I do not work off some of *Mamon's* food.'

'If that is a hint you are hungry, my son, you will have to wait, the meal will be at eight o'clock and not before,' she looked at the clock on top of the cupboard which stored all the games, 'at least another hour.'

'Can I do anything, Matilde?'

'No, not yet, plenty of time, but when the time comes, I think we will use the cutlery you will find in the sideboard, rather than that we have been using.'

Sven had set the board up for chess and asked Pops to show him how to play properly, he seemed to be growing more in confidence in his company.

'Draughts is one thing and needs forethought, but I know this is even more demanding.'

296

'Right. You already know the basic moves; it's the tactics you're after, I suspect,' he offered his closed fists to Sven, each holding either the black or white pawn. Sven thought for a moment then tapped one of Pops' hands.

'OK, you start.' Pops said when he opened his hands offering him his chosen colour.

'Is that good?'

'Statistical research indicates you have a marginal advantage, yes, but probably not just yet.'

Suzanne was kneeling by the board.

'Suzanne, will you do me a favour, dear?'

'Of course, *Mamie*.'

'Would you please close the curtains in the dining room? I think they are still open, then, go upstairs and under your bed, you will find a wooden box, I would like you to bring to me.'

'Of course. Is it your secrets box, *Mamie*?'

'Just a few bits I have kept over the years.'

'I keep mine under my bed too.'

Suzanne went off and closed the curtains ready for dinner before going up to her room to fetch the box for her grandmother which had obviously aroused her curiosity.

A minute later, her terrifying scream ran through the house, shattering the peace of the Sunday evening.

Chapter Eighteen

Matilde started to get out of her armchair.

'I'll go, Matilde.'

I ran up the stairs to Suzanne closely followed by Ricard.

Suzanne was curled up on the bed, her face buried in a pillow, shaking in fear and still screaming. Matilde's box was on the floor by the window.

'Yvonne, it is him, the man in my dream! I knew it was not *Papa*. That man is the one fighting in my dream. It was here, I said I knew where it was, but could not recognise it in my dream.' She lifted her head from the pillow and turned to me, pushing her body into mine. 'Send him away.'

Ricard stood to one side of the window and looked out at his brother without disclosing himself to the man whose attention was now fully on the window.

'Stay here. Keep her away from the window and do not come downstairs.'

I listened to Ricard's steps as he returned down the stairs and then the murmured voices, trying to decipher what was being said. The sound of the kitchen door being opened then closed reached the bedroom before Marianne joined us and sat on the bed. Suzanne shuffled from me to her arms, continuing to shake and sob.

'Who is he?' she whispered.

I moved to the position Ricard had taken at the window and looked down at three men standing stiffly in the yard, forming a rough triangle in their positions. Jules had dropped his backpack on the ground and turned to his father, extending his hand which was ignored by the older man; he made a similar gesture to Ricard who followed his father's lead.

'He is your father's brother,' Marianne answered eventually to break the silence which had fallen as thickly as a deep blue velvet curtain.

'The one who is my godfather?'

'Yes.'

Suzanne slipped from Marianne's arms, off the bed and lay on the floor looking out of the window.

'This is the angle of the yard in my dream, no wonder I did not recognise it, I do not lie on the floor anymore, but I must have been down here when I saw the fighting.'

'So, it was only by the chance request for the box you were down there this evening.'

'Yes, I crawled under the bed to get the box; before I got up, I looked out of the window. The man waved and I was about to wave back but...'

'Come away from the window, Suzanne, your father said for you not to go there.'

She stayed on the floor but turned from the window to look at Marianne.

'This is what my dream is about, my uncle was fighting in my dream. Who is the person he is fighting? Is it my *Papa*?'

'How can it be your dream? You were only eighteen months old; you could not have seen the fight. I was with you putting you to bed,' she wavered, 'wait a minute though, I had left you to get something from the bathroom; when I returned, I found you curled up by the bed, shaking. Something had frightened you, so it is possible you saw the fight from this window as it would have taken time for me to hear the shouting from the bathroom. You must have taken yourself off the bed when I left you. I have never connected it to your dream.'

'It would make sense, somehow this deep memory of the fight is stimulated in the form of a nightmare—or dream—whenever the farm is mentioned.'

Suzanne nodded towards the window and the yard outside.

'Did you know he was coming? Is he the elephant, Yvonne?'

I nodded. 'I couldn't tell you.'

We'd been so engrossed in our discussion we'd not noticed Sven and Pops join the other three in the yard. Ramon and Ricard seemed not to have moved from their original positions and still maintained defensive stances but Jules, with his breath turning into cold vapour as he spoke, was walking around in an aggressive manner, brandishing his arms in a threatening manner one moment and seemed to be pleading the next.

Quietly and with an appeasing gesture of his arm, Pops, wearing a thick overcoat, approached Jules and guided him towards the barn where Troy and Angus were stabled. Sven followed. Jules looked shocked and was obviously questioning who these men were. But Pops just quietly moved on, inviting, by signal, for Jules to follow him. In response to something Ramon said, Pops shook his head and motioned for him and Ricard to go back inside.

'Shall we go downstairs and ask what has been happening? He must be my uncle and godfather. I must ask *Papa* what he wanted and why they have all been acting in this strange way to a family member. If I had a brother and not seen him for a long time, I would want him to come in and talk to us.' She said this last sentence as we entered the kitchen where Ramon, Ricard and Matilde were now sitting at the kitchen table in silence.

'*Papa*, what is going on? Why cannot your brother come inside?'

'Suzanne, eight years or so ago, my brother left here suddenly leaving your grandparents at a difficult time on the farm, he just walked out and has now decided to just walk back in again and expected to be welcomed as if nothing had happened, after all these years without a word to them or me. How do you expect him to be welcomed?'

The response Suzanne gave elicited an exclamation from Matilde.

'Suzanne, dear, your sentiment is in the right place, but when he left, the "prodigal son" did so without guilt, my son did not.'

'What do you mean, *Mamie*?'

Matilde, whose composure all day had been calm, began to dissemble.

'He was guilty of a great sin which he has been hiding for years.'

'Enough *Mamon.*' Ricard put his hand on his mother's shoulder, 'please, stay calm, there is no need for this, it has nothing to do with Suzanne.'

'*Papa*, I may be young, but I know the dream I keep having is something to do with the man in the barn with Sven and *Papi-Pops*, he is linked to—no, not linked—he is the dream. I think I have worked out, upstairs, with Marianne and Yvonne, how I saw the fight in the dream. It was him and you fighting, I should know what it is about, I need to know why, it must be something to do with me.'

Pops entered from the yard leaving Jules outside standing in the light from the open door with Sven by his side.

'Suzanne, come and stand here by me please.'

Ricard took a step forward uttering a protest, against which my father raised his hand and beckoned Suzanne who moved with confidence as instructed. She looked at Ricard as she passed him.

'I have to know, *Papa*,' she pleaded.

'What are you doing, Clive?'

Pops took hold of Suzanne's shoulders and held her in front of him as he replied, 'Hold your peace, Ricard.'

Sven moved a little closer to the door as Pops guided Suzanne to stand in front of him in the open doorway looking out to Jules, who smiled.

'Hello Suzanne, I do not expect you remember me, but I am your fa—'

Ricard shouted, 'No!' and put his arms around Suzanne.

'For God's sake, get her away, Clive.'

Sven moved to close the door.

'That was not—'

'Wait,' shouted Jules, 'I was saying I am your father's brother, your uncle Jules and your godfather,' he continued quickly, shouting, then more calmly, 'it has been a long time since we saw each other, so I doubt we would have known each other if I had not introduced myself.'

Suzanne tried to move towards him but was restrained by Pops and Ricard as Jules took a step backwards.

'No, do not come to me, Suzanne, it will not be safe. See, I must wear gloves now,' he extended his gloved hands, 'but even so they do not protect other people from the skin disease I have. It is something sheep shearers pick up sometimes and I do not want anyone, especially you, my lovely…goddaughter, to be harmed by me,' he moved his eyes, focussing on Ricard, 'in any way.'

'Have you come all the way from Australia with your hands in gloves?' asked Suzanne looking bemused at the sudden change in topic.

For a moment, Jules seemed to hesitate.

'No, I thought it had cleared up before I left, but maybe the European climate stimulated it again.'

'What does it look like?' Suzanne's curiosity took over.

Was she leading Jules into unknown territory, he was obviously thinking hard.

'I suppose the next best thing to describe it is leprosy.'

'Yuk.'

'Yes, yuk.' Responded Jules.

'Can he come in, *Papi-Pops*? It seems silly to have come all this way from Australia and not be able to come into his home.'

'No Suzanne,' Pops looked at Sven who'd spoken, 'perhaps, Jules, if your parents agree, after we have all gone tomorrow, you might like to return in the afternoon to see your parents. You said the infection did not affect people who were used to working full time with other animals, but after we are gone, so we do not catch anything.'

'Yes, I agree, it would be lovely, I would like to although it will mean missing the rest of my family. Is that alright with you, Mother?'

'Yes, my son, that would be wonderful, will you stay long?'

Matilde was so keen to see her son now he had reappeared and was being so reasonable about Suzanne, she tried to go out to him, but Ramon prevented her as Jules took another step backwards, saying, 'No, Mother, do not touch me now. I will see you tomorrow. Father?'

Ramon nodded.

'It was good to see you again, Suzanne. Perhaps godfather and goddaughter should keep in contact in the future.'

'That would be nice, I hope your hands get better.'

'Thank you.'

Jules left and Sven closed the kitchen door on the retreating figure.

'Oh, can I stay then please, *Mamie*? *Papi*? Then I can see more of my uncle.'

'Not this time, my lovely one. I think your grandmother and I would like a little time with our son on our own, I am sure you are old enough to understand. We will find out what his plans are and let you and Ricard know.'

'*Papi-Pops*, you had a long time talking with my uncle; what did he tell you?'

'A great number of things, Suzanne. But now, I am getting a bit tired and would like a drink and specially to warm up. So, you will have to wait until I am ready to put all the information he has told me about his time in Australia into some sort of order before I tell you.'

'I still think it strange he could not come in, after all his parents and brother are here, in fact most of our family.'

'You want to get leprosy?' snapped Matilde.

'To get leprosy takes months of close contact, *Mamie*, not an hour or two or even a day.' Suzanne's response was equally sharp.

'Apologise to your grandmother, Suzanne. You do not speak to her in that manner.'

'Sorry *Papa*. I apologise to you, *Mamie*. It has been a strange evening.'

'You seem to be able to make up any excuse to suit yourself; one minute you say you are grown up and the next you act like a rude child, you cannot have it both ways.'

'No *Papa*. Please excuse me a moment, I must go and get the box *Mamie* asked for some time ago.' She left us, holding back her tears.

I started to follow but was stopped sharply by Ricard.

'Leave her please, Yvonne.'

I nodded.

'How did you manage that, Clive?'

'It only gives you breathing space, Ricard. But please Ramon, may I and Sven have a drink? It was tense and touch-and-go out there; he is one angry and jealous man, though exactly what it is, I am not sure.'

We all moved into the living room where Sven stoked up the fire to a brilliant blaze and drinks were dispensed. We waited till Pops was ready to impart the discussion in the barn.

'Should I wait for Suzanne to be in bed?'

'No, she was upset and may be a while. You can stop if necessary.'

'There is little to tell actually. Essentially, he had come to see all of you, he thought you, Ramon and Matilde, would welcome him with open arms because he presumed you had no idea of what he'd said to cause the fight and assumed you, Ricard, would have been too ashamed or embarrassed to tell your parents about what he'd said about your apparent inability to have children. And of course, Charlotte by then, had gone to her grave.'

'I will kill him if he touches Suzanne. Did he admit doing it?'

'He said he'd already told you so, eight years ago.'

'What does he want? Why has he come back?'

'He said, just to see you all, including Suzanne.'

'You said something about "breathing space."'

'We,' Pops looked at Sven who nodded, 'tried to explain the sensitivities of a young girl and how his bursting in on her would be too traumatic. So as a compromise, we were allowing him to see and speak with her tonight for a short while—'

'On the condition,' Sven interrupted, 'he said only what we agreed in the barn. One word out of place and the door would be slammed in his face, which it nearly was.'

303

'Yes, he tried to pull a nasty trick. The visit tomorrow was part of the bargain but not till we have gone and Suzanne is away from here. Then, I am afraid, Ramon, it is up to you and Matilde to dissuade him from causing any trouble.'

'Unless,' I said; everyone looked at me, 'we jump in before him and explain to Suzanne the circumstances.' Ricard jumped up, but before he had a chance to respond, I continued, 'I have agreed with you until now, your way was right, but then they were theoretical "what ifs"; we now have a situation where Jules is determined to disrupt Suzanne's life—all our lives. I saw his face this evening, the hate he has for you and the almost pathological desire to have Suzanne. I saw him in Leeds, he's not going without Suzanne knowing and his thirst to crush you assuaged, Ricard.'

'Is he really so vicious?'

'Yes, though how Yvonne knew, I don't. But the things he said in the barn reflect exactly what she has said. I am beginning to think Suzanne should be told, carefully and sensitively, by you, Ricard, not with any blame or anger, but with just the straightforward facts.'

'Hardly easy, especially without emotions.'

'I agree and any help you need will be available. But can you imagine the hurt to Suzanne, and you, if you let Jules blurt it out? We may have managed to avoid it for this evening, but it will be hanging over you all the time until he eventually does so. And he will, believe me, he is determined.'

'And I hate to tell you, he has not renewed his passport. It has run out, so maybe he has no intention of leaving until he has made his point.' Sven raised a document in his hand, 'no matter how long it takes. He dropped it in the barn, I was planning to return it to him but he went off in a huff. I'll leave it in the barn where he dropped it.'

'Yes, do, if he finds it missing, it might make him even more angry or determined.'

'I will go now, if he misses it, he might come back this evening looking for it and if he does not, it will have been out there all night in case he questions it.'

A few minutes later, Suzanne came downstairs with Matilde's box.

'I saw Sven going to the barn, is everything alright? And I apologise to you all for my behaviour.' She approached Matilde with the wooden box taken from under the bed. 'Sorry I have been so long, *Mamie*.' She smiled.

'Put the box here for the moment, thank you for getting it,' Replied Matilde smiling in response to her granddaughter.

'*Papi*? Please may I use your computer for a moment? There is a reference in my book I do not understand and would like to check.'

'Of course. Do you remember the log in code?'

Suzanne said she did and went to the office. I followed her, Ricard did not try to stop me.

'May I?' I asked.

'Of course.' She turned on the machine, entered the password then typed into the search line "infections caught by sheep shearers". She read through the information on several such diseases, few if any were transferable—"ORF. A zoonotic disease, etc. etc. etc. which is not possible for humans to pass the virus on to each other. Etc. etc." She turned to me.

'No secrets, no lies. What is going on? What happened in the kitchen? I know I am only a child in *Papa*'s eyes, but I know something is wrong. Please, Yvonne, tell me.'

'Suzanne, I can't, it's not for me to do so. But I'll come with you to talk to Ricard if you want me to, and at any point you want me to go, then I will.'

'This is all to do with my uncle and the fight with *Papa*.'

I nodded.

She looked at the computer before shutting it down.

'My uncle lied about his hands.'

I nodded.

'Has my father ever lied to me?'

'I don't think Ricard would ever tell you lies; he would rather tell you nothing.'

'Keeping silent can also, sometimes, be sort of lies too. But I still think we need to talk. I think the elephant must be here.'

'That is probably an excellent idea.'

She is really stressed. I do wish Ricard would explain to her.

By the time Suzanne and I returned to the living room, the contents of the wooden box were laid out on one of the low tables and neither she nor I referred to our conversation, although Ricard did look up with a silent question which I ignored. It was now up to Suzanne.

'*Mamie*, they are beautiful. Where did you get them?'

The table was covered in exquisite semi-precious gems from different places of the world where Matilde's father had served during his military service. She explained, when they were given to her, they looked like any old bits of gravel, but once polished became these vibrant stones. Some of which she'd made into necklaces and bracelets and sold when money was short.

'A hard thing for her to do.' Said Ramon.

'Only for a second or two, my dear, we needed the money and when was I going to wear these baubles? Milking the cows? They would have run a mile rather than come near those shining stones.' She laughed then getting up, said, 'An overcooked evening meal will be waiting in the kitchen, I will not do it the honour of being served in the dining room. Yvonne, could you give me a hand please?'

I followed Matilde into the kitchen and started to lay the cutlery while she put the cold *hors d'oeuvre* on the table and checked the main course before saying,

'I assume something happened in the office and we are to expect a change of plan.'

'Well, your assumption regarding a happening is correct and it's up to Suzanne to do as she wishes with what she has found out. What happens next, I have left entirely up to her, but said she'll have everyone's support if she needs it.'

'Good. Would you call the others in so we can eat?'

The food was, as always, delicious and overcooked it was not, the conversation seemed to flow gently from topic to topic without any obviously studious avoidance of the four-legged long-nosed animal in the room.

The meal over and with coffee being served in the living room by the fire it was a seemingly perfect ending to a rather traumatic day, when Suzanne asked,

'Do you think we could have one more game, *Papi-Pops*? I know it is getting late, but it might be nice.'

'If you would like to do so, it might be a good idea. OK, set up the board.'

Sven put more logs on the fire and settled down on a settee with Marianne, Matilde and Ramon sat close together, they exchanged quiet observations between themselves, I nestled next to Ricard who was still tension-ridden, he was not feeling any of the peace we'd been hoping for when this visit to Ramon and Matilde, with my father, had first been suggested.

My goodness, how it has been hijacked. C'est ça!

We watched the chess players and heard their murmured "pawn to…" or "king's pawn to…"

After a while, Pops asked,

'Is that move advisable, Suzanne?'

'Yes, I think so, if I did it, it would end the game, would it not?' I noticed she looked long and hard at Pops before moving her eyes to Ricard then everyone in turn except me.

Here it comes!

Pops nodded.

'Yes, but are you certain you want that to happen? Have you thought it through properly?'

She thought for a moment then nodded.

'If you are convinced it is the right thing to do, you had better make it then.'

She nodded as she moved her king. Pops moved his piece saying,

'Checkmate.'

Suzanne gently knocked over her king in the recognised mode of submitting.

'Please, *Papa*, and all of you who I love dearly, please will you tell me all about this uncle of mine and what is going on?'

There was a silence yet everyone was expecting something to erupt.

'I know,' she continued quietly, 'the disease my uncle said he has on his hands cannot be transferred between people, I think he does not have a problem and it is just an excuse you made up to prevent him from coming in. I think *Papi-Pops* and Sven said something to him in the barn and I now know it was my *Papa* and uncle fighting. And I think, though do not know what—there is more to come. So please tell me.'

Silence, apart from the crackling fire logs. So, she continued, turning her attention to Marianne.

'*Mamie-Marianne*, you have lived a great deal of your life with my mother, I agree pretending to be her sister, surely—'

'Yes, Suzanne, but it is not for me to say.'

Suzanne stood up, knocking the chessboard over and screamed,

'You all know, tell me what it is I do not know. What is the big secret?' she stared at Ricard. 'Please, tell me. I cannot see whatever you have to say will ever change anything, please, just tell me.'

Ricard stood and with a voice harder and harsher than I had heard before replied,

'OK, you want to know? Well—'

'Ricard!' I stood up and intercepted him in his advance towards his daughter, 'not in temper. You have no anger towards Suzanne; come away for a bit and calm down. Please.'

I pushed him out of the room towards our bedroom. He could have resisted but thankfully, he had sense to hear me. I looked at Pops and indicated "Five" with my hand and he nodded, understanding I expected him and Suzanne in our room in five minutes' time.

In our room Ricard was, initially, very distant and would not let me hold him but he relented and after I'd held him, he took me in one of his vice-like grips. After a while, he relaxed. I didn't move but said,

'I think, when you have finished, this might also be a good time to tell Suzanne and Pops about the pregnancy. I know it is still early days, but it might help and could reinforce you are Suzanne's natural father.'

Ricard released me and grinned.

'Thank you. If for no other reason, I am happy to tell them, I keep nearly blurting it out anyway, it is a great strain keeping a secret.'

A strain maybe, but you seem to have managed for several years.

'And we do not do secrets any more after this one about Jules is out in the open.'

I agreed.

Pops and Suzanne arrived, luckily a bit later than anticipated. With his usual forethought, Pops brought four glasses and a bottle of wine, Suzanne was carrying a bottle of lemonade and a chair from my father's room, so we all were able to sit comfortably as Ricard told Suzanne of her possible paternal parentage, how Suzanne might have been conceived and thus the cause of the argument and fight. When he had finished speaking Suzanne wiped her hands over her face, rather like pushing a load of sticky spiders' webs to one side, then put her hand through her hair a couple of times.

'So, *Papa*, you expected me to stop loving you, leave you all and go off with this person I do not know, who lied to me the first time we meet—well, almost—who said nothing about what he had done, then insult you by being my godfather. Someone who would not stay and help his parents for a few months longer? Oh, *Papa*, why did you have such a lack of faith in me? I love you, your brother did you wrong. Did you really think I would want to go with him? I was confused at first, while you were telling me the history, why you chose him to be my godfather, but now I understand, at the time, you did not know what he had done.'

They were holding each other tightly when Ricard told Suzanne and Pops about my pregnancy, and how the true sperm report now put doubt on whether in fact Jules is really Suzanne's father, as he had claimed.

'There was no feeling of fatherhood from him. You are my real *Papa*.'

Oh, the simple faith of youth. And does it matter between them?

Pops and Suzanne congratulated us both on my pregnancy and agreed there was now a lot of room for supporting the fact Ricard is Suzanne's father.

Pops and I left father and daughter and re-joined the others and confirmed Suzanne now knew it all, including the fact I'm pregnant. There was relief on the former and congratulations on the latter bit of news. It must have been a good half hour before Ricard and his daughter came and sat by the fire with us.

'I have put your chair outside your room, Clive.' Said Ricard as a matter of fact.

'Thank you.' He responded in an equally quiet tone.

'Well, Suzanne knows the whole situation and for several reasons, although she admits her current thoughts and feelings need to be worked through, she would like it if we all stayed tomorrow and meet Jules in more depth.'

There was a short intake of breath from the rest of us, but no one openly objected.

'Before she goes to bed, and it is getting late on this rather emotional day, Suzanne would like to say something to us all. She has said she will not keep repeating names and what she has to say is to everyone she has known through her life and more recently.'

Her thank you speech was truly short and heartfelt, at the end of it, having said good night to everyone else, she asked if both her grandmothers would go up and say goodnight to her in her room.

Once the three of them had ascended the stairs, Ricard explained, although she was initially confused by who her blood father is, she had no compulsion in saying as far as she was concerned, Ricard was and always would be her father.

'As she said, why do we not just call his bluff and send him away again? It seems she has no desire to be in contact with him and thinks he should hear it from her personally. In fact, she has asked me to go with her to see the vicar to see if there is any way he can undo the godfather bit! Oh, I have so misjudged the strength of my daughter, it makes me feel ashamed.'

'She is her mother's daughter, Ricard.

'Yes, *Papom*, she is and there is also, a strong, probability I am her father as what my brother said about me is wrong, Yvonne is pregnant. I support Suzanne's proposition; we all stay tomorrow and we confront him.'

'Congratulations to you both. It is a bit late to celebrate now, but tomorrow we will.' Said Ramon.

Marianne came down from saying goodnight to Suzanne.

'Matilde has gone to bed and said would you mind kindly locking up the house this evening.'

'What a strange request, I always do! But it is as good a cue as any, for us all to call it a day, but if anyone wants to stay on by the fire, please do. Many congratulations again to you both. Have you known long?'

'She told me here last week, *Papom*, we were not going to say anything till later, but it seemed appropriate now.'

'Yes, probably, goodnight, everyone.' Sven took Marianne by the hand and they left.

Pops followed Ramon into the kitchen, I followed them. They stood outside at the open door talking and taking some air. I started to finish tidying the kitchen of the last dishes left after the meal so it was clear for the morning. They both came in and Ramon locked the door.

'Goodnight, Yvonne, do not stay up much longer, it is already late, so bed soon. Sleep well.'

'And you, Ramon, I think we will all need to do so if we are to face tomorrow.'

'What has Suzanne in mind?'

'I don't know, she didn't say anything to me. Perhaps Ricard knows more. Goodnight.'

'Yvonne, I echo, Ramon, not too long. Goodnight.'

'Goodnight, Pops.'

They left me and I continued, so deep in thought and didn't hear Ricard enter the kitchen.

'Are you coming to bed? It is late.'

'Yes, I'll just finish this and leave the glasses till tomorrow.' I put the last few plates in their place and looked around to make sure I'd not missed anything.

Ricard was wearing a dressing gown but was obviously naked underneath, he pulled me to him and I felt his arousal.

We turned the lights off and went to bed.

He kissed me long and hard before moving off me and going to sleep.

I lay awake listening to him breathing quietly. I wondered, if now, Suzanne's dream has finally been put to rest.

C'est ça!

Chapter Nineteen

I made coffee in the communal area and gave some to Ricard, showered and went to the kitchen where I found Matilde and Marianne busy preparing lunch.

'That looks like rather a lot of food. What's going on?'

'Suzanne thinks Jules might break his word and not wait till this afternoon after we have supposedly left but will come this morning.'

'So, you're giving him lunch? We can go earlier and miss him.'

'Do you not remember? Suzanne wants to call his bluff and face him out. Now she knows he has lied to her and possibly everyone else, she thinks he will come early. She thinks it might be a way to get him to tell the truth if we offer hospitality.'

'Matilde, what do you think?'

'I am biased as I want to see my son and find out what the truth really is.'

'And Ramon?'

'He thinks it is worth a try. Almost kill or cure, if he is worthless, then he can go.'

'But the meal is really your father's idea.'

As if waiting for his entrance line, Pops came in from the yard with Sven.

'Good morning, Yvonne. Matilde, we have put up one of the tables, but we will need to clean it before we can use it to serve food and the other ones too.'

'Pops, what's going on?'

'I have suggested a sort of compromise'

'What is going on?' Ricard had joined us.

'Well, as Suzanne is determined to stay, luckily the weather has helped to clarify my thoughts. It's a beautiful day—especially for this time of year—so what I have proposed is we set up the large trestle tables from the barn for a family luncheon on the patio. I didn't know what food Matilde had planned for today, but she willingly agreed to create an outside meal. I'm sure whatever it is

312

will be delightful. Being outside will ease any tension and reduce the impulse to throw things—or if it doesn't, there will be less damage.'

Was he thinking of Ricard?

'During the conversation, we could elicit from Jules why he left and what he's been doing and why he has returned now. You never know, assumptions maybe quite wrong.'

'He did seem so determined when I met him in Leeds, Pops, and you said yourself he is full of anger.'

'But even though you said he emphasised the daughter part of goddaughter, he never said daughter on its own?'

'He nearly did last night, till Sven reacted.' I countermanded.

Suzanne came into the kitchen.

'I have found the cloth you wanted, *Mamie*. Good morning, Yvonne, *Papa*, I think *Papi-Pops'* idea is good. If I am wrong, then we will have had a lovely outside meal and used the last of the season's sunshine. Look, it is almost eleven so we had better get started cleaning the tables. I will give you a hand, Sven.'

'I hope to God you have not got this strategy wrong, Clive.'

'So do I, Ricard. Come and give me a hand fixing the other trestle table.'

If it all blows up in his face, how will Pops feel? What will happen to our new, vastly extended family?

By mid-day, the meal was laid out on the tables over crisp blue checked cloths. Chairs had been brought from the barn and wiped down. On a side table, bottles of the local wine and water jugs, stood ready.

We waited.

Had Suzanne's hunch been wrong?

Ramon decided to walk down the track and returned with Jules by his side. Ricard told Suzanne to sit between himself and Marianne and placed me opposite the empty chair left for the visitor.

Was he a visitor or just a returning prodigal son, to be welcomed as in the parable?

Jules stood for a moment looking at the gathering, dropped his backpack and lifted the tablecloth to look for the supports before sitting in the only empty chair at the table.

'I do not believe you still have these tables! We used them for the harvest festival parties. The whole village came.'

'Yes, they were happy days, in the main.' Said Ramon.

'Come, eat. I did not spend all morning preparing food for it not to be eaten.' Matilde started to put food onto the plates in front of her and passing them down.

'Help yourselves and pass the dishes round.'

'Well, if it isn't the little miss widow liar! What are you doing here? You said you did not know this part of France, yet here you are.'

There was the same strong aggression I'd felt in Leeds.

'I didn't lie, this area is still new to me although I do work near here.'

'Why are you here now? With my family.'

'I thought I saw a likeness between you, Ricard and your father and knowing vaguely of some family trouble and a little of your travel plans, I told Ricard. And here I am.'

'All those questions make sense now.'

I recognised the anger movements I'd seen him make in the bar in Leeds, I'd not meant to start a confrontation so tried to backpedal.

'Yes, maybe I should have said something to you, I apologise.'

'And the recently widowed act?'

'That is true, not a lie. Did you have a good tour round the UK and journey down here?' I tried to keep my voice level.

The familiar sneer mixed with sarcasm was in his response.

'Yes, so kind of you to enquire.'

'Well, as you are here to see your family and your goddaughter, should you not turn your attention to them, after so many years?'

'Uncle Jules.'

'Yes Suzanne.' Jules turned his attention from me.

'What is Australia like?'

'It is an exceptionally large country and what it is like, is rather like everywhere in the world, it depends where you are,' he stared at me with his familiar smirk, 'some people are friendly others not, some parts are dry and other parts have rain forests, if you come back with me, we can explore it all from Darwin in the north to Sydney in the south and Perth on the west coast. I have not seen much of it as I have been rather stuck in one place.'

'Shearing sheep? How are your hands today?'

'Much better, thank you, although I was not actually shearing sheep, though I did give it a try. I—' Jules did not get a chance to finish as Suzanne said quietly.

'You lied to me, there was nothing wrong with your hands.'

'You are right, it was what is called a white lie, or an excuse just to see you last night.'

'Why did you need an excuse to see your goddaughter?'

'Because I have been away for a long time and I was not sure—'

'Not sure what, son?'

'How I would be received home after so long a time with no communication and no warning of my arrival.'

'So, what have you been doing?' asked Pops. 'If you have not been shearing sheep for eight years.'

'I started out fossicking which led to proper prospecting. I struck lucky. It took a lot of hard work and mind-bending paperwork, but I now have a gold mine. A small one, mind you, but the seam has not yet run out, and I hope it will last for several more years. It is a great life.'

We all managed to eat during these exchanges. I noticed Jules looked at Ricard when he mentioned the gold mine, he had an almost superior winning look on his face.

Ricard did not flinch but asked calmly,

'So, why have you been so silent all these years and returned now, if life is so great in Australia? Do not worry about telling us everything, everyone here knows the story of our antagonism during our teenage years and the cause of our last fight.'

Ricard had stood during this speech but Jules had remained seated.

'Sit down, brother. I have not come to take anything away of yours. In fact, I have not come to take anything, I came to see my family. Parents, brother, niece.'

Ricard sat and Jules stood. He looked at the sky.

'In Australia, we do not have to worry about planning an outside meal. But here, we need to keep an eye on the sky especially at this time of year. So, in case those storm clouds decide to come and drop their load on us, I will speed up and tell you why I have returned after eight years of silence. Well, …'

Jules almost parroted the possibilities Pops and everyone else had outlined earlier in all our hypotheses. His jealous resentment about the money on education, his jealousy over Charlotte and so it went on. He paused at one point during his explanation and Ramon, who I had noticed was getting more agitated, stood and asked in a controlled quiet voice,

'Why did you rape your brother's wife?'

This direct confrontation had not been anticipated by any of us, judging by the looks on everyone's faces.

'I did not. I helped her when the horse kicked and the traces and plough went over. She was tangled in them. I do not know why I said those things to you, Ricard. I suppose I just wanted to hurt you, make you feel bad, ordinary, not have everything I did not have. I did not realise the anguish it would bring me. All those years in Australia should have been fun, but I hated them. My guilt, stupidity, jealousy beavering into me all the time. Hard physical work was the only thing to keep me sane. I was too tired at the end of the day to think. What you saw in me in Leeds, Yvonne, was not who I am.'

'But maybe, the man you have become.' Pops' voice stilled the rampage coming from Jules.

'A possibility I acknowledge. But now I do not have to do all the physical work myself—I can afford better machinery and to employ men—I found with more free time all the emotions were coming back, only stronger and the more miserable I became the more I wanted, no more than wanted, the more I needed to come back. To make amends, to see if anything could be salvaged. To apologise. To see my parents, my brother, my niece and goddaughter. It could have been a great life, but I was just so miserable.'

'Oh! Poor little you!' Ricard exploded as he stood and advanced towards his brother. Sven and Pops stood, but Jules sat down quietly. 'Have you the vaguest idea of the harm and suffering your stupidity, lying and jealousy has inflicted on my parents, Suzanne and me over the years? Let alone on other people in our lives? You lie and cheat and now just want to say sorry because you have been so miserable. What about us? Did you even once think of what might be happening here? You—stupid, stupid, selfish...' He stalked off.

'Papa!' Suzanne stood to follow him but was stopped by Jules saying.

'Stay here, Suzanne, I will go.' Jules followed his brother and we lost sight of them beyond the barn.

Four hours passed in which time we ate and drank, cleared away the meal, putting the remains in the refrigerator.

'I think there will be enough for another meal or people can graze when they feel like it.' Matilde said.

316

The tables and chairs were restacked as the storm clouds threatened and the darkness encroached.

'I will go and get the cows in for milking.'

'I thought *Monsieur Jacques* was milking this evening.'

'Yes, Clive, but I need to do something. I will just bring them in for him.'

Matilde, Marianne and Sven moved to the sitting room while Pops, Suzanne and I stayed in the kitchen.

'It does seem then, there cannot be any doubt *Papa* is *mon père*.'

'It certainly seems that way.'

'What are they doing, *Papi-Pops*? They have been out there for hours.'

'Your guess is as good as mine, Suzanne.'

'I hope they are not fighting.'

'Somehow, Yvonne, I don't think it will come to physical combat tonight. Verbal aggression, yes, but not hand to hand fighting.'

Ramon returned.

'*Monsieur Jacques* has arrived, but I cannot see where the boys are. I walked to the field beyond the barn but could not see them. Mind you, it is quite dark now.' Ramon picked up one of the wine glasses I had washed and placed by the bottles, he looked at me, I shook my head. Pops accepted the offer.

'I will join the others. Will you come?'

'I'll wait here for a while, thank you, Ramon.' Suzanne and Pops stayed with me.

The kitchen door opened.

'May I come in?' Jules stood in the doorway.

'Where is Ricard?' I asked.

'He went to talk to my father in the milking shed.'

'Wait there, Jules. Ramon is in the sitting room. Suzanne, will you please get him.'

Suzanne did as she was requested by Pops and returned with him.

'May I come in, Father?'

'Where is Ricard?'

'Here *Papom*. I thought you were with the cows but found *Monsieur Jacques*. I had forgotten he was doing the milking tonight. I have invited him in for a glass of wine, I hope correctly.'

'Yes, of course. Now, what about your brother? He is asking to come inside.'

317

'It is your house, *Papom*, it is not for me to tell you who you can and cannot have in it.'

'I am asking your advice, Ricard.'

'We have spoken at length about our relationship and exchanged opinions and information about what has happened here during the time Jules has been away. It will take time for whatever relationship finally emerges between him and me, but I think you and *Mamon* need to talk with him and to do so on the doorstep would not be beneficial nor productive.'

'Well, I have heard about diplomacy, but that is the longest way of saying "yes" I have heard for a long time.' Ramon smiled and indicated to Jules to enter. At the same time, *Monsieur Jacques* arrived.

'If this is inconvenient, Letour, I will—'

'No, not at all, Jacques. Come in, do you remember my other son, Jules?'

'Yes indeed. Good to see you again, it has been a long time.' He extended his hand which Jules took.

'You too, *Monsieur*, yes eight years.'

'So, wine for everyone?' Asked Ramon.

'We heard voices, so I have come to see what is happening.' On seeing Jules in the kitchen, Sven moved quickly to stand beside Suzanne.

'It is alright, Sven, I am not going to kidnap her.'

'Come on, there is no point in us all standing around in here. Come Jacques, let us join my wife and Marianne in the sitting room.'

Sven moved towards the back door.

'You not coming, Sven?'

'I need to get some more logs, Ramon. And to visit the barn.'

'Thank you. Good idea.'

'I will help you.'

'Thanks, Ricard.' They left together.

Neither Ramon nor Ricard had told us what they had explained to *Monsieur Jacques* about the family gathering and request for him to do the milking, but he was once again pleasant company. I was glad of his neutral interest in Jules and how he quizzed Jules about his life and work in Australia. Despite the circumstances we were all interested and asked questions to which he happily responded. As Jules began to relax in his childhood home with his parents, he became more expansive and I began to see, despite the positive front he was putting on, there were other emotions underneath.

Earlier, he had expressed a great deal of pain and regret but did not mention them now. There were other, unspoken emotions too. But knowing the pain it had caused Ricard and his parents, my sympathy for him wasn't as deeply felt as maybe it should have been. His was a self-inflicted wound that had festered into a pulsating mass which he now wanted lanced.

And it looks as if it is going to be, by his parents. At what cost to Ricard?

I fetched another bottle of wine for Ramon to serve and left the group to find out what was keeping Ricard and Sven, it shouldn't be taking them so long to collect a few logs. They were not in the wood store, the barn or the milking shed. I went around the back and entered the house by the 'bolt hole' we'd identified. They were sitting in the communal area drinking coffee and working their way through a bottle of brandy one of them had picked up at some point.

'Are you two, OK?'

'Eight years of hate and pain all because of his jealousy and a stupid, pointless lie. And now he has them eating out of his hand.'

'Looks like it.' I commented.

'And you agree with them?'

He took a gulp of brandy.

'No, I don't. In fact, I don't like him very much, possibly because of the way he acted in Leeds, though he is acting the same way here too, towards me anyway, but I think he is also hurting. But there is something more—maybe more lies, I don't know.'

'Good, he deserves to burn in hell for what he has put my parents, Charlotte, Suzanne and me through. All for a fat, stinking lie.'

'And in return you deepen your distrust, possessiveness and jealousy into a vicious hate. That seems admirably sensible and you won't find release in a bottle either.'

'What do you expect me to do? Eight years of—'

'And it's not going to be resolved in four hours, is it? Nor by skulking here.'

'I am not skulking. I am having a quiet drink with a friend while trying to adjust.'

'What I am saying is—'

'Do not start, Yvonne.'

'What do you expect her to do? As you will not listen to me, I will go and join my future wife and return this,' he took Jules' passport from his pocket, 'it

was still where I'd left it. I have tried, Yvonne, but he is as stubborn as Suzanne.'
He grinned and patted Ricard's shoulder as he left us.

I sat down with a sigh and waited for Ricard to speak, he carried on drinking the brandy, we sat in silence for half an hour before Pops came to us.

'Ricard, *Monsieur Jacques* is leaving, Ramon asks if you would please walk him down to the gate.'

Ricard grimaced.

'*Papom* used to get me to do this whenever—'

'You were sulking as a young man, yes, I gather it was a ploy to give you time to think, perhaps it will work this time.'

'Alright, I will be back in a minute,' Ricard took me in his arms, 'I am sorry, I am not sure I am able to forgive him.'

He kissed my cheek and left me to escort the guest, I wasn't too sure how safely, down the track.

'What now, Pops? His anger is back again and a thousand-fold stronger. It will eat him up inside. I don't know if I can face watching him destroy himself.' I put my hand on my tummy and started to cry.

Pops gave me his handkerchief, saying,

'Come on, you're made of stronger stuff, have faith in the man, his love and your love. You have both been through a lot recently and you'll both get through this too.'

We joined the others in the sitting room. The fire was welcoming.

'Has Ricard come back from accompanying *Monsieur Jacques?*'

Matilde shook her head.

'He needs time to think, Jules has gone to look for him.'

I looked at her,

'How do you and Ramon feel about his return? I suppose parents have a different viewpoint, your sentiments go so much deeper than siblings, grandchildren and friends.'

'Maybe, now we know the truth, we are likely to take a more pragmatic view, understand and forgive, but that does not mean I think he did right, because he did not. Immature jealousy is one thing, but such a vicious and blatant lie has no place in anyone's life, he has caused much pain, probably more than he has suffered.'

'Have you changed your mind about your view of the biblical story Suzanne quoted?'

She ignored my question and said she'd put some things on the table from which to help ourselves and bring our plates back to the fire to eat if we'd like to.

§ § §

Ricard and Jules arrived back as the last of the dishes were being taken from the dishwasher, the food having been put away, a cold wind whipped through the kitchen before they closed the door; they were laughing, neither of them said anything to me or Ramon, the only ones still up, about the conversations they'd had in the preceding hours and we did not ask. I looked at Ricard closely and concluded his laughter was genuine but he also seemed a little guarded.

Does this mean he and his brother have, somehow, resolved their differences?

'Father, I understand there are several events expected in the next few months, do you have anything special we can have to drink to them all?'
'I think it is far too late this evening for celebrations. It has been a long day and it is nearly midnight, most of us are already in bed and I suggest you retire soon, we will talk in the morning, there are decisions to be made. If either of you is hungry, your mother has left some food in the refrigerator and some soup you can heat up if you like. Jules, you will have to sleep in one of the guest rooms tonight. Your old room is not prepared for sleeping, it is used as a store and sewing room now. Goodnight.'
I don't know what time Ricard came to bed.

§ § §

I made coffee in the communal area and took both mugs back to bed.
'Are you going to tell me what happened last night?'
'No. At least, not now, it is not a great secret, but I am still trying to work out what happened myself, when I am clearer in my mind, then I will.'
'Please, don't be too long about it.'
Ricard turned on his side and rested on his elbow.
'How are you feeling this morning?'

321

'I'm fine and looking forward to breakfast. But to resolve things between you and Jules so quickly seems strange.'

'Please do not push.'

I knew better than to force him to say anything till he was ready, but I was getting tired of having to wait and do all the work.

'OK, I won't "push" as you say, but we are not going to get anywhere till I know what happened, you agreed, no secrets. I'll go back to London and wait until you have worked it out and can tell me honestly you are not full of the anger and rage which was apparent yesterday.'

'I am not sure I can tell—'

'No Ricard, you go out to escort *Monsieur Jacques* to the end of the track and the next thing, well, hours later, you and Jules are laughing together, I'm sorry, Ricard, it won't do. You say, "no more secrets", yet you carry on, I can't take watching you destroy yourself—and us. And I'm not so sure about Jules, I didn't know the character of the man who left here eight years ago but the one who is here now has the same character as the one I met in Leeds. To use Pops' phrase "perhaps it is the man he became."'

'Yvonne, if you have finished, let me continue what I was trying to say, please. I am not sure I can tell you there is no anger and rage. The uncontrolled raging has gone, most of it was dissipated when it all came out with my parents last week, but I still feel an understandable, but measured, anger. Yesterday it all flared up again when he was being so self-centred about the pain he had been in. Yes, he has changed, during the months before we argued he was pleasant and we got on reasonably well, so maybe Clive's analysis is right.'

'So, are you going to tell me what happened last night?'

'When I am clearer in my mind, then I will.'

'Don't be too long about it.'

'Alright, I heard you the first time.'

We put on dressing gowns and went to the kitchen. It seemed as if no one had been in to prepare breakfast. I looked at the clock above the door and saw it was not quite seven, perhaps Matilde was having an out of character quiet lie in after yesterday's traumas. But not everyone was still in bed. Suzanne was with Ramon and Jules returning the cows to the field after the morning milking. From where we were standing, looking out through the window, she appeared relaxed in her uncle's company. Before returning to the house, they stopped and we watched Suzanne face Jules, giving him a long speech. He took several steps backwards, looking shocked. He turned to Ramon who nodded.

'I think she is telling him about the dream and years of nightmares,' Ricard's voice was quiet, 'do you think she will be alright?'

'Yes, she's strong and after you'd left us in the bedroom on Sunday, when she first saw him and screamed, she said now that she knew the dream, or nightmare, had a foundation, she wouldn't have it again. Now she knows everything, which she didn't before, and knows what it was all about, I doubt it will recur. But she still needs support and certainty that she's safe. You noticed how she took Ramon's hand before she started?'

'No, I did not see, you are so observant.'

'What are we doing today? Going back? Are you letting Suzanne stay?'

'I do not know. I suppose we should address the issue of "expected events" as Jules put it. Do you have to be back in the office today?'

I shook my head,

'I'm no longer on the project, but my gut feeling is we should go home taking Suzanne with us and leave any arrangements about the events to another day.'

'I agree with you, it will give more time for everyone to re-appraise their situations quietly and I should really be in the office tomorrow.'

'Pops and I were supposed to be flying back today, I'll have to contact the airline and sort out other tickets when I know what he wants to do. We won't get the one we are booked on but they might be able to accommodate us on a later flight.'

Sven, already dressed, came into the kitchen and we told him of our decision.

'Thank goodness, I'll get the car prepared and tell Marianne. Is Suzanne coming?'

'Yes, whether she likes it or not!'

Which, of course, she did not.

No-one objected to our leaving, which we did about mid-morning, Suzanne still pleading to stay but was firmly told this would not happen but tried to prolong the farewells, hoping Ricard would change his mind but to no avail. Without it being said, I think Ramon and Matilde were pleased to have some time with Jules. But before leaving, Ricard spoke to his father conveying his and my concerns about his current character. Apparently, Ramon agreed but put it down to the situation and hoped he would mellow with time, if he stayed.

§

It was good to be home; the airline credited our flights for another time, one of the perks of having a company account, and we all felt relaxed that evening.

'He was interesting but there were times I felt he was a bit cold and trying to be nice to everyone, just for the sake of being nice, not really meaning it.'

'Who are you talking about, Suzanne?' asked Ricard rather unnecessarily but probably wanting to hear her confirmation.

'Uncle Jules. I suppose after a long journey and eight years it was hard for him. And you did shout at him, *Papa*.'

'Yes.'

No one spoke for a while, but the silence was not strained.

'We didn't discuss anything while at Ramon and Matilde's, but I would prefer to have the baby after we're married, but I don't want to usurp your wedding, Marianne and Sven.'

'If you wait until after ours, you will be eight months pregnant, which will look a bit odd for a Maid-of-Honour, so I suggest you get on with it.'

'Exactly my thoughts, Marianne. So, the sooner Ricard and I can marry, the better and the happier I'll be. We must decide where, if we want a church wedding in England, we have to give three weeks' notice for the Banns to be read and find a vicar who is willing to preside.'

'The vicar at St Mark's would be willing, Yvonne. We know him and…sorry, you may not want that venue.' Said Pops.

I looked at Ricard.

'That's where Mark and I married and as it happens so did Julie and Paul.'

'Fine by me, you had better start organizing it.'

'What about a civil wedding here? Although the marriage in England is valid here too.'

'I do not think that will be necessary, Clive, but what might be nice would be a blessing at my parents' church in Ortaffa, unless you would rather not, Yvonne. That is where Charlotte and I had ours blessed.'

'History repeating itself for both of us.'

'No!' Suzanne shouted and was frozen in her seat.

'What do you mean "no", Suzanne.'

'You said she would not die if she had a baby.'

324

'My dear, I am so sorry, I had forgotten that part of our conversation. I did tell Yvonne, and we will do our best to avoid all the history. She will be alright, you will see.'

'Promise?'

'I will not lie to you, I cannot promise, but I am almost one hundred per cent sure she will be fine and so will the baby. So do not worry about that.'

'What is this about? Asked Pops.

Ricard explained.

'I see.' Was all he said on the subject. 'Back to a happier topic, if Clementine and I host the wedding in London, do you think Ramon and Matilde would like to host the blessing here?'

'I should think they will be delighted. If we have the wedding as soon as possible, we can then fix the blessing date.'

'Now he is back, will you be asking Jules to be your best man, Ricard?'

'No. I have already asked you, Sven, and I would appreciate it if you would still stand by me.'

'Thanks.'

'While we are on the subject, do you two want a big wedding, lots of people? The full works?'

'Can you leave that for tonight, Pops? Ricard and I'll talk about it later. Anyway, we have rather jumped the gun, haven't we, Ricard?'

'Is a wedding in doubt again, Yvonne? What is the problem now?' asked Marianne.

'Him and his secrets or inability to communicate.'

There was silence.

'I was planning on doing some open sandwiches for supper tonight, we can sit in here instead of the kitchen for a change and have the fire.'

'Are you planning a cosy situation, Marianne?' asked Ricard.

'If it helps, yes.'

'*Papa*, if you do not talk to Yvonne, you will be back where you started and Yvonne will not marry you?'

'She did not say she would not, but she said she would go back to London— and wait. And I did not say I would not tell, just I needed time to analyse it myself.'

'Can I light the fire, Sven?' asked Suzanne.

'I'll supervise her,' said Pops.

'Well, while you do the analysis, I'll get some drinks while Marianne starts on the food, then I'll give you a hand, Marianne.'

She and I left the room.

§ § §

We were eating and drinking by the fire when Ricard started his explanation.

'Yvonne, you asked me what happened to turn the situation with my brother around. It is difficult to identify the exact moment when it changed but I think the pivotal point was when I explained where the money for my, and later his, education came from.

'Jules seemed to go deeper into himself then start to relax. As he did so, so did I. He then just talked about how he had wanted to have a life on the farm, had no desire to go to university, he realised he did not have the sort of brain for, what he called serious study, yet at the same time resented and was jealous of everything I did. To him it seemed as if the whole "shebang" just dropped into my lap. He continued, although he knew we looked very similar, he felt like the ugly duckling and when he saw Charlotte, he realised none of his girlfriends were half as beautiful, intelligent or witty as she was.

'And the night before he went to Australia, my kindness at going to see him and wish him luck just cracked him up and he said the first thing that came into his head. Just to hurt and spite me. He ended by saying he adored Suzanne and had felt very bitter that he was going away from his goddaughter and might never see her again.' Ricard stopped speaking, his eyes welling up.

Ricard accepted the handkerchief Pops passed him.

He smiled, 'Thank you, Yvonne has told me you do this, your laundry bill must be high!'

Then he continued, 'The next half hour or so we both cried, hugged and then started to get to know each other a little before we came back inside, hoping to join you all, but we had not realised the time.'

'Very much what he said at the lunch table then.'

'Yes, I think so, Clive, although I think this was a bit more personal, but I was so het up at the meal, I was either not listening or maybe refusing to hear.'

'Does that mean the wedding is on again, Yvonne?'

'It wasn't really off, but postponed. So yes, if Ricard is still willing. He's had quite an "ear-bashing" today.'

'Worth every bruise! Now, young lady, bed and don't forget your teeth.'

'Goodnight, everyone. I do like being home.' Suzanne left us.

'Pops, now things are settled do you think I should ask Julie and Paul if Ricard could come to their party? We'll keep our engagement and the baby a secret, but it would give him a chance to meet the others before the wedding.'

'If Ricard can stand it, why not. They probably won't object.'

'If she says yes and you two can wait till Thursday evening, I could come with you. I'll have to get a flight back on Sunday or the first one on Monday as I must be in the office then.'

'If you leave me your passport details, I'll ring her tomorrow, see what she says and fix relevant flights.'

'Something worries me though, Clive; both *Papom* and Yvonne agree with me, there is something "odd" or "not quite right" about Jules. When he was talking, it seemed as if he was waiting for me to take the lead—almost to jog his memory—there seemed to be times when there was no spontaneity, as if he had not really been there and was reacting to something he had been told.'

'Probably the effect of eight years in a strange environment. Give him time.'

'You are probably right.'

The fire had died down, the guard put in place and the kitchen left tidy. We all retired.

§ § §

He kissed me briefly saying,

'I do not know when I will finish tonight, so do not hold the evening meal or wait up for me. I have asked Marianne to leave me something in the fridge in case I am hungry, I'll tell Sven not to pick me up, I will get a taxi back.'

As she was on holiday and I had no appointments, Suzanne, Pops and I wandered down for breakfast later. Sven joined us on his return from delivering Ricard.

'I have to clean and return the hire car this morning. Marianne, could you follow me in Ricard's so I do not have to wait for the bus?'

'Of course.'

'Could I come with you?' asked Pops. 'Perhaps you could drop me somewhere to do a little shopping. I would like to find some gifts to take home for the family gathering on Sunday.'

It was agreed we should all go as Marianne needed to get some more clothes for Suzanne and fresh ingredients for the evening meal. Pops found some items he thought would amuse or be appreciated by the family but was flagging by lunchtime. As we were near the bistro owned by the Perez family, I suggested we ate there instead of returning home.

'Yvonne, how lovely to see you again,' Pedro José greeted me with enthusiasm, 'is Sharon with you?'

'No Pedro, she's probably travelling back today. Do you need her for anything? I can ring the London office for you if there's a problem.'

'No problem. One of my sister's is visiting and I would have liked to introduce them to each other.'

'She'll probably be back later; do you know *Madame* Göest and *Monsieur* Emboli?'

'I do not think I have had the pleasure although *Monsieur* Letour has often spoken of you.'

'And may I introduce my father?' They shook hands.

'Please come this way.'

He showed us to a table and left us menus. I explained how Sharon had become a paying house guest in the Perez home and the connection with Ricard and Charles Bassinet.

'Your life over here has been full of coincidences, hasn't it?'

On reflection, it most certainly had. C'est ça.

Suzanne jumped up from the table and ran across to the counter and disappeared behind the bead curtain shouting,

'Gabriella, Gabriella.' Shortly afterwards, two girls were shooed out of the kitchen area and Suzanne dragged her friend over to our table.

'This is Yvonne.' She said with absolute glee. 'Yvonne, this is my best friend at school, she has been longing to meet you. Everyone is. She came to the party I had when you were in Carcassonne with Sven and Marianne. And Gabriella— you know what? She is going to marry my *Papa* and is going to have a baby—'

'Slow down, Suzanne.' Marianne prevented the next flurry of words from Suzanne by telling her proper introductions should be made, and certainly before someone else's personal life should be shouted to everyone in the bistro.

This was how I met the first of Suzanne's many friends.

Pops and Sven found my blushes of embarrassment quite amusing, but I gracefully acknowledged the impromptu congratulations on my future marriage

328

and baby, from customers who had no option but to hear and certainly had no intension of ignoring the news, before returning to their meals as though there had been no interruption and this was a normal daily occurrence.

Suzanne had been invited to spend time in the family room at the back to eat her food with Gabriella, so we enjoyed a lengthy quiet meal before returning home, after arranging to pick up Gabriella tomorrow morning for the girls to spend the day together. Sven and Marianne spent the late afternoon in their own apartment and Pops allowed himself to be cajoled, by Suzanne, into playing chess.

Julie was quite happy for Ricard to attend their party so I made the flight bookings for late Thursday evening. As the stay had been longer for Pops than had been planned, he asked if there was a chance of some laundry being done; Suzanne was dispatched to collect any from Marianne and Sven while I gathered everything in the house which resulted in a small amount of ironing. We spent the evening together and had a light supper, again sitting by the fire.

We were all in bed before a tired Ricard returned. But he found sufficient reserves for a proper welcome and goodnight.

§ § §

Ricard had to work the next day.

'I'm sorry to trouble you, Sven, but could you drive me to town so I could drop into *Monsieur* Bassinet's office to see Sharon? I'll try not to be so much of a bother when I'm fixed up with a car and insurance and so on.'

'It is no trouble, *Madame*, during a working day it is my job to drive you wherever you wish to go. So, unless you will be having any secret assignations, you will not need to drive, unless you prefer to do so. And remember you have arranged to pick up Gabriella at half past ten. Shall we say ten fifteen?'

'Yes, thank you.'

He nodded and left.

'To have your own private transport "on tap" is a luxury worth having, Yvonne.'

'Yes Pops, but it is so strange to switch between employee and family relationships almost at a flick of a switch.'

'You'll get used to it. May I come with you?'

'Of course, and if Suzanne comes too, Sven can bring both the girls back.'

Pops and I spent some time shopping for more gifts he wanted to take home before we joined Sharon and Vivienne at the office and went for coffee. Patrick had been pleased with Sharon's progress even though, as she admitted, not much had been done yet, but the foundations of good relationships had been established.

I called Sven who collected us and brought, at my request, the two girls with him, both wearing thick coats and we went to the lake. When I told him we would walk back, he nodded, strictly in chauffeur mode. The chocolate vendor was still open, which surprised me at first, but as it was school holidays there were several families about and the girls met some of their friends which meant I was able to meet some parents in an informal setting, which I found far less demanding than I would have done at a party. Pops, of course, charmed and flattered all the mothers. As he wanted to work a bit later than his usual office hours, Sven returned Gabriella to the Bistro when he collected Ricard.

'Have you two had any discussion about what sort of wedding and blessing get together you want? Because time is getting on and both I and Ramon would like some idea of how many people. The other evening Ricard, you said you didn't think big ones. What about you Yvonne?'

'Nothing large and elaborate, Pops. We have both had those. I would like just family and a few close friends. If we marry in St Marks then a small reception in my flat.'

'Sounds good to me, Yvonne. And a similar thing for the blessing, with the gathering at my parents' farm.'

'And timing?'

'I think I'd better contact the vicar and ask when he can see us. I'll look him up on the "net" tomorrow and ring him. It would be good to try and see him over the weekend, if convenient for him.'

'A good idea, Yvonne, we should get some straight answers as to what we can and cannot do and what to expect. And I will ring *Papom* and get him to ask *Frère* Macon if he is willing to do a blessing.'

'And if they say "no"?'

'Oh, don't Clive,' pleaded Sven, 'let something go smoothly. And what about your friends you will not be asking? You both must have quite a number.'

'We'll have a big party here in June or July—after your wedding so we can have a big, joint celebration and welcome the baby too.'

'Patrick would be proud of your organisation, dear!'

Patrick—Oh Lord, I've not said anything to him yet.

'I will say goodnight to you, Clive, and go and put out the clothes and so on for the weekend. Will you pack them for me tomorrow, Yvonne? Goodnight, Marianne, Sven.' Ricard left the room.

'That departure was a bit abrupt, Yvonne, is everything alright?'

'I think he needs to meet Patrick to put his stupid thoughts about Patrick and me to bed. Which is where I think I'll go too if you don't mind. Goodnight, everyone.' I looked in on a sleeping Suzanne on my way passed her room.

'You aren't still fussing about Patrick and me, are you, Ricard? Pops noticed you left rather suddenly after he'd mentioned his name.'

'No, I'm sorry if I gave that impression. Nothing too formal this weekend, I hope?'

He took me in his arms and that was the end of the day, Well, almost.

§ § §

I looked up St Mark's and found the 'phone number. After explaining Ricard was only there for a short time, the vicar agreed to see us on Saturday morning.

At two o'clock, Sven collected Ricard from the office, he changed from his formal suit he'd had to wear today to more relaxing clothes, placed the few last-minute items into his case and we were off, having said our farewells to Marianne and Suzanne at the house.

The flight was uneventful with Pops charming the steward, as easily I noticed, as he had the stewardesses on previous flights.

'I am grateful you came, Clive. I am not sure how Sunday would have turned out if there had not been a steady hand on the tiller, as it were.'

'I doubt I contributed much but am glad to have been of some help. But you and Jules did most of the hard work, even if there is more unravelling to do.'

Pops declined my offer of coffee or a drink when we reached my flat saying he would like to get home. Ricard and he shook hands.

'Thank you for everything, Pops. We'll probably come around at some point tomorrow.' I kissed him and waved him off.

'Welcome to my London home, Ricard.'

I punched in the entrance security code. We took the lift to the apartment where I unlocked the door.

'I was expecting it to be cold in here.'

'No, a bit of forethought this time, even so I'll put the heating up a bit.'

I collected the post from the floor by the door on my return from the hall cupboard which housed the controls. A lot of junk mail as usual but also a couple of handwritten envelopes from my siblings.

'Would you like a guided tour?'

'Only as far as the bedroom tonight, thank you. I will bring the bags.'

§ § §

There was no rush to get up in the morning. It felt good to be able to lie in bed together with no one else to worry about for a while, although it felt a little strange not to see Suzanne about when I went to get coffee and tea from the kitchen.

'Goodness! Enjoy the peace while you can!' joked Ricard when I told him. I smiled and snuggled back next to him.

'Ricard.'

'Yes? You sound serious. Have you changed your mind now you are back where you and Mark were happy?'

'No, not about marrying you, but I was wondering about Jules. Do you think he ought to take some responsibility about looking at the properties your father has inherited?'

'No. This did occur to me and I had a word with *Papom* on Tuesday before we left. He would rather we left the arrangement as we have it now. He, like me, has every confidence in your ability. Unless of course with the pregnancy you would rather take it more easily and we can find someone else. But not Jules, we need to see how he settles and what his plans are.'

'It sounds as if you two don't trust him. Is anything wrong? The relationship between all of you is reasonably sound, isn't it?'

'Still fragile, but *Papom* was listening hard and watching him over the few hours we all spent together. He will get to know him better as the next few days pass. He acknowledges Jules has skills but he is not sure he has the analytical ones to ask the right questions, nor the stamina to see the work through. He also thinks he is not stable and, like us, has some question marks over him. *Papom* knows you are a softie on the personal level but thinks, when it comes to business you are a hard nut to crack. So does your father by the way.'

I grunted.

332

'What was Jules' reaction when you told him about the inheritance?'

'He was interested but also a bit ambivalent about it.'

'Maybe he's already a multi-millionaire, he didn't say what his gold mine is worth, just it's small but didn't compare it with anything.'

'Come on. Are we getting up? I ought to go and face your sister.'

'In a minute.'

§

An hour later, I showered and while waiting for Ricard opened the letters from my siblings before we went to Phillippe's for breakfast. Phillippe's reaction was rather cool when I introduced them, there was a moment when they looked each other over before Ricard extended his hand.

'You take great care of her.' Said Phillippe.

'Yes, I will.'

'Good,' responded Phillippe as he took Ricard's hand, 'I have to say you have a high standard to follow and our Gallic charm is not all a woman wants.' He turned to me. 'First Julie, now you. What is going on?'

'It's obviously the Gallic charm! Is Elise here? I would like her to meet Ricard too.'

'Of course, sit yourselves down. Coffee? Anything to eat? How about some eggs Benedict?'

'Sounds good. Thank you.'

The two of them joined us for coffee while we ate, leaving us at times to serve customers. Someone came in and asked for six coffees which they took out on a tray. Ricard watched as the customer entered an office block.

'It is like being at home.'

'Yes, we have tried to bring a bit of France to this corner.'

'Seems as though you have achieved it. Congratulations.'

'Are you going to see Clementine now?'

'No, later. We are visiting Julie this morning. Last time I was over she said she liked to rest in the afternoon. Has she been over to see you at all?'

'She rang Elise a couple of days ago and they had a long talk comparing pregnancies.'

'Sounds fun.' Remarked Ricard. I shook my head, raising my eyes to the ceiling.

'Well, come on then. Let's go. Bus or taxi?'

Chapter Twenty

I recognized the male voice at the other end of the intercom.

'It's Yvonne, Paul.'

'We were not expecting you today.' I heard him say something to Julie then, 'Come on up.'

The security door clicked.

'The apartment is on the top floor, you can walk if you like, I'm taking the lift.'

'I think I will join you. I do not want to expire and give a bad impression on our first meeting.'

Julie opened the door and gave me a hug. I introduced Ricard who willingly exchanged a kiss on both cheeks, she whispered something in Ricard's ear, he stood back, holding her at arms' length; there was an element of tension in their positions.

'You are the second person to say that to me today.'

'Because we care. Sorry, I shouldn't have put you on the spot, come in, let me introduce you to my husband, I don't think you've met him.'

'No, I could not go to the meeting with Marianne.'

The introduction went smoothly, both men comfortable in each other's company, the discussion inevitably turned to the party.

'As I said earlier, Julie, we are sorry to gate-crash your party to introduce Paul to the family, but under the circumstances, we thought it would be an opportunity. But it's up to you if you want to change your minds, we'll understand.'

'Of course not, Paul and I wanted to meet Ricard, I know mother and father have, so no real reason why not and it seems natural the other two should do so too. Of course, we're not going to change our minds, but this is rather a whirlwind engagement, isn't it?'

'I'm pregnant; Ricard knew when I agreed to marry him and we'll be having the wedding as soon as it can be fixed.'

Julie laughed. 'Where has my steadfast, sensible, pre-planning, level-headed sister gone?'

'You are stuck with this one now.'

'She'll do! Congratulations, and to you, Ricard.'

Paul rose and kissed me and shook Ricard by the hand.

'But I don't understand why you didn't tell me everything earlier.'

'It was all rather complicated.'

Ricard explained some of the problems with his brother and why I could not commit before.

'Can we talk about the party and what you need me to do now? I hope you have all the replies and invited everyone you wanted. Has Miguel sorted out the food and drinks you want?'

'I think everything is in order now,' Paul replied, 'but on Sunday morning, Ricard, I would appreciate a hand shifting some furniture, there is not much, as you see, but we think we will move some bits to give a more practical use of the space in the room, and I do not want Julie lifting it.'

Ricard looked at me, 'Can I get over early?'

'Of course, we can both come and do whatever is needed. People will arrive any time from twelve thirty, won't they, Julie?' On her nod of confirmation, I continued, 'things often take longer than expected so we could be here by ten. When is Miguel coming?'

'About eleven thirty.'

'Are you two really up for this onslaught?' I asked.

'We are French.' Was all the response I got.

'I don't want to appear rude, but we have to go to the antenatal clinic soon. You're welcome to stay here if you want to.'

'Thanks, but no thanks. We'll head off to see Pops and Clementine.'

'Do Mark's parents know about you two?'

'No, but they and I have talked about the possibility of me getting married again, I'll go and see them fairly soon.'

We left saying they should call if they needed anything before our return on Sunday.

The meeting at my parents' apartment was comfortable, although we'd not expected to be offered lunch, Grace had anticipated we'd be invited and prepared sufficient for us all. We left them late afternoon and returned home.

To my flat, at any rate.

'After tomorrow, your next hurdle will be meeting Patrick on Sunday.'

Ricard's head jerked up.

'I did not realise he would be there.'

'That's a relationship problem you've made for yourself, Ricard; if you've still any element of doubt, you'd better tell me before we go any further.'

'No Yvonne, it was stupid jealousy. I would not have got this far with you if I had any doubts. I am sorry I reacted as I did.'

I poured some wine.

'Should you be drinking that?'

'It's for you, not me, I'm having soda water, I've cut it right down if you hadn't noticed, except the odd time, even then my glass was rarely emptied or topped up, I've been careful since I knew. I'll get checked out next week. Ricard, I appreciate tomorrow might be a bit difficult for you with the vicar; when I rang, he seemed pleased to hear from me, I don't know if I told you, but he got special agreement from the vicar at the other church to preside at Mark's funeral. Is this all too much, Ricard? Mark and my family?'

'No, of course not. You were thrown in the deep end with all the information about Charlotte and the rest of my family. This is a nice flat, what do you think you'll do with it once we are married?'

'Oh, I don't know. I've not really thought, it has always been here for me during these rocky few years, so the future of it has never entered my head.'

§ § §

The Reverend Matthew Shoreman was coming in from his garden when we arrived at the vicarage. His wife, Teresa, who opened the door to us, was as short and round as her husband was tall and thin. He led us into his office where we were both welcomed with firm handshakes. Teresa brought a tray of coffee and homemade biscuits which she placed on a low table by her husband's side.

'Right. What can I do for you two?'

I asked Ricard to take the lead explaining the full situation, he started, but Matthew raised his hand indicating he should stop.

'My French is not good enough to follow what you are saying.'

Stupidly, it had never occurred to me Ricard didn't speak English and realised all conversations had been in French, with him and his family; with Pops; Clementine; Julie, Paul and Phillippe. However, I felt as I'd asked him to do the explanation, he should continue and I translated.

He started again, saying as neither of us was divorced and both widowed, as far as we were aware there was no reason, in law, why we should not marry in church.

'Are you both certain marriage at this point is what you really want and it is not just because of the baby? It is not many years since we buried Mark, I assume you knew, Ricard?'

'Yes. I would marry her now if I could, but as Yvonne would like a church wedding, with which I agree, I understand the Banns have to be read over three consecutive Sundays. There are also a few other people to consider, specifically my daughter who would probably kill me if we went ahead without her.'

'I doubt we would ever hear the end of it.' I agreed.

'And then there is—'

'Stop. Perhaps you'd better tell me everything right from the start, I don't mean to intrude into areas not of my concern, but marriage is a serious matter.'

'Not to be undertaken lightly,' I said.

'Exactly.'

We retold our story from the beginning.

'You both appreciate the mix of Catholic and Protestant? And neither of you are wanting to convert to the others religion?'

'No, it seems to be working well, now.'

'The operative word being "Now" isn't it? And the child? Will he or she be baptised?'

Ricard's response was fast and emphatic,

'Yes, as a baby—into both churches, when he or she is old enough to make decisions, we will see.'

'You seem to have it all worked out! But tell me. What about the day-to-day life with your—um—I have to work out the relationship will be with Marianne—and the domestic arrangements. There could be tensions there and with your Suzanne, these are where the frictions will arise. Are you strong enough to ride these?'

'We think so, they have been discussed.'

'I think I have quizzed you both enough, yes, I am willing to marry you. Have you both brought your passports with you?'

We handed them over and completed a couple of forms; then agreed a wedding date four Saturdays ahead at twelve o'clock.

Mathew shook hands again at the door as we parted saying,

'Yvonne, please tell the rest of the clan to keep things simple, would you? I think you and Julie have brought me enough potential complications for them as well.'

'See you Sunday week, Mathew.'

'Oh, we'll see you at Julie and Paul's party tomorrow, we might be a bit late of course, I have a service in the morning.' He closed the front door.

'Nice guy, takes his job seriously, does he not? I wondered at one point if he were going to do it, or if we would be going to a registry office.'

'Would you like to have a look in the church while we are here or wait till one of the Sundays when I hope you can be with me to hear the Banns read.'

'Let us go home, I doubt much will change in the church between now and then, I just fancy sitting in your flat and relaxing. Yesterday and this morning have been quite taxing.'

'It's also a build-up of the last few days. I agree, let's hibernate till tomorrow.'

§

The door to Mrs Asher's flat opened as the lift arrived at my floor.

'Oh, my Lord! I forgot you were coming. Welcome.' Portia and I rushed into each other's arms.

'We didn't agree a time and Mrs Asher has been kind enough to let me use her loo, which was my main need. Thank you again, Mrs Asher, you're a lifesaver.'

'Think nothing of it, Portia, it was a pleasure to help and you paid for the service.'

'Thank you for looking after her, Mrs Asher. May I introduce you to my friend Ricard? Ricard, this is Mrs Asher, my incredibly good neighbour.'

Ricard must have been taking lessons from Pops as he oozed charm and kissed Mrs Asher's hand and mumbled a polite greeting in French. She blushed and closed her door.

Portia stood staring at Ricard, then looked at me, with her mouth open. She was still staring as we entered my apartment.

'I think you have gathered who each other is.'

'What did you do in payment for use of her toilet?'

'Changed a couple of lightbulbs.'

I laughed. 'They perpetually need changing, I think we'd better have her in for a pre-dinner glass of something.'

Portia was not at ease in Ricard's company and looked questioningly at me. I realised her dilemma.

'No, no, Portia, this isn't Jules, Ricard is his older brother, but I was right in my hunch, I couldn't tell you what I suspected when I was with you, relax, this one is no danger.'

'Well, you'd better start explaining. Where's the wine? I've had a shock.'

'Hot sweet tea then,' I joked as I asked, 'Red or white?'

'White for now,' Portia kept staring at Ricard, 'uncanny.'

'Portia, do stop staring at the poor man, he's not a museum piece. Are you madly wanting to go out and about tonight? We were thinking of spending this evening in, but I am sure we can manage if you want to go out.'

'No, not me, as you know, an evening with my feet up is a luxury and you can tell me the rest of the tale you hardly started in Leeds.'

Ricard sighed when I translated for him.

'Again? We have just been through it all with Matthew.'

'And we'll probably have to do it all over again tomorrow.'

'Why do we not write it down and distribute it as a handout?' he suggested, 'how many siblings and friends will there be tomorrow?'

'Julie and Paul are probably having the same problem, perhaps I'd better ring her and suggest it.'

I translated the exchange for Portia.

This is going to be a heavy evening.

I found translating small chunks of our history, as the conversation progressed, was easier for me when Ricard was talking. I used some different vocabulary which I hoped expressed his views rather than mine. There were areas he omitted but had to include a censored version of the problem between him and Jules to reassure Portia.

About half past seven I invited Mrs Asher in for a glass of wine, she was delighted to accept, promising not to outstay her welcome. Her command of

French was a great relief to both Ricard and me, my quiet neighbour entertained us with stories of the postings she and her husband had enjoyed all over the world, while he was in the diplomatic service, translating for Portia as she went along. As anticipated, she left after an acceptable time saying she'd intruded into the family long enough.

After we'd eaten and cleared away, Ricard excused himself and left Portia and me to talk, which we did until one thirty.

§ § §

Portia came with us to Julie's on Sunday morning, so the host and hostess were well-prepared when Miguel and his staff arrived. Before the guests began to gather and mingle, we agreed to try and ensure Ricard had a French speaker as a translator with him at all times.

I was in an intense conversation with one of Julie's work colleagues and unaware of Patrick's arrival. I heard his voice following Pops' response to an earlier question he'd asked.

'Oh, that's Ricard Letour, surely Yvonne has spoken about him. Nice man.'

'I knew she had a friend in France she was becoming attached to. There was some problem over her doing the French school project; so, this is the chap.'

'How's your French, Patrick?'

'Not good, I'm afraid, I can say "good morning" and "yes please", then I follow the rest of the British and shout!'

'Ah, let me introduce you then.'

'I hope she's not got herself entangled too soon. I'm fond of her, Clive, I would hate her to rush into anything and make a mistake, I've told her to be careful. I would've thought one French man in your family is quite enough.'

'My goodness, I never took you for being a xenophobe, I've come to like this one a great deal, come and meet him. Oh, excuse me, Patrick, looks like Julie wants me to do the welcome toast to Paul. I'll introduce you afterwards.'

Pops always managed to hit the right tone whenever he had to propose celebratory toasts and this was no exception. Spoken only in English, Ricard would have got the gist of it as he raised his glass with everyone else to welcome Paul, drink to the happy couple, their future and their twins. There was the usual hiatus afterwards, during which no one really knows what to do before conversations started again and Pops returned to Patrick.

Staying where I was, I watched the interaction between Patrick and Ricard. They shook hands, Pops was translating for them both. Patrick looked around the room, on seeing me excused himself, leaving Pops mid-sentence. Instead of coming to me, as I'd expected, Patrick went to Paul and shook his hand then turned to Julie thanking them for inviting him saying he had to leave but would keep in touch.

He left without acknowledging anyone else.

I went to Pops and Ricard.

'What was all that about?' I asked Pops.

'Why did he leave so abruptly?' Julie had joined us, 'he's only been here a few minutes and has hardly spoken to anyone.'

'No idea, they shook hands waiting for me to make the introductions. In French I told Ricard who Patrick is and used English to tell him about Ricard, I'd hardly finished the English introduction when Patrick left us.'

'How much had you managed to tell Patrick, Pops?'

'Not a great deal, only you were engaged to each other.'

'Oh no, we weren't going to say anything today, Pops, the party is for Julie, Paul and their babies.'

I translated and Ricard swore.

'You could've reminded me, I'm sorry, I forgot. Even so, why should good news cause such a response in Patrick? I'd have thought he'd be pleased for you.'

'Excuse me.' I left the flat hoping to catch Patrick before he left the building. I caught up with him in the entrance lobby where he'd been detained by Matthew and Teresa. They were obviously pleased to see him, wanting to talk. It seemed they assumed he'd just arrived and was waiting for the lift.

I exited the lift, they entered and I joined Patrick.

'You two carry on, Matthew, we'll come up in a moment, I need a word with Patrick and it's getting a bit noisy in the flat, you'll find the door open.'

Patrick said nothing at first only stared at me.

'So, this is how you repay my friendship. I knew you had some personal problems, but this...have you done any work recently, or just been snuggling up to...I don't know what. You know how much I care for you.'

'Patrick, we've been through—'

'No, not in that way, but I care for your welfare. I care you have someone who can see things from a friend's point of view, someone who could—and I may add—has supported you for many months when you needed time for

342

wounds to heal. And now, without a word you go blundering on into what in heaven's name… Oh God. Why? Why? Why didn't you tell me everything?'

He broke down in a bitter bout of anger, I stood still and let him continue till he seemed to become calmer.

'Will you give me a chance to explain what's been happening and how this has all come about and why I haven't been able to talk to you? It's been very harrowing for me, Pops, Ricard and his family. I couldn't explain before, but if you'll give me a chance, I'll do my best to do so now. Please, I owe you this, and because of our history, you owe me too. It's a long story which I can't tell you here. But I think you're gravely insulting my sister and her husband on their celebration, and the rest of the family too, by running away. To use your phrase, "I never saw you as a defeatist."'

Patrick had sat on one of the plush chairs provided in the lobby and stared into space.

'OK. I'll come up again, not necessarily to please you, but you are right, it would be a mistake to cause a rift between me and the family, I feel they are as much mine as yours.'

'Thank you. Patrick, before we go back to the party, in case someone says something, I think it only fair for me to tell you, I am pregnant.'

'What? Are you marrying him because you're pregnant?'

'Please keep your cool and your voice down, no one is supposed to mention it today, but just in case, I thought I should tell you. And no, I'm marrying him because I love him and can see a future with him. I would manage the pregnancy and child without him if I didn't.'

Ricard and Paul were hovering at the open flat door. I pulled Ricard out and let Paul lead Patrick to get a drink.

'Alright? I wanted to come and find you, but Paul and Clive said to leave you. What happened down there? Matthew said he had seen you both.'

'Nothing happened, we talked. Well, he shouted at first, he is angry and hurt as I've not been involving him more in my personal life. From his point of view, he thinks I've been taking and not giving in return.'

'How could you have done, what a strange thing to say, from what you have told me he is a very rational man—even if—'

'Yes. Please don't think badly of him. When you eventually get to know him, which I hope you will, I'm sure you'll like each other. Come on, let's go in. And don't tell me off, but I could do with a glass of wine.'

343

Ricard manoeuvred me away from the door and kissed me hard.

'I love you.'

Patrick and Paul had joined Julie who was introducing Francis, who I'd not seen arrive, and decided we had missed each other as he must have walked up the stairs rather than wait for the lift, as I was going down earlier.

I am astounded at how fit he is for someone with such a sedentary job.

I looked around at my family, pleased we could all be together and that Francis had not been called out on a case today.

I wonder what it will be like when all branches get together. How will Marianne and Sven fit in? I will not worry about Suzanne; she'll have them eating out of her hand. How will Portia react to Jules? Alors!

Ricard kept hold of my hand as I moved him to safety with mother who was regaling Portia with the latest exploits in the rehearsals.

'The stagehands are useless, we could do with you Portia on the set, then they might get the right bit of furniture in the right place for the right scene.'

'I doubt our temperaments would add to the jollity of the production, Mother. You and I would be screaming at each other within the first couple of hours, I'll stay where I am, thank you.'

Francis came and joined us and gently pulled my arm taking me from mother, as Ricard was unwilling to leave me, he came too and I introduced them.

'Just want to say old bean, I wish you both every joy. I seem to be getting vibes everything is not yet out in the open and you have not had an easy passage to get this far. Appreciations for your card and if I may be permitted to reciprocate, I am mortified at my omission in the transmission of relevant intelligence concerning the whereabouts and activities of yours truly. Please be reassured every exertion will be generated to rectify the situation forthwith. To this end it beholds me to inform you a lecture tour in Malaysia is on the horizon so I respectfully enquire the date of your jubilant nuptials as a significant urgency, to facilitate my preparations in an endeavour to be in attendance. I have ascertained you had verbal intercourse with our esteemed Matthew, however he is not disposed to divulge information to assist me.'

'Ricard, Francis wants to know the date of our wedding, he must go away on business soon so needs to plan but would like to be here if he can. May I tell him the date?'

'As long as he keeps it to himself for now. I think we have done enough to detract from Julie and Paul today.'

'Four Saturdays' time.'

'Sincerely appreciative of the intelligence.' He smiled, shook Ricard's hand, kissed my cheek and went to mother.

'If you decide to learn English, you will find my brother does not speak as most of us do! Why he talks as he does, I don't know. How do you feel about another attempt at speaking with Patrick? I think he's calmed down and as he's likely to be in our lives in the future it might help to start reconciliations.'

'He seems to be popular with all your family, so perhaps so. But it was nothing I said—I had not even opened my mouth before he charged off, let us get your father in case we need a referee. What did you tell him downstairs?'

'I love you and I'm having your baby. But I will arrange to see him during the week and tell him as much as is relevant.'

'I wish you were coming back with me tomorrow.'

'You know we agreed I'd stay this week. I must see Patrick, go and see Mark's parents, fix to see my GP and hear the Banns on Sunday, then I'll fly over. I seem to have been living at an airport for months. You'll have plenty to do your end before then and we'll come back together the following week. Come on, let's talk with Patrick.'

Patrick realised we were wanting to speak to him and pointedly moved away from Pops to join a conversation with some of Julie and Paul's university friends. Pops grasped this and said,

'Leave it for now, Yvonne. He is more hurt than angry. I tried to explain things have been complicated and fast moving so it wasn't possible for you to keep him informed of everything going on. If I'll be of any use when you meet with him, let me know.'

'I think my presence has caused somewhat of a dampener on some members of the party, Clive, perhaps I should leave.'

'I don't think so, it's Patrick's problem, not yours. I know it's difficult having to use interpreters with some of my family and guests, but they are all eager to know you. Going might seem like running away and you have something to hide.'

'Wait till they meet the rest of my family.' Ricard grinned, the first relaxation of his face for some time.

'Come with me.' Pops removed Ricard's hand from mine and took him to speak with Julie's supervising professor.

Right, I'm not going to be ignored or blamed.

I joined the group with Patrick. I remembered meeting the university friends one summer holiday when I was lucky enough to have some free time. Paul was not on the scene then and Julie and these two invited me to spend a day in the country with them. It was easy to reminisce and I was pleased to see that Patrick was a little discomforted as he was not part of the memory.

You are going to talk to my fiancé whether you like it or not, Patrick.

'Excuse me, I want to chat to the professor, come with me, Patrick, the last time we spoke you said you'd not met him.'

Without making an issue of declining, he'd no choice but to accompany me which inevitably meant he had to join in the conversation. Ricard was in full flow about the charity work he was involved in regarding the hospice movement.

'I admit, Yvonne, I have rather neglected it in the last few months. When we are settled,' he looked at Patrick, 'I must be more active again.'

I translated into English.

'My sister is involved in charity work, as am I.' Pops translated into French.

Patrick had obviously thought he might play the "one-upmanship" game which was out of character and was not a sensible idea as Ricard responded, in an extremely friendly and enthusiastic manner.

'Yes, I know. Yvonne has told me so much about the work you do and it is really through you we met.' He took my hand and kissed it.

Don't push it, Ricard—be careful.

'I am most grateful to you and your sister for bringing this angel into my life.'

The tension which initially emerged as Pops translated the message for Patrick to understand was suddenly broken by Patrick laughing.

'Angel? You must be talking about two different people, young man. You wait till she really gets going!' He took Ricard's hand and shook it firmly. 'You just take care of her, don't ever hurt or deceive her, there is a big clan who wouldn't like it and I will be the leader, I doubt you need any other warning and I wish you both every happiness.'

Ricard's bemused expression changed to a wide smile when Pops translated.

'My apologies for earlier, Yvonne, ring me tomorrow and we can fix to talk. I still want to hear everything—and have my pound of flesh. There are also some office issues to sort out.'

I nodded.

He moved to Julie and Paul, shook their hands and said this time, he must leave as he was reading at the evening service. This second exit was much more acceptable with farewells and waves to everyone.

'Well.' Was all Pops could say.

The party carried on for some several more hours. Miguel was thrilled his choice of food had been appreciated so much there was little left to be placed in Julie's refrigerator.

Gradually all the guests departed, family members staying a little longer at Julie's request.

'I know this party was initially planned, to introduce Paul to you and the other way round, you have all met him now, I can only apologise for not being as open and up front as I should have been. But, as it also turns out Yvonne has some news, which I didn't learn about until yesterday. The four of us agreed we would keep their engagement quiet so as not to detract from the aim of the party.'

'Which didn't quite work out,' Pops took up the narrative, 'the point now is to say I think we should all, informally welcome Ricard to the family; we will do so formally when they are married, which will be soon, invitations will be issued, but please keep the day free and be there.' He gave the date. 'So, I ask you to join me in one more toast.'

He turned as Miguel brought in a tray of glasses filled with champagne.

'Welcome, Ricard.'

The toast was repeated and after some general chat, gradually, we all left Julie and Paul, sharing taxis and heading off to our various homes.

'Why did I never learn French?' Asked Portia.

'Because you were rebelling and refusing to conform.'

§ § §

Portia and Ricard left in the same taxi next morning; one for a plane, the other the train. I was sad to see them go.

It was too early to make any phone calls.

Action, not misery!

So, I stripped the sheets from Portia's bed and put them in the washing machine and cleaned through the flat before heading off, via Phillippe's, for a meeting with Pops and mother to discuss invitation cards.

'I just want to check you are certain about not wanting a big wedding, Yvonne.'

'Certainly, Pops, most of my time with Ricard has been, not so much in secret, but just with close people and we've been through a lot together. We've both had the extravagant weddings and would like to marry in the company of a small and intimate group, quietly and low-key.'

'Would you like the reception in a hotel?'

'No Pops, I'll get Phillippe to do catering and hold it in my apartment, it will be easier than here.'

We sorted out the guest list and the invitations, Pops said he'd finalise the design and e-mail it to the printers when he was satisfied. I went back to my apartment stopping off at Phillippe's asking him if he'd be interested in doing the catering. He was overjoyed and started making suggestions, I asked him to sort something out and price it. Back in my apartment, I made three phone calls; one to Patrick's office and arranged to meet him for lunch the next day; the second to my GP managing to get an early appointment for Wednesday; and the third to Mark's parents when we agreed to meet at the Country Club on Thursday.

I hope the meetings go as smoothly as booking them.

Chapter Twenty-One

Andrea was waiting for me in the foyer when I reached the office, she greeted me warmly and nodded to the receptionist who rang Patrick to say I'd arrived. She hailed a taxi which took the three of us to a restaurant with an upstairs dining area overlooking the river.

A perfect setting, with the sun shining on the river and swans, for a fond or not so fond farewell from Patrick's employment. You have burned your boats here, Yvonne.

A chilled Chablis was poured into three glasses, the bottle set in an ice bucket behind Patrick ready for the waiter to top up the glasses when required.

'A toast to you and Ricard, Yvonne, and to many years of happiness ahead of you.'

'Thank you.'

'As you know, I, and Andrea joins me in this so I should say we, are disappointed you did not tell us what was going on in France and hope you will now enlighten us. We have worked together as colleagues, friends and extended family for years and feel offended. We do not think you have been badly treated, in fact from where we sit, the behaviour you have received from us has been generous, fair and forgiving. I say this now in sadness, not anger as on Sunday. We are not certain your behaviour has been reciprocal.'

'On Sunday, in anger, you accused me of not working during these last few difficult weeks. I assume you mean after the "go-cart" factory contract had been completed.' Patrick nodded, lifting his glass, Andrea and I followed his lead, but I did not drink. 'I can assure you, as far as the English school project is concerned,' I corrected the tense, 'was concerned, I carried out my role and responsibilities in line with my agreement with you and *Monsieur* Bassinet, although not always in the office provided by him.'

'When it became obvious I couldn't carry out the functions as required, for personal and practical reasons, I contacted you and the alternative plan was put in place. I continued with the project supporting Sharon following which I felt I could relinquish the responsibility as she had taken over. If I was in error, then I apologise for my mistake in not clearing my withdrawal with you formally.'

I am not going to lose my temper; I am not going to cry. His pound of flesh indeed!

I sipped my wine.

'As to the personal issue, many factors aren't mine to divulge, they're the property of other members of Ricard's family, who will soon be mine. I can tell you this however, and yes, there will be gaps and unanswered questions, but I'm not at liberty to say more.' I expounded in as much depth as I could, without breaking confidences, the whole story from meeting Ramon and Suzanne at the station in Elne to our current situation.

'Well, that wasn't too hard, was it?' Andrea spoke for the first time at the table.

Yes, it bloody well was, and I haven't told you even half the story.

I made a face between a grimace and a smile.

'What happens now? I'll reimburse your company whatever reasonable figure we agree.'

'Can we select our main course and eat before we continue, Yvonne? I have ordered a variety of appetisers which were recommended while we finish this wine. But you should not drink too much, should you?'

He indicated for the starters to be brought and the menus. With their glasses replenished, we talked about Andrea's family and their antics. I took the opportunity to ask,

'Unless something traumatic happens in phase two of this meeting, may I assume you both, and Frank, will come to the wedding? Invitations will be forthcoming shortly; it will only be a small group.'

'Of course, Yvonne. Thank you.'

Over coffee, Andrea pulled three copies of what looked like detailed project proposals from her briefcase and passed them to Patrick.

I knew a good lunch without business was too good to be true.

Then the bombshell dropped.

'I will soon be retiring, Yvonne, and going to live in France with my sister.'

'Why?' I sounded sharp.

'My health is rapidly deteriorating and I would like a few months, possibly a year, in peace and I can think of no better place than with my sister. You know how lovely her house is.'

'Yes, it's a healing place. Have a rest and come back.'

'No, it is too late now. But to business, this is an agreement between me, you and Andrea to co-manage the company while I have a hands-off overview until I am no longer either capable or interested. There is also a transfer document for co-ownership when the final time comes.'

'Patrick, this is far too pre-emptive a move. Andrea, say something.'

'There is nothing she can say to change my mind. Andrea knows full well; I am beginning to make mistakes, miss things, becoming forgetful. I want to go out at the top, not some fool who ruins everything I have built up because I refuse to acknowledge what is happening to me. I know the company will be in good hands with you two.'

Of course, at the airport, he'd said something about diagnosis being wrong— but he'd meant the wrong person.

'Patrick, your friend and your visit to your sister—'

'Yes, no friend—well, lots of friends, but it is my diagnosis.'

'There must be something that can be done.'

'Yvonne, I have been through so many specialists I have run out of them! I've got to the end of the line and I want to have a productive direction out of the business and a peaceful end to my life. So, let's get on with this, shall we?'

Neither of them would entertain any further discussion about his health and insisted we concentrate on the business plan.

'But Patrick, how can I do this now? I will be in France.'

'What's wrong with the plane? Goodness, you've used them enough recently; the phone, emails? And all the future developing technological communications? I assume you have heard of Skype and such like? We don't have to be constantly in the same room to work. After your wedding—well, I will give you two days!' he laughed, 'we can discuss the various options Andrea and I have put together. I want to be part of the setup and help overcome any unforeseen initial problems and be available in the future for any advice you may need, while I am competent.'

'But what about the baby?'

'You will make a wonderful mother, but I can hardly see you sitting at home nursing it all day; anyway, I thought you said there was another woman living there. I can't recall her relationship to you but it doesn't take two women to run a house and it will probably be a good idea to be out of the way sometimes.'

'You've got it all sorted, haven't you?'

'Not quite all, we need your agreement, commitment and signature.'

'Patrick, Andrea, this is a massive step just now. I'm honoured you both think I'm capable, but I need to think this over carefully and talk with Ricard. I'm about to embark on some work for him on his father's inheritance and I've no idea what's entailed. I'm certain if I said "yes", Andrea and I could work together, but do we have the knowledge and skills between us to run the place? What about Frank? What does he say?'

'He's all for it. In fact, he asked me, if we don't accept, why have we all been working our butts off to build up a fantastic business? Sometimes, under trying circumstances.'

Patrick was about to protest but grunted instead and looked suitably chastened.

Patrick passed Andrea and me a copy of the file.

'Read it with an open mind, Yvonne. Look at it with the objectivity you would do any project—even if your neutrality has been a little skewed recently. Please.'

'It's a strange thing, Patrick, I'm not sure where I stand in your employment now. But I think I'd better tell you, after hearing the Banns on Sunday, I'll be off to France again.'

'You're on paid holiday until a week after your wedding. We will then need to have an answer.'

I nodded.

§ § §

Ricard said the proposal offered by Patrick had a great deal of merit, but agreed we'd have to look at the terms of the contract in detail, not only from the business and financial implications, but how it would affect our personal lives.

There were advantages if I were working full time and away a fair amount, Marianne would have a full role. Neither she nor Sven had intimated they would want to leave once we were married or indeed, following theirs. But how would long, or frequent absences, affect our marriage and my relationship with our child? There was also the matter of how much attention Ramon's inheritance would require; I might get some indication next week; we were in for several long discussions.

§ § §

My appointment with the GP went smoothly. We discussed the future care and she suggested I sort out arrangements in France as soon as I could, unless I planned to be in England for the birth and immediate after-care. In the meantime, I was to arrange with the clinic midwife to have a scan.

§ § §

Peter and Georgina were welcoming. Georgina's eyes travelled to my left hand where I still wore the two rings Mark had given me but she soon noticed the ring I wore on my other hand. Although they were supportive and reiterated their understanding a time would come when I would remarry, I could see, especially in Georgina's eyes, a great sadness. Possibly the last tie to her son's life was about to be broken. It might have been different if we'd had children, but I was leaving to start a new life with a new man in a new country. And with a baby on the way.

Lunch was a solemn occasion, though Peter tried to lighten it at times, but I'd caught Georgina's mood and found it hard to break out of it. I told them about Ricard and his family but withheld most of the details of the history I didn't feel they needed or wanted to know. Now I was moving on had become a fact, as opposed to a possibility, they were less in need of being involved. I experienced an irrational pang of guilt at hurting them. I told them we all hoped they could see their way to coming to the wedding. At this time, they were uncertain but would await the formal invitation before deciding.

'Even if you decline initially but find on the day you'd like to come, you'll be welcome. Although he is quite different from Mark, I think you'll like Ricard and I'd like you to meet him.'

Georgina patted my hand and Peter rose when I did, he gave my cheek a kiss and walked me to the door.

'She gets these very dark days now. I don't think it's all to do with Mark's death and it certainly has nothing to do with your future marriage, we wish you all the joy in the world. Please keep in touch and one day, I hope to meet Ricard. God bless you and drive carefully.'

I watched him walk back to his wife who was still sitting, now staring into space. He put his hand on her shoulder. She looked up and smiled.

I didn't take the motorway back home. I felt I needed a prettier drive. Perhaps life was asking too much of Georgina.

Gloom had descended on me when I arrived home, so, in an effort to dispel this mood, I sorted out my wardrobe putting things aside for the charity shop.

When I rang Ricard, he excitedly told me,

'*Papom* and *Mamon* are over the moon about the blessing venue and they have arranged for me to meet with *Frère* Macon on Saturday. I will drive tomorrow and take Suzanne and try and fix a date for four weeks after the English one. Alright by you?'

'Yes, wonderful. It will also give you a chance to talk with Jules again and see if you can find out more about him and his character.'

'*Mamon* and Marianne have already started to sort out the catering and accommodation.'

'Ricard, I need to think about accommodation this end too. Will Jules be coming to the wedding?'

'No.'

'That was very abrupt, has something happened?'

'Not that I know of, but he has told *Papom* he will stay and look after the farm while they come over to England. But he will be part of the blessing celebration.'

'How thoughtful and kind of him. Maybe I've misjudged him and you may get some more information over the weekend. Take care of Suzanne.'

'Do not worry, my parents and I have agreed she will not be left alone with him, and he is still sleeping in the guest room not the main house.'

'Sounds as if it won't be the most relaxing of weekends. But Ramon has not said anything specific?'

'Just the same niggle as before, but nothing to call hard facts. Do not worry, Suzanne will be well-protected.'

'Alright, take care and I'll see you on Sunday. Love you.'

'Love you too, goodnight.'

What is it about Jules keeping everyone alert? Be honest, Yvonne, you're not unhappy he isn't coming over for the wedding.

§ § §

In the morning, I went to look for something suitable to wear for my wedding. After traipsing around town for several hours, seeking the ideal, I realised this exercise was so reminiscent of—what, I could not think—then it dawned on me.

The time I'd spent in Toulouse seeking a dress for the party. Yes, I will wear it again. Problem solved.

I went to my parents, empty-handed apart from the invitations I'd picked up from the printers earlier but satisfied I'd an appropriate dress to wear. We discussed further the arrangements we had agreed on Monday.

'Are you and Pops concerned about hosting Ramon and Matilde, Clementine?'

'Not at all, dear, your father said they're easy to get on with, and I'm sure they will excuse my rather bad French, it will give me a chance to improve it. My concern is for you, there is a lot to do and you seem to be in France for most of the next two weeks, flying in and out every weekend.'

'Yes, I know. Maybe I'll rethink my travelling but everything seems to have come at the same time. Is Grace happy with the preparations?'

'Yes, she takes things calmly.'

'And I haven't told you about the lunch meeting with Patrick and Andrea.'

'You have kept quiet, we thought it might be because of a traumatic break-up between you.'

'No, in fact, it was quite the opposite and it's a shock. Are you aware Patrick isn't well, and thinking, actively planning, to give up the business?'

'Ah, he's told you,' Pops nodded, 'some time ago he mentioned something about being tired and wondering what to do. What's he decided?'

I explained.

'You've taken on the work for Ramon and Ricard and with the baby, how can you even contemplate it?

'At the moment I'm not, I haven't read the proposal properly, just skimmed it. Under different circumstances I'd jump at it, but I must see about the inheritance first, which might mean just a couple of visits if everything is well. Actually, I'm still reeling over Patrick's news.'

Grace brought some coffee.

'Will you need any help preparing for the guests, Grace? I know it's extra work for you.'

'Not at all, Yvonne. It seems as if you are going to be fully occupied yourself and I was going to offer to help you. This is a good opportunity for me and your mother to clear out a load of stuff she hasn't touched since they moved here.'

'Stuff!' said Clementine, 'stuff? That is my life.'

'Rubbish, your life is not a load of dust sitting festering in boxes. We will keep what is relevant, but old dried-out makeup sticks which are no longer used are "stuff", they can go to the Victoria and Albert Museum, though I doubt they'll want them!'

'Well, I'll be interested in the outcome. Sorry I mentioned it.'

'You are doing me a big favour, Yvonne. By the way, congratulations.' With a look of defiance at mother, Grace left us.

'Shall we start addressing envelopes?' I asked pouring the coffee and passing cups across the table to my parents.' I'll post the ones to the English addresses on the way home and take the ones for France with me.'

I stayed for lunch and mid-afternoon went home planning a quiet evening watching the television, but I was hungry and couldn't be bothered to cook, so went out to get a pizza and met a friend on the same errand. We went to her flat where we chatted till gone eleven. Another person was added to the post-wedding party in June.

§ § §

Saturday was an unusually quiet day. I took my time getting dressed and putting together my overnight bag for tomorrow's flight then spent a few minutes finalising the sleeping arrangements for the wedding weekend. Without Jules it would be much simpler and, although it seemed a bit "daft", I booked a hotel room for Sven and Ricard on the evening before our wedding. I chatted to Mrs Asher, begging a bed for Portia for the weekend. She was more than delighted to help and accepted the invitation to the gathering after the wedding.

I settled in front of the television to watch a film, I must have dozed off halfway through and was woken with a start at the sound of the telephone. Ricard was ringing.

'How did the meeting with *Frère* Macon go?'

'Fine, he says it will be a pleasure to bless our union. I did get a more in-depth scrutiny about the religious upbringing of our children—'

'What! Children? How many does he expect?'

'Well, he did use the plural and intimated time was running out and we should get on with it to increase his flock. How many would you like?'

'Well, if Suzanne is going to get into a tizz every time I'm pregnant, perhaps we should stop at one.'

'Oh. Alright.'

'OK, sixteen.'

'A few too many, my dear! In any case, I told him the same as we did Matthew, which he seemed to accept.'

'I assume you'll be at church tomorrow.'

'Yes, we can think about each other. Yvonne, I just want to be able to love you and call you, my wife.'

'Well, it won't be long now. Just keep loving me. I love you, goodnight.'

§ § §

My parents picked me up on Sunday to hear the Banns read for the first time. It was a bittersweet moment as I remembered first hearing them with Mark and wished Ricard could have been here; next week, he would be. My parents, sitting either side of me, each spontaneously took one of my hands, none of us looked at each other, but I felt their eyes were welling, as were mine.

Afterwards, we dropped mother at their flat so she could have a good rest while Pops took me to the airport. Before he set me down, he asked,

'This might be a bit late in the day to ask, Yvonne. But you are sure about this marriage, aren't you?'

'Oh yes, Pops, very sure. Why do you ask?'

'I just wanted to hear you say it. He's a good man, off you go, see you next week.'

§

357

Ricard had brought Suzanne with him to meet me. Sven and I acknowledged each other and he drove us safely home to enjoy an evening meal, all of us chatting and planning. I took the wedding invitations from my bag and passed them over. Suzanne wanted to take hers to school to show her friends and we could find no reason why not.

'Don't lose it or you won't be allowed in the church.'

'You will let me in, Yvonne.' She smiled.

Don't get your hopes up, my dear. I've not decided yet.

Sven told me while we were eating, his citizenship has come through so his passport application should be alright in time for the wedding.

'Ricard is coming with me to see if we can get it done in person, sometimes it is quicker.'

'Yes, we are going together to get his and Suzanne's done in one go.'

'Congratulations, Sven.'

We cleared away and went to bed.

'Has there been any fallout from the weekend before last? Any more nightmares? And what news from this weekend?' I asked as we lay together.

'No, all seems to be fine now on the dream front, unless she is not saying anything. We all managed to keep her in the company of someone else when she was with Jules. I am not sure if we needed to, but there is something strange about him. I wonder if he had a bad experience in Australia he is not talking about.'

'Not talking about problems and secrets seems to be something in the brothers' blood.'

Ricard released me and moved onto his elbow, looking down at me.

'Yvonne, please, no more digs at me not communicating my problems to you. I will never keep any secrets from you again. So, please, no more.'

'Yes, I'm sorry. I was unfair.'

He relaxed back into the pillows and put his hand on my thigh.

'Is it alright?' he asked.

'What a question; come here.'

§ § §

I kept out of Marianne's way while she sorted out Suzanne for school. Ricard gave me an unopened envelope addressed to him but with a logo of one of Ramon's factories stamped on it.

'Perhaps you could look at this during the day. The first two appointments I have made for you are tomorrow, so take today carefully. For this trip, Sven will drive you, once you are here permanently, we can sort out a car and insurance for you, maybe after the baby is born. The second factory manager has not sent any papers yet, though they might come in today's post. If they do, please open the envelope.'

He kissed me and left.

§

'I am walking into the town later for some fresh vegetables, Yvonne. Do you want to come with me?'

'Yes please, Marianne. I'll just shower and dress.'

'There's no hurry, take your time.'

I wondered why Sven did not drive her. Was this a code for the employees not to abuse their situation? I'll ask Ricard.

We walked side by side in companionable silence along a route I'd not been before, footpaths, not roads. I was beginning to learn, when Marianne had something to say about herself on her mind, she liked to walk and talk.

'I am just checking if you have decided what you will wear to your wedding, Yvonne?'

'Do you know you're the only person to ask me? But yes, I plan to wear the dress I bought and wore for the party.'

'Good, and I am relieved.'

'Why?'

'Because after we get the bread and vegetables, I want to show you something.'

We arrived in the town centre in less time than it took to drive.

Why had I not been told of this route? I'll have to ask Ricard. Was this another secret of his?

The "something" was a silk dress and jacket in dark green.

'I was concerned you might have chosen the same colour, so I could not buy this.'

'It is gorgeous.'

'They have held it for me until I saw you and I was sure the colours would not be the same. Let me try it on again so you can see.'

It fitted Marianne perfectly, but before she had put it on, I was concerned about the dark colour and her dark hair, but the shade was right for her.

'You've got good taste.'

'It costs a bit more than I would usually spend, but this is a special occasion. You have made Ricard so happy, and Suzanne. I showed it to Sven and he agreed it would be appropriate for me to wear at our wedding too.'

'Are you sure you wouldn't rather wear it for the first time then?'

'No, my dear, I think this is right. I will get them to wrap it. Look, there is an in-house café, they will keep this and the shopping for us while we go for a coffee.'

I couldn't resist the cream tart with my coffee and persuaded Marianne to have one too, giving her time for the next question.

'This is really not my business, Yvonne, but you have never mentioned any nieces or nephews.'

'No, none of my family have produced any—at least none they've admitted to—just Julie and Paul's babies on the way, as you know. Why do you ask?'

'It is a matter of whether or not you will be having anything like a flower girl? You know, a small maid of honour.'

'Oh, Marianne, did you want to be her for me as I was going to be for you?'

'No, no, no! Heaven forbid, but you do know who is hankering to do so.'

'I'm afraid I haven't really thought about it, nor forgotten her enthusiasm, I saw it again last evening. It seems so long ago now.'

'Yes, a lot has happened since then. Do not make a rush decision, you might have an old friend in England you would like to ask when you do think about it.'

'I have a feeling Suzanne might have gone a bit further than just thinking about it.'

'Yes, but you do not have to act on her wishes, she has however, found what she calls "the dress". I have tried to tell her not to get her hopes up and not to mention it to you, and certainly not to ask.'

'Has she or you mentioned this to Ricard?'

'Suzanne has been pestering him and he asked my opinion, which is what I have just told you.'

'Am I to suppose "the dress" is in this shop?'

Marianne nodded.

'There's no harm in me having a look at it, but I've not made up my mind one way or the other.'

'I know.'

I paid for the refreshments.

"The dress" came in many colours, some garish and certainly unsuitable but an ice blue one would look good on Suzanne and would complement mine.

'Which colour did she choose?'

'The pale blue one.'

'Nice.'

We retrieved Marianne's outfit and walked back. We didn't refer to the matter again on the return journey.

'Do you and Sven usually eat in your own flat when everyone is out, Marianne? If you do and would prefer to do so, I'm happy to eat on my own.'

'It varies depending on what we are doing. If you are happy with our company, I had planned to eat in the house today.'

Another aspect of domesticity we'll have to agree on.

We went our separate ways till lunch time, each of us having work to do. The envelope contained several years of audited accounts; projected figures incorporating essential and developmental costs. Staffing ratio and gearing seemed to be within sensible bounds and capital, though not massive, was sound. There didn't appear to be anything to be concerned about so I was looking forward to a quick and productive meeting the next day. If all areas of the inheritance were as clear as this one seemed to be, then Patrick's offer might be practical.

After lunch, Sven and Marianne spent some time working in the courtyard clearing leaves. I wandered up the stairs to the landing where, following Lucille, I'd first been aware of the emptiness in the house. Although Marianne kept the whole place spotless there was obvious evidence of wear and tear on the decorations and fabrics and I realised I'd become used to the house and décor and no longer noticed the…

What had I called it? "Bereft" feeling? Yes.

It no longer felt so deeply lovelorn but I felt something was still missing and recognised nothing had changed since Charlotte's death, Ricard had said he'd got used to the place but it seemed as if everything had fossilised and we were living in a time warp, almost in Charlotte's shadow.

A sort of Miss Haversham effect? Was he still mourning Charlotte and we'd moved too fast?

I walked along the landing touching pieces of furniture and the wall coverings until I reached a heavy tapestry I'd seen, but never really noticed. I ran my hand down it and felt a nob behind it, moving the tapestry to one side I discovered a door which opened easily, there was a light switch on the wall which illuminated a carpeted staircase. The space at the top stretched the whole length and width of the building, in all the time I'd been visiting and living in the house I'd never contemplated an attic. I retraced my steps and pulled on a thick coat and examined the external construction which held no indication of the roof space. It was only now I was aware of how much the building rose above the window line of the upper floor.

'Are you alright, Yvonne?'

'Yes, fine, Marianne, I just felt like a bit of fresh air, reading boring reports can get a bit tedious and soporific,' I lied. 'Would you like a cup of something hot? Coffee, tea, chocolate?'

'Not just now, thanks, we will be stopping soon, Sven has to get Suzanne.'

I returned to the attic. There didn't appear to be anything sinister, a few suitcases I didn't open, then I saw the cot and Moses Basket which were obviously old, much older than Suzanne. If they were to be used, they'd need some work. I left the attic, turned off the light and drew the tapestry back into place. Why had no one mentioned this section of the house?

§

Suzanne had gone to bed, Marianne and Sven to their flat before Ricard and I finally settled on the couch.

'What do you think of the idea of Suzanne being a "flower girl" at the wedding?'

'Has she raised the subject?' He asked.

362

'Not to me recently, only the once, weeks ago before anything was settled and she was imagining the future, remember? But Marianne did today while we were buying her outfit.'

'At least she has done what she was told, I said if she raised the matter with you, I was going to veto it, but it is up to you. I just want to get married so we can settle down without all this constant dashing back and forth between France and England.'

'We've agreed on small family groups, and I can't see any of my last bridesmaids clamouring for the role, not that I've asked them. I suppose it won't do any harm to have Suzanne. I'll think about it and put her out of her misery before we go on Friday. She's already picked out the dress, which is quite nice, and I think she'll want it anyway, so why not. She'll be the only child there, so everyone can make a fuss of her.'

'You do not sound over-enthusiastic, do not pressure yourself.'

'I'm tired tonight; those documents were a bit draining and I've been thinking about the future.'

'So have I.' He smiled.

'Ricard.'

'I hate that tone of voice, there is usually a challenge or deep question coming.'

'There are no secrets in the house, are there? Or the way around the grounds?'

'I think all secrets have been exposed now, though they have been coming thick and furious recently.'

'I mean, there aren't any "no-go" areas in the house?'

'No, why?'

'I didn't realise till today there's an attic.'

'Yes, it is massive actually, have you been up there?'

'Yes, I was looking at the landing and thinking and came across it. It's just, you've never mentioned it.'

'Sorry, no particular reason, I suppose I just know it is there. Did you see the cot? It is old, I thought I'd get it down sometime and have it done up, if you would like it. It needs to be checked properly for safety, Marianne used it for Suzanne, I think it came from her mother, but she would be able to tell you.'

'It felt very warm up there, you must be losing a lot of heat from the house.'

'Mmm, maybe. I suspect you are getting a list ready, so put it on the list and we will think about it all. This is your home now, Yvonne. I want it to be as you want it.'

'And the shortcut to town?'

'No secret, but please do not use it when it is dark or at any time you are on your own. It is not safe, that's why we use the car so much to get to town.'

'It's just a bit strange I was never told before.'

'I assumed Marianne showed you the day she took you out on your own.'

'No, we walked the route Sven takes with the car.'

'No wonder you were so long.'

'We ought to go to bed.'

'Mmm, in a minute.' I nestled into him.

'Come on, you cannot sleep here.'

'You and Suzanne did.'

'Circumstances are far from the same.' He said, pulling me up.

§ § §

Both the factories Ricard had arranged for me to visit were situated this side of Perpignan so could be visited in one day and using the dual carriageways meant the journeys were not too arduous.

The first one was running well and profitably. Everything in the documents I'd read were reflected in the factory and work practices. I went with some trepidation to the second, as Ricard hadn't received the information he'd requested. The newly appointed manager of the finance department apologised for this oversight, explaining his concentration was on computerising the current manual system which was proving to be more difficult than he'd initially anticipated, but gave me access to all the "books" and the three previous years' balance sheets and audited accounts. The workforce here, in contrast to the first one, was young and they had an excellent training scheme in place.

At the end of each visit, I told the managers in overall charge I could not give any indication of what Ramon was planning to do but urged them to continue to function as they were currently doing. If they had any queries, to contact me.

§ § §

My detailed report on both factories, which I wrote during the evening, included the recommendation to retain them and, as George Letour hadn't been actively involved in their management, I saw no reason to alter the current system in the interim. But my discussions had highlighted concerns by workforces, at all levels in both factories, about their true position, responsibilities and accountability. The final decisions would have to wait until the whole estate had been assessed.

When he returned from the office, Ricard informed me that his clients had postponed their meetings booked for the next day.

'So I am free and thought it would be a good opportunity to visit the houses. Are you up to it? It will mean an early start as Clermont-Ferrand is a bit over four hours' drive and I've made the first appointment for ten o'clock.'

'Have you the time? Can you afford to be away this week? Wouldn't you use the time better in the office? You might regret taking time out now when you'll be away soon.'

'I hope not; anyway, I've booked four appointments, as these houses are rented, we need to meet the tenants so I have made specific times with the occupiers. The fifth house is unoccupied, I have a key, so we can go there when we have finished with the others. But it will be a long day.'

'Are you having second thoughts about my ability to do the job?'

'Not at all, you are more than capable but I would like to satisfy my curiosity about the houses.'

Ricard decided he would drive and told Sven, before he and Marianne went to their flat, to use a taxi to take Suzanne to and from school.

§ § §

We left the house at six in the morning.

Two of the houses were in the town with small, enclosed courtyards, the other two, situated a little out of town, were larger and had more land. All the tenants were pleasant and they welcomed us with coffee and other refreshments prepared. Ricard had a copy of the tenancy agreement for each house which he asked me, as now the managing agent, to go through with the tenants ensuring both parties were meeting the terms. There was a little slippage in the appointment schedule when we needed to discuss repairs, for which the tenant

365

was asked to obtain quotations and forward them to me. But in the main, we managed to keep to time going through the same process at each dwelling.

As we had been given a variety of cakes and sandwiches with coffee during the visits, we agreed not to stop for lunch and moved on to the unoccupied house in which his grandfather had lived and his father been born. Believing it was unoccupied, Ricard had not anticipated anyone being there, even so he knocked as he took the key from his pocket. His knock was answered by an older woman who was, understandably, reluctant to admit us. She asked us to wait outside while she telephoned the solicitor and having been reassured, she relaxed when Ricard produced evidence of his identity. She introduced herself as Mademoiselle Yvres, the housekeeper.

'Do you live here? Or come in daily?'

'I have a small flat on the other side of the kitchen, it is rent-free and part of my renumeration.'

'If you are content with the current system then I'd be grateful if you would please carry on until my father decides what he will do.'

'Certainly, *Monsieur* Letour.'

'How long have you worked for my grandfather?'

'More years than I care to remember! I came when I was about one and young Ramon, your father, was two. I never knew my father, he died when I was about nine months old, hence mother's need to work, and this live-in job suited her and gave Ramon a play mate for some time.'

'Have you always worked here?'

'Oh no, mother made sure I had a life of my own. I inherited my father's ability with languages and, after university, I was an international translator for many years travelling widely. But as I never found anyone I wanted to marry, I continued to live here and looked after mother when she became ill and later took over her role full time.'

'What about Ricard's grandmother?'

'She was not a strong woman physically, though extremely intelligent and charming. After having Ramon, I understand she lost several children, which was difficult for both parents and when *Monsieur* George sent Ramon away, she was heart-broken and declined rapidly.'

'Senseless waste, *Mademoiselle*.'

'Yes, but it seems he kept a good eye on Ramon and his grandsons.'

'From a distance and with much heartache on both sides and tragedy too.'

Thank goodness, Ricard has made peace with his parents.

'A great pity, yes. Shall I show you around the house or would you like to wander on your own? There is a gardener who comes in several times a week with a boy. I do not know what arrangement he had with your grandfather, but they keep the grounds in excellent order, he might arrive before you leave.'

Ricard requested the housekeeper's company to show us the house. The gardener arrived as we were ending the tour and happily accepted Ricard's offer for him to continue caring for the grounds until decisions were made.

It was a beautiful house and I wondered how Ramon must have felt being practically ejected from this luxurious home to what he described as a small working farm.

As we left, Ricard told them the same as I'd told the factory managers.

'Is that the largest of the houses?'

'I think the largest of the buildings we would call houses, Yvonne. We'll have to visit the big estate one day, it is up in Touraine, near Tours which will take a longer visit and will have to wait till after both the weddings, I doubt we will get there before the Spring. There is an agent who sounds as if he has his head screwed on alright, but he, like us all, would like some indication as to what to do.'

§ § §

Over the evening meal, Ricard told the others about the main house.

'I wonder if *Papi* will remember the lady. It is a pity you had not visited the house before the weekend, then we could have asked him.'

'How did you get on with Jules on your last visit, Suzanne?'

'Oh, very well, I think. He is often quiet and sometimes stops when he is talking as if he is not sure what to say. He says he will have to go back to Australia but might wait till after Marianne and Sven are married, he is not sure yet if he will come back again.'

'And what about the dream? You thought you wouldn't have it again after you knew what it was about.'

'It has stopped now and I do not think I will ever have it again. Thank you for being so kind when I did have it, I was really frightened.'

'Yes, I know. And I'm glad it's over.'

367

§ § §

I'd arranged to see Sharon for lunch and discuss how the project and life at the Perez house were going.

'Smoothly at the moment, but the project seems to get more complicated as time goes on, probably because I now have so much information to categories. And guess what! There are two people who are totally against it.'

'Well, don't waste your previous experience! It's early days and I'm sure you'll find a way around them and you'll probably find peer pressure later will assist in getting them to change their attitude and see the advantages.'

'But life with the Perez family is a breath of fresh air and so welcome at the end of a hard day. I'm so glad we stopped that evening, a hotel room is now unthinkable. Lucy keeps badgering to come over, but I'm not sure about her travelling on her own yet.'

'You could arrange a chaperone. I think some airlines still have them, ask Trish to investigate for you. Any time I am coming or going, I am happy to look after her.'

'I'll bring her with me next school break. And how about you? Is everything settled? You look a bit tired, is everything OK?'

'Yes thanks, it's been quite hectic recently and I had a long day yesterday.' I explained the plans for the wedding, blessing and the party next year.

'It sounds to me, Yvonne, if I may speak plainly, you need to stay in the UK until the wedding. You are running yourself ragged with all these return flights. You'll surely have enough to do at home in the next two weeks.'

'Mmm, my parents said something similar, maybe you're right. But—'

'No buts. Your man will also have enough to sort out, not only work but the blessing. Afterwards will be sufficient time for you to do everything on the inheritance. Have you done anything about medical care here, or do you plan to fly home when the contractions start? Sharon grinned, 'a word to the wise, rest, go to London this weekend and stay there till after your wedding.'

Right, decision made. Look after yourself. Another form of being vulnerable! C'est ça!

When I got back, I told Marianne who thought it was an excellent idea and would support me if Ricard objected.

'Have you decided about Suzanne's role?'

'Yes, I'm not really sure why, but I don't want a flower girl at the wedding.'

'There does not have to be a reason you can express; it is a feeling. The wedding is between you and Ricard, she might be disappointed, but then we all have to take the rough with the smooth.'

'Perhaps I'll come with you when you and Sven go to get her from school and we can go and buy another dress for England and she can have the one she's already chosen for when she's the flower girl.'

'She is growing so fast it will be better to wait and she might change her mind, anyway.'

Understandably, Suzanne was saddened.

'Are you cross with me, Yvonne?'

'I'm far from being cross, I'm honoured you feel so strongly, I really can't explain it because I don't know, it is a feeling.'

'It is good when sometimes you can say you do not know.'

'Do you want to have a look at dresses now? Or shall we have ice-cream or something and you can get a dress with Marianne, another time?'

'Will you bring me another day, please, Marianne?'

'Of course, a wise decision.'

'Ice-creams then please, Yvonne.'

§

After another late night in the office, Ricard, regretting taking yesterday off, was not too enthusiastic when I told him I wanted to stay in London until the wedding.

'But I also wondered, from your point of view, would you rather not come back with me tomorrow, but come over for the third reading next week instead and then stay for the week and the wedding?'

'In fact, it would help a great deal, there is a minor crisis brewing at the office I'll have to attend to, so it would work out quite well.'

My mind returned to Marcel and the fact he'd not been concentrating on business.

369

'Is the crisis because you've not been concentrating on your firm recently? You've been out of the office a great deal.'

'Yes, probably, so I should take your offer and stay here. How you have managed your job and all the flights with everything else going on, I do not know.'

'Not very efficiently in retrospect, and I'm beginning to realise I'm more tired than I thought. You'll have time to make arrangements with your parents, Marianne and Sven and get things sorted for the flights and so on before you leave.'

'Have you discussed her role with Suzanne?'

'Yes.' I told him my decision.

'I am not surprised and I am pleased.'

'Why?'

'Because it makes it a bit more special for me at home; I can involve her at the blessing.'

'I hope you'll tell her, but you were never very eager.'

'I hope I did not put you off.'

'No, it just didn't feel right, and maybe I'd picked up your feeling, which is why I couldn't express it. Will you come to the airport with me tomorrow?'

'Of course. But you must leave me something to remember.'

And then we slept.

§ § §

I was packing more than usual to take back with me. As I was folding the dress I would be wearing at the wedding, Marianne entered the spare room where my cases and many of my things were kept.

'Hang your dress up as soon as you get home, Yvonne.'

'Yes, I don't think it will crease too much, but I will.'

She sat on the bed. 'Yvonne.'

Oh dear, what's coming now?

I stopped packing.

'I need to say this now, before your marriage. When you return to this house, you will be Ricard's wife, regardless of the blessing, which I am sure will be as wonderful as the wedding service in England. Therefore, you will return as "the mistress of the house" and will probably want to make changes to how the house

370

is run. I need you to know, I will listen to anything you have to say and will cooperate as much as I can.

'I know Suzanne has asked about who will be responsible for this job or the other and Matilde has raised the question, as you probably have, if not to Ricard but with yourself at least. I thought now, as you are going away until after the wedding, I would raise the issue with you directly.'

Is she now feeling vulnerable? Alors!

I sat next to her.

'Marianne, I'm not sure what to say. I think I'm grateful for you recognising the fact of my altered status—sorry, I didn't mean to sound so pompous—but with the rather convoluted connections existing in our families, I don't think we should get too worried. I feel we've developed a good relationship and I can see no reason why it should change dramatically. I hope we'll still be open and frank with each other. My concern is you will think I demand too much of you and Sven while I am working and when the baby arrives.'

'I just thought I ought to mention it. You know Sven and I are so happy everything has turned out well, for all of us.'

'Yes, it has taken time and trauma, but we all got there, didn't we? Thanks,' I hesitated, 'Marianne, you and Sven, you haven't any notions of moving away once you're married, have you?'

'Neither of us has mentioned it, I do not think it has ever entered our heads. Why? Do you think we should?'

'Absolutely not, I can't think of anything worse. But if, as you raised the topic, I want changes you disapprove of, I hope you will say so, at least we can discuss our differences even if we have to come to a compromise. I just thought I'd better, to echo you, raise the issue directly with you!'

She smiled and patted my hand.

'I will let you finish packing. There is food in the kitchen when you are ready, you must eat before you fly.'

Ricard insisted I enlist assistance with my baggage at the carousel when I landed and had booked a car to take me home; he'd forbidden me to lift anything before Julie's party and was becoming protective of me. This was a lovely feeling and helped relieve the disappointment over the change in our plans for this weekend and next week.

§ § §

371

Once more, Pops drove me to the church on Sunday following which I went for lunch with them and confirmed I could have their folding bed for Suzanne.

'Tell me again the sleeping arrangements.'

'So simple now Jules is not coming, Clementine,' I said with relief, 'Ramon and Matilde will be here with you two. Marianne, Sven and Suzanne and Ricard will stay at my apartment. On Friday evening, Ricard and Sven will go to the hotel, yes, I know it seems silly, but…then they'll both be back in the flat on Saturday night. Portia is staying with Mrs Asher; I've invited her to join us for the post wedding gathering. When everyone has gone, Ricard and I will spend the following week in my flat before returning to France.'

'Ah!'

'What does "Ah" mean?'

'I've suggested to Ramon perhaps they and the others would like to stay for the week following the wedding and see a little of London. They've agreed, not the best time of year possibly, but it might make a change for them all. Suzanne's school has agreed she may have some time off and it seems Jules is willing to look after the farm for the extra few days.'

'As you say, Ah! But what a good idea. And I'll book a hotel in the Lake District or somewhere for Ricard and me on our own for the week before we all return to France.'

'An equally excellent sounding idea.'

Ricard was pleased when I told him in evening when we spoke. He'd once again been to the village church for the Sunday service with his parents and Suzanne.

§ § §

During the week, I went to the clinic where I'd been booked in for a scan. I carried the picture around, showing it off to anyone who was remotely interested; checked with Phillippe what food he planned to serve and confirmed the wines he thought would be appropriate to order; saw Julie several times; had lunch with my parents again; shopped for food for the family who'd be staying in my flat, although I expected them to be out most of the time; wrote out some instructions about the central heating, water system and fuse box location in case they needed help, although everything was straightforward.

I took time to go through Patrick and Andrea's proposition in detail, marking areas which needed further exploration, though most eventualities had been covered. I met them for a working lunch and told them how far I'd got with the inheritance, which on the surface did not appear to be over demanding, but I'd no idea what Ramon and Ricard would be wanting to do and therefore my involvement. If they really meant they wanted an answer two days after the wedding, I said they would be out of luck and hoped they were joking.

I made another telephone call with my heart rate speeding up a little.

'Peter, do you feel you could meet Ricard before the wedding? I don't want to push you, but I did wonder.'

'Yes, thank you. Georgina is still not sure she can go to the wedding, and even if we do, we'll not go to the reception, so to meet him before would be a good idea. But I will probably come on my own, Georgina is very fragile. When would you suggest?'

'Would next Monday be convenient? Mid-day at the Country Club?'

'Fine. And thank you for asking.'

I'd mentioned this possibility to Ricard before, so I hoped he'd be alright with it.

§ § §

I met Ricard at the airport on Saturday with the car. He'd caught an early flight so we had most of the day together which was spent mainly in the apartment hanging and pressing his clothes which he'd rather slung into his cases. We also started a list of items he'd either forgotten or not considered necessary. I pointed out a tie would be appropriate in this instance, even if he didn't wear one in France.

'You are too rigid.'

'I would just like it to be right. On which subject—'

He interrupted me,

'That tone, what have you in store now?'

'I've fixed for us to meet Peter on Monday,' his face questioned, 'Mark's father.'

'Of course. You mentioned it some time ago. I am still not quite sure why.'

'Put it down to one of my feelings. Georgina probably won't be there and it is unlikely they'll attend the wedding. With your support, I'd like, when with him or them, to remove these,' I pointed to my engagement and wedding ring, 'and place your one on my left hand. It might be stupid, but I feel, again it is the only word I can find—it would be an open and appropriate thing to do.'

'And your other rings?'

'If you don't mind, I'll just swap them over for now. Maybe give them to our son or daughter when their time comes?'

'Will you expect me to do the placing?'

'No, that wouldn't be appropriate. I'll just move them over.'

'Does he speak French? I am sure some things get lost in translation, and this will probably be an emotional meeting for all three, or four, of us.'

'Yes, but I'm not sure how fluently.'

'Are your parents coming to hear the Banns tomorrow or am I being fed to the lions on my own?'

'They said they'd like to come if you're in agreement and they've offered lunch so we can pick up the bed for Suzanne. I said I'd let them know.'

'Fine by me, you had better ring them, it is getting late.'

'Wine or something stronger?'

'Which reminds me, you said you had a scan picture. Can I see it?'

'Of course, sorry, sorry, how stupid of me, I've shown it to so many people I thought I must have shown it to you.' I retrieved it from my bag and passed it to him.

'It is amazing.' Joy and pride filled his face. I left him to revel in his fatherhood again and rang my parents.

We settled on wine for Ricard and I suffered more soda water, hoping the child appreciated my sacrifice! We enjoyed sitting close together, staring at the image before we went to bed.

§ § §

Ricard charmed everyone to whom he was introduced at church on Sunday. Pops and I were having to translate most conversations, Ricard was patient with those using their limited French, although later he admitted, it was excruciating to hear his mother tongue so distorted. I was glad Pops had decided to have the wedding service sheets printed in both languages so, not only Ricard, but also the rest of his family could follow the service easily.

374

'As this will probably be the last time the four of us will have a quiet time together until we meet again in France for the blessing service, we thought we'd have lunch out.'

Pops drove to one of their favourite riverside restaurants, where the water twinkled in the autumn sunshine. While we were having pre-lunch drinks in the lounge, Clementine used English to say,

'I appreciate it is rather late to ask you both. But are you certain you are doing the right thing? You have only known each other for about twelve weeks, not a great deal of time to understand and appreciate your differences as well as similarities. I realize you have both been through a great deal more than you have felt able to tell us, and I wonder if these events have given you time to think through fully what your lives together will be like.'

Pops made a simultaneous translation.

I was dumbfounded but Ricard seemed to see a funny side to her concerns, saying,

'I thought it was the bride who was supposed to have the last-minute doubts, not the parents. Clementine, with what Yvonne and I have been through recently, I think we have learnt more about each other's strengths and weaknesses than a lot of people do after twenty years of marriage. The twelve weeks have been turbulent and with sufficient problems and misunderstanding to last us a lifetime. If we were going to split up—regardless of the baby—we would have had sufficient cause and done so by now.'

Pops had his work cut out with translating the full sentiment in Ricard's response.

'I'm one hundred per cent sure, Clementine.'

'Are you satisfied now, Clem?' Asked Pops.

'Yes, to the bride and groom and many happy years ahead.' She raised her glass.

§ § §

Back in the flat with the folding bed for Suzanne, Ricard said,

'The question from your mother was a bit of a shock, I wonder what made her raise her concerns so late, your father has appeared to support us all the time.'

'He has raised the matter with me recently, but I agree, he has been supportive. Maybe mother felt a little left out of the conversations; we've had more discussions and contact with Pops than her. Maybe my neglect of mother is like our neglect of Suzanne, leading to similar feelings of isolation.'

I have really been too self-centred these last few months.

§ § §

Peter was on his own. The introductions were easily made and the men shook hands, Ricard responding to Peter's smile and welcome.

'Yvonne, I'm sorry, I won't be able to stay for a long lunch, I've managed to get a friend to be with Georgina for a while but she has to leave at two, so perhaps we can eat as we talk?'

We settled for the early light menu served in the lounge rather than the restaurant, Peter telling the waiter to put everything on his account.

'Yvonne has not told us a great deal about you Ricard,' his French was fluent enough for me not to have to translate except when an odd word failed him, 'so will you elucidate at all?'

Ricard gave a quick rundown of his childhood on the farm followed by university and his current law practice. He talked about his marriage to Charlotte and how Marianne came to look after his daughter, then the introduction of Sven into their lives. A resumé on how we met and came together, a simple, uncomplicated "no problems" account.

If only it had been as simple as he'd told it! C'est ça!

'I know Yvonne and Mark were suited and happy together Peter, I have no wish to erase any of their happiness or their memories. What Yvonne and I now have will not disparage what they had, but this is a new love and life and I hope to bring her further joy and contentment.'

Peter smiled and took my hands.

'I wish you all blessings, my dear. And now, I think, is the time to remove Mark's rings—keep them safe—and make room for the new ones.'

How on earth did he know?

I stared at him then removed Mark's rings from my hand.

Eventually, I asked,

'Why did you say to do that?'

'Georgina told me to do so. I told you last time we met she has days when she is depressed. Well, it has now moved on and she has days when she is not at all lucid, but when I told her I was meeting you with Ricard, she said...' he paused, trying to remember her exact words, "'tell her to remove Mark's rings and to move on and continue to be happy.'"

Ricard reached over, took his engagement ring from my right hand and placed it on my left ring finger.

Peter stood and took Ricard's hand.

'Take great care of her.'

Then turning to me,

'Yvonne, I'm sorry I must go. I don't know for how much longer I'll have her with me, she is deteriorating fast. Oh, sorry, this is supposed to be a day looking to your future, not one of misery. Please keep in touch and remember what we said last time we met, you are still part of the family.'

Peter and I embraced and we watched him leave. Neither of us spoke for a while. I put Mark's rings in my bag.

'Yvonne, are you alright?'

I nodded.

'There is still time to change your mind if you are not sure.'

We sat again. I took his hand.

'I am perfectly sure.'

We lingered over more coffee before returning to my apartment.

§ § §

The next two days were spent finalising the arrangements for the beds and the reception. The wine was delivered and Phillippe came and confirmed the arrangements in the kitchen, leaving with a key to let himself and helpers in while we were at the church.

The "people carrier" I'd ordered met everyone at the airport on Thursday, dropping off those who were staying with me then taking Ramon and Matilde to my parents' apartment. Phillippe brought in an evening meal Ricard had ordered at the last moment. It had been a long day travelling, so it was well past midnight before everyone was settled in bed.

§ § §

We arrived back from the rehearsal, which had gone smoothly, to find the apartment empty. The folding bed had been moved from the living room where

377

it had been put for Suzanne, to the spare room used by Sven and Marianne. Suzanne had slept through any noise we had made getting up and making coffee before we'd left. A note indicated Mrs Asher had taken Marianne and Suzanne to have a tour on one of the London City Sight Seeing Busses and they would return late afternoon.

Sven and Ricard packed the things they would need for tonight and tomorrow morning then, the three of us, Sven, Ricard and I had lunch and chatted while waiting for Mrs Asher and the others to return. Ricard and Sven had planned to wait until they came back before going off to the hotel but as it was getting late, left just before the time they had to check into the hotel or lose the room.

'I'll ring you as soon as they get back.' I promised.

'It has been quite some time since I've been out on a bachelor night,' said Sven.

'Well, have a good time and enjoy yourselves. See you tomorrow.'

Shortly after they had left, Portia arrived.

'Oh, have I missed the groom and best man? I was hoping to see them before tomorrow. I am still not sure how I will feel meeting Jules again and had hoped to do so before the wedding.'

'I wouldn't worry about it, he's not coming.' I told Portia about the change of plan. 'But I'm getting a bit worried about where Mrs Asher has got to with the other two, the note said late afternoon, but it's getting on to seven.'

'They'll be alright with Mrs Asher, she knows London like the back of her hand. Can I hang this up somewhere?' She got a hanger from my wardrobe and from her case took a dress which she was to wear tomorrow and hung it in my room.

I froze.

'Nice dress.' I said unenthusiastically and started mentally to search my wardrobe for something I could wear instead of the planned dress, slightly regretting my trip to the charity shop.

'Are you alright, Von?'

'Yes, fine.'

The 'phone rang.

'Yvonne, I am sorry, we really didn't notice how the time has flown. We are eating now and will be back shortly.'

'Where are you now?'

'Covent Garden, we got caught up in some shopping and then outdoor opera pieces and early Christmas carols. Suzanne's enthusiasm is catching!'

'Yes, I know. Look, I know it will cost a bit, but please get a taxi back, I'll pay you.'

'Alright, we'll be with you before nine. I hope you weren't too worried.'

'I was certainly starting to worry.'

I rang Ricard, they were beginning to get more than agitated so I reassured him they were alright and I'd call again when they got here. Finally, about half past eight, the "tourists" arrived back exhausted. Mrs Asher once more apologised for the late time. I rang Ricard.

'We were equally responsible for the time, Yvonne. But it was like total freedom with a perfect guide.'

'And the shopping, Marianne?'

'Today mainly for scarves, gloves and hats. It was colder than I thought and we did not bring any. I must get Suzanne to bed, what is the plan for tomorrow?'

'Portia will use my car and take you all to the church. Francis, my brother, is taking Clementine, Ramon and Matilde to the church then back here afterwards, Pops will collect me and take me to the church. After the service Portia will bring you all back plus Sven; Ricard and I'll come back with Pops. But there will be little to do in the morning except get ready and make sure the place is clear for Phillippe, which means mainly moving Suzanne's bed back and clearing stuff off the dining table, he will sort out what he wants.

'What time do we have to leave?'

'Eleven-thirty, so there will be no great rush in the morning. I'll nip over to Phillippe's for some croissant and pastries unless you'd like something else?'

'That will be fine tomorrow; maybe we'll have some proper English breakfasts before we go home.'

'Pops will arrange those for you while Ricard and I are away.'

We got the bed out for Suzanne, Portia collected her dress and bag and followed Mrs Asher to her apartment, Marianne followed them.

'I just want to say thank you again to *Madame* Asher,' she said. 'I will leave the door on the latch so I can get back if we talk too long.'

Shortly afterwards, Portia returned.

'Why didn't you say something, Von? I didn't know—in fact, I never even thought to ask you what colour you were wearing. Let me look in your wardrobe, you must have something to fit me.'

'Don't choose the green,' Marianne said as she returned. 'I was just so surprised to see the colour, the cut is different but the colour is the same. I wondered if you had changed your mind about a flower girl, so I followed them to ask; Portia is mortified. We will search your wardrobe tomorrow for something stunning but does not outdo you! Goodnight.'

I hugged her.

'Thank you, Marianne.'

'Come in the morning, Portia, it's too late now. Thanks, and goodnight, sleep well.'

'Goodnight, Von.'

Relieved, I went to bed.

About half past two in the morning, my mobile rang.

'Yvonne, the ring, it is in my big suitcase. Will you bring it please?'

'Have a look in your washbag, it is in the original box. You said you'd put it there.'

I heard a scuffle and mumbled exchanges.

'So it is. See you later. Goodnight.'

The 'phone clicked off.

C'est ça!

§ § §

The telephone rang again at eight-thirty as I was going over to Phillippe's.

'Good morning, Yvonne, I hope I haven't woken you, but is it possible to speak to Suzanne?'

'Good morning, Pops, I'm not sure if she's up yet. They were all late, or early to bed last night. Hold on.'

A tousled head, still deep in sleep, lay softly breathing in the dining room.

'She's still fast asleep. Do you want me to wake her?'

'No but get her to call me as soon as she is awake, please.'

'Is everything alright?'

'Fine but there is something I forgot and she might be able to help.'

'Can I—'

He cut me off. I went over to Phillippe's where he handed me a box with the breakfast.

'See you later, hope all goes well at the church.'

'Should do if he remembers the ring.'

'What?'

'I had a 'phone call about two this morning virtually asking me where he'd put it!'

'Bodes well!' He smiled and blew me a finger kiss.

I gave Suzanne the message and told her the number was in the directory on the handset. When she had finished speaking to Pops, she was grinning but said nothing.

So much for not having any secrets!

Marianne answered the door when the bell went.

'Good morning, everyone.' Portia and Mrs Asher went into my bedroom and half an hour later came out clutching a selection of my clothes.

'See you later. I'll collect the car keys when it is time to go.'

We had some breakfast and tidied up.

'We can do no more now, Yvonne, except get changed.' Said Marianne.

Which is what we did. Suzanne had chosen another dress which suited her well and I complimented her. Pops arrived a little earlier than I'd expected and handed Suzanne a small parcel before she left with the others. I was intrigued.

'Service sheets. I'd forgotten I'd not arranged for anyone to hand them out. I thought it might involve her and give her a role.'

Although we were not there to see her do so, apparently, she was adept at the task and relished greeting people, asking, in English, for their names of those she didn't know. Meeting Julie and Paul seemed to be the highlight of her morning. The service went smoothly, Sven handing over the ring which had been found where I'd indicated. Phillippe had everything set by the time we all arrived at the apartment and I found Francis was running a shuttle service for other guests. Once more the family and friends mingled.

Portia, dressed in my clothes and given a French flair by Mrs Asher, looked stunning and had taken photographs in the church and continued here, promising to forward them to us all. Mrs Asher acted as a very able interpreter to take the pressure of Pops and me where needed especially between Patrick and Ricard, but there appeared to be no tension between the two men. Phillippe's selection of food was appreciated and almost totally consumed.

After the toasts and champagne, Pops suggested Ricard and I left, leaving everyone else to stay and to say their farewells when they were ready to leave for trains or other transport. Ricard did not need telling twice and said goodbye to everyone.

I resisted, pointing out we were staying here; he grabbed my hand and said, 'For once in your life, Yvonne, let go of the reins and do as you are told.'

'But—'

'No buts, come on.' He pulled me out of the door and we left.

A taxi was waiting to take us to the hotel where everything we needed could be provided, but I didn't need anything, except my husband.

§ § §

Although we'd anticipated just packing a case and leaving for the New Forest, we found Pops had brought Clementine and the others over to say goodbye again, so it was not till after mid-day we finally settled into my car for a few days on our own.

As we relaxed in bed on the second night of our marriage, in the hotel in the New Forest, I looked back over the last twelve weeks. There had been traumas; bitterness; reconciliations; secrets; surprises; coincidences; some tears; joy; laughter; love; so much travel and work. I wondered how the next phase of my life would pan out. There seemed to be a lot on the horizon: our blessing in France; Patrick's proposal; Ramon's inheritance; Julie's twins—with or without the birthmark; our baby; house renovations and straightening out future relationships.

But for this week, it will be just him and me.

C'est ça!